Private Sitting or Single Bedroom 121

122

120

128 127 126 125

Bed and Sitting Room 124

123

Private

119

118

Ladies Gents

Service

Public Bathroom

108 109

Passenger Lifts

110 111 112 113

117

Telephone

114 115 116

Jerusalem 1946

Winter Garden

Private Sitting Room 11

12

10

Reading and Writing Room

Arab Lounge

Service

9

8

Belle Etage

Passenger Lifts

Reception

Manager

Shop

Bar

7

Office

4

Private Sitting Room 5

6

Cashier

BY BLOOD AND FIRE

By Thurston Clarke

BY BLOOD AND FIRE
THE LAST CARAVAN
DIRTY MONEY

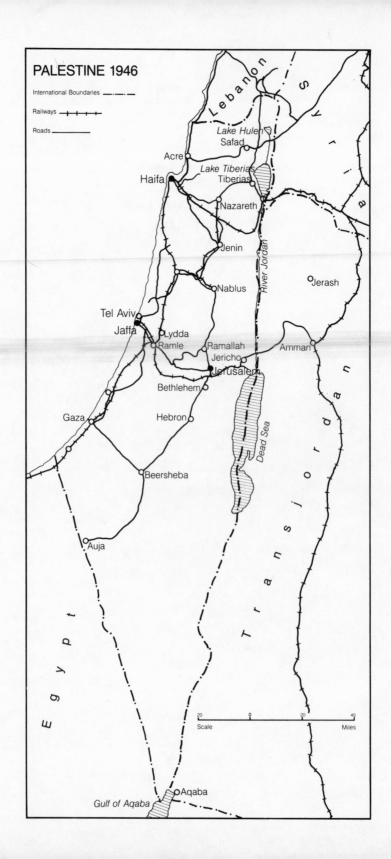

PALESTINE 1946

International Boundaries
Railways
Roads

BY BLOOD & FIRE

The Attack on the King David Hotel

THURSTON CLARKE

G. P. Putnam's Sons
New York

I would like to thank the John Simon Guggenheim Memorial Foundation for its generous support.

—T.C.

Library of Congress Cataloging in Publication Data

Clarke, Thurston.
  By blood and fire.

  Bibliography: p.
  Includes index.
  1. Palestine—History—1929-1948.
2. Irgun Zvai Leumi. 3. Melon ha-Melekh David,
Jerusalem. 4. Terrorism—Palestine. I. Title.
DS126.4.C57 1981   956.94′04   80-24122
ISBN 0-399-12605-8

For Antonia

Contents

Author's Note

This is a true story. Events and conversations have been reconstructed from interviews, official papers, letters, diaries, and firsthand published accounts. Chapter notes follow the text.

In Blood and Fire Judea Fell.
In Blood and Fire Judea Will Arise.
                    —The Irgun Zvai Leumi

The Messiah will not come to the sound
of high explosives.
                    —Chaim Weizmann

PROLOGUE

December 11, 1917

GENERAL SIR EDMUND ALLENBY dismounted outside the walls of Jerusalem and strode toward the Jaffa Gate. An honor guard stamped boots and presented arms. They wore tin helmets and carried grenades. Less than a mile away, the retreating Turkish army fought on. Mortar shells exploded in the distance. Flimsy biplanes sputtered overhead.

Two days before, Allenby's army had captured Jerusalem, ending four centuries of Turkish rule. This victory against Germany's ally had cost Britain considerable blood and suffering but strategically and symbolically it was among the most crucial victories of the First World War.

Assyrians, Romans, Arabs and Turks had each in turn celebrated their conquests of Jerusalem with processions and spectacles. Today no Union Jacks waved from the city's ramparts, no bells rang and no bands played to announce Allenby's triumph. Britain wanted to reassure the world that she would be an impartial and benevolent trustee.

At noon Allenby marched through the Jaffa Gate and into the Old City. The commanders of his army's French and Italian contingents flanked him; his principal staff officers followed at twenty paces. Crowds jammed the Old City's roofs and balconies. Clapping, screaming and sobbing men and women surged against the backs of soldiers lining the sidewalks.

As Allenby passed, priests and monks embraced and crossed themselves. They wore the brown robes of the Franciscan order, the white robes of the Coptic Church and the black cloaks of the Orthodox Church. Arab, Russian,

Greek, Ethiopian and European rejoiced together that for the first time since the Crusades a Christian nation ruled Palestine. An American witness said, "One of the greatest events in history was enacted here before our eyes. We thought this was the Last Crusade."

Tears of joy streamed down the cheeks of black-coated rabbis in the crowd. During the war, deportation, disease and famine had cut Jerusalem's Jewish community by half. Only 25,000 Jews remained, a pitiful remnant of the people who had ruled the city two thousand years before. Now, under the British, they had reason to hope their numbers would soon be swelled.

In 70 A.D., the Romans had exiled the Jews from Palestine and destroyed Solomon's Temple. The remains of this temple, known as the Wailing Wall, became the spiritual center of Judaism, toward which the prayers of millions of Jews in exile were directed when they made the Passover promise of "Next year in Jerusalem."

Today that promise seemed close to fulfillment. Zionism, a political movement advocating the return of the Jews to Palestine, had been born in 1895 when a Viennese newspaperman, Theodor Herzl, published a pamphlet entitled "Der Judenstaat"—"The Jewish State." Its first sentence read, "The Jews who will it, shall have a state of their own."

A turning point in Zionist history occurred on November 2, 1917, when British Foreign Secretary Arthur Balfour sent a short letter to Lord Rothschild, the head of the British branch of the famed Jewish banking family. Its most crucial paragraph said:

> His Majesty's Government views with favour the establishment in Palestine of a national home for the Jewish people, and will use their best endeavours to facilitate the achievement of this object, it being clearly understood that nothing shall be done which may prejudice the civil and religious rights of existing non-Jewish communities in Palestine or the rights and political status enjoyed by Jews in any other country.

This extraordinary, contradictory promise was motivated by a number of factors, prominent among which was Britain's need to secure the support of Russian and American Jews at a crucial juncture in the First World War. Most of all, however, it was motivated by idealism.

Balfour and Prime Minister David Lloyd George wanted to right centuries of wrongs done to the Jews by European Christians. As reparation, they offered Palestine. They offered it because they had been charmed and their consciences stirred by the Chairman of the British Zionist Federation, Dr. Chaim Weizmann. They offered it because, by the standards of this imperialist age, if you captured territory from an enemy, you did with it as you pleased. In 1917, it pleased Britain's rulers to give the Jews a national home in lands they had won from the Turks.

Jerusalem's Arabs—or, as Balfour would have it, the members of the "existing non-Jewish communities"—who cheered Allenby, knew nothing, yet, of Balfour's declaration. Allenby had delivered them from years of starvation and misery under the Turks. They clapped their hands and shouted "Allah Nebi."

By coincidence, "Allenby" sounds identical to "Allah Nebi"—in Arabic, a prophet who, by tradition, would enter Jerusalem on foot and make it a city of prosperity and power. Arab prosperity and power, the Arabs assumed. How could it be otherwise? The Arabs made up ninety percent of Palestine's population and Jerusalem contained the sacred rock from which Mohammed had ascended to heaven. This rock, now covered by a golden dome, was Islam's third most sacred shrine.

In his camp east of the Jordan River, Prince Faisal also celebrated Allenby's victory. In 1915 Sir Henry MacMahon, Britain's High Commissioner in Egypt, had written to the Prince's father, King Hussein, pledging that if the Arabs rebelled against Turkey, Britain would guarantee their independence. MacMahon excluded from this promise only the western portions of Syria. British diplomats later, and not very convincingly, argued that these "western portions" included Palestine.

The officers who marched behind Allenby and the soldiers who held back the crowds were also thrilled by their victory. Education in Britain stressed Latin, Greek and the Bible. Biblical history was studied as carefully as that of the Empire. Today the British rejoiced that the world's holiest city was now part of its greatest empire. A member of Allenby's staff observed, "In Jerusalem, one seldom heard an oath or an indecent word, even though bad language from troops in the field is notorious."

According to T. E. Lawrence, who was visiting Allenby's headquarters, the entry into Jerusalem was "the supreme moment of the war."

The procession halted in front of the citadel. Allenby climbed an open stairway and, standing on a terrace in front of King David's Tower, read a proclamation promising that the holy shrines would be "maintained and protected according to the existing customs and beliefs of those to whose faith they are sacred." After the proclamation was translated into seven languages, he marched to the Turkish barrack square, received the city's notables and then returned to his headquarters. The entire ceremony had taken fifteen minutes.

They were to be the best fifteen minutes of Britain's thirty-year rule in Palestine, the only fifteen minutes when Arab, Briton and Jew celebrated together, and the only moment, until July 22, 1946, when most were united in a single emotion.

The euphoria was brief. Half an hour after the ceremonies, over a luncheon of chicken mayonnaise and foie gras sandwiches, the French attaché, François Georges-Picot, volunteered to set up a civil government.

Allenby's face reddened. He swallowed and jutted out his chin. "In the military zone," he said, "the only authority is that of the Commander in Chief—myself."

This incident was a harbinger of decades of increased Franco-British rivalry in the Middle East. The year before, Georges-Picot and British diplomat Sir Mark Sykes had signed a treaty dividing the Turkish territories between Britain and France. This treaty, rather than the Balfour Declaration or the MacMahon Letters, would determine the immediate future of the Middle East.

In 1922 the Sykes-Picot Agreement was codified by the League of Nations. Palestine and the other Arab-populated Turkish territories became mandates or, in the naive words of the League, "sacred trusts of civilisation" that were supposed to reach independence under European tutelage. The League assigned Lebanon and Syria to France; Iraq, Palestine, and Transjordan to Britain. The year before, Britain had detached Transjordan, a territory east of the Jordan River, from Palestine and given it to Prince Faisal's brother, Abdullah, to rule under the direction of a British Resident.

In the wording of the Mandate for Palestine the League made it clear that Britain's principal task was to establish a National Home for the Jews. But did a "National Home" mean a Jewish State or merely a home for a Jewish minority in an Arab state? The League did not say. It unwisely left this crucial question to be decided by the number of Jews who immigrated to Palestine.

During the next twenty-five years, the level of Jewish immigration became a matter of national survival for both Jews and Arabs. Jews insisted on the right to immigrate and purchase land without restriction. Arabs insisted that unrestricted Jewish immigration automatically violated their rights. What greater political right was there, they asked, than that of a majority to govern its own land?

Throughout its rule in Palestine, Britain struggled to do the impossible: strike a "fair" balance between these uncompromising and irreconcilable positions while at the same time pursuing its own strategic and economic interests in the region. "Fairness," however, was the last thing either Jews or Arabs wanted; both wanted Palestine for themselves.

Until 1933 Jewish immigration was modest and only once, in 1925, did it exceed 14,000 a year. In two separate years, more Jews left Palestine than arrived. Nevertheless, Arab leaders protested and Arab mobs frequently rioted, killing Jewish civilians.

When Hitler came to power in 1933 Jewish immigration to Palestine increased dramatically. The harsh Nazi laws directed at Jews proved the Zionist contention that the Jews were a people, and a people who did not belong in Europe.

Sixty thousand Jews immigrated to Palestine in 1935, fifteen times as many as had come four years earlier. The Arabs calculated that at this rate the Jews would become a majority in only ten years. In 1936 they rebelled against British rule. Arabs now killed British officials as well as Jewish civilians.

The British Army and police force resorted to harsh punishments and reprisals to defeat the rebellion. In 1939, in order to forestall future Arab unrest, Britain issued a White Paper, or statement of policy, restricting Jewish immigration to a total of 75,000 during the coming five years. After that, any immigration would depend on "Arab consent." Britain hoped this White Paper would guarantee the support, or at least the neutrality, of the Arabs in Palestine and neighboring countries in case war broke out with Germany.

The Arabs considered the White Paper a minimal concession: the beginning, rather than the end, of a redressing of the injustices of the Balfour Declaration. For the Jews it was a betrayal of Balfour and a violation of the League's mandate, proof that Arab terrorists had succeeded in intimidating Britain. The virtual closing of Palestine to Jewish immigration at a time when Jews in Europe were subjected to persecution convinced some of a sinister British plot to prevent their escaping Hitler.

The practical effect of the White Paper, when combined with the reluctance of the United States to accept large numbers of Jewish refugees, was to condemn many Jews to death in Hitler's gas chambers.

Four months after the issuance of the White Paper, Britain was at war with Germany. Ben-Gurion ordered the Yishuv—Palestine's Jews—to "fight Hitler as if there were no White Paper, and fight the White Paper as if there were no Hitler." Palestinian Jews obeyed and enlisted in the British Army.

When the European war ended in May 1945, the Yishuv believed Britain would rescind the White Paper. The reasons seemed to them overwhelming: they had supported Britain during the war, while the Arabs had not; the British Labour party, which had just come to power, was more pro-Zionist than the Conservatives and had frequently attacked the White Paper; and most important, hundreds of thousands of Jewish refugees, the pitiful survivors of Hitler's "Final Solution," were stranded in Europe.

Most of these refugees were afraid to live in Europe and wanted to emigrate to Palestine. No other country in the world wanted them. During the first eight months of 1946 the United States admitted only 4,767 Jews. The Arabs of Palestine argued that it was unfair for them to bear the entire burden of these refugees, particularly since European Christians, and not Arabs, were responsible for their suffering.

By the end of the summer of 1945, it became clear to the Yishuv that Clement Attlee's Labour Government had no intention of permitting large-scale Jewish immigration to Palestine. The Soviets now threatened Britain's position as a Middle East power and the Empire's lines of communication. The White Paper was still needed to protect British strategic and economic interests—the Suez Canal and the oil fields—and to guarantee Arab friendship during the next war, the Cold War. British Foreign Secretary Ernest Bevin, not fully comprehending the trauma of the Holocaust, believed that most Jewish refugees should be resettled in the European countries in which they had lived before the war.

The Yishuv was bitterly disappointed. In September 1945 the three Jewish underground groups, the Haganah, the LEHI (also known as the Stern Gang) and the Irgun Zvai Leumi (the "National Military Organization"), commanded by Menahem Begin, put aside their substantial differences and joined in a rebellion against British rule. They sabotaged railway lines, police stations, and the radar and police launches used to trap boatloads of illegal immigrants smuggled out of Europe by the Haganah.

On July 22, 1946, the Jewish rebellion reached a point crucial for Britain, the Arabs, and the future Jewish State. And on this date, for the first time since Allenby's triumphant procession twenty-nine years before, Britons, Arabs and Jews were united, but this time not in celebration.

PART ONE

July 22, 1946
5:30 A.M.–10:30 A.M.

1

5:30 A.M. ISAAC SANDLER parked his dark blue Plymouth taxi near the intersection of Tel Aviv's Frishman Street and King George V Avenue. Someone had ordered his cab for 5:30, seventeen minutes before daybreak.

For the last three weeks Palestine had suffered a heat wave. Tel Aviv had been hot and humid; Jerusalem hot and dry. To escape the heat, laborers awakened in darkness and worked at first light. Trains and buses started running at 5:30; shops and offices opened between 7:30 and 8:00. Travelers started journeys in the half-light of dawn, so this early call was not surprising.

Two men approached the taxi. One opened the rear door and climbed in, the other drew a revolver and ordered Sandler into the back seat. He was blindfolded and shoved onto the floor. The engine started and the taxi lurched forward. The journey had begun.

Two hours later Sandler was sitting under guard in the walled courtyard of a house in Petah Tikva, a suburb of Tel Aviv. Forty miles to the east, a young blond man was driving Sandler's taxi past the two- and three-story stone villas of Rehavia, a prosperous Jerusalem neighborhood favored by German Jews. He stopped at intersections, yielded at traffic circles and stayed clear of bicyclists, donkeys, and pushcarts. An accident or traffic violation would attract a policeman who might ask why a journalist was driving through Jerusalem in a Tel Aviv taxi registered to Isaac Sandler.

The blond man would have had no answer. His license identified him as a reporter for *Davar*, a Hebrew-language newspaper published in Tel Aviv, but he was not. The Palestine Police index of terrorists correctly listed him as Yitzhak Avinoam, Jerusalem commander of the Irgun Zvai Leumi.

Avinoam shared the taxi's front seat with a hulking Polish Jew who had chosen the name "Chaim-Toit"—"Alive-Dead." Everyone in the Irgun chose an underground name. Their real identities remained secret, a protection against traitors. Most preferred the names of Old Testament heroes: David, Gideon, Saul.

Chaim-Toit had taken his name during an Irgun training program in the Judean hills. His instructor had told him, "You have joined the Irgun until you die."

"No! I'm going to live!" he said.

"You may be lucky. But we're giving you the chance to die for Eretz Israel."

"All right. Now I'm alive, soon I'll be dead. That'll be my name, 'Alive-Dead.'"

Although he joined in 1938, he did not become active until 1943, the year another Polish Jew, Menahem Begin, became Commander in Chief, and the year the Red Cross reported that Nazis had hanged his sister and brother-in-law in the main square of their Polish village.

Now, three years later, Chaim-Toit was one of four members of the Irgun's National Planning Committee. He selected targets for sabotage from among the government's army camps, airfields, police fortresses and offices. He planned how to enter them and how to destroy them.

While Avinoam drove, Chaim-Toit turned and scrutinized other cars. Rationing had made gasoline expensive and scarce and most private cars belonged to policemen, army officers and government officials. Anyone following would notice that during the last thirty minutes the taxi had picked up only Jewish boys in their late teens and early twenties. The boys waited at street corners and on doorsteps. Each was delivered to the same address, the Beit Aharon religious school on David Yellin Street.

Avinoam braked in front of a two-story house on Rashba Street. A tall, fair-haired German Jew climbed into the back of the taxi. Six months ago "Yanai" had been a corporal in the British Army. Now he was the Irgun's only army-trained explosives expert.

As the taxi started he poked his head over the front seat. "An operation?" he asked.

"Yes, an operation," Avinoam said.

"Good. What's the target?"

"You know the rules. No one knows until the meeting."

"But it means I'll be gone all day, and I told a girl friend I'd meet her at a café at eleven. She's the daughter of an editor of *Haaretz*. I missed one date with her yesterday and she'll wait all day unless I call. Let me go back and telephone her."

Avinoam continued driving.

"Let him make his call," Chaim-Toit said. He was grooming Yanai to become Chief of Operations in Jerusalem and knew about his reputation with women. There were always dates with two or three different ones; always someone new in love with him.

Avinoam refused to stop. Today he would follow the rules. For five generations his family had lived in Jerusalem and paid taxes to Turkish and British rulers. He was determined that during his lifetime his people would finally govern his city. To this end he had sacrificed his youth, his education, and, perhaps, his future.

An attractive, twenty-six-year-old man, he took pleasure in wearing the finely cut English suit that was part of his disguise as a journalist. And yet he denied himself the pleasure of a girl friend. "I could be arrested tomorrow and hanged a month later," he told one girl who became interested.

Although he had been an excellent student, Avinoam left school to join the Irgun. Now he slipped into Tel Aviv once a week to attend a law class under a false name. The Palestine Police had hunted him since 1941. He lived alone, moved often, and seldom went out at night. "I have to live seven floors underground," he told his comrades.

He hoped that today would reward his years of sacrifice. In January he had met Menahem Begin for the first time. "I am beginning to believe that soon we are going to succeed," Begin had said. "It will not be long before the British leave Palestine."

At the time Avinoam had been skeptical; now he was not. If they succeeded today, how could Begin's prophecy not be fulfilled?

7:45 A.M. Sir John Shaw strode through the gate of the German Hospice. Sergeant Bill Jennings snapped to attention and saluted. Shaw turned left and strode down the center of Lloyd George Street, a narrow lane lined with single-story stone houses, high stone walls, and metal gates. German pilgrims had built the houses and walls just before the turn of the century. Shaw and his wife lived in a hostel managed by German nuns.

Jennings cradled a Thompson submachine gun. Shaw carried a .38 caliber pistol in a holster under his gray seersucker jacket. He disliked the pistol and never fired it, even in practice. He liked to say, "I only carry this fool thing so that if they attack I can take one of them with us."

On July 22, Shaw was the most important British target in Palestine. Three days earlier his only superior, High Commissioner Sir Alan Cunningham, had gone to London for consultation. As Chief Secretary, Shaw was in charge of the local civil servants and British Colonial officers who administered the country. Now he was also AOC—Acting Officer in Charge—with an additional responsibility for 80,000 British soldiers.

Not only was he the most powerful Briton in Palestine, but at six feet seven inches he was also probably the tallest. His young son told a family friend, "If they wanted to disguise Father they'd have to chop off his legs."

"Any fool could hit me," Shaw said to a British journalist. "Precautions are nonsense."

He knew he could be killed if he chose to drive to work. Jewish terrorists belonging to the Stern Gang had murdered Lord Moyne as he sat in his official car outside his Cairo residence. They had made six attempts to kill High Commissioner Harold MacMichael as he motored around Palestine, even though his car was always preceded by police vans or armored cars.

He could be killed as he walked down a busy city street. The Sternists had shot Tom Wilkin, a Hebrew-speaking Palestine Police inspector, as he walked alone down St. Paul's Road. He died two hundred yards from police headquarters.

He could be killed in an empty field. Inspector Ralph Cairns had stepped on a land mine the Irgun had buried in the middle of a dirt path leading from his house in the German Quarter. He was walking to work.

Shaw and Jennings emerged from the German Colony's claustrophobic lanes and started up a steep hill toward the King David Hotel. People and goats had trod countless paths among its olive trees. Every morning Shaw chose a different path, "varying the route."

Jennings dropped back even farther and turned his head from side to side as he walked. Twenty-five yards to the left traffic struggled up Julian's Way, a two-lane asphalted road that began near the German Colony and ran past the King David's front door. Jennings knew that a burst of Sten gunfire could come from a stolen taxi, or an armored car could stop and turn its machine gun on them. Terrorists often stole army vehicles and masqueraded as soldiers.

Terrorists might be hiding behind olive trees. They could emerge from behind the Montefiore windmill twenty yards to their right, fire, and then disappear down the hill into the narrow streets of Yemin Moshe. One of the Bedouin herders using the slope to feed his goats might pull a Sten from underneath his cloak.

Shaw and Jennings both checked out every Orthodox monk that passed them on the path. Was he carrying anything? Was he wearing his habit properly? Was he really a Holy Father or a Jewish teenager slipping a safety catch off the pistol hidden in the folds of his robes?

A few weeks before, some thieves, it was presumed they were terrorists, had broken into a Greek monastery and stolen a dozen habits. These habits were an informal Jerusalem laissez-passer. Guards at roadblocks and government buildings usually waved on those wearing habits without a search.

Shaw pictured squads of terrorists in stolen habits preparing to dynamite buildings and assassinate officials. "What's the good of telling me," he snapped at the police inspector who called with news of the theft. "Get your damned force out and do something about it."

The police swept through the Old City searching and checking the identity of every monk and priest. They repeated the exercise frequently during the following weeks, but without results. Many of the Christian-Arab police constables were reluctant to disturb the Holy Fathers.

The possibility that a group of "killer monks" was preparing an atrocity haunted Shaw. It was the only thing that had truly frightened him since he had arrived in Palestine two and a half years before.

Shaw stared straight ahead as he walked through the olive grove. When he did glance behind him it was to shout a question about Jennings' wife or infant daughter or to comment on the weather.

For the last two weeks a hot, dry, desert wind, known to the Jews as the "sharav" and to the Arabs as the "hamseen," had blown into Jerusalem from the east. Usually it ended before July, but this year it lingered. It drove temperatures into the nineties by noon, caused necks to stiffen, livers to malfunction, and touched off migraines. It made people quarrelsome and uneasy. Even now, at eight in the morning, the sun had already turned pale white and a haze of dust from the Jordanian desert was forming above the barren hills encircling the city.

Twenty years before British urban planners had designated this olive grove as a park because of its stunning view. To the north Shaw could see Mount Scopus and the Hills of Moab. The soldiers who had died during Allenby's campaign lay buried on Mount Scopus in a military cemetery. Shaw had been a young lieutenant in Allenby's army.

To the east, steeples, domes and minarets rose above the medieval walls of the Old City, home of most of Jerusalem's 60,000 Arabs. These eight miles of walls, over thirty feet high, encircled the most sought after, fought over and bloody square kilometer in human history.

Half a mile to the west Shaw could see the tops of modern office blocks and villas. This part of the city contained the Jewish cafés, cinemas and stores, most of the banks and modern commercial enterprises, and the majority of the city's 100,000 Jews.

A few hundred yards north, directly ahead of him, a massive, stone building rose from the like-colored earth to dominate the city's skyline. It was the King David Hotel.

Shaw preferred to walk to work at the hotel. The police had tried to dissuade him, but he insisted. It was his only physical exercise and he thought it important for everyone to see that Britain's senior civil servant in Palestine walked the streets unafraid.

Symbols and prestige had played a central part in the career Shaw had followed for half his fifty-two years. After the First World War he had spent fourteen years as a Colonial officer in West Africa. He was in Palestine between 1935 and 1940 and then in Cyprus until Christmas Day, 1943, when he returned to Palestine as Chief Secretary.

Since then he had often told Arab and Jewish leaders: "I am not pro-Arab or pro-Jewish; I am pro-British." Neither believed him. To the Arabs, being pro-British meant being a Zionist; to the Zionists it was a clever way of disguising anti-Semitism. For Shaw it simply meant viewing events in Palestine through the prism of British interests.

At one time being pro-British had indeed meant supporting Zionist aims. As Shaw put it, "If you beat an enemy into a cocked hat, as we had done with Turkey, you could more or less do as you liked with their territories. We conquered Palestine. It was ours to administer, or give away. We had a perfect right to say, 'Since we have conquered this little insignificant country the size of Wales, this country that was nothing under the Turkish Empire—just a district in the Vilayet of Damascus—then we have a perfect right to promise the Jews a national home in it.'"

Later on, as British policy changed, being pro-British meant enforcing the White Paper. It also meant preserving the symbols and prestige of the Empire and keeping the King David functioning as a civilian hotel. In Shaw's view, closing it to guests would have been a symbolic victory for terrorism, a blow to Britain's prestige and, given the shortage of hotel rooms in Jerusalem, "damned inconvenient."

At 8 A.M. Shaw climbed the six wooden steps over the wall separating Julian's Way from the King David's south wing. Since 1939 this wing had housed the headquarters of the British government in Palestine. It was known as the "Secretariat."

A British Palestine policeman emerged from a stone guardhouse on the other side of the wall, saluted, and demanded Shaw's security card. The year before, one of the young assistant securities had put a picture of a dog on his security card. In the space provided for "any peculiarities," he had written, "walks and talks like a dog." For weeks he had used this card to enter the Secretariat, but under Shaw such laxity was no longer the rule.

Shaw handed over an orange card. The officer checked it carefully. Even though he recognized the Chief Secretary, he knew the importance Shaw attached to security. A few months before, Shaw had written to the army security officer complaining that soldiers were entering the building without showing their passes:

> My officers and I take a great deal of time and trouble by personal daily supervision to ensure the security of this building as far as possible. I myself invariably show my pass twice daily at the entrance— and I suppose I am not less well known than private soldiers and A.T.S. [Auxiliary Territorial Services]. . . . If such personnel are allowed to come and go freely without checking of passes, it is futile for me to attempt to ensure the security of the building (which, incidentally, affects your headquarters as much as it does mine since bombs or fire would not discriminate).

Shaw stepped into one of three compartments in a wooden turnstile. The policeman pushed a pedal and he swung through into the hotel grounds.

He walked twenty yards along the path flanked and covered with coils of barbed wire. To his left, huge nets designed to catch grenades tossed from the street hung over the first-floor windows of the government offices. To his right, telephone poles supported high-intensity searchlights that lit the hotel grounds at night.

Shaw's arrival in Palestine had coincided with a rise in Jewish attacks on the government and he had personally suggested many of the security features that protected the Secretariat. At his request the number of searchlights was doubled. Sappers with mine detectors swept the hotel grounds every week. Electricians installed a silent alarm system. Guards, as well as the hotel's cashiers and manager, could summon the police simply by pushing a pedal or leaning against a hidden button.

The procedure for entering the Secretariat was also tightened. Two sets of guards searched every visitor. There were complaints that it took forty-five minutes just to enter and leave.

Two extra coils of barbed wire were added to the necklaces that already surrounded the garden and rear of the hotel. Army engineers strung trip wires through the wire and buried mines that rang bells and triggered magnesium flares.

The devices worked. Stray cats sent flares rocketing. When the son of the hotel manager trained a flashlight on the hotel walls, police cars raced to the King David.

In addition to its own police and military guards, the hotel was protected by frequent army foot patrols along Julian's Way, police radio vans cruising the neighborhood, the two hundred soldiers who worked in army offices in the hotel, and the four hundred soldiers stationed in an army camp three hundred yards away. The perimeter fence of this camp intersected with the wall of the King David's garden, giving these soldiers easy access to the hotel.

Shaw climbed three steps to a door at the southern end of the building. Police Sergeant Ronald Woodward and two corporals examined his pass and admitted him.

He walked up two flights of stairs to a corridor that ran the length of the Secretariat's south wing. A concrete wall in front of him blocked the main north–south corridor that had once connected the south wing with the rest of the hotel.

He turned right, walked to the end of the short corridor and stopped in front of a wicker door. Someone peered at him through the slats, pressed a buzzer, and the door swung open. Sir John Shaw walked into his office.

2

AVIDOR PICKED up a length of wire from the floor of the Beit Aharon classroom and bent it into the shape of a monocle. He held it in front of one eye and walked around the room shaking hands with the other teenage boys with exaggerated formality.

"Good morning, old chap," he said. "Jolly good of you to pop in. Meeting will start soon. Won't keep you long." Except for the words "jolly" and "old chap," which he said in English, he spoke in a parody of the clumsy, heavily accented Hebrew of the few Britons who had learned the language. The other boys smiled and laughed. One tried to knock away the monocle.

By eight o'clock he had welcomed fifteen young men and a woman. They perched on narrow wooden benches and leaned against the bare, whitewashed walls. Most wore the unofficial "uniform" of the Palestinian Jew, khaki shorts and a white short-sleeved shirt. Most were oriental Jews born in Jerusalem or recently arrived from Arab countries. Their dark skin and Semitic features made them indistinguishable from Arabs. Most were under twenty-one; the youngest was sixteen. All were veterans who recognized one another from previous operations—the bombing of the immigration office, the attack on Lydda airfield, the mining of the Tel Aviv railway—or from training courses in the Judean hills or in moonlit orange groves. Some were students at the same Jerusalem high school.

They knew that this sort of meeting often, but not always, preceded an operation. None had attended a meeting in which so many soldiers had been gathered together.

They whispered the same questions Yanai had asked Avinoam and Chaim-Toit in the taxi. "Is it an operation or just a meeting?" "The target? What's the target?"

"An operation. It has to be an operation," Amnon, one of the oldest boys, told the others. "Why else would they risk gathering so many of us in one room?"

Fifteen months ago Amnon had come to Palestine from Tunisia for one purpose: to build a Jewish State, not by farming or trading but by fighting. He had grown up in Tunis where he had belonged to the Betar, a Zionist youth organization that preached the inalienable right of Jews to live in a state that included the West Bank of the Jordan River and Transjordan.

The brief Nazi occupation of Tunis proved to him that the Betar was right: Jews could be secure only in their own country. During this occupation he risked death by plastering Tunis with Zionist posters. During the British occupation that followed, he risked jail for putting up the same posters. He saw little difference between the Nazis and the British. They both opposed the Jewish State.

In 1945 he arranged to marry a Tunisian Jewess. Her brother lived in Palestine and she held an immigration certificate. As soon as they arrived in Tel Aviv, he divorced her and contacted the Irgun.

Two weeks later another girl led him to the door of a stone house outside Jerusalem. She disappeared and he walked in. A Star of David flag covered a low table. A pistol and Bible rested on the flag. A curtain hung from the ceiling. Flickering candles revealed the outlines of three men behind the curtain.

"Why do you wish to join Irgun Zvai Leumi?" asked a voice.

"To build a Jewish State," he answered.

"Do you understand that if you are captured by the police you could be tortured? Could you keep our secrets?"

"Yes."

He answered questions about his willingness to suffer pain, obey orders and sacrifice his personal life. His examiners reminded him that the Irgun was a temporary organization with one goal: to force Britain to leave Palestine immediately and to bring about a Jewish State on both banks of the Jordan.

His answers satisfied them. One man ordered him to "put [his] left hand on the gun and the Bible and repeat the oath."

Amnon repeated: "I do solemnly swear full allegiance to the Irgun Zvai Leumi and to its commander, to its goals and its aims. And I am ready to make every sacrifice, even my life. I will give preference at all times to the Irgun above my parents, my brothers, my sisters and my entire family until we build an independent Israel or until I die."

Amnon kept one secret from his examiners: he feared and hated guns. He had never served in any army and he loathed hunting. Until the oath he had never touched a gun in his life.

During his training he tried to overcome this fear by using the logic instilled in him by a French education. He had come to Palestine and joined the Irgun in order to help create a Jewish State, he reasoned. A great number of Jews were needed to build this State, certainly more than the 600,000 then living in Palestine. The survivors of death camps wanted to come but British laws prevented them. Therefore, in order to build a Jewish State he had to fight the British. In order to fight the British, he had to overcome his fear of guns.

He considered his fear of firearms to be part of the hateful personality of the Diaspora Jew—servile, hesitant and accommodating. He was determined to effect a total transformation—to become the brave, defiant, fighting Hebrew who would drive Britain from Palestine. He chose an underground name, Amnon, that would symbolize his new personality.

Amnon had been a leader of the German Jews during the twelfth century. Because of his popularity, the Bishop of Mainz demanded that he renounce Judaism and convert to Christianity. Amnon asked for three days to decide. When he failed to appear on the third day the Bishop ordered his legs amputated "because they did not bring you to our meeting on time."

Amnon asked the Bishop to "cut out my tongue because it did not immediately refuse the demand that I become a Christian." He was tortured to death, but his martyrdom inspired other Jews to resist Christian conversion. In 1946 the story of a Jew defying a German torturer was inspirational.

Amnon overcame his fear of firearms but a year after his training he had still not lived up to his name. His own operations against the British struck him as petty. He laid mines in the streets near police stations and army barracks, then fired a shot in the air. Armored cars and police vans raced from their garages and ran over the mines. The vehicles suffered minor damages, the soldiers and police minor casualties. Such mines would never build a Jewish State.

The number of soldiers gathered in Beit Aharon and the presence of a few older men, presumably commanders from Tel Aviv, convinced him today would be different. He noticed particularly a tall man in his mid-twenties with black bushy eyebrows and glittering dark eyes who stood alone in one corner. Amnon asked the other boys if they knew him, but none did.

Shortly after eight this man stepped to the front of the classroom. The boys pulled the benches into a semicircle facing him. When they quieted he took a stick of red chalk from his pocket and began drawing a diagram on the whitewashed wall.

Amnon watched as the diagram began to take the shape of a building—a building that, thirty-two years later, would still trouble his conscience and haunt his dreams.

*   *   *

"How can Gaillard cook *pilaf financière?*" Max Hamburger asked his assistant manager, Emile Soutter. "He doesn't have all the proper ingredients."

"He is substituting a compromise *pilaf financière* because of rationing," Soutter said.

He was accustomed to Hamburger's objections. Every morning he brought the menu cards for the table d'hôte luncheons and dinners to Hamburger's office in the lobby of the King David Hotel; and almost every morning Hamburger found fault. If he approved the menus he initialed them. If he disapproved, he drew a line through the unsuitable dish and Soutter returned to the kitchen to negotiate with head chef Paul Gaillard.

Hamburger laid the menus on his desk and pulled *Le Guide Culinaire* from his bookshelf. He referred to Escoffier's book as "my Bible."

"'*Pilaf financière*,'" he read, "'contains quenelles of veal or poultry, olives, mushrooms, a cock's kidney's and comb, and truffles.' There aren't any truffles in Jerusalem. Tell him to cook something else."

Hamburger accepted that rationing made it impossible for the hotel to offer a *grande cuisine*. He had decided at the beginning of the war that a simple omelette executed according to Escoffier was preferable to a bogus pilaf. He had sent Gaillard a letter instructing him to "make the menu less complicated and stop offering such variety . . . seasonal fruits and vegetables should be used to the greatest extent possible. Sometimes we must have menus without meat."

The morning ritual typified two of Hamburger's cardinal principles: attention to detail and maintenance of the standards of a European grand hotel in the Middle East. These principles had served him well.

He had become an assistant manager at Shepheard's Hotel in Cairo while still in his mid-twenties. In 1937, at the age of thirty, he was named manager of the King David. If the war had not intervened he would have achieved his goal of managing a grand hotel in Europe.

Certainly his tenure at the King David had proven him capable. In some respects the King David surpassed the grand European hotels. When it opened in 1930 it was immediately the most modern in the Middle East. It charged more for its rooms than any hotel on the Asian continent and boasted of conveniences second to none—steam heat, a rose garden, a tennis court, two restaurants and bars, a banquet hall and a palatial lobby.

For all its modernity, the King David was built and operated in a time-honored Middle Eastern fashion. Azra Mosseri, a Jewish-Egyptian banker, had purchased a four-and-a-half-acre lot in Jerusalem from a Greek Orthodox monastery. To finance construction, he sold shares in Palestine Hotels Ltd. to American and Egyptian Jews, and to Swiss investors, retaining for his family a controlling interest. A Swiss architect designed the hotel, a Jewish architect supervised its construction, and Arab workmen built it. The company hired

Swiss and Jews to manage it, French and Italians to cook, and local Arabs and Africans from the Sudan to wait on tables, clean rooms, mop floors and wash dishes.

Another Mosseri company, Egyptian Hotels Ltd., owned and operated the best hotels in Egypt: the Winter Palace on the east bank of the Nile in Luxor, the Mena House next to the Pyramids, the Semiramis and Shepheard's in Cairo. Shepheard's had become the most celebrated hotel in the Middle East, a center of social life and intrigue and a crossroads of empire where, according to Kipling, if one sat in the bar long enough, one would meet everyone one knew. Mosseri planned for the King David to become "Jerusalem's Shepheard's."

By the time it registered its first guest in December 1930, the hotel was already a Jerusalem landmark. In only eighteen months the Jewish architect, Tommy Chaikin, and his Arab laborers had erected a massive rectangular six-story structure faced with khaki-colored stone that dominated but did not clash with Jerusalem's landscape.

The stone matched the hills that surrounded the hotel and the buildings that sat in its shadow. Its rectangular shape imitated the angles of the walls of the city that faced it across the Valley of Hinnom. The cypress and palm that dotted its grounds were like those shading the tomb of King David on Mount Zion, the Tomb of the Virgin Mary on the Mount of Olives and the Dome of the Rock.

At the time of the hotel's opening, the *Palestine Bulletin* said: "Nothing about the building jars with its surroundings. View the Valley of Hinnom, Mount Zion, and the walls of Jerusalem with the so-called citadel of David (whence the hotel took its name) from any of the terraces overlooking the spacious formal garden and you feel that those sights, and the Hills of Moab beyond, properly belong there. And if the position were reversed and you looked from any of these places at the hotel you would have the same feeling about the new structure . . . the rightness and distinction of the whole to the surroundings which are Jerusalem."

The hotel resembled Jerusalem's older stone buildings but it had been constructed somewhat differently.

In 1927 a series of earthquakes rocked the city. The walls of the El Aqsa Mosque and the Holy Sepulchre cracked, the Auguste Victoria swayed, and a few smaller stone structures collapsed. The Swiss architect, Emile Vogt, designed the hotel so it could withstand small earthquakes and the type of aerial and artillery bombing that had destroyed so many stone and concrete buildings during the Great War.

He built the King David in the shape of a flattened "H," with a long rectangular body joining together wings at the north and south. To protect the structure from earthquakes, he mandated a particularly large expansion joint between each wing and the main body. These joints were designed not only to absorb the expansion of the building in hot weather, but also to contain the shock waves from an earthquake or explosion. If one section of the building collapsed, the joint would, it was hoped, enable the other two to remain standing.

In order to increase the structure's resistance to shock waves from explosions, Vogt asked for extra steel reinforcement in the concrete pillars and floors. Only one thing could destroy the entire building: a direct hit by a bomb.

The stone covering the King David's walls gave the building an image of strength and durability. In 1921 the British Governor of Jerusalem, Sir Ronald Storrs, had ordered that all new buildings be faced with stone dug from local quarries. His purpose was to harmonize the New City and its suburbs with the stone walls and buildings of the Old.

Many Jews protested. Since most stonecutters were Arabs, the law was, in effect, forcing them to employ Arab labor. Storrs refused to compromise. Jerusalem's new buildings were faced with stone of various colors. Just as the hills and valleys surrounding the city had different, subtle shades—some darker, some pinker, some with a greenish tinge, some a pale brown—so too did the buildings faced with their stones.

A quarry near the Jericho Road supplied the stone chosen to cover the King David's facade. According to Jewish legend, when Roman legionnaires destroyed Jerusalem and massacred its citizens, a stream of Jewish blood rushed down a dry riverbed toward the Dead Sea. Midway between Jerusalem and Jericho a mountain blocked its way. The blood seeped into the mountain, coloring its rocks red. These rocks were used to build the King David. Every evening the setting sun gave the King David's stones a reddish hue and Jerusalem was reminded of the legend.

Gray-green marble slabs from another quarry covered the pillars, floors, and ceilings of the lobby, bar and main restaurant. In these public rooms the interior decorator, Hufschmid of Geneva, tried to re-create King David's Palace. "A faithful reconstruction was impossible," Hufschmid admitted, "so the artists tried to adapt to modern tastes different Jewish styles."

Except for an alcove overlooking the garden, these public rooms were completely without curves. In the main lounge, guests and visitors reclined in square green leather chairs modeled on Hittite thrones. Four thrones surrounded each of nine rectangular marble-topped tables. The tables stood on rectangular carpets into which were woven the symbols of the tribes of Israel: lions, snakes, wolves, fruit, hinds, etc. Rectangular pillars rose two stories to the lobby's ceiling. A geometric frieze depicting the crenellations in the Old City's walls ran along the molding. Slabs of marble covered walls, ceilings, floors and pillars. Wooden doors, twelve feet high, opened onto the banquet hall and a writing room known as "The Arab Lounge."

One expected the doors to swing open for King David himself, or for King Solomon and the Queen of Sheba. Instead one saw Nubians, carrying trays of drinks. The rooms might have been the set for a Hollywood biblical epic, the ticket hall of a fascist railway station, or the Egyptian wing of a museum built just after the discovery of King Tut's tomb. According to Hufschmid, "the object was to evoke by reminiscence of ancient Semitic styles the ambience of the glorious period of King David."

The royal ambience suited the guests. Kings, emperors, queens, princes, dukes and princesses made pilgrimages to Jerusalem's shrines and stayed for weeks, sometimes months, at the King David. King George V of Britain, King Alfonso of Spain, and Emperor Haile Selassie of Ethiopia had all perched on the Hittite thrones and made entrances through the enormous doors. The Emperor left after two nights, protesting that the King David was too expensive. The Italians had forced him into exile and he had to watch his money.

The Duke of Segovia, the Duke of Alba, the Maharaja of Tikari, Emir Abdullah of Transjordan and the Mahendra of Nepal threw banquets in the Phoenician Hall and sipped brandies in the main bar. This bar was decorated in an English Tudor style that was, according to Hufschmid, meant to evoke "nostalgia for King Solomon."

Princess Eugénie of Greece, King Farouk's mother Farida, Queen Sophie of Albania, and the Princess de Bourbon Parma wandered through the rose garden, took high teas in the main lounge and discussed the mosaics, silver trays, rugs and religious relics they purchased during "pilgrimages" to the Old City.

The Christian and Moslem royalty was joined at dinner dances or for cocktails on the terrace at sunset by a Jewish aristocracy of Rothschilds, Warburgs, Sulzburgers, and Guggenheims; by Christian princes of industry— Walter Chrysler and Wilhelm Von Opel; by artists like Arturo Toscanini; and by British warlords—Allenby, Mountbatten, and Churchill.

These guests attracted a mixed band of celebrities, hypnotists, vegetarians, mystics and healers. One frequent guest, a Dr. Voronof, claimed to have reversed the aging process by transplanting the glands of apes into human beings. Queen Mothers were reported to be intrigued by "The Voronof Method."

For the wealthy and titled, the world outside Europe during the 1930s and '40s was small. They ran into one another at Government House receptions, in the first-class drawing rooms of liners bound to or from Suez, India and Malaya, and in the clubs and grand hotels of Palestine, Egypt, Singapore, and Hong Kong.

Like ocean liners, these hotels—the King David, Shepheard's, Raffles—were a world unto themselves. Just as the passengers on an ocean liner ate, drank, and met in the same restaurants, bars and public rooms, so the guests at the grand hotels stayed within the hotel grounds, confident that they would find there the city's finest restaurants, liveliest bars, and most pleasant gardens.

Inside the ocean liner and the Colonial hotel, bands played, waiters served iced drinks, couples in evening dress danced, chefs prepared exquisite dishes and stewards turned down linen sheets.

Outside the liner, storms raged and icebergs appeared out of the fog. Outside the hotel there was poverty, filth, incurable disease and terrorist gangs; mosques, temples, pagodas and shrines; the Terrible Turk, "wogs," "chinks," "kaffirs"; and, in Jerusalem, bloody skirmishes between the "Towels" (Arabs) and "Beards" (Jews).

In 1938, just a year after Hamburger became manager, the King David ceased to be a neutral Swiss refuge from Jerusalem's horrors. In October the British Army requisitioned the forty bedrooms and seventeen bathrooms of the hotel's fourth floor for its Palestine headquarters. A month later, the civilian government appropriated forty-five rooms in the south wing as its "Secretariat." These rooms were on the ground floor, mezzanine and first three bedroom floors. The top floor of bedrooms in the south wing was already in the hands of the army.

When the war began in 1939 the army seized the bedrooms in the center and north wings of the third floor. Engineers installed an army communications center in the basement and in the bottom two floors of a garden annex. Hamburger was left with less than a third of the hotel's rooms—sixty-two bedrooms and twenty-four bathrooms in the center and north wings of the first two floors.

The army moved into the King David because it needed more space. The number of troops stationed in Palestine had increased, first because of the Arab revolt, and then because of Palestine's strategic value in the war.

The civilian Secretariat moved because it needed more security. During the Arab revolt the Secretariat had been located in a former German nunnery which overlooked a busy street near the Damascus Gate. Between 1936 and 1939 Jewish and British Secretariat employees were beaten and shot at as they entered and left the building. The King David was more secure. Its neighborhood was less populated and access to its rooms easier to control.

The government assured Hamburger that the occupation was temporary. An architect had already been contracted to design a permanent Secretariat and Army HQ. However, groundbreaking ceremonies for this huge diamond-shaped fortress were postponed, postponed again, and then canceled because of the war. The Secretariat and army renewed their leases at the King David.

The Secretariat's occupation of the south wing posed the fewest problems for Hamburger. Workers and visitors to this wing reached the offices by a side door and a set of rear service stairs. The military, however, had to use the main entrance. They mingled in the lobby with civilian guests, jammed the bar and used the washrooms.

Hamburger tried to minimize the damage. When the army renewed its lease in 1942 he inserted a clause stating that "in no circumstances whatsoever shall orderlies, male or female clerks, typists, secretaries be allowed to use the passenger or luggage lifts of the hotel whether going to or from their place of work." Only officers were permitted in the lifts; others had to trudge up a narrow flight of service stairs.

During the war soldiers stayed in the sixty-two bedrooms still open to the public. As many as six or seven crowded into a single room and Generals Auchinleck, Montgomery, Alexander and Patton and their aides-de-camp stopped at the hotel on their way to and from the Asian war theater and conferences at Teheran and Yalta.

When the war ended the army kept its offices on the third and fourth floors but relinquished the bedrooms on the first two floors. Civilian guests began returning to the hotel. Statesmen, politicians and journalists arrived to study the Palestine problem. A few of the wealthy and aristocratic came for their annual pilgrimages.

Like Government House and the Club, a functioning grand hotel such as the King David was visible proof that the Empire continued.

Nineteen forty-six was a year of illusion for the British Empire. Britain was bankrupt and its wartime defeats, especially in Asia, had irreparably damaged the Empire's prestige in the eyes of its subjects. Nevertheless, it seemed to many Britons that the Empire might survive. Nowhere was this illusion more convincing than in the eastern Mediterranean. Here the British Army occupied Greece and Libya. A British general commanded Transjordan's army and British influence was strong in Iraq. There were British military bases in Egypt and Palestine, and British High Commissioners ruled Cyprus, Malta and Palestine.

Just as Britons believed, or pretended, that the Empire could return to its prewar power, so too did Hamburger believe that the King David could return to its prewar elegance; that it could remain a civilized oasis of Swiss neutrality despite the Palestine troubles; and that despite food rationing, he could insist on Escoffier's standard of truffles in the *pilaf financière*.

3

AMIHAI PAGLIN finished drawing the diagram on the schoolroom's white-washed wall. He had carefully labeled Julian's Way, the French Consulate, and the David Brothers Building. The largest building was in the center of the diagram. It dwarfed the others.

He put the chalk in his pocket and stepped back. Now the others could see, and as they realized what he had drawn, what their operation was to be, one soldier whistled while another clapped his hands and stamped his feet. The rest were silent, paralyzed with shock and excitement. For the first time, Paglin spoke.

"We are going to attack the headquarters of the British Army and Government. We are going to blow up the King David Hotel."

Amnon was elated. "At last I've been chosen for something important," he thought.

Paglin was as excited as the young soldiers. The King David was the British Mandate's equivalent of the American Pentagon and Congress; its War Office and Parliament. To penetrate and destroy it would be an act of guerrilla warfare unequaled in history. No partisan band in World War Two had succeeded in destroying German headquarters in any occupied European country. Today the Irgun would write history.

For four years Paglin had wanted to mount an operation that would demolish a symbol of British power. The symbols he planned to attack had changed but his determination had remained constant since one afternoon in March 1942.

On that afternoon, he and two high school friends, David and Eliahu, had sat on the steps of his house in Tel Aviv. They had just graduated but none of them could find an exciting job. They were bored and aimless. A great war was being fought but Jews were only playing the part of victims.

For Paglin it was particularly frustrating. He came from a family noted for its patriotism. His father, an emotional Tsarist, had been driven from Russia by the Bolsheviks in 1918. He transferred his nationalist fervor to Zionism and named his first son born in Palestine, "Amihai," "My Nation Lives." For the next twenty years the family was poor but politically active.

Every day Amihai's father walked five miles to Tel Aviv to search for work. He usually returned empty-handed and in tears. On these days he made a point of telling his sons, "Never think that I regret having come to Palestine instead of America."

During the 1929 Arab riots, the family was saved by its poverty. An Arab mob broke into the house, but while they fought over the only object of value, a sewing machine, the Paglins escaped.

During the 1930s the family became more prosperous and Amihai, at a late age, attended high school. His father, aunt and brothers joined the left-wing Mapai Party and his brothers became members of the Haganah. And still, Amihai, to his own disgust, accomplished nothing. "Let's think," he often said to David and Eliahu. "We are young, we owe no allegiance to anyone, we can think clearly—what shall we *do*?"

A parade of demonstrators carrying banners and flags marched down the road a few feet away from where the three boys sat. Several marchers carried posters bearing the picture of a distinguished-looking man. Underneath the picture were the words, "Sir Harold MacMichael, known as the High Commissioner of Palestine, WANTED FOR MURDER of 800 refugees drowned in the Black Sea on the boat *Struma*."

The *Struma*, a rickety Danube River cattle barge, had left the Rumanian port of Constanţa on the Black Sea in December 1941. Its destination was Palestine; its cargo, 769 Rumanian Jews fleeing Fascist persecution. Hours after departing, its engines failed and it was towed into Istanbul. The Turkish government refused to allow the Jews to land and the Palestine government refused to issue immigration certificates, because the White Paper quotas had already been filled.

The refugees sat in the boat for two months. No country in the world would offer them asylum. Finally Turkish tugboats towed the *Struma* out to sea and cast it adrift. A few hours later it exploded. The only survivor said they had been torpedoed.

Numerous Jews in Palestine had had relatives aboard the *Struma* and this afternoon's demonstration was one of many.

Paglin saw a red sports car driven by a Palestine policeman wheel into the marchers. The policeman jumped out and grabbed a Zionist flag from an elderly man at the head of the procession.

"The demonstration is over," he shouted. "Everyone back to your homes." He ripped up the flag, crumpled it into a ball, and walked back to his car.

Paglin was incredulous. "Look at that!" he shouted to his friends. "Nobody challenged him. One British policeman can intimidate a thousand Jews. That's how they rule, by prestige."

Eliahu jumped off the steps, ran into the street and leaped onto the policeman's back. The policeman wrestled him to the ground and yanked him up by the wrist. Eliahu grabbed the flag with his other hand, squirmed out of the policeman's grasp, and ran.

He met Paglin and David around the corner. Paglin burst into tears. Amihai, "My Nation Lives," his father's tears, the family's escape from Arab terrorists— what was it worth when one policeman could insult and intimidate a thousand Jews?

"Look at the masses of people we have," he cried. "And what do we do? Nothing. Eliahu just risked his life. For what? For nothing. To save a flag. If we are going to risk our lives, let's risk them for something important. Let's do something that will really shake the British. Something that will shake the world."

They decided on the spot to form a three-man underground cell. The following week Paglin stole a bayonet from a sleeping British soldier. Eliahu and David bought pistols. They all debated what action would "shake" Britain and destroy its prestige. Paglin finally said, "All right, then, let's kill the High Commissioner."

One Sunday night a month later they crouched in a ditch outside Government House, a stark, white, two-story fortress surrounded by gardens and pine trees and perched on an otherwise barren hilltop known since biblical times as "The Hill of Evil Counsel." They were scouting Government House. Later, they planned to return and dynamite it.

Suddenly MacMichael's silhouette flashed across the blinds of his bedroom. "Oh, God, if only I had a knife!" Paglin thought, "I could climb up the drainpipe into his bedroom and slit his throat." He almost cried with frustration.

But the next day he confessed to his friends, "I'd never be able to use a knife. But if I had an ax, maybe I'd have enough courage to lift it up and then by the power of will I'd order my muscles to let it fall of its own weight. Perhaps that would do the job. Because if I touched his skin I'd recoil. I could not touch the living flesh of a man and then kill him."

Paglin decided that if he was going to shake the world he would have to cultivate a split personality. One was Paglin, the man of thought and sensitivity, who gave the order; the other was Paglin the emotionless technician, who carried it out—logic ordered, conditioned reflex acted. The logical Paglin raised the ax, the mechanical Paglin let it fall.

He and his friends worked hard to transform themselves. When they practiced shooting with live ammunition they fired three times in quick succession—One! Two! Three! This would destroy the target. They were afraid that if they fired only once they might stop and help a wounded victim. Instead, they concentrated on pulling the trigger and letting the technician take over. *He* always fired three times, always quickly, always to kill.

When Eliahu was out of ammunition he practiced by banging a stick against a tin can again and again. One! Two! Three! One! Two! Three!

Paglin never dropped the ax on the High Commissioner. For weeks the three boys crouched in the hills bordering the Jerusalem–Tel Aviv road waiting for his car to pass so they could detonate mines buried in the road. When MacMichael finally appeared, the mines failed to explode.

Paglin decided to return to his original plan and dynamite Government House. To do this he needed hundreds of pounds of TNT; to get the TNT he needed the cooperation of one of the established underground groups. At the beginning of 1943 he arranged to meet with Yaacov Meridor, the Commander of the Irgun.

The Irgun had come into being during the Arab revolt as a reaction to the policies of the Haganah, the Jewish defense organization that was controlled by the Yishuv's elected representatives. In 1936 almost every Jewish male in Palestine belonged to the Haganah.

During the Arab revolt Haganah commanders ordered their soldiers to protect Jewish settlements but not to mount offensives or retaliate against Arab civilians. Haganah soldiers who opposed this policy of restraint left to form the Irgun Zvai Leumi. If Arab terrorists bombed a Jewish market and killed Jewish women and children, the Irgun placed bombs in an Arab market and killed Arab women and children. If Arabs ambushed a Jewish bus, the Irgun ambushed an Arab bus. And so on.

At first Vladimir Jabotinsky, the founder of the right-wing Revisionist Party from which the Irgun drew its members, opposed this retaliatory terror. He told Irgun commanders, "I can't see much heroism or public good in shooting from the rear an Arab peasant on a donkey carrying vegetables for sale in Tel Aviv."

Later, reluctantly, he agreed to the terror, although he told his biographer, Joseph Schechtman, "What kind of people are they [the Irgunists]? I know them very little. Their plans, their innermost thoughts, just don't reach me."

In 1939, when Britain published the White Paper, the Irgun began attacking British offices and policemen. After Britain declared war on Germany the Irgun called a truce and offered to cooperate with the British Army in the Middle East. David Raziel, the Irgun's previous commander, was killed while fighting with a British expedition sent to Iraq in 1941 to crush a revolt led by the pro-Axis politician Rashid Ali.

Montgomery's victory at El Alamein in 1942 ended the threat of a German invasion of Palestine. The Irgun, now commanded by Yaacov Meridor, resumed its rebellion against British rule. It published leaflets, stole arms and broadcast propaganda. Meridor, however, feared British reprisals and the wrath of the Haganah, and some Irgunists considered him too cautious.

Paglin had resisted joining the Irgun. His family disapproved of its violence and he thought he could accomplish more on his own. He wanted to see Meridor for one reason: he needed dynamite.

They met at night in a tin shack outside Tel Aviv. Paglin explained his plan: he and his friend would slither into the High Commissioner's garden and mine the foundations of his house with enough dynamite to demolish it, killing MacMichael and his aides. The Jewish and Arab servants of Government House would, of course, also be killed.

Meridor was appalled. "If you boys do this maybe the next day the British will act like Germans and kill the entire Jewish population as revenge. Given the situation of the Jews in Europe this would mean the end of the Jewish race. As chief of the Irgun I could never accept such a responsibility. The Irgun cannot be involved. Of course, if I was on my own I might do it."

Paglin was dismayed. This was not the tough, brave Irgun commander he had imagined. "Listen, it doesn't make any difference to me," he said, "but my friends Eliahu and David want the approval of the commander of the Irgun. That's all."

"OK, I approve it."

"In addition to the approval, how about a bag of dynamite?"

"OK. That too."

Afterward Paglin told his friends, "I haven't felt so happy since the first day of a school vacation."

Finally he had enough dynamite to change the course of Jewish history. "This will be the most important action ever staged by Jews in Palestine," he said. "We're going to destroy an important symbol of British prestige, and kill the most important Briton in Palestine. We're going to put our names in the history books."

Again he was to be disappointed. Two days later he received a note from Meridor. "A new alliance has been formed with the Haganah and this alliance has decided to adopt our plan. I promise that you will not just get a bag of dynamite but the entire Irgun supporting you. We will blow up all of Palestine's important police stations on the same day."

Paglin was suspicious. The Haganah had never before approved this type of operation. The day before the charges were to be placed, the Haganah changed its mind. Only a dissident faction within the organization had given its approval. When the members of the Haganah's High Command learned of the joint operation they canceled it. To ensure that the attack would fail, Haganah soldiers exploded grenades on the road leading from Jerusalem to the Hill of

Evil Counsel. An armored car and a large detachment of police was immediately sent to guard Government House.

Paglin returned to free-lance sabotage. Using the explosives meant for the High Commissioner, he and his friends blew up construction equipment in the yard of the largest British contractor in Palestine. The following night they put up posters in Tel Aviv. "THIS IS THE BEGINNING. We give Britain two months to leave Palestine. Otherwise we will destroy every British building."

Several months later a messenger from the Irgun stopped Paglin in the street. "Begin has heard about you and admires what you're doing. He wants you to join the Irgun."

On February 1, 1944, two months after assuming command of the Irgun, Menahem Begin had issued a proclamation of war against Great Britain: "There is no longer any armistice between the Jewish people and the British administration of Eretz Israel which hands our brothers over to Hitler. Our people are at war with this regime—war to the end. . . . we shall fight, every Jew in the Homeland will fight. The God of Israel, the Lord of Hosts, will aid us. There will be no retreat. Freedom—or death."

At last, Paglin thought, here is a man who will fight. Stirred by Begin's leadership, he joined the Irgun. His own group had already fallen apart. Eliahu had left to join the smallest and most violent of the three underground armies, the LEHI (Lohamei Herut Israel—"Fighters for the Freedom of Israel").

The LEHI was started in 1940 by Irgun members who disagreed with that organization's wartime truce with Great Britain. It was small, never more than three hundred members, and it believed in and practiced personal terror, the assassination of important Britons and the random murder of British soldiers, policemen, and civilians.

The British and its numerous enemies within the Yishuv called LEHI "The Stern Gang," after its founder and first leader, the brilliant and charismatic Abraham Stern. His followers called him "Yair"—"The Illuminator." He was a poet:

> Like a rabbi
> Who carries his prayer book in a velvet bag
>   to the synagogue
> So carry I
>   my sacred gun to the temple. . . .

Eliahu tried to persuade Paglin to join. He refused. He hated the British administration, not the British. He saw a purpose in killing MacMichael and blowing up a police station but not in shooting a corporal sitting in a barber's chair.

On November 6, 1944, Eliahu and another LEHI boy, Eliahu Hakim, assassinated Lord Moyne, Britain's Minister of State in the Middle East. Hakim pumped three bullets into Moyne's chest. Eliahu shot Moyne's driver, Lance Corporal Fuller, three times—One! Two! Three!

Meanwhile, Paglin had become chief of the Irgun's Tel Aviv assault unit and a member of its four-man planning group. In April 1946, the Irgun's Chief of Operations was arrested and Begin summoned Paglin to a late-night meeting in an orange grove near Tel Aviv. It was the first time Paglin had met his commander. Begin announced that he was making him the new Chief of Operations. At the age of twenty-five, he would be the youngest member of the Irgun High Command.

He accepted on one condition, that he be allowed to break into British police amps and armories in order to steal his favorite weapon, dynamite.

Paglin deserved the promotion. He had planned and led attacks against the RAF airfield at Qastina—three Halifaxes destroyed and eight damaged—and the Ramat Gan police station, where thirty weapons and three hundred rounds of ammunition were stolen. He had proven himself a uniquely talented saboteur.

He was courageous and had a genius not only for guerrilla tactics but also for inventing and constructing the devices necessary to execute his plans: tamperproof contact mines for railway sabotage, a gigantic barrel-bomb mounted on a truck, a remote control mortar with an acid fuse and a range of four miles that admiring army engineers dubbed the "V3."

In 1945 he sent V3s hurtling toward police stations in Jaffa and Sarona. He buried six in the olive grove south of the King David. Three were aimed at the government printing press, three at the King David. The Haganah learned about them and Teddy Kollek of the Jewish Agency tipped off the British. Army sappers dug them up before Paglin's D-Day, the King's birthday.

Now he was ready to try again. This time he had the approval of the Haganah; this time he had devised a more elaborate plan to shake Britain and destroy its prestige.

"We considered three plans for this operation," he told the soldiers sitting in front of him at Beit Aharon. "The first was to reserve rooms and then carry bombs into the hotel in our suitcases. After checking into our rooms we would sneak the bombs downstairs into the basement, activate their fuses and escape.

"We eliminated this plan for numerous reasons. We estimated that we needed 350 kilos of explosives and we could never carry so many heavy suitcases into the hotel without arousing suspicion. The corridors and lobby are always full of soldiers, and if there was any fighting inside the building we'd have been sure to lose. We have also learned that the British have installed automatic machine guns in the corridors. A soldier pushes a button and the guns fire a murderous crossfire.

"Our second plan was to create a diversion and storm the hotel from the road. This risked too many casualties. The guards are armed with submachine guns and the soldiers who work in the headquarters carry sidearms. There are hundreds of other soldiers stationed nearby." Paglin pointed to an area of the diagram south of the hotel, the army camp.

The Irgun soldiers stared at the red chalk marks on the wall. No one moved or spoke as Paglin began explaining the final plan, the plan to destroy the British headquarters.

4

GABE SIFRONY limped through the King David's lobby greeting waiters, guests, and regular customers by name. He peered into the bar, Winter Garden, and Arab Lounge, strolled out onto the terrace, looked down into the garden and then returned to the lobby. The usual collection of Jewish and Arab politicians, pilgrims and merchants, army officers, policemen and spies sat on the Hittite thrones sipping coffee and whispering.

Ever since its opening the King David had been Jerusalem's most important neutral gathering place. For the first eight years of the hotel's life the intrigues and conspiracies hatched in its bar and lobby centered around the Arab-Jewish conflict. When the war started, these intrigues took on a global dimension.

Palestine was important because it was near the vital Suez Canal. It was also a stop on the air route to India and the Asian war, a contact point for refugees and agents from the Balkans, and a base for operations against the Vichy French regimes in Syria and Lebanon.

The Palestine Police Criminal Investigation Department (CID) and army Intelligence recruited many of the King David's waiters, chambermaids, bartenders and guests to keep track of suspected Axis agents and monitor their contacts, often made in the hotel's lobby, with Arab politicians. The most notorious of the British agents was the beautiful, self-styled "Druze Princess," who had left her husband in Vichy Lebanon and taken up residence in the hotel. In exchange for information, army Intelligence picked up her hotel bills.

Soon she was boasting about her job and calling herself the "Mata Hari of the Middle East." The British stopped paying and Hamburger evicted her.

When the war ended, Palestine's strategic and political importance increased. The United States and Britain feared a Soviet military threat to Iran and the Persian Gulf. Palestine provided a military and political base from which to counter the Russians.

At the same time Palestine menaced the stability of the Anglo-American alliance. Britain's refusal to open the country to Jewish refugees had enraged American politicians and Jewish leaders. They threatened to block a loan Britain desperately needed for its postwar recovery.

In 1946, the West was also beginning to realize the extent of the Middle East's oil reserves and oil executives sensed that the Palestine dispute could harm their relations with Arab oil producers.

Aviation executives considered Tel Aviv's Lydda Airport a key stop on their round-the-world air routes. They sent representatives to Palestine to lobby for landing rights.

By the middle of 1946 Jerusalem had become a center of postwar intrigue and the King David Hotel its epicenter. Everyone stayed there or came regularly to its restaurants and bars: weapons salesmen and smugglers, American politicians, officials of the Jewish Agency, diplomats, Committees of Inquiry, oil men, journalists, religious fanatics, and Intelligence agents.

Haganah commanders who specialized in smuggling illegal immigrants were there, as well as Jews of every political persuasion: Arieh Altman, the president of the Revisionists who wanted a Jewish State on both sides of the Jordan River; Judah Magnes, who wanted a bi-national state; and lawyer and Haganah commander, Dov Joseph. Jerusalem's noted Arab hostess, Katy Antonius, patronized the King David, as well as moderate Arab nationalists such as Musa al Alami and Wasfi Tell. Policemen and spies—Richard Catling, the Palestine Police Jewish expert; Nick Andronovich, the American OSS agent; John J. O'Sullivan of the DSO (Defense Security Organization); Martin Charteris and Ernest Quinn of Military Intelligence; and Boris Guriel, a member of Shai, the Haganah's Intelligence organization—all came to exchange information over glasses of rough Cyprus brandy, tap telephones, bribe hotel employees for information, or spy on the Jewish and Arab politicians and on Jerusalem's rabbis, patriarchs and bishops.

In the morning they gathered in the lobby. Before lunch they moved into the "Best Informed Bar In Jerusalem." The intrigue in this bar made Bartley Crum, who visited Jerusalem in March as part of the Anglo-American Committee, feel "like a character in a Hollywood mystery film":

> Here we found ourselves in the center of an extraordinary social-political ferment. Every special pleader in the Middle East was on hand, and here levantine intrigue flourished unashamed. . . .
> Appropriately enough a Swiss bartender presided. . . . I found

myself drinking cocktails with an Arab journalist and member of one of the best-known Arab families, who proceeded to tell me of the deep hostility between the Nashashibi family in Palestine and the Husseinis, of whom the former Mufti is the head. He would depart and his place would be taken by Harry Beilin, the Jewish Agency liaison officer, who would relate yet another unpublished story of bravery behind Nazi lines by Haganah parachuters recruited by the British. Beilin would leave and I would find myself tête-a-tête with a toothy French correspondent whose secret explanation for anti-Semitism was that all Jews were circumcised and all Christians were not. I spoke with Arabs of every political persuasion from Fascist-clerical to Communist, and with Jews of every political color. . . .

In the later afternoon everyone regrouped in the lobby. A string quartet played between four and five while Sudanese waiters pushed tea trollies between tables. In the early evening guests walked in the garden or sat in wicker chairs on a terrace facing the Old City. The moon, faintly visible in the afternoon sky, now became brighter, and a fresh wind blew away the heat. The pink stone of the buildings glowed, rooftops turned blood red, the sky darkened, church bells rang, and red-jacketed waiters arrived with drinks.

According to Richard Crossman, one of the British members of the Anglo-American Committee, "The atmosphere is comic as dusk falls and the groups drinking on the terrace whisper to each other and the various members spy suspiciously on each other to see what sub-rosa contacts each is making. And all around us detectives every ten yards under the bougainvillaea, grinning and saluting."

As Gabe Sifrony limped through the lobby on the morning of July 22, he noticed to his astonishment that he was one of the only journalists in the hotel. The night before a report had swept through the main bar that Bedouins in the Jordanian desert had discovered a boy who had been raised by gazelles. Jimmy Gammill of Pathé had hired jeeps and drivers and at sunrise a large party of reporters and newsreel cameramen had set off for the Transjordan. A few hours later another group of journalists drove up to Mount Scopus to tour Hebrew University and lunch with its president. Sifrony was one of few pressmen to avoid both junkets.

It was a rare day that he could sit in the King David's bar without being joined by groups of reporters. He was the unofficial dean of the Palestine press corps and foreign journalists usually sought him out as soon as they arrived. He introduced them to the leaders they wanted to interview, found them apartments, and told them how to contact the underground.

Although he was a Jew, he had close friends in every community. His physical appearance put people at ease. He was under five feet tall and limped as a result of a wound received while covering the Italian invasion of Ethiopia. He seemed perpetually grinning and cheerful and, most important, he was useful.

He carried messages between those who found it inconvenient to meet in person, between Arab and Jewish leaders, even between terrorists and British policemen.

Every Jew in Palestine had his "Good Arab," and every Arab his "Good Jew." Many prominent Arabs considered Sifrony their Good Jew. He had been raised in an Arab village and spoke fluent Arabic. The prestigious Cairo newspaper, *Al Ahram*, published his articles and Katy Antonius invited him to her parties as her token Jew.

Jerusalem's Christians trusted him. He had been educated by Russian nuns, spoke Russian and was so knowledgeable about Christianity that his American- and Arab-Christian friends insisted he join the Jerusalem YMCA, where again he was the token Jew.

British policemen and government officials believed he was a "safe Jew." His articles appeared in British newspapers otherwise unsympathetic to Zionism and unlike many Jewish and American correspondents, he did not vilify Britain. The British made him a member, the only Jewish member, of the Jerusalem Sports Club.

He did not play tennis or squash, nor was he interested in the golf course the members were building near Mount Zion. But he liked to visit the bar. He grinned, listened to conversations and sometimes reminded the guests that "I am the indispensable Jewish ingredient in your club, the milk to make your porridge white."

The Jerusalem commanders of the Haganah, Irgun and Stern Gang also trusted him.

The Irgun trusted him because he had written for right-wing Hebrew newspapers sympathetic to the Irgun. Avinoam's private secretary and courier, Adina, often appeared at his house with messages.

The LEHI trusted him because he had been a close friend of their leader, Abraham Stern, before he was killed by the police. Sifrony had often left the King David bar or one of Katy Antonius' parties to join Stern in a basement room. Both loved chess and sometimes played until dawn.

The Haganah trusted him because he gave information to the Shai, their Intelligence organization, and had persuaded the Sternists to call off an attack on the government's information office in the David Brothers Building. This office was as much a headquarters for journalists as the King David. It contained a bar and canteen and a convenient telegraph service—"The Blue Train"—which enabled reporters to reach London or New York within an hour. Any attack on David Brothers would have killed a number of foreign journalists.

Because Sifrony listened, grinned and never ventured a political opinion, all the various factions believed he had no opinions of his own, or agreed with theirs.

They were wrong. Passionately and secretly he was loyal to one undergound group. Today would test that loyalty.

Paglin finished explaining the plan. X's and arrows covered the diagram.

"We're going to attack the King David in order to save Eretz Israel," he said. "We're going to damage British prestige and destroy important documents the British have stolen from the Jewish Agency. These documents are being kept under guard in the Secretariat. The leaders of the Haganah have approved this operation because they fear that unless these papers are destroyed there will be no Jewish State."

Paglin was finished. After announcing that Gideon would be in command, he stepped away.

A short, frail blond boy walked to the front of the classroom. The Irgun High Command considered Gideon the bravest and most experienced commander in Jerusalem. He was eighteen.

He was sixteen when he and other Irgun soldiers donned the uniforms of British constables and carried bombs into the heavily guarded headquarters of the Palestine Police. The other boys left and Gideon was surprised by a British police inspector as he was setting the fuses. His English was too poor to answer the inspector's questions. Instead, he drew his revolver and began firing. The Englishman fell, mortally wounded, and Gideon calmly returned to the fuses. For this, and other operations, he gained a reputation for bravery under fire.

Promotions followed. First he commanded ten boys, then twenty-five. He destroyed railway trains and sections of track. He blew up Jerusalem's electric transformer so that, during the ensuing blackout, a second Irgun unit could attack CID headquarters.

He commanded the unit that robbed Barclays Bank in Nablus. During this operation the telephone rang as he herded customers and tellers into the Arab manager's office. He picked up the manager's phone. A voice on the other end said in Arabic, "Hello. Police calling in for the daily check. Is everything in order?"

Gideon answered in fluent Arabic, "This is the director. Everything is fine, thanks be to God." The policeman rang off and Gideon's soldiers cleaned out the vaults.

After this operation one Irgun commander remarked that Gideon was fulfilling the prophecy of his underground name. The original Gideon was the fifth of the Israelite Judges, a twelfth-century B.C. leader who led Jewish tribes into battle against the nomadic Midianites.

Gideon's most famous battle occurred at Ain Harod. Thirty-two thousand Israelite soldiers gathered at the southern edge of the Jezreel Valley, a few miles from the Midianites' camp. Gideon reduced his force to three hundred, preferring a small, mobile band to an unwieldy army. Then, according to the Bible, "He divided his three hundred men into three companies and he put a trumpet in every man's hand, with empty pitchers and lamps [burning torches] within the pitchers."

When it was dark, his guerrilla band crept up to the Midianite camp, spread out and surrounded it. Gideon blew his trumpet and they attacked from every direction, blowing trumpets, smashing pitchers and waving blazing torches.

"A sword for the Lord and for Gideon!" they shouted. The Midianites panicked, struck each other with their swords and fled in confusion. A hand-picked group of commandos had vanquished a larger army through surprise and cunning.

Now, at Beit Aharon, Gideon divided his twenty soldiers into three units—"attack," "porters" and "diversionary"—and gave each soldier a specific assignment.

Although the Irgun was organized along paramilitary lines with "commanders" and "units," its operations were often executed by soldiers who had been carefully selected from a number of units. Gideon, Avinoam, Chaim-Toit and Paglin had chosen these twenty from the approximately one hundred combat soldiers in Jerusalem.

They had chosen some for their marksmanship and some for their strength; some because they spoke Arabic and others because they spoke English. They chose only soldiers with combat experience and eliminated those with European features. They chose only one brother or sister from a family. They picked an explosives expert, a mechanic and a nurse. They also, unknowingly, picked a traitor.

5

THE MESSENGER steered his bicycle off the main highway and onto a dirt lane in north Tel Aviv. The winter rains had carved ruts in Yehoshua Bin Nun Street; the summer heat had filled them with dust, which the messenger's bicycle stirred into dense plumes.

The messenger pedaled past one- and two-story concrete structures built in the same monotonous squares and rectangles, all with ugly boxlike terraces and flat roofs; all yellowed and cracked by the city's heat and humidity.

He passed a home for abandoned dogs and then a slaughterhouse. The dogs howled for their freedom; the animals wailed for mercy. Nobody lived on Bin Nun Street by choice. The public works department ignored the road's surface; the police ignored its inhabitants. It was the frontier of a frontier, the last road on the northernmost edge of Tel Aviv.

The messenger braked opposite a two-story house and walked his bicycle through its neglected garden. Beyond the yard the dust of the street merged with the dust of empty fields and rotting orange groves, and the dusty banks of the sluggish Yarkon River.

After leaving the bike in the rear yard, out of sight of the road, he entered the first-floor apartment through a back door. The kitchen was dark. Curtains and venetian blinds blocked light and trapped humid air and cooking odors. When his eyes had adjusted to the perpetual twilight he handed an envelope to the man sitting at the kitchen table.

An index card in the Palestine Police terrorist file described this man as

"Polish, b. Poland 1906 [his actual birth date was 1913]—5 ft. 9 in., medium build. . . ." A wanted poster described him as clean-shaven and "thin-faced with bad teeth." "He has a long hooked nose," it said, "and often wears horn-rimmed spectacles." The poster's illustration matched the description, so unflattering as to be almost an anti-Semitic cartoon. The CID believed that a plastic surgeon must have changed the wanted man's face. How else could he have evaded capture for so long?

The man at the kitchen table bore little resemblance to the picture. His hair was thinner. He had changed his spectacles to wire rims and grown a mustache and beard. He looked fifteen years older. His overall appearance was delicate rather than ugly, gentle instead of fierce. His most distinguishing characteristic was his pallor. His skin was pure white, almost translucent.

Menahem Begin had lived in Palestine only four years, the last two spent hiding in darkened hotel rooms and houses such as the one on Bin Nun Street. He passed most days agonizing over the Irgun's political strategy, and deciding which targets to attack, whether an operation conformed to the Irgun's "honor code," and what risks it posed to innocent civilians and his "boys."

Despite the opportunities for contemplation afforded by his years of isolation, he was not considered a particularly original or innovative political tactician. Arthur Koestler, who had been the General Secretary of the Revisionists, the political party linked to the Irgun, was bitterly disappointed when he met Begin in 1945. "He gave me an emotional lecture," Koestler said, "a recitation of biblical arguments supporting the Jewish right to the entire mandate. He had no conception of realpolitik or compromise."

Begin became so nervous and exhausted by his continual decision making that his wife sometimes chided him in front of the High Command. "Relax, Menahem," she would say. "You have to relax and not take every question, every discussion so seriously."

He met with the Irgun High Command in the Bin Nun Street house. When he had to confer with the commanders of the Stern Gang or Haganah, cars fetched him at night and returned him at night. If the meeting lasted until dawn, he returned to Bin Nun Street on the following evening. Sometimes he put on a long black coat and visited the local synagogue where he was known as Israel Sassover. None of his neighbors suspected he was Menahem Begin.

He kept busy during his voluntary imprisonment by reading, listening to the radio and helping his wife with housework. He changed his infant daughter Hasia's diapers and minded his three-year-old son, Benny. He mopped floors and washed dishes.

His wife, Aliza, shopped. Otherwise, she too remained inside for most of the day. She knitted and read, became thin and stooped and suffered from chronic asthma. Her sacrifices were equal to his.

His only frequent visitors were the seven members of the Irgun High Command. Usually they came one by one to avoid arousing neighbors' suspicions about why this quiet, sickly Israel Sassover was suddenly having so many guests.

When they did meet as a body, they reached decisions by consensus. Begin hated dissension. He listened and consulted. The other men respected him like a father and admired his sacrifices and uncomplaining isolation. He referred to his soldiers as "my boys" and became severely depressed whenever one was captured or killed.

His other contact with events outside his shuttered windows—and his only contact with the British enemy—was the radio. He listened to the BBC faithfully and used it to practice his English. Unlike the leaders of the Haganah or the Jewish Agency, Begin had never met or negotiated with Palestine's British rulers.

He had had even less contact with the Arabs. Toward them he adopted the philosophy of his hero and mentor, Vladimir Jabotinsky, whom he venerated as "the father of resurrected Hebrew heroism."

Jabotinsky dismissed the Arab problem with a simple analogy. You are going into a railway carriage. In the compartment there are eight seats; two are already occupied. Naturally, those who are already there may be disturbed by your entry, but it does not harm them, and eventually they will reconcile themselves to it.

Begin, too, believed that Arabs would accept the inevitable Jewish State. Those who resisted did so only because they had been incited by British agents. "We told the Arabs," he said, "that we had no desire to fight or harm them: that we were anxious to see them as peaceful citizens of the Jewish State-to-be."

Under his leadership the Irgun scattered leaflets in the Old City. One of them read as follows: "TO OUR ARAB NEIGHBORS: We want to regard you as good neighbors. There is enough room in Eretz Israel for you, for your children and your children's children and for millions of Jews who have no other place to live but in this land. The Hebrew Government will accord you full equality of rights. . . . The Hebrew State will be the common home for all of us."

Begin believed that only Britain prevented the Arabs from embracing his generous offer. "The treacherous government does not want this," the leaflet continued. "It tries to sow friction between us, to incite you against us, and us against you."

It ended with a warning: "Do not try to raise a hand against the Jews or their property. For if, against your national and personal interest, you do raise a hand against us, we shall be compelled to cut it off without delay by the force of our arms. And both you and the whole world have learnt that the power of the new Hebrew youth is great."

The Arabs learned of Jewish power because Begin went to great lengths to teach them. Irgun soldiers distributed leaflets and posters in Arabic describing in vivid detail their attacks on government installations and personnel. "The Arabs, it is true, do not read much," Begin later wrote, "but their curiosity to find out what the underground was saying was very marked. Often an educated Arab would read aloud to an eager audience. . . ."

Begin lived in his shuttered house suspended between the past—the destruction of European Jewry—and the future—the rebirth of the survivors in a Jewish State on both banks of the Jordan River.

He listened to the events of 1946 on his radio. First the BBC, then the Haganah's "Voice of Israel," then his Irgun station, "The Voice of Fighting Zion."

He received reports about Palestine from his lieutenants. He saw his new country at night, from the windows of the automobile speeding him to meetings. He thought about it constantly. But he never experienced it. To Begin, the Palestine of 1946 was like the transient Britons who ruled it and the superfluous Arabs who lived in it: less than real, the world seen from a prisoner's cell.

Begin's reality was the Zionist program of his idol, Jabotinsky, whom he called "the greatest Jewish personality of our era after Herzl." Jabotinsky believed that the entire original Palestine Mandate, including Transjordan, should become a Jewish State. A verse of the Revisionist Party song, which he had written in 1925, proclaimed:

> Two banks on the Jordan;
> One is ours, so is the other.

In 1925 the Jewish population of the Transjordan was two; in 1946 it was zero but Begin clung to Jabotinsky's dream. In the past, not only Jabotinsky's dreams but his nightmares had become Jewish reality. In 1938, he had delivered a brilliant speech predicting the Holocaust:

> For three years I have been pleading with you, the Jews of Poland, the cream of Jewry. I have warned you again and again that the catastrophe is approaching. My hair has turned white and I have aged during these years because my heart bleeds that you, my dear brothers and sisters, cannot see the violence which has started to spew out the fire of extermination. I see a terrible sight. Time is short, but it is still possible to be saved. In the name of God let each and every one save his soul while he still can. And I want to tell you one more thing. Those who insist on getting away will be privileged to witness a moment of great Jewish rejoicing: the rebirth of a Jewish State.

Begin's reality was the truck convoy of his friends who heeded this warning and tried to flee Poland a few days before the Germans attacked. When they reached the border, the Rumanian authorities turned them back into Poland, even though they held valid transit visas. Begin later learned that British diplomats in Bucharest, correctly believing the Poles were illegal immigrants heading for Palestine, had persuaded the Rumanians to deny them transit privileges. Almost every Jew in this particular convoy was later killed by the Nazis.

Begin's reality was his flight on foot from occupied Warsaw and his arrest by Soviet police in eastern Poland. He spent over a year in Soviet prisons and concentration camps and was finally released only on the condition he join the Free Polish Army. By a stroke of luck his unit was posted to the Transjordan for its training. In May 1942 he crossed the Jordan River and was reunited with his wife, who had entered Palestine in 1941 as an illegal immigrant.

His reality was that Palestine, a country he had dreamed about, longed for, but never visited, was his true homeland. The moment he crossed into Transjordan, he fell on the ground and buried his face in the soil of his Eretz Israel, rubbing his cheeks against its rocks and inhaling the fragrance of its wild flowers. One of the non-Jewish Polish soldiers accompanying him was astounded at this emotional display and asked him why he was behaving so strangely.

"I'm a Zionist," Begin answered. "This is my homeland."

But even in Palestine, reality for Begin was the horror of the Holocaust: his father and brother machine-gunned by Nazis on a riverbank in Brest-Litovsk; his mother murdered in a Warsaw hospital; two of his three sisters murdered, he didn't know where or how; "the cream" of world Jewry exterminated.

His reality was the hatred that consumed survivors of the Holocaust. As he later wrote:

"We had to hate, first and foremost, the horrifying, age-old, inexcusable utter defenselessness of our Jewish people. . . .

"We had to hate the humiliating disgrace of the homelessness of our people.

"We had to hate all those who . . . barred the way of our people to physical salvation . . . and ruthlessly withstood their attempts to regain their national honor and restore their self-respect.

"Was there hate in our actions, in our revolt against British rule in our country? . . . to such a question the sincere answer is 'yes.'"

His reality was the all-consuming mission thrust on him because he had survived the Holocaust. After arriving safely in Palestine he told friends, "I could have died in a Soviet concentration camp or been blown up by German bombs in Poland; I could have fallen into German hands and died at Auschwitz. Instead, I survived. God has given me the rest of my life as a gift. I'm determined to use this gift to make sure that a Holocaust will never again be possible; that never again will Jewish children be murdered."

His reality was that Irgun soldiers were "fighters for freedom" engaged in a "revolutionary war of liberation," waging the type of heroic partisan war fate had denied him the opportunity of waging against the Nazis.

He ignored the fact that the European partisans had been applauded by the democracies, not just because they were allies, but also because of the nature of their enemy. They were employing terror against the century's greatest terrorists. But responsible world public opinion had never equated the British regime in Palestine with the Nazi occupation of Europe. The British Mandate was sometimes repressive, undeniably undemocratic, and capable of being cruel and arbitrary, but it was not a regime of terror. During the Mandate's thirty years, fewer than a dozen Jewish underground fighters had been executed. No Jewish villages were blown up or ploughed under and most Jews convicted of political crimes under the harsh Defence Emergency Regulations were accorded "special treatment" by British judges and segregated in prison from common criminals and Arabs.

He ignored, too, that the European partisans had been supported by majorities within the populations of the countries they sought to liberate. The Irgun was not. In 1946, two-thirds of Palestine was Arab and it certainly did not support any "liberation" which would lead to a Jewish State. Democratic elections had proved that ninety-five percent of the Jewish third supported the Jewish Agency and the Haganah. The Irgun was a minority within a minority.

Now, in the house on Bin Nun Street, Begin opened the envelope the messenger had just handed to him. Inside was a one-line note typed in Hebrew on notepaper pulled from a looseleaf binder. In the lower right-hand corner was the date, 22/7. The note said: "You should hold on for the time being the Jerusalem operation." It was signed by the Haganah.

Twice during the previous week he had received similar orders and twice, after hours of thought and consultation with his High Command, he had reluctantly obeyed. Now he had to decide again: How long could he afford to postpone the Yishuv's revenge for Black Saturday?

PART TWO

June 29—July 21, 1946

PART TWO

6

June 29, 1946, Black Saturday

H.Q. PALESTINE AND TRANSJORDAN OPERATION INSTRUCTION #68, 23 JUNE 1946. FROM LT.-GENERAL EVELYN H. BARKER TO ALL DIVISIONAL COMMANDERS:
HMG has authorised the High Commissioner to put into effect Operation AGATHA. D-Day for this operation will be decided after consultation, but the target date I wish worked to is Saturday 29th June. . . .
This operation means a declaration of war against the Jewish extremist elements. . . .

3:45 A.M. British troops in full battle dress, revolvers drawn and faces blackened with grease, burst into telephone exchanges in Jerusalem, Tel Aviv, and Haifa. They tore headsets off civilian operators and ran past banks of switchboards, pulling plugs, disconnecting calls, and isolating every home and settlement in Palestine.

Convoys consisting of troop carriers and buses stopped at points along King George V Avenue, Mamillah Road, and Keren Hakayemet Street. Soldiers jumped out and took up positions around the Jewish Agency. Within five minutes they had sealed off the organization recognized by the League of Nations as "a public body for the purpose of advising and coordinating with the Administration of Palestine in such economic, social, and other matters as may affect the establishment of a Jewish National Home."

A raiding party of policemen and soldiers arrested the night watchman and threw open the Agency's front door. More police and soldiers ran into the building.

In the main conference room they pried off doors and walls in their search for code books, documents and weapons.

In the offices of the Jewish National Fund they pulled down an electric wall map and broke colored light bulbs identifying new agricultural settlements and industrial projects.

They burst into a small second-floor room decorated to resemble Theodor Herzl's library in Vienna, scattered books on the floor, and rummaged through the desk on which he had written "Der Judenstaat."

They ignored the "Relatives' Room." They knew that the only documents to be found there were files containing the names and particulars of Jews killed during the Holocaust. These files covered tables and chairs, reached to the ceiling, and overflowed into the corridor.

The offices of the Agency's Executive received the roughest and most thorough search. Desk drawers were yanked out, letters and speeches ripped from typewriters, locked file cabinets prised open, and wastebaskets emptied onto tables.

The soldiers threw papers into boxes and carried them downstairs to the conference room where Palestine Police Superintendent Richard Catling and two Colonial officers from the Secretariat selected some for translation into English.

Catling, an expert on the Jewish underground groups, later declared himself "one hundred per cent in favor of the searches." He hoped to find documents proving that the Jewish Agency Executive had approved the sabotage of Palestine's bridges by the Haganah's elite shock troops—the Palmach; documents proving the existence of the alliance between the Haganah and the more violent Stern Gang and Irgun; and documents that could be used later to shock moderate Jews in Palestine, Europe and America into reconsidering their support of the current Jewish leadership.

Catling thrived on the intrigue and the challenge of matching wits with the Jewish underground armies and aboveground politicians. He considered it a "glorious, complex game." Several years before, he had been driven blindfolded to a deserted orange grove for a midnight meeting with the Irgun leadership. There was no specific purpose for the meeting. He was simply curious about his elusive enemy, and the Irgun leaders wanted to meet the man they considered their most dangerous and clever foe.

When the blindfold was removed, Catling found himself facing a group of men wearing black hoods. Expecting an exchange of political views, he was astonished at the conversation that in fact ensued. The Irgun representatives complained endlessly about their need for money and the difficulty they were having surviving as an organization. This was why, they explained, they had recently kidnapped a wealthy Rumanian Jew and were holding him for ransom.

Finally Catling became exasperated and said, "I don't give a damn about you as a bloody organization but if you break the law I'll whack you and whack you good."

The Irgun was now more of a threat, less the joke it had seemed then, and Catling hoped the Jewish Agency papers he was translating would enable him to "whack" the Irgun and the other underground groups.

While the army and police searched the Agency, a company of Argyll and Sutherland Highlanders wearing sneakers crept through a garden and cordoned off the house of Rabbi Yehuda Fishman, the acting chairman of the Jewish Agency Executive during Ben-Gurion's absence. Other soldiers pounded on Fishman's doors with fists and rifle butts.

The seventy-two-year-old Fishman awoke in a panic. "What do you want?" he screamed.

"Police. Open the door."

"Never!"

"We'll break it down."

"Never!"

For fifteen minutes soldiers banged on his door and shouted threats. Finally he opened up. A British police constable and five soldiers commanded by a Lieutenant Holyoake stood on his doorstep.

"Pack!" Holyoake ordered. "We're taking you into custody."

"I want to call the police."

Holyoake said no. He had already strayed from his orders. "Locked houses are to be forced open with minimum delay. The emphasis of this operation is speed and prisoners must not be given time to make lengthy toilets; clothes can be forwarded later."

The orders described the Jewish leaders marked for arrest as "the enemy."

Fishman saw trucks parked outside. "I'll agree to accompany you if I'm allowed to walk. My religion forbids riding in automobiles on the Sabbath."

Someone promised he could walk to the local police station and the rabbi left his house. The moment he reached the street two soldiers grabbed him and tossed him into the back of a truck. One slapped him when he screamed in protest.

David Hacohen, the president of the largest Jewish contracting firm in Palestine, awoke to the sound of the telephone ringing in his Tel Aviv apartment. He looked at his watch—six A.M. The sun was balanced on the horizon. He picked up the phone.

"Daddy!" It was his six-year-old son calling from the family home in Haifa. "Soldiers have blocked the street and there are men and trucks in front. A policeman came to the door and wanted to know where you were."

"Did you tell him?"

"Yes."

Hacohen turned to his wife. "It's finally happened. They're coming to get me."

The doorbell in Dov Joseph's seaside cottage rang again and again. As Joseph rushed to the door he worried that some tragedy had befallen a friend or relative.

He opened the door to a young army officer pointing a revolver at his stomach. Two other soldiers leveled rifles at his chest. Behind them was a shamefaced Jewish constable. More soldiers and British policemen stood in his garden and sat in a truck blocking his driveway. Since martial law had not been declared, the civilian government was technically making the arrests and at least one policeman had to accompany each of the military parties.

"Excuse me, sir, are you Dr. Joseph?" The officer was nervous and overly polite.

"Yes. I am."

"I'm terribly sorry, but I have orders to take you into custody."

Joseph thrust out his hand. "Show me your warrant." He was a member of the English Bar and had studied law at London University.

"I've nothing in writing. I was given the order by my superior officer."

"Then I must ask you to leave. I suggest you inform your superior that you cannot arrest me without a warrant." Joseph was the Agency's legal expert, responsible for monitoring and protesting the government's rigorous security laws that covered curfews, detention, and censorship.

"My orders are to arrest you. Warrant or no warrant, you'll have to come along."

"All right then, I demand the right to telephone the Attorney General."

Four days earlier Joseph and his wife had thrown a party for a retiring British police superintendent. All the important Britons had attended: Attorney General Fitzgerald, Catling, Shaw, Charteris of Military Intelligence, and many others. They had already secretly ordered his arrest but they had drunk his tea and eaten his cakes.

"You can't call anyone," the officer said. "We've cut your wires."

Joseph was relieved. If the phones were out, his arrest was not an isolated incident. They had to be picking up all the Jewish Agency leaders considered to be "activists." He wondered where they'd be sent: Exile in the Sudan? Eritrea? Kenya? Mauritius? He hoped for Cyprus.

He was correct, except that arrests were not being limited to Agency executives. The army and police had been instructed to arrest Moshe Shertok and Yitzhak Greunbaum of the Agency Executive; David Remez, the President of the Jewish Parliamentary body (Vaad Leumi); and two dozen others who were designated by the British as "VIJs"—Very Important Jews.

None of the "VIJs" were too surprised by the arrests. Relations between the

Jewish Agency and the Mandate had deteriorated badly ever since the underground groups had started their coordinated attacks on the government in 1945. The British correctly suspected that the Agency, despite its semilegal status as an administrative authority, was secretly approving and directing the Haganah's sabotage.

Some "VIJs" escaped capture. The Chairman of the Agency, David Ben-Gurion, was in Paris. The commander in chief of the Haganah, Moshe Sneh, and Palmach commander Yitzhak Sadeh were warned of the impending arrests and moved to more secure underground hideouts.

In order to prevent the "VIJs" from fleeing and to guard against street demonstrations and a sudden counterattack by the underground, British security forces effected a strict curfew. Most Palestinian Jews awoke to find their neighborhoods and settlements under siege. Police vans cruised city streets, their loudspeakers screaming, "Curfew! Curfew! Everyone remain indoors until further notice!"

Low-flying planes circled Jerusalem. Soldiers fired volleys into the air to scare Jews away from windows and balconies. Roadblocks code-named for game fish—salmon, trout, and pike—ringed the city preventing movement and, for the hunted, escape. Policemen flagged down trains and escorted passengers home. Fire trucks and ambulances had to obtain special passes before responding to emergencies. Military policemen guarded workers at the electric plant and waterworks.

Throughout the morning the Palestine Broadcasting Corporation repeated the official announcement: "At 0415 this morning the army occupied the Jewish Agency's buildings in Jerusalem and certain buildings in Tel Aviv which are being searched. Numbers of persons are being detained. The operations are proceeding. Curfew has been imposed over wide areas. Searches are also being carried out in the settlements. . . ."

The settlements resisted.

At 7 A.M. tanks and armored cars smashed through the gates of Kibbutz Yagour. British soldiers, some grim-faced, others scared, marched into the largest Jewish agricultural settlement in Palestine. Beyond the gate, a barricade of tractors and other farm machinery blocked their way. Beyond the barricade, hundreds of men, women, and children lay on the ground, their legs and arms intertwined.

The night before, a British policeman had visited Yagour and unofficially warned its mayor, "Be prepared, you're going to be attacked tomorrow morning."

The mayor called an emergency night meeting. Two weeks before, Sylvia Lupatkin, a veteran of the Warsaw ghetto uprising, had delivered a fiery three-hour speech describing the extermination of European Jewry and the heroic resistance of the Warsaw ghetto. Perhaps inspired by this memory, the settlers now voted to resist the British.

British tanks shoved the tractors into fields. Soldiers dragged Jews off the road and rolled them into ditches. Troop carriers and trucks carrying coils of barbed wire drove into Yagour. Army engineers erected tents and barbed-wire cages in a field near the dining hall. Barbed-wire corridors connected them.

When she saw the cages, a seventeen-year-old girl who had survived Auschwitz ran through the settlement screaming, "Make them stop! Make them stop! They're turning Yagour into a concentration camp!"

The commanding officer told the mayor, "The police have come to check the identity of the men in your settlement. You must tell them to gather in the cages."

The mayor stalled. "It's the Sabbath. I cannot order anyone to do anything."

The soldiers fixed bayonets, advanced on a group of men, and tried to herd them into a cage. Women threw themselves between the men and the bayonets. Children hugged their fathers' legs. Some men lashed themselves together with rope.

The soldiers retreated and fired tear gas. Settlers smothered the canisters with sandbags and wet towels.

The soldiers grabbed some men and shoved them into a cage. People ran into the dining hall and barricaded the door but soldiers fired tear gas through the windows.

"Gas!" shrieked a woman. "Oh God, they're gassing us!"

The settlers covered their faces with wet dishcloths and threw chairs through the windows to let the gas escape.

An armored car approached the dining hall. A man recently mustered out of the British Army recognized it. "It's a fuel carrier, for flamethrowers," he shouted. "They're going to burn us out!"

The armored car swiveled its nozzle and fired a stream of noncombustible oil through a broken window of the dining hall. Choking on fumes, slipping on the oily floor, dripping in oil, humiliated and in tears, the settlers dismantled the barricade and marched outside.

Some men resisted attempts to push them into the cages. Soldiers hit them with rifle butts, prodded them with bayonets, and dragged them through the dust. Women who grabbed their husbands' legs were pulled away by the hair and tossed into the women's cage.

Throughout the morning those in the holding cages were led through barbed-wire corridors into interrogation tents. The Jewish constables stationed in Yagour had refused to cooperate, so the interrogators were all army officers and British policemen. They sat behind trestle tables covered with photographs and lists of known Palmach members.

General Barker's orders had been emphatic: arrest as many members as possible of the Palmach—the Haganah's elite strike force. The British had excellent Intelligence information on the Palmach including lists of units, membership, and which settlements were used by which units as bases. They knew that many of the young men in these Jewish communal agricultural settlements, the kibbutzim, belonged to the Palmach. The more violent Irgun and Stern Gang were left outside the scope of Operation Agatha because, according to Barker, "Our Intelligence regarding them is insufficient to permit any preconceived plan of extermination."

The police interrogators in the tents asked the settlers to identify themselves. Most answered: "I am a man of Yagour" or "A woman of Yagour"; "A Jew of Eretz Israel."

Their refusal to give their names made it impossible for the interrogators to know if they were confronting Palmach members or innocent settlers. To resolve this dilemma they decided to arrest everyone who defied them. All but twenty of the settlement's 325 men were loaded into open trucks. As they drove away, the women, bleeding from scalp wounds and bayonet cuts, wailed and sang the Zionist anthem "Hatikvah" ("The Hope").

The British Army had not finished with Yagour. An officer noticed two pipes protruding from the earth underneath some farm machinery. A corporal stabbed the ground with his bayonet and hit metal. He scraped away earth and uncovered a concrete slab, an air compressor and a lever.

The officer pulled the lever. The concrete slab slid back and an odor of oil and gunpowder filled the air. Below was a subterranean arsenal of rifles, pistols, mortars, grenades, ammunition, and dynamite.

The Haganah had purchased them from smugglers, stolen them from the British and captured them during the Arab revolt. Jewish soldiers had pulled them from the hands of dead Germans in Europe and North Africa. The British Army had supplied them to Yagour when Rommel menaced Egypt and Palestine. Over the years all had been regularly cleaned, oiled, and fired; each weapon stood ready for use in case of an Arab attack.

The government had not launched Agatha to confiscate illegal arms. It feared that large-scale arms seizures would provoke a general insurrection. Barker's orders said: "The search for arms will be incidental and only [carried out] when it can be done without interfering with the main objects of the operation."

Nevertheless, now that the army had stumbled onto some of Yagour's arms, orders were given to look for more. Search parties ripped up tiles in a bathroom and found 5,000 rounds of ammunition. They pulled paneling off walls in a children's nursery and found a dozen rifles. They scattered heaps of grain in a cowshed; beneath were five cases of gelignite. They dismantled a stone bridge to find another cache. They drilled holes in the dining-room floor, cut the water supply, ploughed up acres of vineyards, and dug up saplings.

Three days of searches left Yagour's buildings and crops severely damaged. The army displayed its final haul for the press: 500 weapons, 4,000 grenades, 800 pounds of explosives, and 300,000 rounds of ammunition. It was the largest arsenal ever found in a Jewish settlement.

Yagour was one of twenty-five settlements searched on Black Saturday. At other settlements, too, Jews lay in the road, fought back, and refused to identify themselves.

In Rehovot, youths built roadblocks out of cars and buses. In Tel Aviv they tossed stones at a truckload of soldiers and a Jew was shot dead for violating curfew. In Tel-Yosef an army truck rolled over Jews lying in the road. A Jew in Yagour who had served with the British Army put on his uniform and medals and insisted he be arrested by someone of comparable or higher rank.

In another kibbutz a Jewish veteran handed his arresting soldiers a box containing his army medals and awards. Their only answer was, "You killed our soldiers in Tel Aviv." They were referring to an act of terrorism committed by the Stern Gang only a few months earlier. On April 25, the Stern Gang had murdered seven British soldiers, some as they lay sleeping, during a raid on a military parking lot.

The recent murder of these comrades and the resistance of the settlers to the searches enraged some British soldiers.

One search party marched into the dining hall at Givat Brenner shouting "Heil Hitler!" and singing the "Horst Wessel" song. Another party scrawled red swastikas on the walls of the settlement's classrooms.

While searching the Bank Haopolim in Tel Aviv a British officer shouted at one of the clerks, "What you need is the gas chamber."

In Tel-Yosef a corporal told a group of settlers, "Hitler did a good job. Too bad he didn't have more gas chambers."

Twenty-five thousand soldiers participated in Operation Agatha. Only a small minority was responsible for these incidents, but they made a powerful impression. Accounts of the incidents, often exaggerated, spread rapidly through the Jewish community.

Many Jews were traumatized by the similarities between Agatha and a Nazi roundup: the predawn raids; policemen pounding on doors; hurried arrests without warning or explanation; the segregation of men and women into separate holding cages; the removal of the entire male population in some villages; and the detention camps with their guard towers, dogs, and endless coils of barbed wire.

As soldiers dragged her into a cage, a woman who had spent three years at Belsen shouted, "Don't let them take me to the gas chambers!"

A Czech girl from Auschwitz was seriously ill but refused to notify the British doctor at the Athlit detention camp. She told friends she feared if the authorities learned she was sick she would be "selected out" and gassed.

A concentration camp survivor in Beit Hashita was beaten for refusing to give his name or fingerprints. "Even when the Germans took me away they did not treat me like these soldiers," he shouted.

As she was herded through a barbed-wire corridor, a thirteen-year-old girl screamed again and again, "This is what the Nazis did before taking us to the gas chambers! This is what the Nazis did!"

Women at Tel-Yosef ripped their dresses to expose concentration camp numbers tattooed on their arms. Some soldiers were ashamed and looked away. Others said, "You killed our soldiers in Tel Aviv."

None of the British leaders had anticipated that Agatha would trigger these echoes of the Holocaust.

The British High Commissioner, General Sir Alan Cunningham, announced on the radio that "[The arrests] are not directed against the Jewish community as a whole but solely against those few who are taking an active part in the present campaign of violence and those who are responsible for instigating and directing it. . . ."

The Assistant District Commissioner in Ramle, Ivan Phillips, wrote his father that the operation was "long overdue and a step in the right direction. We had carried appeasement and conciliation to the limit."

When Joan Gibbs, the wife of a young Colonial officer stationed in Palestine, heard the loudspeakers and saw a plane circling Jerusalem, she told her husband, "This should finally help matters. At last the army is becoming involved."

"No," he said. "It won't help at all. It's only going to bring terrible reprisals."

At 9:45 A.M., Sir John Shaw held a press conference in Jerusalem. He began by telling the fifty local and foreign journalists in attendance, "Large-scale operations have been authorized in an effort to end the state of anarchy existing in Palestine and to enable law-abiding citizens to pursue their normal occupations without fear of kidnapping, murder, or being blown-up."

Shaw approved of Agatha. For months he had urged his superiors either to partition Palestine into Arab and Jewish states and then leave, or to disband the Jewish Agency and govern. He had no patience with the ambiguity of the present situation. The Jewish Agency was a parallel administration that ran its own schools, hospitals, and villages. It claimed semilegal status as an administrative power and yet also secretly supported the underground war. Agatha would teach the Agency it could not do both.

"How long will soldiers occupy the Jewish Agency?" asked one reporter.

"As long as necessary to achieve the purpose of the operation," Shaw answered.

Agatha had purposes besides those Shaw would admit to the press. The government wanted to bolster the morale of the army, cripple the Haganah's military power and forestall a Jewish coup d'etat.

On June 10 members of the Agency's Executive and the Haganah High Command had met with a delegation from the Stern Gang and Irgun in Tel Aviv. According to an American Intelligence report, British Intelligence learned that "the delegation gave information that the two groups they represented had decided to ask the entire Yishuv officially to participate in a future coup d'etat for the proclamation of a future Jewish State and the interruption of all relations with the existing Palestine Administration."

On June 16, "The Night of the Bridges," Palmach units blew up eight railway and road bridges linking Palestine to neighboring countries. The following evening the Stern Gang attacked railway workshops in Haifa. The next day the Irgun kidnapped six British officers and announced they would be released when General Barker commuted the death sentences of two Irgun soldiers.

The attack on the bridges was the boldest, most skillful act of sabotage yet mounted against the government. Its purpose was symbolic—to protest Britain's refusal to follow the recommendations of a recent Anglo-American Committee of Inquiry and admit 100,000 European Jews. It was also meant to demonstrate that if Britain closed Palestine to Jewish refugees, the Haganah was capable of closing the country to everyone.

The Haganah miscalculated the British reaction. Rather than intimidating British leaders, "The Night of the Bridges" convinced them the Haganah had become too powerful. Because the act occurred in apparent concert with the attacks of the Irgun and Sternists, it was interpreted as evidence that the Haganah might be willing to join them in a coup. (In fact only the Haganah and Stern operations had been coordinated. The Haganah opposed the idea of a coup and disapproved of the Irgun's kidnapping the officers.)

For months the British Army had lobbied for permission to attack the underground groups. High Commissioner Cunningham had opposed military action, particularly against the Jewish Agency. In March he told a member of the Anglo-American Committee, "No, I should not want to see the Agency disbanded. . . . The Palestine Government may not like it but it cannot ignore it. It is a force to be reckoned with."

After "The Night of the Bridges" Cunningham changed his mind. On June 20 he and Field-Marshal Bernard Montgomery met in London with the Cabinet. Montgomery, who had just returned from visiting Palestine, was outraged at what he considered the Yishuv's ingratitude to the British Army. His victory over Rommel at El Alamein had saved Palestine from Hitler and the Yishuv from certain extermination. Now, four years later, Jewish terrorists were murdering his soldiers, sixteen of whom had been killed during the previous six months. He argued that some form of military action in Palestine was crucial to maintaining his army's morale. Operation Agatha was Montgomery's plan, and the Cabinet approved it.

Cunningham reluctantly went along and hoped Agatha would lead to a political solution. With the activists imprisoned, he believed he could persuade Dr. Chaim Weizmann to form a new Jewish leadership of pro-British moderates.

Jewish journalists attending Shaw's press conference considered such hopes naive. One questioned the wisdom of attacking the Jewish Agency and the Haganah's Palmach while ignoring the more violent Stern Gang and Irgun.

Another reminded Shaw of Cunningham's statement that "the door to negotiation and discussion is not shut" and asked, "With whom can the Government negotiate now that the leading members of the Jewish Agency are under arrest?"

"There are many moderate leaders who have not been detained," Shaw replied. "We have not, for example, detained Dr. Weizmann."

7

June 29, 1946—4 P.M.

THE BLACK SEDAN, led and followed by jeeps full of red-capped military police, sped up the steep grades and around the hairpin turns through the Judean hills to Jerusalem. The sedan overtook convoys of troop transports and passed trucks taking Jews to detention camps in Latrun and Athlit. Soldiers raised barriers and waved it through mazes of barbed wire.

Dr. Chaim Weizmann, President of the World Zionist Organization, sat in the back seat wrapped in blankets and shivering with chills from an attack of bronchitis. The seventy-year-old Weizmann, a tall, handsome man known to many as "King of the Jews," also suffered from high-blood pressure and diabetes. Cataracts had left him partially blind. According to his 1946 medical report, his chronic illnesses—headaches, weakness, and high blood sugar—were psychosomatic and tied to the political situation. "Aside from his eye cataracts, which would require an operation," the report continued, "his health is good."

His wife and his personal doctor sat beside him. He had refused their pleas that he remain in bed. Shertok, Joseph and the others were his friends. According to his wife, their arrests had left him "beside himself with fury and indignation."

Since persuading Lord Balfour to write his fateful letter promising a Jewish homeland in Palestine, Weizmann had continued to charm and stir the consciences of prime ministers, Colonial secretaries and high commissioners.

His charisma and understanding of the British ruling class had won numerous political victories for Zionism.

According to one British politician who came under his spell, "No man knew better than he the art of using the conscience and ambition of British politicians . . . in the interests of the Jewish State."

Weizmann's motorcade pulled into the circular driveway of Government House. One of the High Commissioner's aides opened the car door. Weizmann ignored his greeting and outstretched hand and strode inside.

The aide invited Mrs. Weizmann to wait in a sitting room. She shook her head and stared straight ahead. A servant appeared with a tray of cold drinks. She refused them and remained in the sweltering car.

Weizmann met Cunningham in the main lounge. With its high ceilings, huge fireplace and overstuffed sofas, the room was reminiscent of an English manor house, except for the view. A set of double doors opened onto a luxuriant garden. Beyond, framed by palm trees and cypress, was the Valley of Hinnom and, two miles away, the walls and spires of the Old City. No one in Jerusalem lived in greater isolation or at a greater distance from the city than the High Commissioner.

Jerusalem was Cunningham's first civilian post. He was a fifty-nine-year-old career soldier and a bachelor ("I have courage for everything but marriage") who liked hunting foxes, growing roses and eating rare roast beef.

He had distinguished himself during the Ethiopian campaign by routing an Italian army thirteen times the size of his own. Newsmen said that his motto— "Hit them, hit them again, and hit them hard!"—had inspired his troops. A year later he was relieved of command of the Eighth Army in North Africa because, according to a letter from Auchinleck to Churchill, "he had now begun to think defensively."

Since coming to Palestine in 1945, he had repeatedly tried to persuade the Colonial Office to announce a political solution or issue immigration permits to the relatives of Palestinian Jews. He wrote to Colonial Secretary Hall, "I believe that if, during this interim period, the question of immigration into Palestine was tackled by HMG from the angle of allowing in proved destitute close relations, a start might be made in separating the humanitarian from the political issues."

Like most Jewish leaders, Weizmann considered Cunningham neither the best nor worst of the British high commissioners. Their previous meetings had been cordial. But according to Mrs. Weizmann's memoirs, the meeting that day was "stormy."

Weizmann said, "I demand you release the Jewish leaders and withdraw your soldiers from the Agency immediately. The searches in the kibbutzim must stop. These are particularly cruel. Their weapons pose no threat to you but without them these villages are open to Arab attacks."

By attacking the settlements the army had attacked the foundation of Weizmann's Zionism. He believed a Jewish majority would emerge in Palestine not through terrorism, open revolt, or war with the Arabs, but through the creation of new facts—the arrival of new immigrants, the construction of new settlements, the reclamation of more land, and the transformation of the urban Jew of the Diaspora into the new agricultural Jew of Palestine.

Cunningham could not stop the searches or release the leaders without gaining concessions. To do so would be an admission that Agatha had been a mistake. "If we agree to stop the operation," he said, "can the Agency guarantee to stop all terrorism?"

Weizmann knew it could not, especially with the Agency's most influential leaders under arrest. "The door to negotiation is still open," Weizmann said. "The admission of 100,000 refugees from Europe would satisfy the Yishuv. If this is done I will personally guarantee the restoration of peace and the end of violence."

"No. Negotiations can only resume when the Agency is reformed and placed under government control. The Agency must surrender any information it has about terrorist armies. We can no longer allow the existence of a state within a state. I am hoping you will agree to restructure the Agency, choosing, of course, more moderate men to lead it."

Cunningham began reading a list of moderates.

Weizmann interrupted. "An Agency controlled by the government would never be acceptable. You know that."

Cunningham was overestimating Weizmann's influence. Britain's failure to keep its wartime promises, its refusal to implement the recommendations of the Anglo-American Committee, and now Black Saturday had conspired to undermine Weizmann's position with the Yishuv. In private he had taken to describing British policy as "an appalling fraud on the hopes of a martyred people," and complaining that "the world is divided into two regions: countries where Jews are forbidden to live and those where they are forbidden to enter." However, to the Jewish public he remained a symbol of Anglo-Jewish cooperation.

To the Stern Gang, Irgun, and activists in the Haganah he was a British stooge and one of the "Shadtlonim"—Jews who pleaded with Gentiles for Jewish rights. Many believed that his style of leadership—leadership which had won the Balfour Declaration—had also led to the White Paper and Auschwitz. His willingness to meet Cunningham on the day Britain declared war on the Yishuv would soon be attacked as "collaboration."

Weizmann told Cunningham he would not be Palestine's Quisling. He would not choose pro-British moderates to staff a new Jewish Agency. "What you ask is impossible," he said. "I have not been empowered by the Yishuv to give guarantees or form governments. There is nothing more to discuss."

He stood up, faced Cunningham and held up his wrists. "You may as well arrest me too."

Cunningham refused. Before turning to leave Weizmann said, "These arrests will have world-wide repercussions. In Palestine they may unleash terrible violence."

Weizmann, although not a pacifist, feared this violence for the suffering it would cause and the damage it would inflict on Zionism.

He believed that the Jews had a mission to create a nation like no other; "a holy land of a holy people with a holy mission"; a nation dedicated to social justice and respect for human life; a nation of humane socialists who, by transforming the land and building a nation brick by brick and house by house, would transform themselves and build a socialist utopia. To achieve this utopia he was willing to exercise a patience that seemed obscene to many survivors of the Holocaust.

Menahem Begin was one of these survivors. He wanted a Jewish State immediately and was willing to use violence to get it. Violence to him was proof of the Jewish will to live. He later wrote, "We fight, therefore we are." Weizmann, on the other hand, saw violence as moral decay, a Jewish death wish. In his view, it reduced Zionism to the level of other national movements. It threatened his creed that Zionism was unique, a nationalism no one needed to fear, a nationalism at no one's expense. "When Jews come to Palestine," he said, "they create space for others; they do not fill the space of others."

Violence, he felt, endangered Zionism more than it did other nationalisms. The Jewish right to settle Palestine had been given, not won, and given largely on moral grounds. "The Balfour Declaration was given . . . to the Jewish people as a whole," he said, "and the entire people must accept it with clean hands and a pure heart."

Violence undercut his dream of a peaceful accommodation with the Arabs. It made a lie of his promise that "Palestine must be built without violating the legitimate interests of the Arabs. Not a hair on their heads shall be touched. The Zionist Congress . . . has to learn the truth that Palestine is not Rhodesia, and that 600,000 Arabs live there who, before the sense of justice of the world, have exactly the same right to their homes in Palestine as we have to our National Home."

Violence had already proven itself fatal to Jewish progress. Weizmann had seen a single act of terrorism frustrate the emergence of a Jewish State.

On November 4, 1944, he had met with Prime Minister Churchill to discuss a postwar partition of Palestine. Churchill promised to support the establishment of a Jewish nation large enough to absorb a million and a half Jews within ten years. He told Weizmann, "As soon as the war with Germany is over I want to bite into the Palestine problem . . . if Roosevelt and I come together at the conference table we can carry all we want."

Two days later the Stern Gang murdered Churchill's political ally and close friend, Lord Moyne. In his eulogy to Moyne delivered in the House of Commons, Churchill said, "A shameful crime has shocked the world and affected none more strongly than those like myself who, in the past, have been consistent friends of the Jews and constant architects of their future. If our dream for Zionism should be dissolved in the smoke of revolvers of assassins and if our efforts for its future should provoke a new wave of banditry worthy of the Nazi Germans, many persons like myself will have to reconsider the position we have maintained so firmly for such a long time."

Churchill did reconsider his support for a Jewish State. A month after the end of the European war he sent Weizmann a curt note confirming his change of heart. "There can, I fear, be no possibility of the question [of a Jewish State] being effectively considered until the allies are definitely seated at the peace table."

The rebuff shattered Weizmann. He knew it might be months, perhaps years, before the Allies defeated Japan and gathered at a final peace conference. In the meantime, there would be no Jewish State to absorb the survivors of the Holocaust.

Weizmann also opposed terrorism because he had seen it lead, ultimately, to dead Jews. It had touched members of his own family.

At 6 P.M. on July 6, 1938, shoppers, merchants, donkeys and pushcarts had jammed the narrow lanes of Haifa's Arab vegetable market.

A few minutes after six a grenade thrown from a passing automobile by an Irgun terrorist exploded near the crowded entrance. Metal splinters tore into pedestrians and an Arab policeman. Shoppers panicked and ran toward the melon stalls.

A milk churn packed with explosives had been left next to a melon stall by Irgun terrorists disguised as Arabs. It exploded seconds after the grenade.

Bodies flew into the air. The wounded writhed in pools of blood. Policemen vomited as they tried to comfort the wounded and dying. Among the mess of iron, glass, and melon pulp were the blood-soaked remains of donkeys and horses and the mangled bodies of eighteen Arabs. Five more later died of wounds.

Arab survivors grabbed iron bars, ripped wooden planks from shattered stalls, pulled pistols from underneath cloaks and ran into surrounding streets screaming "Jehudi! [Jews!]"

The first Jew they encountered was Weizmann's brother-in-law. Tuvia Dounie, an engineering contractor who had built the Jerusalem Post Office and the YMCA. He had left his car to help a wounded Arab policeman when an Arab boy in the crowd shot him through the head. Four other Jews who happened to be near the market were also murdered by Arabs.

This Jewish bomb, the first terrorist bomb planted by the Irgun, had killed twenty-three Arab men, women, and children and provoked the murder of five Jews, among them Weizmann's brother-in-law.

Throughout the summer of 1938 the Irgun exploded bombs in Arab markets. Each was in retaliation for Arab attacks against Jewish civilians; after each, Arab mobs killed Jews. In Weizmann's view, Palestine was too small, its people living too close for terrorism not to ricochet.

In 1938 most Palestinian Jews shared Weizmann's hatred of terrorism and his vision of a peaceful, human Zionism. They condemned the Irgun's retaliatory terror and, in the face of Arab terror, followed a defensive policy known as "Havlagah," the Hebrew word for restraint.

During the Arab revolt the Haganah told its soldiers, "Your duty is to beat off attacks, but not to let the smell of blood go to your heads. Remember that our meaning is in our name, Defense [Haganah], and that our only aim is to provide security for creative work. Your organization is subordinate to this ideal; it is the instrument that enables us to live and work; it is the servant of this purpose; it must never become its master."

Most Haganah soldiers followed Havlagah. Arab attacks against kibbutzim were repulsed with a minimum of force and bloodshed. The Haganah did not mount large-scale offensive operations or terrorize Arab civilians. (There were some exceptions. A British officer, Orde Wingate, led his Jewish "night squads" on raids against villages from which Arabs had mounted attacks.) It was as if settlers in the American West had shot back only when attacked and refused to raid Indian camps for fear of compromising their moral precepts.

A British commission sent to Palestine in 1937 to investigate the disturbances praised the Haganah's restraint. It reported that "The Jews, as compared with the Arabs, are the law-abiding section of the population; and, indeed, throughout the whole series of outbreaks, and under very great provocation, they have shown a notable capacity for discipline and self-restraint."

This restraint was even more remarkable because, as the report also stated, "The elementary duty of providing public security has not been discharged. If there is one grievance the Jews have the undoubted right to prefer, it is the absence of security."

The Holocaust transformed Havlagah. Centuries of persecution had taught Jews that resistance to a superior power brought disaster. The Holocaust taught that not resisting brought annihilation. The philosophical foundations of Havlagah, liberal humanism and nonviolence, were found wanting. Liberal humanists in the Christian world had failed to rescue Jews and Jewish nonviolence had abetted the Holocaust.

By 1945, many in the Yishuv had decided they could no longer afford the luxury of separating the offensive and defensive aspects of warfare. The Haganah and the Jewish Agency split into two factions: moderates such as Weizmann, who continued to believe in the traditional application of

Havlagah; and activists led by Moshe Sneh and David Ben-Gurion, who wanted to wage an offensive underground war against British rule. (By and large it was these activist leaders within the Jewish Agency that the British had arrested on Black Saturday.)

After the announcement by the Colonial Office in August 1945 that the White Paper would continue, the activists led the Haganah into an alliance, "The Joint Command," with the Stern Gang and the Irgun. Beginning in October 1945, units from all three groups staged separate coordinated attacks on government installations. Because it was the most powerful member of the alliance, the Haganah had the power to veto operations proposed by the Stern Gang or Irgun.

The activists constructed elaborate arguments to convince moderates (also known as "Weizmannites") that these sabotage operations were defensive and not a departure from Havlagah. They argued that more Jews were needed to protect the Yishuv from Arab attacks. Therefore the sabotage of installations, such as radar towers that tracked down illegal immigrants, was done to protect the Yishuv's defensive capabilities. It constituted "Defense of the Defense."

The activists also argued that since the soldiers manning these radar towers traveled to them by train and road, blowing up railway and road bridges was also "Defense of the Defense." This logic enabled them to justify attacking any target in Palestine while still claiming to be "defending the defense" and exercising restraint. Activists further corrupted the doctrine of Havlagah by announcing that counterattacks were permissible if "the scope of the Jewish reprisal is equal to the magnitude of the British attack."

During the first half of 1946 Weizmann and other moderates fought these compromises. They denounced the Haganah's alliance with the Sternists and Irgun, tried to minimize the number of sabotage operations approved by the Joint Command, and denounced as immoral operations which posed *any* threat to human life. Yet, although most moderates feared that violence would corrupt Zionism, they also sympathized with the outrage that motivated the activists and terrorists.

Weizmann expressed the dilemma facing moderates when he addressed the Anglo-American Committee in March.

"I hate political violence," he said. "I am uncompromisingly against it. It can only do us harm; it can never do us any good . . . but I cannot help understanding the reason why these young men are driven to despair. They have lost faith in humanity in the war. Why, if I talk to a young man and he asks me, 'Why is not my father allowed to come? Why has he not been allowed to come during the war? If he had perhaps he would be alive today.' I have no answer and we stand before them as people who have failed them in the sacred task which they have entrusted to our hands, and our influence is therefore very, very small."

After the Anglo-American Committee left Palestine the Joint Command stepped up its attacks. In desperation Weizmann wrote to Churchill and begged him to persuade the Labour Government to reach a decision about Palestine's future that would undercut terrorism. He wrote:

> You will know that conditions here are difficult. My friends and I are doing everything in our power to keep things quiet, in spite of the very great strain under which the Jewish population is labouring. But our power dwindles as time goes on. We deeply deplore some of the things that happen, but we know them to be no more than the product of black despair which is overwhelming our people. . . . I hope that you will realise that I am appealing to you *in extremis*—as an old friend with whom it has been my privilege to work for nearly thirty years. . . .

In May, British Foreign Secretary Bevin announced that he would carry out the Anglo-American Committee's recommendation to admit 100,000 Jews only if the United States bore some of the cost of settling and policing them and only if the Jewish underground armies disarmed themselves.

Bevin knew these conditions could never be met. They were pretexts not to follow the recommendations of a commission he had proposed and whose report he had promised to implement. The Yishuv was bitterly disappointed. More moderates became activists and on June 16 the activists launched "The Night of the Bridges." British and Arab guards were wounded and fourteen Jews killed when a bomb exploded prematurely.

Weizmann was appalled. On June 23 he drafted a letter to Moshe Shertok, head of the Agency's political department, threatening to resign unless the Agency ordered the Haganah to suspend all military operations.

Weizmann agonized over the letter, decided not to send it, but then redrafted an even stronger ultimatum on June 27:

> In the eyes of all men of good-will, our movement is sinking to the level of gangsterism.
>
> Our only force is moral force—as we showed during all the years of the "troubles" [the Arab Revolt]. . . . A policy of destruction can rebound only on ourselves, and it is we who, in the end, will be part destroyed. . . .
>
> I cannot continue to play the part of a respectable facade screening things which I abhor, but for which I must bear responsibility in the eyes of the world.
>
> Unless political violence is abandoned, definitely stopped, and every effort is made to bring the Etzel [the Irgun] and the Stern people to obedience to moral discipline until the organization has had a chance to review the whole situation at the next Congress, I shall feel compelled to resign my office now. . . . This letter serves notice that the very next act of sabotage will automatically result in my resignation. . . .
>
> A vicious circle is being created which can only be broken by our

movement's return to those moral standards to which it has clung in the past, in spite of everything.

P.S. The sending of this letter has been delayed owing to my illness.

Weizmann hesitated to make such a momentous decision while he was ill. He held on to this second letter for two days. Before he could decide whether to send it, the British launched Agatha and arrested Shertok.

Weizmann feared that Agatha would provoke the underground groups to still greater violence ("The scope of the reprisal must be equal to the magnitude of the attack"). He tried to head off this violence by asking Cunningham to release the leaders. The High Commissioner refused. Now Weizmann's only hope was to persuade the activists to forgo the counterattack he was certain they would begin planning once the government lifted the curfew.

He was determined to stop their dangerous violence.

8

June 30—July 2

THE GOVERNMENT lifted the curfew at six on Sunday morning. Within the hour teenage boys and girls with handkerchiefs tied over their faces raced through Jewish neighborhoods slapping up posters. Crowds gathered quickly. It was a challenge to read the posters before the police could rip them down.

The Irgun posters bore their familiar, distinctive emblem, a rifle held high in a fist over a map of Palestine and Transjordan. Underneath was the motto "Only Thus!"

They described the "Nazi-British Enslavers" as "Blood-Thirsty Fascist Hooligans" and "Exterminators" whose hands were "stained with boiling Jewish blood." The Palestine Police were "The British Gestapo"; the army, "The British SS"; and Foreign Secretary Ernest Bevin, "Adolf Bevin."

One poster said: "The rulers of Britain actively helped the Nazis destroy the Jews of Europe."

Another promised that "Rivers of blood [would] flow," for the Irgun had sworn "an oath to take revenge on the Nazi British enemy and repay him, the destroyer of our nation, the murderer of our children."

The Haganah posters also promised retribution and compared the British to the Nazis:

Britain has declared war on the Jewish people.
The Jewish people will reply with war.
Jewish resistance will continue,
Jewish resistance has only begun.

Down with the Nazi-British regime.
Out with the unclean sons of Titus from the
    Holy Land.
Long live the Jewish State.

A year before it was the Irgun, not the British, that Haganah posters had described as "fascists," and "the enemy of the Jewish people." Haganah youths had ripped down Irgun posters or covered them with black paint.

A year before, the Irgun had called Ben-Gurion a "Quisling" and "The Dwarf Dictator." The Jewish Agency had been "a clique of degenerate leaders . . . who groveled like willing slaves before every Nazi-British official . . . who drew up lists of suspected Irgun members and handed them over to the enemy's secret police."

A year before, the Haganah had condemned the Irgun attacks on police stations. Every Haganah broadcast had begun pointedly with the Sixth Commandment—"Thou Shalt Not Kill."

The Irgun radio station had replied with a quotation from Exodus—"Life for life, eye for eye, tooth for tooth, hand for hand, foot for foot, burning for burning, wound for wound, stripe for stripe."

These antagonists had been united by the continuation of the White Paper and now by Operation Agatha. At 8:30 this Sunday evening the Irgun clandestine station, "The Voice of Fighting Zion," broadcast a five-minute appeal for revolt:

> The arrest of the heads of the Yishuv is a step in the campaign of liquidation, carried on systematically and brutally by the bloody British regime against our people. This act of aggression was preceded by many acts of hostility, resulting in the destruction of one-third of the people, which have brought us to the edge of the abyss, and which have all had one purpose: To put an end to the aspirations for Hebrew freedom; to rob us forever of our country; to turn us—as in the diaspora—into dust and to blot us out from under God's heaven.
>
> The oppressive hand of the enemy—the teacher of Hitler and the executor of his plans—has been raised against the Jewish people. The existence of the nation is at stake.
>
> In this situation there is no other way but to fight. In this situation vacillation is a misdeed, delay and retreat are crimes. In this situation the whole people—in Zion and in the far-flung diaspora—must rise as one man and smite the cruel enslaver, and by every means and in every way, until he is brought low.

On the same evening, the Haganah's "Voice of Israel," skipping between wave lengths to foil British jammers, broadcast a remarkably similar appeal. It listed the settlements attacked by the army and charged that "Yagour has become another Lidice."

Lidice was a Czech village destroyed by the Nazis in reprisal for the murder of the Nazi governor of Czechoslovakia, Reinhard Heydrich, by Czech partisans. German soldiers shot every man over the age of twelve, burned the village to the ground and shipped its women and children to concentration camps.

Smashed windows and ploughed-up vineyards did not make Yagour another Lidice; nor did swastikas scrawled on walls make the British Army the equivalent of the SS. But in their anger and hysteria after Black Saturday, many in the Yishuv saw only the superficial similarities between Yagour and Lidice, the army and the SS, not the enormous differences. Some also reasoned: if the British were similar to the Nazis, then were not those who fought them heroic partisans? Throughout the war the Allies had praised the terrorism of the partisans.

The Haganah announcer concluded his broadcast by saying, "The British Nazi government, under the so-called Labour Party, has declared war on the Jewish people. The government will have to destroy all the Jewish settlements as it has destroyed Yagour if it intends to find arms, but our reply will come."

Early on Monday morning, July 1, six members of the Haganah High Command met in a Tel Aviv apartment to plan the Yishuv's "reply."

The Haganah's stocky thirty-six-year-old commander, Moshe Sneh, proposed coordinated attacks on the government by all three underground organizations. (Until now, he had used the Joint Command primarily to restrain the Irgun and Sternists.) The attacks would prove to the world that no amount of British force could intimidate the Yishuv.

"They want to demonstrate their military superiority," Sneh said. "So we will demonstrate to them the superiority of a people fighting in their own country for their freedom. The Palmach will raid the British arsenal at Bat Galim and retake the arms taken from us at Yagour. The LEHI [Stern Gang] will bomb the David Brothers Building [which contained the offices of the Palestine Information Office] and the Etzel [Irgun] will blow up the government and military headquarters in the King David Hotel."

Sneh insisted that all three operations fell within the doctrine of Havlagah. The raid on the arsenal was "Defense of the Defense." He said, "Their aim was to take our arms; we will be taking them back."

He argued that the King David operation fulfilled the condition that the scope of reprisal equal the magnitude of the attack. "They attacked our government body and sought to paralyze it; we will attack and paralyze their government bodies."

The High Command approved the operations unanimously. Once they had accepted Sneh's skewed premise that destroying the King David and searching the Jewish Agency were equivalent acts, then blowing up the King David became not an act of terrorism but a reasonable military operation, a justified counterattack.

Sneh left the Haganah's apartment and hurried to the offices of an agricultural society on Allenby Street where he had called a meeting of the top-secret "X Committee."

In 1945 the Jewish Agency had set up this five-man committee of activists and moderates to be the Haganah's moral brakes. It could veto any military operation on the grounds that it posed too substantial a threat to human life. Sneh, as commander of the Haganah, was automatically a member, so was the Haganah's treasurer Levi Eshkol (who later became one of Israel's prime ministers). Two other current members, Rabbi Fishman and David Remez, had been arrested on Black Saturday. They had since been replaced.

The X was not told the specific target or date of the operations it considered. Sneh described both in general terms. A few months earlier he had presented the X with an Irgun plan to bomb the King David. He described it as "harming a central building of the government." The X had vetoed it.

On the morning of July 1, Sneh asked permission "to undertake an armed operation called 'Return the Lost Items,' which will recover arms stolen from the Yishuv by the British Army."

The X approved.

Next he asked permission for "an attack directed against two central buildings of the Palestine government."

One member of the X said, "We must be careful to choose operations which will mobilize world sympathy and will also be supported by public opinion in Palestine."

"These proposed operations will have those effects," Sneh said. "The public will see them as counterattacks."

The X approved both operations by a vote of three to two. In both cases Eshkol was in the majority. Sneh believed the committee had guessed the identity of the "central buildings."

While Sneh was securing the approval of the X, the representatives of the principal Zionist organizations were meeting in a Jerusalem hall near the occupied Jewish Agency. In attendance were Golda Meyerson (Meir) and David Horowitz, two of the most senior Agency officials to avoid arrest. Neither knew of Sneh's plans. The British had picked up the Agency leaders who were in closest touch with the Haganah and most capable of controlling it. In fact, Meyerson was somewhat insulted not to have been arrested with her colleagues. Her disappointment was aggravated by David Ben-Gurion's wife, Paula, who had telephoned every few hours throughout Black Saturday saying, "Golda, you are still at home? They didn't come to take you?"

The meeting lasted the entire day. Prayers were offered for the four Jews killed, the eighty wounded, and the 2,700 arrested on Black Saturday. Representatives from the settlements gave exaggerated accounts of the brutality of the troops and the damage at the kibbutzim. A resolution was passed threatening nonviolent civil disobedience if the searches and arrests continued.

Weizmann's doctor had forbidden him to attend. He sent a statement which his wife read aloud. "Show courage and restraint," it said. "Do not allow yourselves to be provoked into rash action. Abstain from violence."

At midday on July 1, a Haganah courier left a letter in the mailbox of a Dizengoff Street apartment house which served as the Tel Aviv contact point for the three underground groups. To avoid seeing one another, couriers visited the box at different times of day.

During the afternoon an Irgun courier picked up the Haganah's letter and delivered it to Menahem Begin. The same letter had also been sent to the Stern Gang. It said:

> Shalom!
> (a) You are to carry out as soon as possible the Malonchick [code name for the King David Hotel] and the House of Your Slave and Redeemer [code name for the David Brothers Building]. Inform us of the date. Preferably simultaneously. The identity of the organization which carries out the operation should not be made public, either implicitly or explicitly.
> (b) We are also planning something. We will inform you of the details when the time comes. . . .
>
> "M" [Moshe Sneh]
> 1.7.46
> 11:00

After reading the letter Begin's first thought was, "How can we do it so my boys can escape after leaving the bombs?" His second thought was, "How can we avoid killing civilians?"

He immediately notified Paglin that the Haganah had decided to activate "Chick." (The Irgun shortened the code name from "Malonchick"—small hotel—to "Chick"—small—for the sake of security.)

The following day Paglin repeated the message to Adina Hay. Adina made five courier runs a week between Jerusalem and Tel Aviv for the Irgun. The police had never searched her and she never forgot a message or failed to arrive on time. According to one Irgun wife, she was "shy, pretty, and terribly punctual. If she were due at any specific hour she would arrive as the clock was striking."

She was sixteen. Eight years before, Arab rioters had murdered the husband of her favorite teacher. The entire school marched in procession to the cemetery to witness his burial. Afterward she asked everyone why he had died. His son was her age. Now he was fatherless. Why?

A teacher said that the British, not the Arabs, were responsible. He had died because the British prevented Jews from protecting themselves.

Five years later, in 1943, the Irgun leaflets pushed under the door of her family's apartment contained the same message. Adina discussed the leaflets with an older cousin.

"Aren't you going to do something about it?" the cousin demanded.

"Yes. But what?"

"Join the Irgun."

"But who knows where they are?"

"I do. I'm a member. If you want to do something for Israel I can arrange a meeting. It'll be dark and you'll have to swear an oath. They'll ask you questions about your beliefs and dedication. They'll also ask your age. Don't admit you're only thirteen. Say you're sixteen."

Adina admired her cousin and the meeting sounded exciting. Two weeks later she took an Irgun oath with twenty other teenage girls in a classroom in Mrs. Spritzer's Private School. She agreed to risk her own life but not, she quickly added, the lives of her parents.

One of her examiners said, "You may be tortured. The police would pull out your fingernails to get information."

"I don't care," she answered. But her knees shook and for days she avoided looking at her fingers.

She mixed flour and water on her mother's stove to make paste. Then she and an Irgun boy would walk through Jerusalem hand in hand, arm in arm, sweethearts. When they were alone she would pull the paste from her bag and the boy would reach under his shirt for a poster.

Later she discovered a more efficient way to distribute the Irgun bulletins. She and another girl would climb onto the roof of a building overlooking Zion Square and balance a stack of leaflets on a round tin of shoe polish—a "Kiwi"— packed with gunpowder and armed with a sixty-second fuse.

When the cinemas began emptying they lit the fuse, dashed downstairs and ordered ice cream sodas in a nearby café. Seconds later the "Kiwi" exploded. Leaflets fluttered down over the bus intersection. Pedestrians snatched them out of the air and stuffed them into their pockets. Drivers stopped, scooped some off the pavement and sped away. Policemen arrived and swept them into piles. Adina and her friend spooned ice cream and giggled.

In 1945 she became the commander of fifteen girls and went to Galilee for training. She learned how to fire a Sten and throw grenades. She was outdoors and camping with people her own age. She had a grand time. Her parents thought it was a school camp.

When she graduated, Avinoam chose her as his personal secretary and courier. She had an exceptional memory and quickly learned the names and addresses of dozens of Irgun soldiers. If the police had caught her and extracted those addresses, they could have smashed the entire Jerusalem network.

They never did. She was young, dark, and beautiful. Soldiers and police at checkpoints never suspected her. The one time they stopped her she burst into tears. "I forgot the time of the curfew," she said. "I want to go home. My mother will be worried." The sentries escorted her past the cages holding other curfew breakers and sent her off with a warning.

By the summer of 1946 she was spending her entire day on Irgun business. She collected and left messages at her Jerusalem drops—a barbershop, a hardware store, and an eggman's wagon. She delivered money to the families of imprisoned Irgun soldiers and carried lunch pails to men in jail. Their handles concealed letters.

Nothing scared her except the dark. Every evening she had to climb a dark staircase to her family's apartment. Her mother would stand on the landing above calling out in a soothing voice, "Adina . . . Adina . . . Adina. . . . It's all right. I'm here. You can come up now."

Every morning she checked into school and then sneaked away or pretended to have a headache. When the usual methods failed, her schoolmates rolled in a smelly bog during recess. The teacher canceled the next class and sent them home to wash (they tried to miss English, the enemy's language). Adina, who had avoided the bog, ran off to meet Avinoam.

On July 2 she met Avinoam on a street corner in Jerusalem and recited Paglin's message: "We have received an approval for Operation Chick. Proceed immediately with your preparations."

That same evening she visited the New British Drug Company, a Jewish-owned pharmacy on the Jaffa Road, Jerusalem's busiest shopping street. She whispered a message to the young delivery boy, Israel Levi, and then left without making a purchase.

"I don't feel well," Levi told the proprietor. "I'd like to go home early."

Levi had worked in the pharmacy for six years, since the age of twelve. Before then he had been one of the cleverest students in his elementary school. He had skipped a grade and gained admission to a prestigious high school. A year later he withdrew because his father could not afford the expense.

He believed the setback was temporary and that soon he or his father would earn enough for him to resume his studies. Two years later he was still a delivery boy. He gave up his dream of a formal education and joined the Betar, a paramilitary Zionist youth movement founded by Vladimir Jabotinsky in 1923.

Jabotinsky described the Betar as "a blend of school and army camp." Betar members wore brown uniforms and armbands, marched in torchlight parades, and attended camps where they learned "outdoor skills," obedience to their leaders, and the uniqueness of the Jewish race. A verse of the Betar anthem proclaimed:

> Even in poverty the Jew is a prince
> Jew! Whether slave or tramp you have been created a prince.

The Betarim idolized Jabotinsky, the "Rosh Betar" [Leader], and scrupulously followed his dicta to speak quietly, dress neatly and keep themselves impeccably clean. One Betar youth, sentenced to death in 1938 for participating in an Irgun attack on an Arab bus, brushed his teeth just before leaving for the gallows and asked witnesses to "tell Jabotinsky I will die with his name on my lips."

The Betar had its largest following among Eastern European Jews. Left-wing Zionists attacked it as a Jewish version of the fascist youth movements flourishing in Europe during the 1930s and referred to Jabotinsky as "Vladimir Hitler."

Ties between the Irgun and Betar were close. The Betar was the youth movement of Jabotinsky's Revisionist Party and the Irgun was its military organization. Menaham Begin had commanded the Betar in Poland.

In 1942 Israel Levi's Betar teacher, Sike Haroni, took him aside and said, "The Irgun will soon attack the British and force them to leave Palestine. Are you willing to help?"

Levi said yes without hesitation. Betar was his only school and Haroni, whom he idolized, his only teacher. He knew his parents would approve. His father often reminded him that "a Jewish State in Palestine is your birthright. Our family has lived in Jerusalem for three generations; the British have only been here for twenty-five years."

Levi joined the Irgun and assumed the underground name "Gideon."

Gideon found Avinoam waiting around the corner from the British pharmacy. As they walked Avinoam said, "You have been appointed to command an operation against an extremely important target. Tomorrow Chaim-Toit will contact you with the details. Be ready."

"What target?" Gideon asked.

Avinoam shook his head.

Gideon persisted. "When? How many men?"

Avinoam smiled and walked away.

9

July 3—July 5

THE NEXT morning, July 3, Chaim-Toit began stalking the King David. He walked up the driveway, pushed through the revolving door and wandered around the lobby. He strolled down the lane that led past the hotel's north wing to the French Consulate and he peered over a stone wall into the garden.

He spent the next three days near the hotel. One day he wore a hat, the next he went bareheaded. He dressed in workmen's overalls, in shorts, in long trousers and a jacket.

He walked alone in the daytime; in the evening he strolled arm in arm with Yael, a young Irgun woman named for a biblical heroine who impaled an enemy general on a spear. He counted the cars parked along Julian's Way and whispered their license numbers to her. She copied them into her school notebook and asked, "Why? What are we doing?"

"We're preparing a plan," he said. "We may use it, we may not. There's no date."

In February he had sent Gideon, Eliahu, and two women inside the hotel. They had drunk champagne and danced in the basement nightclub. Afterward, Gideon reported that the nightclub's four concrete pillars appeared to support the entire south wing.

This told Chaim-Toit where to place the explosives but, weeks after the visit, he had still not devised a plan for smuggling them into the hotel. It did not matter. The Joint Command had vetoed the operation and the Irgun transferred him to Tel Aviv. Now Paglin had ordered him to return to help Avinoam and Gideon penetrate the only building in Jerusalem that had ever stumped him.

He sat on the stone wall bordering the YMCA and watched the soldiers guarding the turnstile and main door. Every four hours Arab Legionnaires in spiked helmets replaced Scotsmen in tam-o'-shanters, Englishmen from the 2nd Oxford and Bucks, or Irishmen of the First Ulster Rifles. They were all armed with Thompson submachine guns.

He counted British officers with red epaulets and with pistols strapped to their sides as they pushed through the King David's revolving door on their way to military headquarters.

He too was a soldier, a Jewish soldier. Ever since Polish boys in Lodz had taunted, stoned, and beaten him as he walked to school through a Christian neighborhood he had wanted to be a Jewish soldier. He wanted revenge: first against the Polish boys; then against the Germans, who had hanged his sister and brother-in-law; and finally against the British, whose immigration laws had prevented their escape. As soon as he joined the Irgun he had dynamited the Immigration Office.

Now he counted and memorized the cars pulling into the hotel's circular driveway. Staff cars brought army officers from the Allenby Barracks. Police cars delivered important Colonial officers from their homes in the Greek and German colonies. Jeeps or armored cars preceded the cars of senior officials. At midday taxis delivered journalists, clerics, and a few tourists from the railroad station. If a particular car arrived at the same time every day, Chaim-Toit would cross Julian's Way and examine it closely.

He could watch the service entrance from the Shell gasoline station opposite the north wing. Every morning Arab porters pushed wooden carts loaded with vegetables and fruits down the steep driveway and stopped next to a green basement door. Trucks arrived with beer and milk. A truck collected garbage.

Homsi and Salameh's antiquities store was opposite the King David's south wing. While Chaim-Toit pretended to gaze at the Holy Land souvenirs on sale there, he was observing the Secretariat employees present credentials and swing through the turnstile.

He waited for a bus at the stop on Julian's Way and watched passengers get on and off.

He often passed Gideon, Avinoam, and Adina in Julian's Way. Adina also copied down license numbers. She and another girl stayed five or ten paces behind Avinoam and Gideon as they strolled past the hotel in the late afternoon, young Jewish friends enjoying the sunset.

Gideon circled the YMCA and its soccer field and saw army officers parking their cars in the YMCA lot. As he walked he whispered to himself the English phrases he would use if a policeman stopped him for questioning. Sometimes they arrested any Jew who stuttered, hesitated, or appeared nervous.

Chaim-Toit was more reckless. He was so exhausted after living underground for two and a half years that he almost welcomed the possibility of arrest and internment.

When a policeman finally stopped him for an identity check he thought, "So what? If he arrests me I'll be able to rest, regain my strength, perhaps even complete my studies. I'll be out of danger. No one will be able to kill me."

The policeman returned his forged papers and walked away. That same evening, after three days of surveillance, Chaim-Toit told Paglin he had a plan.

"Do the British want to destroy me?" Weizmann asked. "Is that the purpose of the arrests?"

No one spoke.

"It's lunacy," he continued. "They've arrested the only people who can control the underground. But why? Can any of you tell me why they didn't arrest me? Did they want to undermine my authority?"

"It's the same old story," said *The Guardian*'s correspondent Jon Kimche. "You can only push an imperial power so far. If you push them over the edge, they react. In fact, they usually overreact."

"No. It's the leadership," said Weizmann. "The contrast between these British leaders and the others is shattering. On the one hand you have Balfour, Lloyd George, Milner, and Curzon, men who understood the Bible, history, culture; on the other hand, Bevin, Attlee, and Hall [the Colonial Secretary], trade union leaders who understand nothing. . . . Weisgal! Stop it! Don't think I'm that blind, I can see you pinching my cigars."

The others laughed and relaxed. The mood of "The Chief" had suddenly changed. All afternoon Kimche, Meyer Weisgal, and Gershon Agronsky, the editor of the *Palestine Post*, had listened to Weizmann harangue them about the British. He was bitter and sick, almost in tears one moment and then laughing the next.

Kimche had come to Weizmann's room in Jerusalem's Eden Hotel hoping to persuade him to agree to meet again with Cunningham. Since arriving in Palestine two days before, Kimche had heard rumors that the underground groups were preparing a counterattack. He thought it could be stopped if the British and the remaining Jewish leaders reestablished communications and if the British made some concessions; at the minimum, they would have to release some of the arrested leaders.

At present, Britons and Jews sat in different rooms. The British did not know which Jews to call or where to reach any of them. In the meantime Kimche, who was a British Jew, had become the principal intermediary. In a cable to London, Cunningham described his efforts as "backstairs intrigue."

Kimche was discouraged by today's meeting. He had never seen Weizmann so bitter, angry, and determined to forgo negotiations.

The following morning he visited Sir John Shaw. Before he could speak Shaw said, "How can we arrange another meeting between Dr. Weizmann and the HC? He must agree to see him again. Somewhere, somebody has to make a start. We'll try to be as liberal as possible, as flexible as possible. But you must make him understand that we have to worry about the Arabs and the army."

Kimche sensed that Shaw feared the army had gone too far. He wanted to undo the damage and to compromise. But compromise with whom, Kimche wondered.

"You've played into the hands of the terrorists," the journalist said. "Now that you've arrested the leaders you've no one to talk with, and the terrorists are running around free plotting something."

"Well, what do you suggest?" Shaw asked.

"Free Shertok and some of the others as a sign of goodwill and then Weizmann will see the High Commissioner."

"I'll have to discuss it with Weizmann first. Can you persuade him to see me without conditions?"

Kimche agreed to try. He walked downstairs, around the front of the King David, through the revolving door, took an elevator upstairs to his bedroom and called Weizmann.

The identification card carried Gideon's picture, the signature of a CID officer, and said: "The person holding this certificate is employed by the municipal electric company."

The Arab plainclothes policeman standing in the King David's service driveway looked at the card and then at Gideon, who wore blue overalls and carried a tool box. A genuine employee of the electric company stood next to him. The policeman let them pass.

Inside the basement the electrician started checking the fuse boxes. Gideon checked the three entrances. There was a service stairway leading to the lobby, a door that opened onto the garden and, at the southernmost end of the corridor, the Regence, a nightclub.

He began walking toward the Regence. Chaim-Toit had told him that upstairs, concrete barriers separated the Secretariat from the rest of the hotel. Did similar barriers exist in the basement? Was there a police checkpoint inside the Regence? Chaim-Toit had ordered him to find out.

The electrician grabbed his arm. "Don't go any further," he whispered. "A manager just asked what we're doing here. He said that electricians put in new electric meters last week so the government and hotel bills could be separated. He's getting suspicious, we'd better go."

While the electrician packed his tools, Gideon discussed the routine in the basement with the receiving clerk, Johannes Constantides.

"I have to stand here all morning," Constantides said. "The vegetables come at nine, the bread at ten, the milk at eleven. The vegetables are the worst. Everything has to be separated, weighed, checked, and their weight and price entered in a ledger. The workers steal and the merchants cheat. I'm supposed to stop them all."

Gideon commiserated. "My job is no better. Last week I was doing some rewiring and I got one hell of a shock."

Constantides appreciated the sympathy. As he complained, Gideon thought, "The next time I come here, it will be to blow all this up."

The following evening a CID officer stopped two Jewish couples in the lobby of the King David and demanded identification. He looked first at Chaim-Toit's card and then at those of his companions, Yael, Eliahu, and Zeppora. When he recognized Zeppora he smiled.

Chaim-Toit was relieved he had hired her. No policeman would suspect the companions of Jerusalem's most notorious prostitute. "Enjoy yourself," he had told her. "You're going to have a grand time. We'll drink and dance. Nothing more."

They strolled past the reception desk, turned right and at the end of the corridor descended a flight of stairs to the Regence. Chaim-Toit was looking forward to the evening. No one would shoot at him. Avinoam had given him money and he wore his best dark suit.

Yael was nervous. Earlier in the day Chaim-Toit had told her, "Dress in your best clothes and meet me at eight o'clock in front of the King David."

She had rummaged through her closet, but nothing looked nice enough. Finally she persuaded her sister to lend her green dress. She put on nylon stockings for the first time. Walking into the Regence in these clothes with Chaim-Toit and the prostitute seemed a bigger challenge than carrying messages through roadblocks or placing mines under armored cars. Her father, an Orthodox rabbi, approved of her underground work, but what would he think of nightclubs, nylon stockings and dancing?

She had joined the Irgun because of him. Every evening he lectured his five daughters and seven sons about the treachery of the British and the Arabs. He had been among the first pioneers to leave the Old City and move to Givat Shaul, a Jewish village near the Jaffa Road almost encircled by Arab settlements.

The family lectures had begun in 1936, the same year Arab terrorists had killed his eldest son. Afterward he told his children, "We must now learn how to kill Arabs." His family had lived in Palestine for generations. He threatened to disown them if they left home instead of remaining to fight.

He addressed the lectures to his sons. He wanted his daughters to stay home, lead modest lives, and marry Orthodox husbands, but they also listened.

Yael was so moved that she joined the Betar. When she turned eighteen in 1944 she joined the Irgun. Her father became suspicious. Why was she away from home so often? She lied and said she was at Betar meetings. He suspected a boyfriend.

Her brother Gal said, "You can't tell us you're at Betar every morning and evening. Betar doesn't have that many meetings." He was a year and a half older, her closest brother in age and her best friend. She loved him and could not lie.

"I thought so," he said after she told him the truth. "Tell them I want to join too."

He quit his job as an automobile mechanic and worked only for the Irgun. When his father learned the truth he congratulated him but scolded Yael. Another brother joined. Their mother washed their clothes and cooked nourishing meals so they could survive on an Irgun allowance. She also cooked for the British major they kidnapped. She thought he looked thin and gave him particularly large helpings. The family house became a center of Irgun activity, a place for meetings and a storehouse for weapons.

Yael sensed her father becoming secretly proud of her. If he learned of her visit to the Regence she hoped he would believe she had gone there as a soldier.

A young Swiss headwaiter led them to a table set with china bearing the hotel emblem, King David's Tower, and presented menus embossed with the same emblem.

The Regence offered what Hamburger called a "snack menu." There was caviar, foie gras, and other delicacies; for dinner, sole amaral (with shrimps), English mixed grill (kidneys, sausages, bacon, and lamb), elaborate snacks like "Le Club Sandwich," "Les Saucisses de Berne" (pork sausage), or "Le Croute Regence" (toasted ham-and-cheese sandwich). Nothing was kosher.

Yael ordered wine, Chaim-Toit fruit juice, the prostitute whiskey, neat. They asked for coffee and cakes later.

During the next hour they joked, gossiped about friends, and discussed the food and service. Yael liked her cake. The prostitute drank too much and said she'd never had a better time at the King David. Sudanese waiters removed plates, swept crumbs off the pink linen cloth, replaced the candle, poured coffee and, Chaim-Toit assumed, eavesdropped for something to peddle to the CID.

While the others talked, he studied the room. Copper mugs and pitchers hung behind the bar. Copper cocktail tables reflected the candlelight. Blue leather covered the barstools and banquettes. The four important pillars stood near the center of the room. Each was a meter and a half wide. They supported the barbershop, the southern corner of the lobby, three floors of government offices, and the military offices on the top floor.

At nine o'clock the band began playing and the room filled. Army officers, merchants, and journalists sat on the barstools. English and Arab hostesses presided over small dinner parties.

The King David advertised the Regence as a "Gay and Intimate Snack Bar" offering "Comfort, Relaxation and Jollity." By 1946 it had become a British sanctuary. Upstairs in the lobby and main bar the British discussed politics and terrorists. They came downstairs to the Regence to forget Jerusalem; to flirt, dance, and watch "Eugene Ferrar the Talented Juggler," "Irene and Gordon—Tap Dancers Direct from London's Piccadilly Hotel," and "Wendlard," a magician who made cigarettes, scarfs and a wireless tuned to Prague vanish. Tonight, "Mandelbaum's Three Musketeers" played dance music.

Chaim-Toit and Yael danced around the edge of the tiny floor. Chaim-Toit saw iron-barred windows in the south facing wall, a fireplace in the east, and velvet curtains in the west. "Push yourself into those curtains," he whispered. "I want to see what's behind them."

Yael stumbled and fell backwards. There were stacks of chairs and a wall, no windows or doors.

They danced back to the middle of the floor and a British officer tapped Chaim-Toit on the shoulder.

"Excuse me," he said. "Do you mind?"

"I do," Yael said. "I've danced enough for one night. We're just about to leave."

"Please, you must go back and dance with him," Chaim-Toit implored as they left the dance floor. "I'm not finished."

"I am. I don't like the British and I didn't come here to dance with them."

"We'll have to go then. He'll be suspicious if we stay. Quick, go to the ladies' room and memorize the location of every door and window. You'll have to draw a plan after we leave. I'll meet you in the corridor."

As soon as she left, he walked past the men's toilet and through an unmarked door. He was in the kitchen. Chefs labored over stoves and counters. Waiters pushed through swinging doors from the Regence. At the opposite end of the room another set of swinging doors had been propped open. On the other side he could see the green walls of the basement corridor. A Sudanese waiter blocked his way.

"Mister, what are you doing here?" he asked.

"I'm lost."

The waiter pointed toward the Regence. "That way out."

Yael was waiting in the corridor. "Let's go," he said. "I've found what I wanted." He had found the King David's jugular.

10

July 6—July 8

"IN EVERY country in the world it is customary that the President is also the
Commander in Chief of the military forces," Weizmann said to the Jewish
leaders not arrested on Black Saturday. They were gathered in his home in
Rehovot. "I have never before needed to use this authority and have never
interfered. But now, for the first and only time, I must demand this right and
demand that you cease all military activities."

The leaders promised to do their best to restrain the Haganah and assured
him they knew of no military action under consideration. They also authorized
him to negotiate with the High Commissioner and Chief Secretary and to
promise that if the leaders were released the Yishuv would surrender any
weapons not needed for defense against the Arabs.

Golda Meyerson, who was present at this meeting, urged Weizmann to
support a campaign of nonviolent protests. "If you call upon the Yishuv to
adopt a policy of civil disobedience toward the government of Palestine," she
said, "it will show the world that we cannot acquiesce in what has happened.
Only you have the necessary authority to make this proclamation effective."

"All right," Weizmann said. "But I must be assured by the Haganah that
nothing will be done—no actions taken—until the Jewish Agency meets in Paris
in August."

Mrs. Meyerson promised to make every effort to secure such an assurance
"from the five people [the X Committee] who decided these matters."

The following afternoon Sir John Shaw drove to Rehovot to attend the meeting with Weizmann arranged by Jon Kimche of *The Guardian.* Since speaking with Kimche, Shaw had consulted the High Commissioner. Britain's terms for releasing the leaders were stiffer than he had first imagined. The Haganah had to liquidate the Palmach, stop all illegal activities including immigration and put itself under the control of the Palestine government.

Weizmann rejected this government proposal. The Yishuv would never agree to stop illegal immigration. He repeated the offer of the leaders to surrender unnecessary arms but defended the Haganah. "The other leaders have assured me," he said, "that there has been no contact between the Haganah and the dissidents [the Stern Gang and Irgun] except an occasional attempt to exercise restraint."

Shaw knew this was false. Recently the British had broken the Jewish Agency's code and intercepted telegrams that mentioned the alliance between the Haganah and the dissidents. "Your advisors are misleading you," he said. "There has been contact, and for evil purposes."

"How do you plan to destroy the King David?" Haganah Chief of Staff Yitzhak Sadeh asked Amihai Paglin.

"By putting three hundred and fifty kilos of explosives in the restaurant underneath the Secretariat," Paglin answered. He did not explain Chaim-Toit's plan. Neither Sadeh nor Moshe Sneh asked for details.

The three men sat around the kitchen table in the Tel Aviv apartment Sneh had chosen for a hideout. Sneh wore a disguise; Sadeh was growing a beard. Government press bulletins described them as "wanted terrorists."

Like Sneh, Sadeh believed in active resistance to the White Paper. He had been the first Haganah leader to advocate attacking Arab terrorists outside the boundaries of Jewish settlements during the Arab revolt.

In 1941, he had founded the Palmach with the encouragement of the British Army. Modeled on the European partisan armies, its original purpose was to resist a Nazi occupation. It eschewed secret oaths, military discipline, and the mystical hero-worship favored by the Sternists and Irgun. Sadeh believed that "we must teach our youth to fight but not to hate."

Now he was planning the most ambitious underground attack in history with the representative of Menahem Begin, a leader who believed "It is axiomatic that those who fight have to hate—something or somebody."

Today was the first time he or Sneh had met Paglin. Both had been shocked when he walked through the door. Paglin's older brother had died while on a British-Haganah commando raid against the Vichy French who had ruled Lebanon during the war. The Paglin family were ardent socialists and supporters of the Haganah. It unnerved them that this slight, intense young man, whom they recognized as the brother of a Haganah martyr, was the military genius of the right-wing Irgun.

"I'm surprised you're only using three hundred fifty kilos of explosives," Sadeh said. "Are you sure it's enough?"

Paglin was stunned. The Haganah usually wanted to decrease the amount of explosives. Now Sadeh asked for more. Was he ignorant of what 350 kilos would do to the King David? Or had the Haganah changed its policy?

"If we place the explosives around the supporting pillars," Paglin explained, "the force of the blast should reach the roof. The entire wing, perhaps the entire building, will collapse. If we use more explosives, we'll increase the possibility of a total collapse. Is that what you want?"

Without answering, Sadeh raised more objections. "But you've promised to give a warning. If you place the bombs in the center of a restaurant, won't the British find them and dismantle them?"

"I've devised a bomb that can't be dismantled."

"But can you assure us the operation will result in absolutely no loss of life?" Sadeh asked.

"It is our experience that the British abandon a building quickly once they've been given a warning."

"Are you sure?"

"Of course."

Paglin was exaggerating. He believed the King David would be evacuated but he could not be sure. At first the British had evacuated buildings whenever they received a bomb warning. Recently, however, so many of these warnings had turned out to be hoaxes that some Britons had begun disregarding them. For example, a favorite ploy of the Irgun was to call a rural police station and warn that mortars targeted on the station had been buried in the surrounding hills. The mortars were armed with automatic fuses, the Irgun would say, that would launch them sometime during the night. Sometimes these calls were hoaxes, sometimes they were real but, fearing they would be ambushed if they left their stations, the policemen never evacuated.

Paglin was perplexed by Sadeh's attitude toward the warning and the explosives. First he had worried that the explosives were inadequate, then he worried about casualties. He and Sneh appeared nervous. Were they afraid of being arrested? Perhaps, Paglin thought with great satisfaction, they were cowards. Black Saturday had proved them incapable of taking elementary precautions. Now their best soldiers sat in detention camps, their largest cache of arms was in a British arsenal and they were running to the Irgun for help. They were contemptible. He had detested them ever since "The Season."

After the assassination of Lord Moyne, David Ben-Gurion, fearing a political challenge from the dissidents, had announced that the Yishuv had a "common interest with the British in rooting out terrorism." But instead of attacking the Sternists, who had killed Moyne, he declared war on the Irgun. Paglin believed he had chosen the Irgun because he knew Begin would not retaliate.

This underground civil war became known as "The Hunting Season," or just "The Season." Haganah commanders ordered schoolchildren to rip down Irgun posters. Headmasters expelled students who belonged to the Irgun or Betar.

Irgun soldiers and their families were dismissed from their jobs. The Haganah hunted down and kidnapped Irgun soldiers, tortured them for information, and then turned them over to the British police. Many were deported to East Africa. Begin refused to fight back and shed Jewish blood. It was his finest hour.

Sneh had masterminded "The Season." Paglin had never forgiven him.

Sneh thought the Irgun fascist. The Haganah took orders from the Yishuv's democratically elected representatives. The Irgun took orders from one man. Sneh suspected the Irgun was financed by a rich bourgeoisie that planned to use it to frustrate the socialist state that would arise in Israel under the direction of the Agency.

After meeting Begin in 1944 Sneh wrote, "Begin made a pathetic impression. He is incapable of framing his thought without resorting to rhetorical riddles. And when he uses rhetoric, he tends to become emotional."

Sneh considered Begin's concept of revolt destructive and simplistic. He wanted to throw out the British, that was all. He gave insufficient thought to the Arab menace. The Haganah's policy of armed struggle *and* illegal colonization and immigration was constructive. These immigrants and settlements would be important in the Arab war the Haganah considered inevitable.

"How much time are you allowing for the evacuation of the King David?" Sneh asked Paglin.

"Forty-five minutes."

"Too long," Sadeh objected. "It gives the British time to save documents as well as people." The Haganah leaders had another purpose besides retribution for attacking the King David. They hoped the Irgun's bombs would destroy the possibly incriminating documents the British had seized from the Jewish Agency. In their hysteria after Black Saturday, some in the Haganah believed the British might use these documents to arrest and execute the entire Jewish leadership.

"Don't worry about any documents," Paglin said. "When the British learn we've mined a building they don't waste time picking up papers."

Sadeh wanted to be certain the papers were destroyed. He insisted the Irgun use a fifteen-minute fuse. After considerable discussion and argument Paglin proposed and Sadeh agreed to a compromise, a thirty-minute fuse.

"It's evident, isn't it?" Begin said after Paglin summarized the meeting. "They want to be sure we destroy the documents the British stole from the Agency."

They sat in the perpetual twilight of Begin's kitchen sipping tea. Paglin wore blue plumbers' overalls. To complete the disguise he had carried a box of wrenches and plungers into the house on Bin Nun Street.

Paglin agreed with Begin's analysis. It fitted in with his belief that the Haganah were incompetent and cowardly. They had lost these important papers and now they had to beg the Irgun to destroy them. It also explained Sadeh's curious insistence on increasing the amount of explosives and reducing the evacuation time. Sneh had even said it: they did not want to give the British time to save the "documents."

He assumed the documents proved the secret links between the Haganah and Irgun and the less secret ones between the Haganah and the Agency. Sneh had to be afraid the British would use them as a pretext for outlawing the Agency and arresting its remaining leaders. Under British law the penalty for assisting a "terrorist" organization was life imprisonment or death.

Nevertheless, Paglin could not let the Haganah's predicament influence his judgment. "I still recommend we allow forty-five minutes for an evacuation," he said. "My fuses will detonate if British sappers play with the bombs."

Begin was a political, not a military tactician, an amateur in questions of fuses, blast effects, and evacuation times. The highest military rank he had achieved was corporal, a filing clerk in the Free Polish Army. He believed in armed revolt but had never fought a battle, fired a gun in anger or planted a bomb. He risked arrest, imprisonment and execution, but not death in combat.

The question of how long it would take the British to evacuate a building the size of the King David was one only Paglin could answer. But the decision to give a warning in the first place was more a political one and he had made it.

He had decided on a warning because the purpose of Operation Chick was not to kill as many Britons as possible, but to humiliate them and terrorize them into leaving Palestine by destroying their supposedly impregnable headquarters.

He wanted to give a warning because Jewish civil servants worked in the King David and Jewish lawyers, accountants, and politicians visited it throughout the day. Any bomb exploding in the hotel without warning would kill scores of Jews. A year after the Holocaust, Jewish life seemed especially precious. The Irgun could not be responsible for the mass murder of Jews. Avinoam had recently dissuaded the Sternists from blowing up a brothel patronized by British officers by pointing out that Jewish prostitutes would also be killed.

Begin would also warn the King David because in July 1946 the Irgun's "honor code" demanded it. This unwritten code required that Irgun soldiers go into battle wearing armbands ("uniforms"); that the Irgun claim responsibility for its attacks; that an enemy be "executed" only after an Irgun "military court" had reached a verdict of "guilty"; and that warnings be given to targets when civilians might be endangered. According to this code it had been "immoral" to attack the British Army while it was fighting Hitler. After the war it had become morally acceptable to kill British soldiers.

Begin applied the Irgun's code of etiquette erratically, particularly in the case of bomb warnings. Later on, after the King David operation and after the Joint Command was dissolved, the Irgun exploded bombs without warning when British soldiers and policemen and Arab civilians were the only potential victims.

But in July 1946, because Jews and other civilians worked in and visited the King David, because the Irgun was in a joint command with the Haganah and the Haganah insisted on a warning, and because the Irgun's flexible honor code allowed for it, Begin would give the British time to evacuate the King David before he destroyed it.

He approved Paglin's thirty-minute compromise and instructed him to make certain that warnings were telephoned as soon as the bombs were fused. "I did not want any casualties in that operation," he said later, "not even one and therefore I insisted we give ample time for an evacuation."

He assumed that if Paglin armed the bombs with thirty-minute fuses the British would have at least twenty-five minutes to evacuate, provided everything went according to plan.

11

July 9—July 11

"THE JEWS kidnapped me and hid me in a cellar," nine-year-old Henryk Blaszczyk told his father. "I saw the bodies of fifteen Christian children they had murdered." The story was a lie, the infamous anti-Semitic lie of ritual murder. The boy told it to avoid being punished for disappearing from home.

"Jews are killing our children!" The lie spread quickly through the small Polish city of Kielce and police confiscated pistols owned by the small postwar Jewish community.

Twenty-five thousand Jews had lived in Kielce before the war. Now there were scarcely two hundred. They had returned from Russia, from hiding places in surrounding forests, from Auschwitz and Buchenwald. Most lived in large communal houses and worked as laborers in local factories and workshops. They planned to live together in a kibbutz in Palestine and were practicing communal living while awaiting visas.

On the morning of July 4, 1946, five thousand Christian Poles attacked the two hundred Jews of the commune. Jews were stoned, beaten, slashed with knives and hatchets. Men in police uniforms joined the pogrom. Government officials and the army did nothing. Seven hours later forty-two Jews were dead.

The survivors fled the largest, but not the only, attack on Jews since the end of the war. The remaining 100,000 Jews in Poland panicked. Roads leading west and south were choked with Jews fleeing to displaced persons camps in western Europe. Kielce and other Polish towns were again "Judenrein"—Jew-free. The papers said that when young Blaszczyk learned of the result of his lie, "he shrugged his shoulders."

Accounts of the Kielce pogrom reached Palestine on Sunday, July 8. They electrified the Yishuv. Here was vivid proof that, as one newspaper said, "Jews can never be secure in a Christian nation." Here too was vivid proof of the inhumanity of the White Paper. If the gates of Palestine (or the United States) had been open, the forty-two Kielce Jews would have survived. If British policy killed Jews, what alternative did the Yishuv have but to resist?

The day after the Yishuv learned of the pogrom, Weizmann held a press conference in a crowded room in the Eden Hotel. Pale, ill and wearing sunglasses because of his eye condition, he sat in a chair while a Jewish Agency official read extracts of a speech he had just delivered to Zionist leaders.

The speech reflected his conflicting emotions, his anger over Kielce and Black Saturday and yet his determination to keep Zionism from being contaminated by violence.

> I am the last to justify the breaking of the Law, but even in the administration of the Law, account is taken of extenuating circumstances. Is there a people in this whole world which has endured such terrible trials as my people?
>
> For more than a decade now the Jewish people have been subjected to a continuous and terrible ordeal: under Nazi Germany, torture and death; and since the Allied victory, hope deferred. Throughout the many storms that have passed over us, I and the Executive of the Jewish Agency have endeavored with all our strength to preserve the purity of our movement, the sanctity of our ideal. The fire burning within us, a fire that might have consumed others to ashes, our people have transformed into a mighty force for the creation of spiritual and material values in the land of our fathers. This fire will not be extinguished. . . .

Weizmann wanted to be certain this fire did not consume the Yishuv and turn three decades of accomplishments to ashes while he was in London undergoing an eye operation. He was not convinced by the assurances of the Jewish leaders that the Haganah was not planning anything. Shaw had encouraged his doubts.

The day after he met with Shaw the Haganah radio announced: "The Jewish Resistance will choose its own time and its own methods of counterattack and retaliation for British military attacks carried out against the Jewish community in Palestine."

The Irgun radio said: "Our reply to British aggression is war—war for liberty, war for justice. We shall wage this war as long as there is breath in our bodies and blood in our veins."

After the press conference Weizmann sent his personal assistant Meyer Weisgal on a secret, delicate mission. If the mission succeeded, he could leave

Palestine certain that there would be no attacks by the underground groups during his absence.

Paglin bought the explosives from an Arab dentist. The dentist's wife was Jewish and they both detested the British. He often returned from his clinics in Ramle and Gaza with his car's trunk stuffed with weapons and explosives (Arabs were not thoroughly searched at the roadblocks). He resold some of these explosives to Paglin.

The explosives were ten years old. Arab terrorists had stolen them from the British Army during the Arab revolt and hidden them in Hebron. Paglin paid for them with money donated by supporters and "confiscated" from banks and merchants. He stored them in the Irgun house in Petach Tikva.

Paglin took the weapons for Operation Chick from the Irgun's own arsenal. The Irgun owned a hundred small weapons—pistols, rifles, and submachine guns. Many belonged to a floating Middle East arsenal that was traded from people to people, even between enemies, and had plagued Britain and France since World War I.

The Druze, one of the Middle East's numerous religious minorities, had used this arsenal during their uprising against the French Mandate in Syria. In 1936, Palestinian Arabs had used many of the same weapons to kill British officials and Jewish settlers. The Second World War increased the arsenal. Bedouins in the Western Desert salvaged weapons abandoned by the British, German and Italian armies. Smugglers moved them to Palestine by road and rail.

The Irgun and Stern Gang purchased their weapons from Arabs or British soldiers or stole them from military arsenals. They never had enough; they always needed more. Each weapon was in perpetual motion, passed between soldiers and commands, used again and again. Each had a history. Ballistics experts determined that the pistol that killed Lord Moyne had been used to commit eight other terrorist murders.

The Irgun treasured every weapon. Each pistol and round was catalogued. During training, recruits were allowed to fire three live bullets—one for single fire and two for rapid. Quartermasters distributed weapons just before every operation and collected them immediately afterward. Only a few soldiers were given revolvers or machine guns; the rest carried homemade grenades.

Paglin planned every operation so that the Irgun would gain rather than lose weapons. He had taken particular care with Operation Chick since to this operation he was allocating one-fifth of his "army's" entire arsenal—one Tommy gun, five Stens, and eleven pistols. If the King David was destroyed but these weapons lost, the operation would not be considered a total success.

In Jerusalem, Avinoam and Gideon also made last-minute preparations to execute Chaim-Toit's plan for penetrating the King David. Paglin had told them to be ready to attack the hotel at a moment's notice.

Young oriental Jews slipped into Arab neighborhoods and mingled with crowds in the Via Dolorosa and in front of the Damascus Gate. Some were recent imigrants from Syria, Iraq and North Africa; others belonged to families that had lived in Jerusalem for generations. They spoke fluent Arabic and resembled Palestinian Arabs, the same dark skin and brown-black eyes and the same Semitic features. They walked with the same cadence, touched with the same intimacy and bargained with the same intensity.

They made their purchases carefully. They exchanged elaborate greetings with the merchants, argued over price and quality, left one tailor, bargained with another and then returned to the first to make a purchase.

They bought workmen's overalls, red fezzes and the blue robes worn by Arab laborers and hawkers. One man persuaded a Sudanese waiter from the King David to sell his entire uniform. The Sudanese reported it stolen.

Like every grand hotel in the Middle East the King David employed tall, dark-skinned Arabs from the Sudan as waiters and cleaners. Many had worked in Shepheard's and other Egyptian hotels and were following a tradition begun by their fathers and grandfathers.

About a hundred Sudanese worked at the King David. They surrendered their passports to Hamburger and were forbidden to work elsewhere. They earned upwards of a pound a month (scarcely more than the cost of high tea in the Arab Lounge), lived in the dormitory annex, and wore red fezzes, white pantaloons and crimson or green jackets embroidered with gold braid.

They appeared before the King David's guests as picturesque Ali Babas carrying silver trays of gin and tonics through the lobby or as tall, silent specters gliding into rooms to draw blinds, make beds, and lay out clothes.

According to Naim Nissan, the King David's chief maitre d'hôtel, they were "honest and efficient, devoted to their jobs, loyal to the hotel and hard-working. They took orders gracefully, had good posture, and were fanatical about cleanliness. They were a people born to serve. When you put them under the management of Swiss hoteliers you had a unique combination."

During 1946 this combination came under considerable strain. One rung below the cool and efficient Swiss managers were temperamental French and Italian chefs, headwaiters, accountants and housekeepers. They fought constantly with the Sudanese and Arab workers who, like other Africans and Asians, had started rebelling against European authority.

A Sudanese cleaner assigned to the first floor repeatedly burst into bathrooms while guests were in the tub. Sometimes he locked them in their bathrooms. He refused to wear his fez.

Every morning a Sudanese on the second floor purposely omitted one important item from a guest's breakfast tray. Hamburger reprimanded him in a letter: "When a cup is not lacking, a spoon is; when there is salt, there is no pepper; when there is bread, there is no margarine, etc., etc."

Helmut Werner, the young Czech refugee who managed the second floor, became so enraged that he punched this difficult Sudanese. His file, like those of many other Europeans, bulged with letters of complaint from the Arab and Sudanese workers. One charged him with following the wrong procedure for replacing beers, another with signing chits in an illegible handwriting.

The most bitter staff dispute centered around a cigar. On June 19 Enrique Ubelhardt, a European headwaiter, overheard a lobby waiter, Abdel Hussein, brag about stealing and smoking one of the cigars offered to guests in the main dining room.

Soutter docked the price of the cigar from Hussein's salary and fired him. Hussein complained to the Palestine Labour League, a Jewish organization to which all of the King David's workers belonged. (Some Arabs charged that Arab workers were recruited into the League to prevent Arabs from lowering wages, thereby forcing higher-paid Jewish workers out of work in case of a postwar depression.)

The dispute divided the hotel. Jacob Cohen, a lawyer for the Labour League, demanded a hearing. Five Arab waiters denied hearing Hussein brag about the cigar. The hearing was adjourned and both sides gathered more evidence.

The Cigar Incident touched off more disputes. On June 25 Cohen argued that "this case continued to be responsible for waves of bitterness among the employees."

The next day Rosemarie Polushny, an Austrian refugee who managed the basement commissary, refused to give a Sudanese waiter, Ibrahim Khalili, an extra cup of yoghurt. He shouted an obscenity, she screamed back. He was enraged that a woman dared scold him. He grabbed her wrists and shook her. She was furious that a Sudanese dared to touch her. She dug her fingernails into his neck and drew blood. He chased her into a storeroom and boxed her ears. She threw a soup tureen at him, slicing a wound in his head.

Incidents such as these led Hamburger to complain to Jerusalem's resident American Intelligence agent, Nick Andronovich, that "the situation at the hotel has become impossible."

Even though many of the Sudanese could not read, Hamburger fought back with letters. The most picayune offense resulted in an employee receiving an elaborate letter of reprimand. For example, Hamburger wrote to a second-floor waiter:

> No less than two years have elapsed since your coming here during which time you could have easily adapted yourself to the type of clientele patronizing this hotel and the quality of the service required by them . . . complaints by guests on your floor in reference to your

bad service are getting more and more insistent and frequent until I am afraid that the service on the second floor of the King David will lose its reputation entirely, which of course I am not willing to tolerate.

The letters increased the strain and widened the distance between the management and staff of the King David. Soon this distance would have consequences more serious than a squabble over a cigar or an extra cup of yoghurt.

Meyer Weisgal sat blindfolded in the back seat of an automobile driven by Haganah soldiers. Since beginning the journey a half hour earlier in Tel Aviv he had counted turns, noted when the car slowed or stopped at intersections, estimated its speed, and listened to the sounds of traffic. He believed they were still in Tel Aviv, perhaps on Allenby Street.

During the last twenty-five years he had performed numerous delicate and secret missions for Weizmann. He had served as Secretary of the Zionist Organization of America, established a branch of the Jewish Agency in New York, had been Weizmann's personal representative to the United States. His devotion to Weizmann was total. His political opinions mirrored those of his "Chief."

He had recently attempted to make sense of his conflicting feelings toward violence and terrorism by writing down his thoughts on scraps of paper. He titled these notes, "Random Thoughts of a Bewildered Zionist."

He wrote that on the one hand:

> The world seemed to have a double standard as far as we are concerned. . . . Political violence in other parts of the world, and there is plenty of it, is given the name of patriotism, resistance, revolt, partisan warfare, Marxism, de Gaullism, revolution. In Palestine it becomes a very simple thing: terror.

Yet, much as he resented this reaction to Jewish violence, he, like Weizmann, believed it corrupted Zionism. He wrote:

> We owe nothing to the goyim. We owe them no apology. Nothing that we can do will ever expiate their sins. But it has no relation to your acts. What is more important is the question: What does it do to us? It eggs on evil as an end in itself. But there is no compromise with evil. This is at the root of our mistaken policy. We thought that by dealing with the Etzel or the Stern Gang we would influence them to a more rational policy. But the reverse happened. We are smeared with the blood on their hands. What is happening in Palestine is the greatest triumph of so-called Christian civilization. It has succeeded in dragging us down to its own level.

The purpose of tonight's mission, probably the most important Weisgal had

ever undertaken for his Chief, was to stop Jewish terrorism from further
corrupting Zionism and dragging it down to the level of Christian nationalisms.

The car slowed, turned off Allenby Street and stopped. The door opened and
Weisgal's guards led him, still blindfolded, into a house, up two flights of stairs
and into an apartment. The blindfold was removed. He was standing in the
middle of a dentist's office. Moshe Sneh sat in the dentist's chair.

Weisgal pulled a notebook from his pocket and read, "Dr. Weizmann has
asked me to bring you the following message: 'We are standing on the edge of a
precipice. If you continue your operations this will be the equivalent of a
declaration of war on Great Britain. I am certain Britain will fight back and
everything we have worked for may be destroyed.

"'I am still the president of the Zionist Movement and in Democracies it is
generally accepted that the President is the Commander of all the armed
forces. . . . I am now using this authority. I demand that you stop all operations
by all three underground groups.

"'If you are unable to stop the others I demand that you cancel all Haganah
operations until the Jewish Agency Executive is gathered [at the August meeting
in Paris] in the broadest possible composition and can decide how to conduct
the struggle.

"'You must decide immediately. You must give Weisgal a clear answer now,
yes or no. If you say no I will resign immediately and publish the reasons for my
resignation.

"'My resignation will harm the movement. It will split the leadership and our
people. I would like to avoid it but I am certain that military operations would
be even more damaging.'"

Sneh believed it crucial for the Haganah to continue the military struggle and
for the King David and the other two retaliatory attacks to proceed as planned.
The documents had to be destroyed and the Yishuv had to prove it had not been
intimidated by Operation Agatha. Otherwise, the British might be encouraged
to believe they could get away with imposing a political solution on Palestine
unfavorable to the Yishuv, without having to fear a full-scale Jewish uprising.

He disagreed with Weizmann's argument that resistance would cause further
destruction in the settlements. If he rejected Weizmann's ultimatum he was
certain the underground groups and a majority of the Yishuv would support
him.

But if he defied Weizmann he would split the Yishuv. The moderate
politicians still supported Weizmann. The military and political leadership
would be at odds. The public would receive contradictory instructions. The
British would exploit their differences. The only way to avoid these catastrophes
was for an authorized, democratic Jewish institution to rule on Weizmann's
demands. He decided to submit the matter to the X Committee.

"I can't answer yes or no immediately," he said. "The Jewish Agency has given me general authority to conduct a military struggle. I am facing a conflict between my responsibilities to Dr. Weizmann and to national bodies that have authorized certain military actions. Others have collaborated with us. I cannot act alone. I must have time to think and consult. You'll have my answer as soon as possible."

12

July 12—July 14

M ANY IN the Yishuv besides Sneh and Weisgal reexamined their loyalties and principles after Black Saturday. Some were in equally, if not more, delicate positions.

Several days after the arrests Julius Jacobs, a British Jew who was the senior Jewish civil servant in Palestine, stopped Sir John Shaw in a corridor in the Secretariat.

"I feel I must warn you," he said. "I am under tremendous pressure to disclose information acquired in the course of my official duties. . . ." His voice trailed off.

"Who's putting this pressure on you, Julius?" Shaw asked.

Jacobs was shy and sensitive. He blushed easily, doted on his children and read poetry for relaxation. Black Saturday had broken his heart. His government had arrested his friends; his people had attacked his government. He wanted to be true to the Jews without betraying the British.

"My friends, neighbors, everyone is pressuring me," he said.

Shaw did not expect him to name them. He knew Jacobs could no more betray them than betray the government. He was British, and Jewish, and one of two Jews in the government with access to the gray-covered top-secret files which the regulations said "are to be seen and handled by British officers only."

He was a British Army officer who had come to Palestine with Allenby's army and had decided to stay; a Zionist who, like Weizmann, believed that the National Home would flower under a British administration. Unlike

Weizmann, he had become a Zionist by chance. Passion, not politics, had drawn him to Palestine.

His parents, comfortable middle-class Manchester Jews, thought the First World War had deranged him. He had survived Flanders and the Somme. He had a degree in chemistry and a promising career awaited him in England. Instead he chose to remain in Palestine. "It's a tragedy," his mother told her friends. "Julius is burying himself in the desert."

In 1921 he married Nahama Dondikov, the beautiful daughter of one of Rehovot's founders. They set up house in two tents, one for living, the other for her Steinway grand piano. She was the daughter of Zionist pioneers as well as a talented pianist.

He taught organic chemistry at Hebrew University and worked under Moshe Shertok in the Jewish Agency. After the birth of a son he resigned from both positions and joined the British government. He needed more money to support his family.

Since then he had been torn between his allegiance to Britain and the Yishuv, between friends in the Jewish Agency and those in the Secretariat. During the day he was a hard-working assistant secretary known for staying late and finishing the work left on his colleagues' desks. In the evening Dov Joseph, Shertok, and others arrived after dinner, closed the door to his study and asked for advice—how could the Agency best respond to this or that British policy?

He had almost resigned from the government twice, once in 1939 to protest the White Paper and a second time in 1945 when British Foreign Secretary Bevin announced the White Paper would continue. Both times friends in the Agency persuaded him to change his mind. They said the Yishuv needed him in the Secretariat, not as a spy—they knew he was too honest—but as an intermediary.

His Saturday afternoon musical parties symbolized his position in the middle. Golda Meyerson, Teddy Kollek, David Horowitz, Gershon Agronsky and other prominent Jews (except for David Ben-Gurion, whom Mrs. Jacobs loathed and held responsible for the terrorism of the dissidents) gathered at the Jacobses' sprawling house in Rehavia for tea, drinks, conversation and music. Mrs. Jacobs played her Steinway and the foremost musicians in Palestine gave recitals. The music of string quartets echoed through the barren hills around Rehavia.

Jacobs was secretary of the Palestine Philharmonic. He had often interceded with chief secretaries and high commissioners to allow "illegal" musicians to remain in Palestine. He supported them until they became settled and Mrs. Jacobs' Steinway was the first instrument many had touched in years. "It plays by itself," they marveled.

Neither the Arabs nor the kind of Britons found in the Colonial Office were particularly musical. They came to Jacobs' parties to meet prominent Jews and exchange political opinions. The fact that the Jacobses served whiskey also helped make the music bearable. (Although one Briton remembers that "they were always doing something like having a man play the cello in the garden to coax the nightingales into song. We never appreciated that sort of thing very much.")

Sir John Shaw and the Financial Secretary, Geoffrey Walsh, were among the most regular British guests.

Mrs. Jacobs liked Shaw. "He was neither anti-Semitic nor pro-Jewish, just a decent man. However, none of us had any illusions about him. He had to do what they—Whitehall—told him."

Walsh was also popular. "A jolly man and a real friend of the Jews," said Mrs. Jacobs. "Although sometimes he appalled the Jewish Agency people by saying things like, 'No one should have a nation. Hasn't the war taught us that? One passport, one nation. We need fewer nations, not one more.'"

The Arabs who came to the Jacobses' were Christians who had kept up their Jewish friendships despite the Arab revolt and Jewish terrorism.

In 1942, when Rommel appeared to be heading for Cairo and Palestine, Mrs. George Salameh had taken Mrs. Jacobs aside and told her, "If the Nazis come, send Ruth [their daughter] to us. We'll adopt her. We all look the same, no one will know. The Germans won't be able to tell us apart."

After the war Mrs. Jacobs continued her parties. Fewer Britons and Arabs came. The Jews were more sensitive to anti-Semitic slights and the Arabs and British more likely to make them. At one postwar party Mrs. Nashashibi tried to be sympathetic. "It's tragic that the German Jews lost so much," she said. "I remember that before the war they owned all the German banks."

Mrs. Jacobs did not remember the Jews "owning all the banks" when she had visited Germany. She remained silent, but wondered, "Are these friendships futile? These gatherings doomed?" Here, even among the "best" Arabs and Britons, were reminders of the necessity for a Jewish State.

There were no parties after Black Saturday. The British guests had arrested the Jewish guests and the Arab guests had applauded.

At the time, Mrs. Jacobs was visiting London. She wrote her husband and begged him to accept the Colonial Office's recent offer of a job in Britain. "Let's spend these easy, well-paid years in London," she wrote. "Our son is in Oxford. We can be near him and escape the troubles."

He wrote back, "I belong in Palestine." He told her he had tried to resign after Agatha but the Agency had insisted it was more important than ever that he remain in the Secretariat.

"The pressure has become intense," he told Shaw. "So intense that"—he chose his words carefully—"soon I'm afraid I'll be unable to resist."

Shaw was reminded of his years in Africa, of natives under pressure from relatives to "pinch the till."

"What would you have me do, Julius?" he asked.

"Transfer me. Put me where I won't have access to important information."

Shaw had never seen him so upset. These days everyone was upset and uncertain, even his own wife. She had taken to saying things like, "Well, if the Nazis were in England I'd fight tooth and nail and that's what we are to the Jews, an occupying power."

Mrs. Shaw had been pro-Arab when they first came to Palestine but during the last year of the war she had become sympathetic to the Jews through her Red Cross work tracing Jewish relatives in Europe. Time and again her letters of inquiry were returned stamped "Addressee Unknown." This meant, as the Jews she had to inform knew, that a relative was either dead or in a concentration camp.

Now in private she told her husband that the British immigration restrictions were "wrong and evil." "It all depends on how much you can imagine what the Jews have suffered," she said. "How much you can imagine the emotional effect of what happened in Europe."

Shaw was offended by the arrogance of the Jewish leaders and outraged when they lied by claiming they had no control over the Haganah or the terrorists. Yet he too was "beginning to have suspicions that our immigration policy was wrong."

Jacobs' confession saddened him. "Obviously I must honor your request," he said. "But I'm truly sorry, Julius. You're valuable where you are. Since you insist, I'll shift you to a less sensitive position."

The next day Jacobs was transferred to the economic section. He packed his belongings and moved from the annex behind the King David's garden into an office on the first floor of the Secretariat, directly above the Regence.

Approximately thirty other Jews worked in the Secretariat. A few were British, most were Palestinians. In the days following Black Saturday all came under intense pressure to declare their loyalties.

Victor Levi had also come to Palestine with Allenby and stayed to marry a Palestinian Jew. His position, Deputy Assistant to the Financial Secretary, was less important than Jacobs' but he too had made important contributions to the Yishuv. He was known as the unofficial representative of Tel Aviv inside the government and had fought for the loans and land that had made the city's growth possible.

Jacobs and Levi and their families were extremely close and their wives were currently visiting London together. Both had sons who had fought with the RAF and daughters whom they suspected of belonging to the Haganah.

Levi had recently told Jacobs, in jest, that the Haganah had become so militant he worried "one day my daughter will put a bomb under my chair."

The Mandate had spanned a generation. Older Jews could remember when relations between Britain and the Yishuv had been friendlier. Younger Jews knew only the White Paper and the Holocaust.

If Black Saturday was the start of a British–Jewish war, it would be, for some Jews, almost a civil war. The first battles would be fought within their own families and within themselves; between their affection for Britain and their anger at its policies; between their dislike of violence and their fear of extermination if they ruled it out.

Boris Guriel commanded the British section of Shai, the Haganah's Intelligence agency. While serving with the British Army in Crete during the war, he had written to the immigration office in Haifa begging for a visa for his mother. She lived in Latvia and he feared she would be trapped by a Nazi invasion. He reminded the immigration office that he was risking his life in His Majesty's Forces.

He received a form letter in reply. The White Paper quota for the year had been filled. No visas were being issued. Guriel memorized the letter. It was, in fact, his mother's death sentence.

Guriel himself soon fell into the hands of the Nazis. Taken prisoner during the Battle for Crete, he spent four years in a German prisoner of war camp. His fellow British prisoners showed him great kindness and no anti-Semitism. When he was released he had no doubts about the difference between the British Army and the SS.

He returned to Palestine and continued to be a moderate. He supported Weizmann. He believed the British were wrong, not evil, and opposed both terrorism *and* the White Paper.

His service in the British Army made him an effective Intelligence agent. He had learned about Agatha from a sympathetic British major the afternoon before. His warning had enabled Moshe Sneh to avoid capture.

Thirty-two thousand Palestinian Jews had fought with the British Army. For most, the return to Palestine was traumatic. They discovered that the British Army—until recently *their* army—had become the enemy of their people. Instead of receiving the hero's welcome they had expected, children had taunted and stoned them.

A former Haganah commander who had served in the British Army was advised by an officer in Cairo to change into civilian clothes "for your own safety" before boarding a train for Jerusalem. On reaching Palestine he found that "the Yishuv had undergone a severe psychological transformation. Hitler and the Holocaust had sucked the idealism out of Zionism. The altruism of the early kibbutzim, the self-sacrifice necessary to build a rural socialism, had been replaced by the morality of the Holocaust, the morality of the concentration camps—'How can we survive?'"

When they returned to Palestine most of these 32,000 former soldiers joined or rejoined the underground groups. The majority chose the Haganah; only a few enlisted in the Stern Gang or Irgun.

Avinoam, Gideon, and Chaim-Toit now met two or three times a day on street corners and in the "Tin House," a tin-roofed shanty on the outskirts of Jerusalem with six dirt-floored rooms built around a communal courtyard. The

Irgun's room contained a rough wood table, chairs and a cot. The window was small, the room perpetually dark.

They met to make final preparations, to pick a site for the Operation Chick briefing and to choose the men and women for the assault unit. They chose Ariela to nurse the wounded; Peri to drive the taxi; Gal and Abu Jilda to distribute weapons; Amnon to guard the entrance; and to set the fuses, they chose Yanai.

They also decided to make Yanai second-in-command. If Gideon were captured or killed, he would decide when to retreat and signal to the Irgun soldiers stationed outside the hotel.

Gideon knew Yanai was brave. Together they had mined sections of the Jerusalem–Tel Aviv railway. Once a British patrol surprised them and despite heavy fire, Yanai had set the fuses before taking cover.

Chaim-Toit knew he was eager. He had groomed him to take over as Chief of Operations in Jerusalem. During a tour of potential targets he kept asking: "When will we attack this building? Why not now? What are we waiting for?"

These qualities had dispelled any doubts they had about choosing a German, perhaps the only German Jew in the Irgun, for such an important assignment. But aside from the fact that Yanai was brave and had emigrated from Germany in 1935, the Irgun knew almost nothing about him.

Friends outside the Irgun suspected him of being a secret Christian convert, or perhaps part-Christian. He belonged to the Jerusalem YMCA and when he moved from Haifa to Jerusalem brought a letter of introduction from a priest to the head of Jerusalem's Scottish Church. It said he was "anxious to learn something about Christianity."

Yanai also had a secret social life. Most Irgun soldiers followed the Betar's ascetic code, sexual restraint and no drinking or gambling. They lived in near-poverty, dependent on a meager Irgun allowance and the support of their families.

Yanai lived in Rehavia, Jerusalem's wealthiest neighborhood. He played high stakes bridge and poker and attended elegant parties given by his lover, "Mrs. L." She was married to an army buddy of Yanai's, and they had met when he delivered to her a package from her husband. They soon became lovers and she loaned him money to support his expensive tastes. "You are not to think of the small loan I have given you," she wrote. "After all, it is a pleasure for me to give you these small services."

Yanai was tall, fair-haired and handsome. Many women adored him. Pasia, a girl friend of seven years, wanted to marry him. Rachel wanted him to "destroy my letters as soon as you read them."

He had three affairs while stationed with the army in Europe. His Dutch girl friend Daisy now sent weekly letters and frantic telegrams to Palestine. She pressed a daisy in each letter and begged him to return. "I cannot live without you, sweetheart of my dreams," she wrote.

He could not decide among them. He kept none of their pictures (the only picture later found in his wallet was of a dog, a long-dead childhood pet). He kept his personal life secret from friends and family. Just as he concealed Mrs. L., so too did he conceal his membership in the Irgun from his stepmother and sister and from close friends such as Palestine policeman Max Schindler.

Schindler and Yanai had met at the Safed police station in 1938. Schindler, a regular Palestine policeman, had been a lawyer and police inspector in Berlin. Yanai had joined the police as a Temporary Additional Constable (TAC) for the duration of the Arab revolt. These two German Jews who had recently emigrated to Palestine quickly formed a close friendship. Yanai's father had been murdered by the Nazis. Schindler treated Yanai like a son.

When the army posted Yanai to Europe, Schindler and his wife sent food parcels. Yanai reciprocated with books of poetry for Schindler's daughter. Throughout 1945 they exchanged long and affectionate letters.

Schindler encouraged Yanai to confide in him. "By all means continue to write such personal letters as your last one."

He worried about Yanai's future. "Did you start to make any plans for postwar times? You could of course rightly answer that there will be none, especially here. But still, if you have I would like to know about your plans."

He lectured him about the new immigrants to Palestine from eastern Europe. "Most of them are not a desirable type, they forget that we older ones [immigrants] too have rights."

He wrote: "Crime is very high. We had the murder of a jeweler on Hadar Street in his shop, and an enormous series of break-ins and thefts. All parts of the population are taking part but we can book a novelty in the shape of Polish ex-soldiers. The human material brought in by the Agency is partly very bad."

He condemned terrorism as representing "a lack of moral discipline." To his mind, it diminished Eretz Israel. "It is no consolation that the other nations are not better than we are."

It robbed Zionism of its mission. "I am very worried about the future of our country. I wonder whether our chances would not be better if we would realize the human way of the prophets. But are we entitled to fight with moral weapons? Only if we are morally justified can we dare to appeal to the justice of the best of the world?"

When the war ended Yanai trekked across Europe searching for the remnants of his family. He found a second cousin in a displaced persons camp in Czechoslovakia and gave him money and medicine. He found his sister in a Belgian camp. He could not get her a Palestine immigration certificate because the quotas were filled. He returned to Palestine in February 1946. She remained in Belgium, waiting for the precious certificate.

Back in Palestine he felt not the relief of a homecoming but restlessness. He had no purpose or avocation, only choices. Should he return to the Netherlands and marry Daisy? Emigrate to Australia or the Dutch East Indies? Line up at the

American Consulate for a visa? Become a sports instructor at a local high school? Resume his studies at Hebrew University? Settle in a kibbutz?

One girl friend urged him to join her in the Stern Gang. His best friend Finkelstein wanted him to join the Irgun. He chose the Irgun, but he had doubts. He had saved all of Max Schindler's letters.

Neither Chaim-Toit nor Gideon suspected his friendship with Schindler. So many recruits had joined the Irgun that to run extensive background checks on all was impossible. They had no way of knowing they had chosen a potential traitor, someone torn between Schindler's beliefs—the Zionism of Weizmann—and the reality represented by his family's destruction in the Holocaust: Begin's Zionism.

One week after Operation Agatha, Katy Antonius, Jerusalem's foremost Arab hostess and the widow of celebrated Arab historian George Antonius, gave one of the gayest and most enjoyable of her numerous parties. One British guest remembers it being "almost a celebration of the arrests and searches."

It was held on the kind of summer evening that persuaded Britons it was worthwhile staying in Palestine regardless of the risks. A balmy breeze had blown away the heat of the day, the stars sparkled, and the sky darkened to blue and then black.

Strings of colored lights illuminated the patio. Waiters circulated with trays of drinks and Arab *mezze*—grape leaves, olives, radishes, and houmous. Servants heaped grilled meats and salads onto plates.

Couples disappeared into the dense shrubbery of the three-tiered garden or sat on the patio's stone wall and admired the view. Mount Scopus was above them, beneath them and down a valley were the walls and lights of the Old City.

Inside, past heavy wrought-iron doors, Arabs in suits and Arabs in headdresses played chess and dominoes and chatted with Britons in dress whites. The prettiest and cleverest young Arab women in Jerusalem sat on Katy's French furniture and flirted with the British. Couples waltzed and fox-trotted across the glistening parquet floor to music from a record player. To most Britons these Arabs appeared amusing and civilized, tragic yet gay. Immensely more interesting than the tense, bourgeois Jews.

Everywhere the "Little Lawrences" of the British Army and Colonial Office pursued the elusive Grail of Arab friendship. It was never difficult to overhear anti-Semitic comments at Katy's parties and this night a British general was overheard to say, "Every bloody Jew should be taken out and hanged!"

Katy had invited two Jewish journalists to her party, Gabe Sifrony and Jon Kimche. Sifrony, everyone's contact man, listened patiently as Katy launched into one of her explanations of the links between Zionism and Soviet Communism. Sifrony knew he had been invited not to argue but to exist, to prove to the British guests that Zionism, not the Jews, was the enemy of the Arab people.

No one suspected that he sympathized with the Irgun and the Stern Gang. Adina, whom he called "that pretty, bright little Irgun girl," often came to his home with messages and news tips but out of allegiance to his dead chess partner, Abraham Stern, his greatest loyalty was to the Sternists.

Sifrony said he allied himself with the right wing because, "like everyone in the Yishuv, I was ashamed of not having done more during the war to help the European Jews. My feelings of guilt were raw, immediate, and had to be satisfied.

"I kept telling myself that I should have done something, fought somewhere, shot someone. I also blamed Britain for not allowing the Yishuv to form an army and do more to help the other Jews. After the war I decided that Stern's methods were the most certain to force Britain to leave Palestine."

Sifrony limped between groups of guests at Katy's party listening, grinning, and then moving on. When he heard talk about "Bloody Jews!" he never reacted. He was so small that many guests never noticed him.

Everyone, the army officers and policemen, White Russian refugees and socialists, archaeologists and journalists, pilgrims and fanatics, was busy discussing politics and Palestine's future. If political heat could generate light, the King David Hotel and Katy's parties would have lit up Jerusalem's skyline.

Uncertainty over Palestine's future produced this energy, as well as the shrillness and excess drinking, the wariness and distrust that characterized most Jerusalem parties in 1946.

The Jews were suspended between suffering and statehood, between extermination in Europe and their fear of extermination by the Arabs. The Arabs were suspended between their frustrated dreams of a nation and their terror of disinheritance. The British were adrift. Would they be asked to enforce a partition? Promote the bi-national state recommended by the Anglo-American Committee? Or continue to be the target for the hatred and terrorism of both parties?

During this nervous in-between time loyalties were pushed and pulled by conflicting considerations of race, religion, nationality, morality and politics. They crossed and recrossed, merged and separated and became tangled again like the colored threads in Katy's Persian carpets.

The pattern was confusing. Everyone moved in intersecting circles. Jews, Britons and Arabs worked together in the same government departments. Arabs belonged to the Jewish labor union. Jews had Arab colleagues; Arabs had Jewish friends. Most Britons sympathized with the Arabs but a few, particularly the military officers, sided with the Jews. It was often difficult to know where one's own loyalties or those of one's friends and colleagues lay.

—A British major warned the Haganah about Operation Agatha the day before it occurred. Sneh and other Haganah commanders changed hiding places and escaped capture.

—The British policeman who warned Yagour about Agatha was unknown to the settlement. The mayor believed his warning was "an act of conscience."

—Colonel Martin Charteris of Military Intelligence assisted in planning and executing Operation Agatha. Yet his wife had boarded with the Dov Josephs when she arrived in Palestine, he had a family connection with the Balfours and had been introduced to Chaim Weizmann by Balfour's niece, Baffy Dugdale.

He went to Rehovot every fortnight to lunch alone with Weizmann. "I had great affection and admiration for him and thought he was one of the greatest men I had ever met," Charteris said. When Charteris visited Weizmann a week after Black Saturday, "it was very painful because I was very fond of the old boy. I was very embarrassed. I was already having some doubts about Agatha. I was not at all sure that it was the right thing to do. I imagine that my fondness for Weizmann encouraged these doubts."

—A Jewish nurse served during the war with the British colonel who now commanded a regiment stationed near Haifa. During an afternoon tea party on Mount Carmel she hinted to him that the Stern Gang was planning a major operation in his sector. He put his troops on alert and that evening a Stern unit did attack the Haifa railway yards. The colonel's regiment threw up roadblocks, cut off their escape route, and killed eleven Sternists in an ambush.

—Many soldiers in the Irgun and Stern Gang also belonged to the Haganah and moved back and forth between these three organizations depending on political events and personal whim. All three groups also had agents planted in the other two. Amnon, one of the soldiers picked by the Irgun to attack the King David, belonged also to the Stern Gang and secretly reported to them on Irgun activities.

—The political representative of the Stern Gang was a bluff, hearty man who also was an executive of the Palestine Potash Company and extremely popular with many British officers. When he visited them in their offices in the King David he always said, "Come on now, here I am, better cover your files, don't want to let any secrets out." They laughed and were of course too embarrassed to cover their files.

—Hesse's Restaurant was a favorite with the British Army and police as well as the Jewish Agency leaders. The British felt secure there and believed it was kidnap-proof because it had only a single front door. They did not know that the Stern Gang had tapped the phone and recruited some of the employees.

—Stacey Barham, the head of the CID in Jerusalem, said, "We were always finding out that people we thought were close friends were members of these organizations. Why, the little pianist at Hesse's who played all our favorite songs, a funny little chap who smiled all the time—we later discovered he was with the Sternists. Then there was the bartender in a little pub near Zion Square. He was also a great favorite. He even lent us money. As it turned out he was also with Stern."

Jerusalem was too small to contain all these intrigues and conflicting loyalties without casualties. Under these conditions, terrorism ran the risk of becoming fratricide.

Sometimes Katy's parties were interrupted by explosions on the horizon. From the patio, guests could see flashes of fire. Afterward, those who sympathized with or belonged to the underground groups that had set the bombs crowded around the buffet, drank and traded jokes with those who, if they had not happened to be there that evening, might easily have been the victims of those distant explosions.

Katy Antonius made no secret of her loyalties. She was English and Lebanese, had grown up in Cairo and had come to Jerusalem when her husband took a position in the Mandate's education department. She was passionately pro-Arab.

She was appalled at the Anglo-Arab society she found in Jerusalem in 1925. "No one entertained or lived well. The British rarely gave parties, and when they did they served their guests on tables fashioned out of steamer trunks."

Haj Amin al-Husseini, the British-appointed "Mufti of Jerusalem" and the most powerful Arab politician in Palestine, had run out of funds before he could complete an elegant two-story house he was building on the outskirts of Jerusalem. Katy bought it, finished it, filled it with furniture from Paris and built a stone archway over the door that carried the Arabic inscription, "Enter and Be Welcome." The house became a center for Jerusalem's small but growing circle of Arab intellectuals.

At first Katy had included Jews in every party. The sudden surge of Jewish immigration after 1933 upset her but she could see some benefits. The German Jews were cultivated and educated and "they knew how to make the most delicious chocolates." After the Arab revolt she restricted her Jewish guests to journalists, British Jews working for the government, and, during the war, Egyptian Jews who, according to Katy, said, "Now we have to come to Jerusalem, to Katy's parties, in order to be gay."

The Palestinian Jews were suspicious of her parties. They imagined sinister bacchanals at which beautiful Arab women seduced British officers to the Arab cause and everyone hatched anti-Semitic plots.

If so, the seduction was so subtle that many Britons were caught unaware. According to Martin Charteris, "Katy's parties were really political salons, but not grim ones. No one pushed the Arab views on us, it was more delightful than that. Of course, there was no love lost between Katy and the Jews, but the main thing that benefited the Arab cause was that she gave good parties and attracted people to her house."

The Jews' suspicions had foundation. In 1938, her late husband, George Antonius, had written *The Arab Awakening*, a brilliant history of the rise of Arab nationalism and the first book to describe rationally and persuasively the injustice done to the Arabs by the Balfour Declaration.

Antonius wrote that the Arab claims to Palestine "rest on two distinct foundations: the natural right of a settled population, in great majority agricultural, to remain in possession of the land of its birthright; and the acquired political rights which followed from the disappearance of Turkish sovereignty and from the Arab share in its overthrow, and which Great Britain is under a contractual obligation to recognize and uphold."

His book was influential because it described in English the rage and feeling of invasion experienced by Palestinian Arabs as they watched Zionist settlers carve out of their land a land for themselves; as they watched them encircle it with watchtowers, barbed wire and sentries and train an army to defend it.

Antonius called the Zionist invasion "moral violence." The fact that it was nonviolent and accomplished through immigration and land purchases made little difference to the victims. The result was the same as if they had been dislodged by an invading army. "But the logic of facts is inexorable," he wrote. "It shows that no room can be made in Palestine for a second nation except by dislodging or exterminating the nation in possession."

For him, the terms "moderate Zionist" and "nonviolent Zionist" were self-contradictory. He saw both Weizmann and Jabotinsky as enemies of Arab nationalism. According to Antonius, fourteen months after Weizmann had persuaded Britain to issue the Balfour Declaration he had tricked King Faisal into signing an agreement expressing Arab support for Jewish settlements by "giving him [Faisal] assurances that the Zionists had no intention of working for the establishment of a Jewish government in Palestine." Weizmann later, in his opinion, showed his true colors when he stated that Palestine should become "just as Jewish as America is American and England is English."

Like most Arabs, Antonius blamed Britain for Zionism. Britain had issued the Balfour Declaration and ruled Palestine during the twenty years (1918–1938) when its Jewish population increased from eight to twenty-nine percent.

From America the Arabs had received their political heritage. American missionary teachers in Beirut during the eighteenth century had encouraged pride in written Arabic and the literature and intellectual ferment that stimulated Arab nationalism.

From France the Arab upper classes had received their cultural heritage, their tastes in food, furniture, foreign literature and architecture.

From Britain they had received military training, and the Jews. This stark fact, so inescapable to the Arabs, and particularly the Palestinian Arabs, somehow escaped the many Britons who, despite Arab neutrality or collaboration with the Axis during the war, still believed in the myth of Anglo-Arab friendship.

Although many Arabs were encouraged by Operation Agatha, few believed it signaled an important shift in British policy. One Arab newspaper charged it was a smoke screen thrown up to hide a cunning Anglo-Zionist conspiracy.

Within weeks, the paper charged, Britain would announce a solution to Palestine favorable to the Jews.

Another Arab newspaper said: "Jewish terrorism and the fight against it are a matter between the Jews and English themselves. The Arabs are interested in something else, namely, stoppage of immigration and land sales and the setting up of a national government."

The Arabs were mistaken. Jewish terrorism was about to become an Arab matter, as Katy Antonius, whose crowded engagement book contained an appointment for lunch at the Regence on Monday, July 22, would soon discover.

13

July 15—July 18

THE X Committee reversed its earlier decision and voted three to two to respect Weizmann's ultimatum and cancel the attacks on the Bat Galim arsenal, the David Brothers Building, and the King David Hotel. Levi Eshkol, who had also learned of Weizmann's feelings from Golda Meyerson, was the member who changed his mind and cast the deciding vote.

Sneh, who had cast one of two dissenting votes, resigned as Haganah commander and made preparations to leave for Paris where he hoped to persuade Ben-Gurion to overrule Weizmann. In the meantime he followed the orders of the X, up to a point.

He instructed the Palmach to cancel its attack on the Bat Galim arsenal but he did not tell Begin or the Stern leaders about Weizmann's ultimatum or the decision of the X. Instead, he informed them that their operations had to be "postponed."

His strategy was to string Begin along with a series of postponements. Once he returned from Paris with Ben-Gurion's support he planned to resume command of the Haganah and unleash Begin. The military struggle would continue, the King David would be attacked and the unity of the Joint Command preserved. He explained to his lieutenant, Israel Galili, that he feared that if Begin learned the truth "he would fall into despair and go ahead on his own, no longer under our control."

On Wednesday, July 17, Galili met with Begin and the Sternists and asked them to postpone their operations for a short but unspecified period of time.

The Sternists agreed readily. They were having difficulty coordinating their attack on the David Brothers Building with that of the Irgun on the King David. The targets were less than a quarter-mile apart. If the explosions did not occur simultaneously, one or the other of the groups would be trapped when the police cordoned off the neighborhood after the first blast.

Begin reluctantly agreed to the delay. The Joint Command had already asked him to delay Operation Chick several times during the preceding week because of problems of coordination with the Stern Gang and Palmach. "These postponements are becoming increasingly dangerous," he told Galili, "especially because so many people know about the operation." He referred to the fact that the High Commands of the Stern Gang and Haganah both knew about Chick.

Begin knew nothing of Weizmann's ultimatum or Sneh's resignation. He did not even know about the existence of the X Committee. He had no reason to suspect that this new delay was motivated by anything other than technical considerations. He instructed Paglin to prepare to attack the King David at the end of the week, on July 19.

On July 17, the same day that Galili asked Begin to delay, Weizmann departed for London to have his eye operation. He left believing that Weisgal's mission had succeeded. There would be no bloodshed while he was away.

On the morning of his departure the Agatha detainees in Athlit and Latrun went on a hunger strike. The rest of the Yishuv staged a one-day general strike in sympathy. It was a sign to Weizmann that the Yishuv was expressing its anger nonviolently.

There were other encouraging signs. The government had ended the occupation of the Agency, suspended the arms searches and begun screening and releasing the least important detainees. But the one step which might have defused the crisis, releasing the leaders, was not taken. No one in Latrun knew about Sneh's planned counterattack. "If we had known," said Dov Joseph, "and if we had been free, we would definitely have stopped it."

Unaware of Weizmann's opposition, the Irgun prepared to attack the King David on Friday, July 19. Avinoam summoned Adina five or six times a day. They walked through empty lots and on the road near her high school, mingled with shoppers in the Mahane Yehuda market, and strolled down lanes behind the Jaffa Road.

He recited the names of Irgun soldiers. She contacted some with orders to leave Jerusalem; others she instructed to move the Irgun's arms caches to hiding places outside the city.

At the same time as men and arms were traveling west toward Tel Aviv, an Irgun car and truck loaded with explosives traveled east toward Jerusalem. The car passed easily through the British checkpoints. Its driver, Eliahu Spector, slowed to make certain that the truck also passed inspection.

Spector's wartime service with the British Army had taught him that the army enforced two levels of security; one for the natives and another for Britons. He tried to place himself in the second category by dressing in English clothes and greeting the guards at every roadblock in a hearty British military accent.

The soldiers manning the roadblock on the edge of Jerusalem passed Spector but stopped the truck. Sacks of grain were heaped in its rear. A soldier poked at one with a bayonet. There was a clang of metal against metal. He lifted a sack warily. Underneath was a milk churn. The churns and feed went together, a truck belonging to a dairy farm.

The soldiers raised the barrier. The explosives had arrived in Jerusalem.

Golda Meyerson and David Horowitz had both attended the meeting in Rehovot on July 6 at which Weizmann, invoking his power as Commander in Chief, ordered that "you cease all military activities." After Weizmann's departure for London, they continued their efforts to persuade the government to release the leaders and the underground groups to follow Weizmann's orders.

Meyerson sent a message to Sneh: "Don't rock the boat while the Old Man is in London."

She also ordered her personal representative, Harry Beilin, to meet with Major Ernest Quinn, the officer in charge of Intelligence while Colonel Charteris was on leave. She instructed Beilin to reassure Quinn that the Haganah would not start a new round of hostilities. There was no reason to delay releasing the leaders or to plan further searches.

Beilin telephoned Quinn and made an appointment to come to his office in the King David at noon on Monday, July 22.

David Horowitz telephoned Roderick Musgrave, a young Colonial officer at the Secretariat, and proposed they meet that evening in his room in the Pension Rita Asher. Much to his surprise Musgrave agreed immediately. It took courage for a Briton to visit a Jewish quarter alone, and in the evening.

Horowitz had known Musgrave since 1942 when they had served together on a committee to investigate municipal wage scales in Tel Aviv. Musgrave was then an assistant district commissioner and Horowitz considered him "an intelligent and charming man who had an affable way with people and possessed a keen sense of humor."

He also knew that this "handsome young Englishman" was popular with his British colleagues as well as being sympathetic to the Yishuv. Israel Rokach, the Mayor of Tel Aviv, had told Horowitz, "Musgrave firmly believes in the establishment of a Jewish State." When the government moved Musgrave to Jerusalem, Rokach filed an official protest.

Musgrave had come to Palestine in 1936 at the age of twenty-two as an ordinary police constable. Within five years he was the youngest deputy police superintendent in the Empire. In 1942 the Colonial Office plucked him from the police force and made him an assistant district commissioner in Tel Aviv.

More than three decades later one former colleague described him as "having everything: good looks, intelligence, and he was a very debonair, charming man. Everyone loved him. He had the most uncanny ability to make close friends in all three communities, and on the first encounter."

According to another friend, "Musgrave was a Kennedy type, possessing a great charisma."

In his free time Musgrave painted and attended concerts. He loved classical music and enjoyed sitting in cafés discussing it. These were Jewish pastimes and because of them he made Jewish friendships easily.

He also appealed to the Jews because he understood their rage and hysteria. "Even when Musgrave was a policeman he was different," said one friend. "He didn't just dismiss the natives as 'beards and skirts' and turn back to his beer."

One of his closest friends was the Irgun's first Commander in Chief, Moshe Rosenberg. They met in 1938, just after Rosenberg had resigned from the Irgun "in order to devote myself to my family." Musgrave wanted Rosenberg to help identify Nazi spies within Jaffa's German Colony. Soon they were meeting weekly in a Tel Aviv café to drink vodka and exchange information.

At their first meeting Musgrave said, "Look here, Moshe, if I was a Palestinian Jew I'd be a Revisionist and I'd probably have joined the Irgun as well. Believe me, I'm not just saying this to make you like me."

Rosenberg believed him. "I knew this wasn't just bluff. He was sincere. He was truly sympathetic to us. After the *Struma* sank he told me, 'MacMichael [the High Commissioner] is a bloody dog. If I were a Jew I'd fight the British.'"

After 1939 Musgrave became one of the principal intermediaries between the Palestine Police and the Irgun. During these early war years, when the Irgun was still cooperating with Britain, he met frequently with the new Irgun commander, David Raziel.

He also kept up his friendship with Rosenberg and lobbied to have Irgun members released from detention camps. On one occasion he wrote to Rosenberg:

> I deeply appreciate your Christmas wishes and drink to your health with Vodka; wishing you all the best and hoping our association will go on being as delightful as it has been for me now for over a year.
>
> I very much regret that I shall be unable to attend the dance as there is a function at Government House. I have excellent memories of last year's dance and I am most disappointed that I cannot come this year. . . . I should have liked to get Arieh and Kurt [two Irgun members] out [of jail] in time for this occasion. Believe me, Moshe, I have tried hard and I am very sad that nothing has happened yet. Please convey my sympathy to their wives.

Even after Begin assumed command and issued his declaration of war against Britain, Musgrave kept up his sub-rosa contacts and friendships with Irgun members. When he was transferred to the Secretariat in 1945 Rosenberg said, half-joking, "Well, Roderick, now you're really in a good position to help the Jewish people."

Musgrave stared back and, suddenly serious, said, "Believe me, Moshe, I'll do my best."

Musgrave arrived at the Pension Rita Asher punctually at seven o'clock. Horowitz handed him a glass of vodka and offered him the only straight-backed chair. Horowitz sat on the edge of the bed.

Musgrave stated the official government position on Agatha and said that Jewish terrorism had become the chief obstacle to any understanding between the government and the Yishuv.

Horowitz replied by explaining why the Jewish Agency and Haganah activists had departed from the traditional policy of defense and restraint, and why he and other moderates found it difficult to condemn them wholeheartedly.

"There are moments in the history of nearly all people," he said, "when the bulwarks of law and order collapse under the grim pressure of reality and the demand for justice, when these conflict with the demands of law and order. A whole population cannot be coerced into obeying a universally detested law that all are prepared to oppose.

"Is there no validity at all in the mood of a people of whom one-third, about six million persons, were massacred? Is there any explanation of the fact that the might of an Empire, its navy, army and air force, were for years engaged in preventing the survivors of the Jewish tragedy in Europe from reaching their sole haven of refuge in Eretz Israel? And at the same time that Jewish troops fought alongside British troops against the common enemy, seven hundred Jewish refugees fleeing from the Nazi inferno were drowned in the Mediterranean because the route to that haven was blocked by the White Paper?

"Can you find in human history a more moving tragedy, or a more profound vindication for the conflict between justice and the forces of law? Is there a stronger power incapable of propelling people into acts of desperation and lunacy, into bitter reaction and revolt?"

Musgrave made no attempt to justify Agatha. Instead he said, "All right, then, but what's the outcome of all this going to be? The important thing now isn't an argument over the merits of your case. . . . What is important at this stage is to find some way out of the mess we're all in.

"I have myself submitted a memorandum to the government urging it to refrain from any further measures, and I am in favor of releasing the detainees. My opinion hasn't of course been accepted, but its time will probably come. Some sort of understanding must be found and your fanaticism and impatience aren't making the situation any easier."

For the next two hours they discussed every aspect of Anglo-Jewish relations. Musgrave warned that if the Yishuv called a general strike and used other nonviolent weapons it would worsen the situation and delay the release of the detainees. The only hope he would offer was that some of his proposals would be accepted by the government.

"My authority is limited," he said. "My position is insecure because of my views. But in the past I have been able to prevent the government from taking measures which would have further irritated our relations."

The following morning Horowitz smuggled a letter summarizing the exchange to Moshe Shertok in Latrun.

Shertok wrote back, "The talk between Abu Dan [Horowitz's code name] and Musgrave was splendid for its dynamism." He instructed Horowitz to schedule more meetings.

Horowitz was delighted. He believed Musgrave was sincere and would lobby for the release of the leaders. Perhaps these contacts at a lower level would bear fruit. He called him back and they agreed to meet on Monday, July 22, in Musgrave's office in the King David Hotel.

Chaim Weizmann.
*(Central Zionist
Archives, Jerusalem)*

Sir John Shaw *(right)* greets High Commissioner Sir Alan Cunningham upon Cunningham's arrival in Palestine. *(Imperial War Museum, London)*

Moshe Sneh.
(Haganah Archives, Tel Aviv)

Menahem Begin *(center)* with members of the Irgun. *(Jabotinsky Institute, Tel Aviv)*

Black Saturday. British soldier on guard duty during the search of Kibbutz Yagour. *(Central Zionist Archives, Jerusalem)*

Black Saturday. The Jewish Agency leaders arrested by the British at the Latrun Detention Camp. From left: David Remez, Moshe Shertok, Yitzhak Greenbaum, Bernard (Dov) Joseph, David Adiri, David Hacohen and Haim Halpern. *(Haganah Archives, Tel Aviv)*

Black Saturday. Soldiers remove boxes of documents from the Jewish Agency. *(Imperial War Museum, London)*

Left, the bar at the Regence. *(Author's collection)*,

Below, King David Hotel—rear view. At right is the YMCA tower. Julian's Way and the main door are on the other side of the building. *(Author's collection)*

Bottom, Sudanese waiters stand at attention in the main lobby of the King David. *(Author's collection)*

"I WANT TO LIVE"

The Fighting,
Hebrew Resistance Way

"I WANT TO LIVE"

The Submissive,
Jewish Agency Way

Posters showing the Irgun's contempt for the Jewish Agency. *(Jabotinsky Institute, Tel Aviv)*

Above, from left to right, Amihai Paglin *(Jabotinsky Institute, Tel Aviv);* Yitzhak Avinoam *(Author's collection);* Yael *(Author's collection);* Adina *(Author's collection)*

Fake identity card used by Gal. *(Author's collection)*

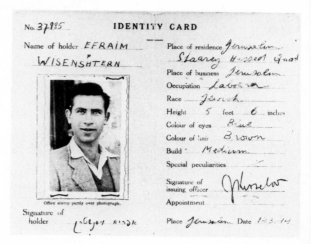

14

July 19—July 21

"**F**OOD!" JOAN GIBBS shouted to her husband after opening a huge box sent by an American school friend. "Brian, just look at all this lovely food!"

She pulled out chocolates, coffee, preserves, boxes of dried fruit, cans of cranberry sauce and more; delicacies unseen in Palestine since rationing had made oranges and olive oil the staples.

"What shall we do with it?" she asked.

"Give a party," he said. "Let's give a tremendous party and invite everyone."

"Yes, let's!"

Ever since Operation Agatha she had noticed him drinking and smoking more than usual. A party might relax him. Besides, wasn't it better to eat the food as soon as possible? Palestine made her want to do everything at once. "Do it now. Do it now," she kept thinking. "Tomorrow, who knows?"

On the evening of Saturday, July 20, Freddie Bleinkensop, William Bradley, Jerry Cornes and his wife, the Smith-Dorriens and other young Colonial officers who worked at the Secretariat gathered at the Gibbses' to devour an eclectic supper of chocolate, canned pineapple and cranberry sauce.

They sat on packing cases in the Gibbses' living room. After months of requesting a transfer, Brian Gibbs had finally been posted to Aden, a steamy port near the entrance of the Red Sea. He and his wife were prepared to leave the moment his replacement arrived.

As they ate, the Colonial officers talked, as they did on most occasions, about the "troubles." Brian Gibbs was particularly incensed at *The Guardian* and Jon Kimche for "always taking the Zionist side." He said, "Of course the Zionists *do* have a case, but it's so infuriating that simply everyone seems to be on their side. It's not fair to the Arabs."

Most of the Britons in Palestine shared Gibbs's opinion. They shopped in Arab markets, lived in Arab neighborhoods, and preferred the Arabs as social companions and as subordinates. The Jews knew it.

Most Jews dismissed their preferences as simple anti-Semitism. They were mistaken. Britain had a relatively small Jewish population. Anti-Semitism was an absentminded habit, not, as it was in Europe, a passionate belief. The preference of Britons for the Arabs and their sympathy for the Arab cause was more often a result of their experiences in Palestine.

According to Ivan Phillips, a young assistant district commissioner in Lydda, "I went to Palestine with a perfectly open mind. Of course I had known a few Jews at school and so on, but otherwise I was more or less ignorant of the problem, and I think this was more or less true of most of us."

It was also true that most Britons came to prefer the Arabs for what they considered to be political and moral reasons. Also the Arabs were more subservient than the Jews, less educated and more the typical Colonial "native."

A Palestine Police inspector in charge of training young British recruits reported that, "All our men are pro-Arab, except in areas where they can meet and go out with Jewish girls. And they will go anti-Jew when they are forbidden to marry a Jew, as they are. One must remember that we British can feel superior to the Arab but we know that the Jew is a good deal abler than we are. And the Jew doesn't often permit us to forget it."

Many of the Jews encountered by the police and Colonial officers belonged to an artistic and intellectual elite. There were world-famous musicians and physicians, skilled attorneys and celebrated university professors.

"The Jews were on the average intellectually superior to the average English official," said Sir John Shaw. "But this didn't bother me in the least because *I* didn't have any pretensions to being an intellectual.

"I remember once I went to a party at Shertok's house where five different languages were being spoken and Shertok was turning from one man to the next translating, equally at ease in all five. I envied him. I thought it was a wonderful performance. I didn't resent this sort of thing at all but quite a few of the others did.

"For example, there was always a great deal of talk about music at Jewish parties. I remember one time there was talk about some obscure Jewish composer. I said I'd never heard of him and the Jews were simply amazed.

"'Now you must have heard of him,' they all said. Of course I hadn't. Now this is just the sort of comment that antagonized a great many Englishmen. Of course it didn't bother me."

It did bother some Colonial officers. They were not Blimps posted as a punishment to an obscure African capital. They had been hand-picked to serve in the most demanding, challenging country in the Empire. Palestine was an honor, recognition that they were dedicated, intelligent and promising.

In most cases they were. Brian Gibbs had earned a triple first, the highest graduating honor, from Cambridge. George Farley had been an outstanding scholar at Trinity College, Dublin, and one of the youngest men to be appointed to the Colonial Office. Jerry Cornes had won a silver medal in the 1500 meter race at the 1932 Olympics in Los Angeles. Peter Smith-Dorrien came from a distinguished military family. During the war he had become the army's youngest brigadier.

Like most Britons in Palestine, they were more comfortable with the Arabs, who generally behaved with the kind of good manners the British expected. The Jews, on the other hand, were abrasive and rude; they made no attempt to disguise their hatred of British policy. One British police inspector said he preferred the Arabs because, "An Arab pots you in the leg at night, you go around and investigate, and he gives you a cup of coffee."

Ivan Phillips gave similar reasons. "The Arabs were for the most part great hosts . . . this arose naturally from the Muslim tradition of hospitality. On the Arab side one met great courtesy—one would drink cup after cup of sweet coffee. On the Jewish side, on the other hand, and I am thinking particularly of the eastern Jews, there was nothing like that; in fact they could be most rude— quite extraordinarily rude sometimes—for no apparent reason. . . . I think they thought of us really in terms of Russian or Polish officials."

Leah Ben-Dor, a reporter for the *Palestine Post*, witnessed countless meetings and conversations between Britons and Jews. She believed that "most Jews made the mistake of thinking that because British policy was hostile, all the individual Britons in Palestine were hostile to them. They didn't understand that these were just employees, bureaucrats who wanted to be successful, not people sent from England to destroy the Yishuv. This was a big mistake. They just wrote off all the British as anti-Semites, treated them with incredible rudeness and naturally alienated them."

Some Britons became so tired of hearing endless litanies of Jewish sufferings—Britain too had suffered in the war—that they came to view even the Holocaust as, in the words of one, "a tiresome political argument for the Jews to beat us over the head with."

Shaw thought "the news of the Holocaust turned the Jews into emotional wrecks. There hardly seemed to be a Jew in Palestine who didn't have a relative who'd perished in one of Hitler's gas chambers. Of course they reminded us of it at every opportunity . . . every time I toured a Jewish village someone would say something like, 'Come and see my chicken coop and by the way my brother died at Belsen.'

"Later I often thought how I would have felt if the Germans had invaded England and done this to my countrymen while I'd been in Cyprus. Of course I would have talked about it all the time. However, at the time, I didn't have the time to reflect too much on this. I was simply too busy."

Separated by so many social, emotional and political barriers, Britons and Jews in Palestine remained mysteries to one another.

The British Colonial officers worked together at the Secretariat and relaxed together at the Jerusalem Sports Club and at parties in one another's homes. They were encouraged to keep to themselves. One Colonial Office directive advised them "not to attend too many functions on one side or the other for fear of showing favoritism."

Most of the guests at the Gibbses' party would have been happy never to attend another function in Palestine. They envied Joan and Brian Gibbs their packing boxes and their transfer to Aden. They too wanted to leave.

They were professional administrators trapped in a country in which they could not make an administrative decision without being vilified. Every time they promoted a Jew or Arab, opened a bridge or installed a new water pump, someone protested. They could not do justice to the Arabs without doing an injustice to the Jews, and vice versa. Each held them responsible for the other's success, the other's nationalism, the other's terrorism.

The situation was so frustrating that one assistant secretary declared, "Sometimes I don't know who I hate more, the Jews or the Arabs. I think I despise them all, equally."

Arabs and Jews both accused the Colonial officers of promoting Jewish and Arab revolts in order to further a secret British plan for Palestine. Begin called it the "British Master Plan" for taking control of Palestine for all time and believed it was "clear and consistent, both in purpose and content."

If Britain did have a "clear and consistent" policy it was a secret to those who administered it. Sir John Shaw complained that "there seems to be no policy for Palestine's future, nothing to work toward or believe in." Two years earlier he had become so exasperated that he and his wife sold their china and furniture and returned to London without warning. It took months for the Colonial Office to coax them into returning.

Since the end of the war the British government had repeatedly postponed any decision on Palestine's future. Conferences were called and committees formed but nothing happened. The government was deliberately stalling, hoping for a miraculous solution that would satisfy the United States, the Palestinian Arabs and Jews, and at the same time preserve British economic and strategic interests in the Middle East.

In the meantime, the Colonial officers in Palestine enforced a status quo that satisfied no one and enraged everyone. One Colonial officer compared their situation to that of a rear guard protecting a retreating army. "Like a rear guard we were fighting for time, trying to delay the inevitable; and also like a rear guard we were expected to suffer heavy casualties."

Many Colonial officers, and particularly their wives, wanted to leave Palestine before they became casualties. When they first arrived Bernard Bourdillon and his wife Joy had preferred Palestine to their previous post in Nigeria. The climate was better, their daughter healthier and they could live an almost European life. Three years later they were desperate to leave.

Repelled by the hatred between Jew and Arab, Bourdillon requested a transfer back to Nigeria and wrote friends there: "I am looking forward to returning to a country where people don't spend all their time and energies hating one another."

The violence terrified his wife. Whenever she heard an explosion she rushed to the telephone and called the Secretariat. She worried when her husband returned home late from a meeting, when she overheard Geoffrey Morton, the police officer who had killed Abraham Stern, offer to drive him to work ("The last thing anyone wanted to do was drive anywhere with Geoffrey Morton") and when, during a dinner party at the Regence, someone said, in jest and to much laughter, "Well, if anyone wanted to blow up the Secretariat, this is how they'd do it—mine the Regence!"

George Farley's wife, Doreen, had come to Palestine during the Arab revolt. On their wedding night loud explosions rocked their house. Doreen felt her husband's body stiffen. Thinking the bombs signaled the start of another Arab riot he jumped out of bed, dressed and left for the office. Minutes later he returned. Someone had set off large fireworks under their window in celebration of a Moslem holiday. Since then she "had died a thousand deaths any time there was an explosion or any time he was a minute late."

Finally the nightmare was going to end. During a visit to London in May, George Farley had accepted the offer of a position in the Home Office. Knowing how thrilled she would be, he cabled her immediately: "I wish I could see your face when you learn this. . . ."

"It's almost too good to be true," she shouted to her mother when the cable arrived. Her sons would grow up in England and she and her husband would survive.

On July 19 Weizmann looked in on the Zionist office in London. According to Baffy Dugdale, Lord Balfour's niece, who was in the office at the time, "[Weizmann] thinks only his presence has so far restrained 'rivers of blood,' for the Army were longing for an excuse to wipe out the Yishuv, and on the Yishuv's side the hatred and anger against Britain will never be wiped out except by partition and a Jewish State."

Two days later Weizmann elaborated on these thoughts in a letter to Palestine's chief rabbi. He wrote:

But I am afraid that since the events of Saturday, June 29th, the situation has changed fundamentally. Something has definitely snapped in the relationship between Jews and British in Palestine, and I, as a firm believer in, and champion of, that relationship, am forced to realize that what has been destroyed is so deep, so vital, and of such moral significance, that it cannot be restored by projects, resolutions, and kind words.

Cunningham had arrived in London the day before to report on Operation Agatha and discuss long-term policy with a delegation of American diplomats. The notes he wrote in preparation for a meeting with the Colonial Secretary show that he had drawn all the wrong conclusions. Under the heading FUTURE he wrote a single word, "Weizmann." Under the word RESULT (of Agatha) he had written, "Jews: Strengthened hands of moderates—Sneh puzzled—50% realise futility of violence."

"In a couple of hours we will attack the King David Hotel." It was Friday afternoon, July 19, and Gal was speaking to Zvi Barzel and three other Irgun soldiers in the basement of a building in Jerusalem's Bukharian Quarter. These four were being briefed first because the plan called for them to arrive first at the hotel. The others would assemble later.

Gal was a "quartermaster." Besides conducting this briefing he would distribute and collect weapons.

"We are dividing you into two teams," he said. "One team will stand north of the hotel, the other south. One man in each team will be armed with grenades and pistols, the other will carry matches for lighting the fuses. Gideon will give you the signal."

Gal was disappointed not to be in the assault unit. He was three years older than Gideon but had joined the Irgun three years later and commanded fewer operations.

Eighteen months before, he had been an automobile mechanic. After his sister Yael admitted her Irgun membership, he had resigned from the Haganah and moved back to Jerusalem to join as well.

The Haganah demanded nothing, only that he belong. The Irgun, however, was a way of life. But he was up to its demands. Garages were closing because of rationing and the Irgun needed his skills. There was only one drawback: Leah, his sixteen-year-old girl friend, lived and attended school in Petach Tikva. He missed her desperately.

They corresponded through a Jerusalem post office box. On the back of each letter she printed, as instructed, "for Sarah." He had been forbidden to explain his sudden move and this mysterious address.

She begged for a picture. He said that a friend had destroyed his pictures "by mistake." In truth, an Irgun comrade, worried that he would break down and send one, had ripped them up on purpose.

Instead of pictures Gal sent poems:

> I wish you were here beside me
> So I could stroke your hair
> And look into your eyes,
> So I could see love.

He hinted at what he was forbidden to say, that he fought in the underground and risked his life:

> In the street people are happy;
> In her home they are sad.
> The night is moonless
> The shades are drawn
> Her window is black.
> Her boyfriend is gone
> And will never come back.
> Now in the street the Jews are sad
> And heroes hang from every lamppost.

He told her he loved her:

> I love you, my sweet child.
> The light in your eyes
> Your neck like a swan's.
> I love you.

He told her he loved his struggle:

> I come to you with a poem
> Because we parted with a poem.
> Soon I will return to where we parted
> Soon I won't have to live in a basement
> Soon I won't have to live in poverty.
> Like a hero my heart is happy,
> My will to conquer is strong.
> For me, the streets of Jerusalem are too narrow.

He told her he loved her and his struggle:

> I kiss you both,
> You and my pistol.

"As soon as the operation is over," Gal told his soldiers, "take Arab buses to Jaffa and reassemble in the Tel Aviv field we use for target practice. Anyone who can't escape from Jerusalem should hide in the insane asylum in Givat Shaul."

Before he could finish, a messenger arrived with a letter. He read it and then told the four soldiers, "The operation is postponed. You can go home but don't tell anyone about this meeting. You'll be contacted again."

A few hours earlier Begin had received a note from Moshe Sneh which said:

19 July 1946   11:30
Shalom!
My friends have told me about the recent talk [the talk between Galili and Begin on July 17 at which Galili asked Begin to delay Operation Chick]. If you still have respect for my personal appeal, I ask you earnestly to delay the operation which is on the agenda a few more days. . . .

This was the second request for a delay Begin had received from Sneh in three days. He decided it would be the last one he would honor. He interpreted "a few more days" to mean three and informed Sneh he would reschedule Operation Chick for Monday, July 22.

Sneh replied with a message asking Begin to postpone the operation beyond the twenty-second. He wrote:

20 July 1946   9:30
Shalom!
. . . We are told that on the coming Thursday, July 25, the coming policy of non-cooperation will be announced [by the Jewish Agency]. This is another reason why no operations should be carried out before then.

Sneh became nervous when Begin failed to respond to this message. Early on the morning of July 22, while he waited in Haifa to be smuggled aboard the ship that would take him to France, he sent Begin a third and final note:

22 July 1946
Shalom!
You should hold on for the time being the Jerusalem operation.

PART THREE

July 22, 1946

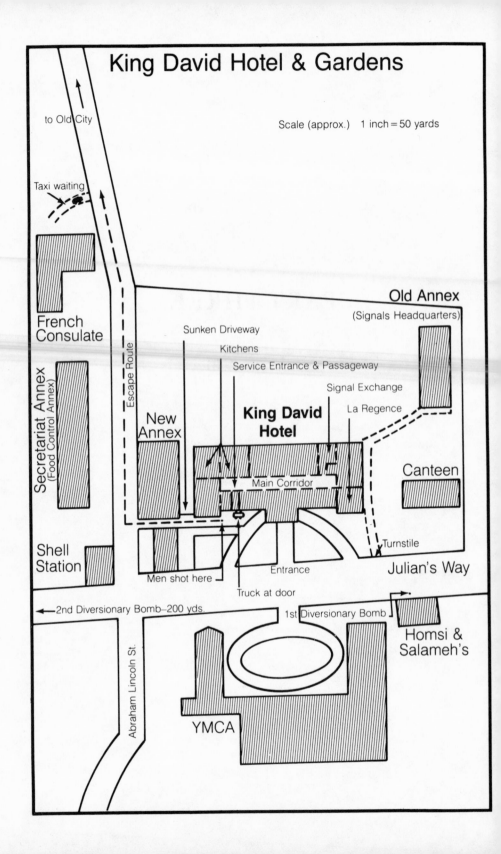

15

July 22, 1946

7:45 A.M.

J OAN GIBBS closed her front door and listened. The sound of her husband's
retreating footsteps echoed down the corridor. As he descended a flight of
steps, it became fainter. He walked outside and the sound disappeared. He was
gone.

Every morning at 7:45 she listened to him leave. Every afternoon at 2:00 she
prepared their lunch, watched the clock, and waited to hear the familiar click-
clacking of his heels against the landlord's new tiles. Every morning and every
afternoon she had the same thought: "One day I won't hear that sound."

She prepared for that day. When she was stranded in India during the war she
had saved his letters in a special file. She was afraid that, except through these
letters, her newborn son would never know his father. When she returned to
Palestine she kept the file and added to it. She still feared her children would
need his letters.

She tried to banish these premonitions, but they surfaced whenever she read
the *Palestine Post* or talked with the wives of the other young British Colonial
officers. "Someday, the day I don't hear his footsteps, someone will have to
come here and tell me he's been killed," she thought. "Will it be this woman?
Or her husband? The police? I wonder who it'll be?"

She was not, by nature, morbid. Her friends considered her a jolly woman
and she admitted to "being fond of food, drink and the general business of
living." Her fears did not drive her to tears; she accepted them as part of

Palestine. They had begun eight years ago, when she married Brian Gibbs.

They had met on a liner bound for England. She was returning from two years with her parents in India, he from three years in Palestine as a Colonial officer. After their engagement he went back to Palestine. It was 1937, the Arab revolt was at its peak and he was an assistant district commissioner in an Arab district.

When he came to England in January for their wedding she was appalled at his condition. He cringed when champagne corks popped. He jumped when a waiter dropped an ice bucket. For an instant he thought terrorists had infiltrated his wedding party.

They returned to Palestine together. The night they arrived in Haifa, her first night in the country, Arab terrorists blew up a police station next to their hotel. The following morning Gibbs was sent to Safed to replace a recently assassinated district officer. Arab terrorists immediately placed him on their "blacklist" of Britons condemned to death.

He had to witness the hangings of condemned terrorists and the dynamiting of villages that had harbored them. Martial law made the punishments mandatory and he was forbidden to grant clemency. The brutality revolted him. He had not, he told his wife, "joined the Colonial Service to be a policeman or a judge."

He had joined, after studying anthropology and geography at Cambridge, hoping to be made an administrator in an African colony. Instead, he supervised hangings in Palestine.

The Second World War brought a respite from terrorism. During the war he filed frequent reports about the theft of arms and ammunition from arsenals in his district. The thefts convinced him a Jewish revolt was imminent. "I've gone through this once with the Arabs," he told his wife. "I'm not going through it again with the Jews. I'm not going to die for a Jewish National Home if I can help it."

In 1946 he was transferred from Hebron, now a "safe" Arab city, to the Secretariat in Jerusalem. Soon afterward he and his wife began discussing strategies for surviving their second terrorist war. The government issued guns to the assistant secretaries but he refused to carry one. "If they want to kill me, they'll shoot first. Anyway, if I carry a pistol I'll probably just shoot myself by mistake," he said.

The police advised Britons to vary their route to work. Gibbs thought this a stupid precaution. He lived less than half a mile from the King David; there *was* only one route between his home and office. "I can walk there six different ways but if they want to kill me, they will."

His wife believed he was most in danger when he walked to and from work. He had assured her the Secretariat was safe. "Blowing up police stations is fair game but I'm safe in the K-D. Too many Jews work there."

She agreed. After the Holocaust it seemed inconceivable that Jews would risk killing one another.

In the spring of 1946 he told her, "We're trapped here and it won't get any better. I want out." He was thirty-four and had spent twelve years, his entire Colonial Office career and a third of his life, in Palestine. He applied for posts anywhere else in the Empire. A few weeks later, London agreed to the Aden transfer.

Immediately he and his wife packed their belongings and shipped their furniture. They hoped to leave any day, as soon as his replacement arrived from Britain. In the meantime, she didn't mind living out of suitcases and stumbling over packing cases. Soon they would escape; her husband would live.

A maze of walls surrounded her; thick walls without ceilings or doors; white walls that reflected the sun, shot up into the clear Jerusalem sky and disappeared in a haze of heat; walls that suddenly swayed, crumbled and collapsed with a roar.

For the fourth straight night the same nightmare haunted Pauline Mantoura. Over breakfast she described it to her husband and son. It disturbed them because they thought her dreams prophetic. This was her first recurring dream.

Atallah Mantoura, an Arab Christian, took every threat, even one in a dream, seriously. He was the government's second-ranking Arab civil servant and a British citizen. Some Arab nationalists considered him twice a traitor. Twice in the last ten years they had tried to kill him.

Mantoura blamed Britain. He understood why some Arabs considered him a collaborator. He himself had belonged to an earlier generation of Palestinian nationalists.

During the First World War he had worked for British Military Intelligence. Afterward, like most Arabs, he believed that in spite of the Balfour Declaration, Britain would honor its promises and create an independent Arab state in Palestine. He joined the government to prepare himself for a position in this state.

Fifteen years later he was bitter and disillusioned. Iraq and Transjordan were on the way to independence but Palestine, whose Arab population was more skilled and educated, was still ruled as a British colony. Meanwhile the Jewish population had grown from 65,000 in 1918 to 400,000 by the end of 1936.

Since he was in daily contact with the Jews who worked in the government, he understood better than most Arabs their dedication to Palestine and determination to rule it. By 1935, frustrated by British vacillation and Arab impotence, he had concluded that his people would never govern Palestine.

This conviction determined the rest of his life. In 1936 Britain awarded him a CBE (Commander of the British Empire) and offered him a citizenship in recognition for his long and faithful service to the Mandate. He accepted. If he was right and the Arabs had no future in Palestine, his own family would always have a country.

His decision angered and puzzled those who knew him. "You blame Britain for 'selling Palestine to the Jews,'" his son Jack said, "and yet you work for the British government and have even become British. Why?"

"One day you'll be happy I did," was his father's only answer.

One Arab neighbor, Doctor Canaan, had many Jewish friends and hoped for a compromise. Mantoura disagreed. "Whatever you or I do won't make the slightest difference. There is no hope for Arabs in Palestine. Look out for your family."

Mantoura's wife overheard him. "If you're so pessimistic," she said, "why don't you sell your properties and we'll leave?" (She was half Italian and half Austrian.)

"I refuse to sell my heritage," he replied. Instead, he gave it away. Neighbors, colleagues, street vendors, relatives, and relatives of relatives called frequently at the Mantoura house. They described misfortunes and asked for "favors"—loans which he knew they could not repay. He never refused. Some came every month, some every week. His father, a prominent judge in Jaffa, had left him a sizable estate but by 1946, except for two small parcels of land in Jerusalem, he had given it away.

He kept his philanthropy a secret from his wife and sons and borrowed so they could live in a style commensurate with his position. By the summer of 1946 he was deeply in debt.

Arab terrorists still plotted to murder him. The year before, a terrorist had poked a rifle through his open bedroom window. His wife saw the man's reflection in a mirror and screamed. He grabbed a rifle and the assassin fled. After that incident, he covered his windows with metal shutters and his front door with an iron gate. At 7:00 every evening he closed the shutters and locked the gate.

The family ate breakfast in their darkened kitchen as they discussed Pauline Mantoura's nightmare. The shutters muffled the sounds of morning traffic and allowed only slivers of light to slip between the metal slats. No one could explain the dream. The walls of their house were of dark stone, not white.

At 7:50 Mantoura pressed a buzzer. The front door snapped open. Two blue uniformed Palestine policemen stood in the street beside the family's ancient Dodge. Until the last attempt to kill him he had walked to work. Now British policemen drove him to his office in the King David Hotel. Jewish or Arab policemen could not be trusted.

Before leaving he turned in the doorway and faced his wife for his morning inspection. She centered his bifocals, rearranged the handkerchief in his breast pocket, brushed lint from the lapels of his brown suit—it pleased him that

Englishmen often asked for the name of his tailor—and handed him a cane and a brown hat to match his shoes. This morning he wore his favorite shoes—brown wing tips with thick rubber soles.

As he walked to the car she traced a cross in the air and mouthed a silent prayer.

16

July 22, 1946
10:30–11 A.M.

B EGIN DECIDED not to postpone the King David operation. The bombs had been in Jerusalem for three days; they might be discovered. Soldiers in the Irgun, LEHI and Haganah knew the target. One of them might reveal it.

The last-minute note from the Haganah—"You should hold on for the time being the Jerusalem operation"—was too vague. It offered no explanation, no final date. The Joint Command had authorized Operation Chick and this authorization, as far as he knew, had never been withdrawn.

Gal and Abu Jilda carried eleven pistols, five machine guns, thirty grenades, a box of sandwiches and a crate of soda pop into the Beit Aharon classroom. Immediately afterward they would station themselves near the hotel and collect the precious weapons. As a joke, Abu Jilda had named himself after a famous Arab terrorist who, during the Arab revolt, bragged of being able to kill three Jews with the same bullet. In 1939, the real Abu Jilda murdered a young Englishman, Michael Clarke, as he rode his motor bike between Rehovot and Tel Aviv. Clarke was a school friend of Chaim Weizmann's son Michael, and was in Palestine visiting the Weizmanns.

The soldiers ate the sandwiches, drank the pop, and got dressed. Gideon climbed into baggy white trousers, wrapped a red cummerbund around his waist, slipped into a short red jacket and vest and centered a fez on his head. Only his height and skin betrayed him. The waiters at the King David were slightly taller and darker.

One boy put on the blue overalls worn by most Jerusalem truck drivers and deliverymen. The others became Arabs in long blue cloaks and white and red checkered headdresses. They pointed at one another, laughing at the clothes, joking in Arabic and performing pirouettes.

They played games. One man pulled a headdress over his face and challenged the others to guess his identity. Soon everyone was gliding around the room, pretending to bargain and tugging on one another's robes.

Ariela the nurse told Amnon, "If there were Arabs as attractive as you, I'd marry one."

Amnon worried. Did he really look like an Arab? Arabs walked with a distinctive step, the gestures they made with their hands could not be copied. He'd be discovered and the operation would be ruined.

The other soldiers were also apprehensive. They knew that during the last six months operations less hazardous than this one, against targets less carefully guarded, had resulted in serious casualties. David Sternglass had died while attacking an army arsenal in Tel Aviv; another soldier had been killed during the raid on the Qastina airfield; two more had died and thirty-one were captured during the April 2 attacks on the railways. The heroic Dov Gruner had been wounded and captured and two other soldiers killed during the assault on the Ramat Gan police station. Joseph Shimson and Michael Ashbel had been captured while attacking the army post at Sarafand. Colonel Michael Fell, the hated British military judge, had sentenced them and Dov Gruner to be hanged.

All of these operations had achieved their objectives but, since there were only a hundred Irgun soldiers qualified for the assault units, the victories had come at great cost. Yet none of these targets had been as heavily guarded and fortified as the King David. Attacking the Ramat Gan police station had posed the same degree of difficulty as assassinating a Nazi general. To the soldiers gathered at Beit Aharon, attacking the King David seemed the equivalent of attempting to kill Hitler.

The boy wearing blue overalls groaned and clutched his stomach. "My stomach is turning over," he said. "Cramps . . . so bad I can't drive."

Avinoam and Chaim-Toit had the same thought—"He's so scared he's become sick."

Gal volunteered to take his place. Avinoam had no choice but to waive the rule prohibiting quartermasters from joining assault units. No one else was left, the other Irgun soldiers in Jerusalem having already been evacuated. Gal was elated. He helped the driver undress and then put on his overalls.

A few minutes later, Abu Jilda volunteered to replace a soldier who had been too nervous to report to Beit Aharon. Gideon agreed and put him in command of the "porters."

Yanai was also nervous, but for another reason: he had decided to defect to the British and betray the operation. His letters, which were later seized by

Irgun agents, support the conclusion that he was motivated primarily by moral and political considerations. Certainly his close friendship with Max Schindler, his friend on the Palestine Police Force, and Schindler's abhorrence of terrorism were crucial influences.

Earlier that morning, when Avinoam had collected him from his house in Rehavia, he had attempted unsuccessfully to use the excuse of calling an imaginary girl friend in order to get to a telephone and alert Schindler. Now he tried the same ploy again.

He took Paglin into a corner of the schoolroom, out of earshot of Avinoam, and begged for permission to call his "girl friend."

"It's almost eleven o'clock," he said. "She's waiting for me. Let me go and telephone her at the café."

Paglin refused. "No. No one can leave after they know the target."

Yanai persisted but Paglin was adamant, and worried. First the driver and now Yanai were afraid. If the soldiers remained in the small schoolroom much longer there might be others. He blamed the delays. He had scheduled the attack for 11 A.M. Three minutes later the LEHI, who had also ignored Sneh's request for a postponement, was supposed to mine the David Brothers Building.

Throughout the morning messengers had shuttled between Beit Aharon and the LEHI briefing room. the LEHI commanders still feared that if the Irgun failed, the British would cordon the entire neighborhood and catch their soldiers outside the David Brothers Building.

They wanted to begin the two operations simultaneously. Paglin refused.

They wanted to delay a few hours more. Paglin refused again. They'd delayed too long. Finally the LEHI announced they were canceling their operation. Paglin decided to attack the King David as soon as Spector delivered the explosives. But where was Spector? Already he was more than an hour late.

For the last hour a formation of Argylls had paraded back and forth along David Yellin Street. Eliahu Spector, who had stopped Isaac Sandler's taxi two blocks away from Beit Aharon, could not decide if the soldiers were practicing, being disciplined, or waiting to arrest him and seize the explosives. A few yards behind Spector, two Irgun soldiers sat in the cabin of a wood-paneled pickup truck which they had hijacked early that morning.

A few minutes before eleven the troops marched away. Spector parked in front of Beit Aharon, went inside and began explaining the explosives and their special fuses. As he talked he noticed that Yanai was pale and dripping with perspiration. Clearly he was not paying attention to this important briefing. Yanai was the explosives expert, the second-in-command. How could he set the fuses if he didn't listen?

"Yanai!" Spector shouted. "What's the matter with you? Why aren't you listening?"

Yanai apologized. Afterward he told Paglin, "I was distracted because I suddenly realized I left letters mentioning the Irgun sitting on my desk. The police are watching me and I'm afraid they'll search my room after the operation. Let me go home and hide them."

Paglin was relieved. This explained Yanai's nervousness. "I'll arrange to have someone take them away," he said. "Give me your keys."

Yanai had failed again. Now his only hope was to alert the British or stop the operation while he was in the hotel, and before he was forced to activate the tamper-proof fuses.

General Sir Evelyn ("Bubbles") Barker, the General Officer Commanding (GOC) all British troops in Palestine, laughed and looked at his wristwatch. "Well, we'd better be quick," he said. "I understand we're due to be blown up this morning."

Colonel Andrew Campbell felt a nerve twinge. He and Barker sat at a long table in the third-floor briefing room at the north end of the King David. "Morning prayers," the daily briefing for staff officers, has just ended. Campbell had stayed behind to discuss the approaching trial of some Stern Gang members caught broadcasting from an illegal transmitter.

"Don't worry, Andrew," Barker said. "We've got a few hours of peace." He laughed again.

"What do you mean?"

"We've been tipped off."

"How serious is it?"

"Oh Christ, don't worry, we've had these warnings so many times before."

Campbell did worry. He was responsible for organizing the military courts and prosecuting terrorists. He knew more about the Irgun and the Stern Gang than anyone in the army. He had seen the hatred in the eyes of the captured terrorists, a hatred so intense that it almost stirred the air in the courtroom. He prosecuted them, he tried to send them to the gallows, but he respected their determination. It was this determination that made them so dangerous.

Barker's tip did not surprise him. The previous week he had told his friend Hugh Niven, "It's not going to be long before they tackle the K-D. We're wide open."

Obviously Barker did not agree. Campbell, like most officers, admired Barker. He was a brave, forthright, professional soldier who had commanded a division and then a corps from Normandy to Germany with great distinction. By temperament and training he was ideally suited to lead men into battle in a conventional war, but not to fight an undeclared war against Jewish terrorists.

In 1945 General Barker's corps liberated the German concentration camp at Belsen. He said: "I visited it two days after it was liberated. It was so awful that it made very little impression on me. I made a quick inspection tour; I didn't linger. I'm not the kind of chap on whom things make a terrific impact. When you've seen two world wars it's hard to shock you. It didn't in the least make me more sympathetic to the Palestinian Jews."

When he was sent to Palestine in May 1946, Barker was annoyed that the Jews were so ungrateful for what the British Army had done for them. "They didn't realize that it was thanks to us that they hadn't been occupied by the Germans during the war and were now going to get a country at all."

Barker liked Palestine: "It was a lovely country, entirely ruined by its inhabitants. I shot ducks and played polo. I enjoyed life there."

He preferred the Arabs: "I always had a sneaking affection for the Arabs because it was their country, whether you liked it or not. Why should they be pushed out by the Jews because [the Jews] had such an unfortunate time during the war . . . from my point of view the Arabs were just nicer characters than the Jews."

Campbell worried that Barker "hadn't grasped the significance of modern terrorism and didn't understand how to handle it." The attitude of most other officers in HQ reminded Campbell of that of a boys' school sixth form— everything was "great sport." "It never occurred to them that they could be killed. They thought that you shot, fished, womanized, boozed and enjoyed yourself. Life was a joke. This attitude had served them well in the war."

Fighting an undeclared terrorist war was another matter. They assumed they were safe in the K-D because of the barbed wire, the frequent security checks, the armored cars and foot soldiers patroling Julian's Way, and because so many Jews visited and worked there.

They were not. During the last two years Campbell had seen the terrorists foil every British security measure.

The army and Palestine Police had surrounded army camps and government buildings with double and triple coils of barbed wire and erected barricades on the roads leading to them.

The terrorists, however, ignored the barricades and avoided costly frontal attacks. They entered buildings in disguise and by guile. The barbed wire isolated their targets and made it easier for them to attack without risking injury to the civilian population. "Congratulations!" Teddy Kollek once said to a Palestine Police inspector. "You have finally succeeded in rounding yourselves up."

The army and police printed special passes that allowed the holders to enter certain buildings and sectors of Jerusalem and to travel on specific roads at specific times. They changed the colors and emblems on the cards often and only issued them to civilians after a thorough investigation.

Terrorists had no trouble stealing or counterfeiting the passes. They always flashed impeccable credentials and guards arrested and alienated only the innocent, those who left their identity cards at home or forgot to renew them.

Every night the army blocked the roads leading to Jerusalem and only allowed holders of special curfew passes to enter or leave the city. They removed the roadblocks at seven the following morning.

The Irgun soldiers driving Isaac Sandler's taxi arrived in Jerusalem at 7:15 A.M.

The government issued fifty paragraphs of Defense Security Regulations that put the entire country under virtual martial law. The regulations suspended habeas corpus and permitted any military commander to destroy homes or entire neighborhoods from which an illegal firearm had been discharged. One article made it a crime punishable by death or life imprisonment to belong to an outlawed organization. Another prescribed life imprisonment for owning an illegal gun. This law, if enforced, could have meant the jailing of ⌐lmost the entire male Arab and Jewish populations of Palestine.

None of the laws were fully enforced. No democracy could execute scores of Jews a year after the Holocaust.

To protect its headquarters in the King David, the army installed an iron gate on the stairs between the civilian bedrooms on the second floor and the army offices on the third and fourth. Anyone entering had to present a pass or identity card to soldiers sitting at a table behind the gate. Visitors were announced by telephone, their hosts came to the door, vouched for their identity and escorted them to their offices.

However, no one was searched and the guards just glanced at the identity cards of soldiers in uniform. Only civilians were scrutinized. This was the sole army checkpoint. Anyone could walk into the hotel, drink at its bars, eat at its restaurants or register for a room without being questioned.

The government appeared to have the manpower to fight terrorism. There were 5,800 British policemen and 80,000 soldiers to police the 136,000 Jewish males between the ages of sixteen and forty-nine. A quarter of the soldiers belonged to the famed 6th Airborne Division, veterans of Arnheim and the Rhine crossing.

But the army's morale was low. Most saw Palestine as the last, unforeseen and unnecessary act of the World War Two nightmare. Many had been on troopships heading for the Pacific war when America dropped its atomic bombs on Japan. They had rejoiced and assumed they would be demobilized. Instead, they were sent to Palestine. According to one officer, "The men felt cheated. Palestine was one last tiresome bit they had not really signed on for."

The soldiers were imprisoned in rows upon rows of canvas tents or ramshackle wood huts on hot, dusty plains surrounded by barbed wire and searchlights. Much of the time they were forbidden to patronize Jewish shops, cinemas and restaurants and were ordered to carry loaded rifles and walk in pairs when visiting civilian areas.

They suffered terrible boredom. They stood guard all night at curfew posts and then returned to sweltering camps during the day. Twelve hours later they stood guard again or walked foot patrols or manned roadblocks. Sports were their only release. Everyone drank.

In Jerusalem the officers drank at the Officers Club in Goldschmidt House, at Hesse's Restaurant, at the lobby bar of the King David, at a special "canteen" on the fourth floor, and at home.

To relieve the boredom, Andrew Campbell and the officers with whom he shared a Jerusalem house kept two dogs, boxers named Punch and Judy (over time, Punch's name was lengthened to "Punch You Bugger"). They also took turns firing a shotgun at an old baby carriage. Whoever moved it farthest along the road with a single blast was declared the winner.

In the summer of 1946 many British soldiers in Palestine were as desperate and hysterical as the Jews. They had survived the European war and been reprieved from the Asian one but instead of reentering civilian life they rotted in primitive army camps in Palestine. The suicide rate was high.

Andrew Campbell thought the graffiti on a wall near his house expressed the dilemma perfectly. A Jew had scrawled TOMMY GO HOME in large letters.

Underneath was a soldier's reply, I WISH I FUCKING WELL COULD.

17

11–11:55 A.M.

A T 11 A.M. Paglin began dispatching his soldiers from Beit Aharon at predetermined intervals. The first to go were Nissim, Amatzia and the Arab porters, then Amnon and Peri, then Abu Jilda and his five porters and last of all the largest group, Gideon's assault unit.

Nissim pushed a wooden wheelbarrow carrying four milk churns through the gate at Beit Aharon and into David Yellin Street. He wore baggy white trousers, a loose-fitting smock shirt and headdress—the traditional uniform of an Arab porter.

Amatzia followed a few paces behind. He wore khaki shorts and an open-necked white shirt. Together the two men were a common Jerusalem scene—a shopper returning from market and a porter carrying or pushing his purchases.

Two minutes after leaving the school, they joined the stream of other shoppers and pushcarts, automobiles, donkeys and horse carts that choked the sidewalks and pavements of the Jaffa Road.

They passed Sudanese peanut vendors squatting next to piles of nuts and sweets, news vendors arranging and rearranging racks of Yiddish magazines and newspapers and Jews sitting at the Café Europa's zinc-topped tables. In the windows, refrigerated cases protected trays of Sacher torte from the hot desert winds.

The churns were heavy. Nissim strained to hold back the cart as they descended past the Egged bus station to the center of Jewish Jerusalem, Zion Square. Here a black-visored British policeman stood on a pedestal directing traffic from under an umbrella. The nearby Zion Cinema was showing *They Were Expendable*.

Ten minutes later they crossed Mamillah Road and Nissim pushed the cart up Julian's Way. They passed the King David's main entrance and stopped just beyond the Secretariat wing, directly in front of Homsi and Salameh's, an antiquities shop.

Nissim stretched out on the ground as though resting. Amatzia sat next to him—a tired Arab porter, a patient Jewish shopper.

Two hundred yards beyond the hotel's north wing another Arab porter and Jewish shopper stopped opposite Deen's Indian Tailor. Their pushcart was heaped with melons and vegetables, a cargo which looked different from Nissim's but which was, in its most important respect, identical.

Amnon dropped back and stared at Shaul as they walked from Beit Aharon to the bus stop on the Jaffa Road. Shaul was an Iraqi Jew who spoke fluent Arabic and had grown up among Arabs. Amnon did his best to imitate his gait and mannerisms, trying at the last minute to become a convincing Arab.

The bus driver was Jewish and by chance a friend of Shaul's. "Why are you dressed like an Arab?" he shouted in Hebrew.

Shaul shrugged and paid his fare.

The driver repeated the question.

"I don't understand Hebrew," Shaul answered in Arabic. He and Amnon took seats in the rear of the bus, as far away from the driver as possible.

Peri turned Isaac Sandler's taxi off Julian's Way and onto a narrow dirt lane running past the hotel's north wing. He parked three hundred yards down the lane in a driveway next to the French Consulate.

Abu Jilda and the five "porters" got out and stood next to the taxi. Ariela remained in the front seat. The taxi was now an "ambulance" and she and Peri would use it to transport any casualties to the Tachemoni School near the Wailing Wall. There another nurse waited in a shuttered room. Ariela's medical supplies consisted of an army field dressing kit, bandages, cotton wool, a pain killer and rubber tubing for a tourniquet. Anyone seriously wounded would have to get to the Tachemoni School quickly.

Gal and Yanai jumped into the cab of the hijacked pickup truck. Gal started the engine and someone tossed three burlap sacks into the rear. Avidor, Katsina, Gideon and Aharon climbed in and leaned against seven milk churns, the property of Fluger's Dairy.

The churns were three and a half feet high and a foot and a half in diameter. They were carafe-shaped—a wide mouth, tight neck and circular body and base. They had handles to facilitate carrying and metal lids to prevent spillage and keep the milk clean and cool. Each carried thirty liters of milk and weighed thirty-five kilos when full.

Today, however, each churn weighed over fifty kilos. Two days ago Paglin had packed them with gelignite and TNT, fitted Yale locks on their lids and drilled holes in their sides. A copper pin stuck out a half inch from each hole. The truck lurched forward. Gideon reached into one of the sacks and released the safety catch on two Thompson submachine guns, "Tommy guns." Each held a twenty-round magazine. The other sacks contained a Sten gun, six Italian hand grenades and ten gelignite flash bombs.

Gideon pointed the barrels of the Tommy guns at the rear of the truck. The other men reached under their cloaks and slid the safeties off their Smith & Wessons.

For eighteen-year-old Leila Canaan, today promised to be one of the most exciting of her life. She spent the morning in her room, trying on clothes, primping and preparing for her first unchaperoned date (she had not told her parents), a drink with Wasfi Tell.

Tell planned to open an Arab Information Office in New York. He needed an assistant and Leila Canaan had volunteered. She had just completed a journalism course at the American University in Cairo. In truth, the Information Office did not interest her. Like many Arabs of her generation she was bored by politics. Furthermore, she saw no reason to fear the Jews when her own parents had such good relations with them.

It was, in fact, a Jewish matchmaker, Miss Landau, the headmistress of the Montefiore School, who had arranged her parents' marriage. Her father had made a list of the twenty most eligible and attractive women in Jerusalem and Miss Landau had narrowed the list to three. He had married one of her selections—the daughter of Egyptian-German parents.

Leila's father, Atallah Mantoura's neighbor, was the first Arab doctor in Jerusalem, but no Arab was willing to trust another Arab to treat him. Six months after leaving medical school he still had no patients. Finally, a Jewish doctor arranged for him to practice at the Orthodox Hospital in Mea Shearim.

In spite of their Jewish friendships, her parents supported the Arab revolt. They hid an Arab leader from British search parties and her father treated Arab detainees. Nevertheless, they sheltered their daughter from politics. Only once had the Palestine conflict touched her.

During the Arab revolt, Arab children scattered nails in the street to puncture the tires of British jeeps and police cars. She walked after them picking up the nails, which she needed to complete her treehouse. An Arab saw her and slapped her hand. Two nails pierced her palm, the rest scattered onto the street. She still carried the scars.

If the Arabs had staged a revolt in 1946 she could have been a great asset, if she had cared. She resembled a German Jew more than an Arab. She had many Jewish friends, spoke fluent Yiddish and German, and could enter Jewish neighborhoods and buildings without arousing suspicion.

She used her appearance and languages to escort Arab friends to Jewish cinemas. She particularly liked Disney movies and a few weeks before had taken two friends to see *Fantasia*.

Today's meeting with Tell was not a sign of sudden interest in the Arab cause. She was not going to this trouble to discuss Arab offices in New York, but to flirt. It promised to be an exciting adventure—a noontime drink with an attractive man in the most glamorous place in Jerusalem, the King David Hotel.

"Why is a pretty girl like you sitting here all alone?" an elderly Arab man asked Adina.

She ignored him. She had been sitting on a bench across from the King David since 10:30.

He sat down beside her. "Why aren't you in school?"

"I had a fight with my parents and I've run away from home." She got up and paced the sidewalk, looking at her watch and pretending to wait for someone.

Yael stood farther north of the hotel, directly opposite the Shell station. She worried that someone would notice she had been there over an hour.

A boy from her office stopped and asked what she was doing; why wasn't she at work? She ignored him.

A middle-aged Jew stared at her from across the street. He had stood in the same spot ever since she arrived.

A British soldier approached her and said something unintelligible. She looked the other way but he persisted. "What's your name?" he asked.

Now she understood, he wanted a date. "Meri," she said. It meant "revolt" in Hebrew. She knew it would sound like "Mary" to the soldier. She glared at him and he shrugged and walked away.

Avinoam appeared. "Be patient," he said. "It's been postponed until noon."

She pointed to the man across the street. "He's been there all morning, watching me, watching the hotel."

Avinoam looked at him. "Don't worry, I know him. He's an observer from the Haganah. He'll disappear when we attack."

Early this morning he had called Yael away from her job as a secretary in the Jewish Health Insurance office and briefed her. "We'll attack at eleven," he had said. "Make sure you wait until the last soldier leaves the hotel, then follow Adina. If anything happens to her, you make the calls." He wanted to be certain the calls went through. His cousin Leah Bachrach worked as a typist in the Secretariat.

During the Secretariat's ten-minute tea break, Leah Bachrach modeled her new shoes for her co-workers. Leah had beautiful legs and delicate ankles and she bought shoes that showed them off. Everyone agreed the shoes were attractive. Any shoes were attractive on Leah.

In George Farley's office on the first floor, Lubah Wahbeh drank tea, ate biscuits alone and thought how much she missed the jolly tea break in the confidential pool. Just this morning "Father Antippa," the elderly and popular Greek who supervised the typists, had transferred her from the pool.

She had dreaded the move but George Farley was so courteous that she quickly forgot her disappointment. He rose from his chair whenever she came in to take dictation. When she left, he rose again and opened the door.

One floor above her, the women of the confidential pool brewed tea and unwrapped sweet rolls. They were the elite, the fastest and most accurate typists in the building. The other women called them "the hand-picked darlings."

Aside from this minor jealousy, relations among the women who worked at the Secretariat were good. The Arabs had all attended Schmidt's Girls School and knew each other from childhood, but they included their Jewish, British, Greek and Armenian colleagues in their frequent parties and outings.

For one of the Armenian typists, twenty-seven-year-old Eugenie Markarian, the Secretariat was everything. She worked to support two invalid aunts and spent her free time with the other typists going on picnics, attending concerts and holding dinner parties.

During the tea break the women in the pool liked to discuss the appearance, characters and foibles of the British civil servants. "They're real English gentlemen," one woman said. "They treat us like queens instead of typists."

"The light comes from their faces as if they were saints," said another.

"They're too polite and gentlemanly," said Grace Baramki. "They don't search the visitors carefully enough."

The others were surprised. Miss Baramki was thirty-four, a "secretary-stenographer," and known for being unflappable. They reminded her of the guards, the barbed wire and the turnstile.

"But what about the back of the hotel?" she said. "There are back doors."

Max Hamburger was on the prowl, inspecting the hotel and taking notes for letters of praise or reprimand. His black hair was slicked back, his striped trousers and swallow-tailed morning coat immaculately cleaned and pressed. He insisted that everyone, staff and guests, follow his example.

He stood at the corner of the reception desk and scrutinized the morning arrivals. If a prospective guest arrived improperly dressed, if he seemed loud, vulgar, or for any reason unsuitable, he signaled discreetly. The reception clerk, Otto Kupferschmidt, would tell the guest the hotel was full and suggested he try the Eden or the Pentiles.

Hamburger only paused in the bar for a moment. The bar did not please him. It had become, especially in the evening, a rowdy beer hall, a place where army officers and policemen let off steam and drank without fear of assassination. Recently he had ordered three policemen to stop singing lewd drinking songs. It was 10:30 P.M. and they were disturbing the guests. They tackled him, rolled him up in an oriental rug, propped him in the corner and then toasted him with their vulgar songs.

In the dining room, Hamburger bent over and measured the starched tablecloths with a ruler. Each had to be exactly centered on the table.

In the lobby, he peered into ashtrays—were they being emptied every thirty minutes? He timed the waiters as they brought drinks from the bar.

In the upstairs corridors he counted utensils on the room service trays and looked into the public bathrooms. He had ordered the Sudanese to scrub them the minute a guest finished his tub.

At 11:00 every morning, first maitre d'hôtel Naim Nissan came downstairs from the suite he shared with his mother and began his own tour of inspection. Nissan, an Iraqi Jew, had been a headwaiter at the palace of the Iraqi royal family in Baghdad, at a Greek nightclub in Jerusalem, and at the Regence. Now he was the King David's chief headwaiter, responsible for overseeing all the kitchens and dining rooms. He worked closely with Hamburger and thought him strict but professional, "an excellent teacher."

Nissan was a good student. Every morning he walked down to the basement kitchens to taste sauces and sample desserts. Upstairs in the pantry he smelled cheeses and checked for bruises on the pyramids of fruit. He took the day's menu upstairs and presented it to VIP's staying in the hotel. They could make substitutions for dishes they disliked.

Throughout the morning, particularly on Mondays, telephone calls interrupted his rounds. Only he could take table reservations. Most people called on Monday to reserve for the festive Saturday night dinners.

Upstairs in the bedrooms Mathilde Papadoupolous counted dirty sheets, towels and pillow cases, and noted the room number in her ledger. Then she counted out the same amount of clean linen, examined it for spots (although Madame Louise rarely sent a dirty one up from the laundry), and gave it to a Sudanese. He remade the bed and cleaned the room. Before the end of the morning she would count sheets in each of the sixty-two rooms still open to the public.

She also arranged flowers in the suites and ran her finger along the furniture and drapes, checking for dust. She rose at six each morning to supervise the Sudanese and Arabs who mopped the corridors and public rooms. But of all her jobs, the most important and time-consuming was counting the sheets.

She had come to feel more like a detective than a head housekeeper. Since the beginning of the war, the King David had been cursed with theft, drinking, espionage and a more tiresome set of royal families. The war prevented European royalty from coming to the King David and Middle Eastern royalty from leaving to visit their favorite European spas. Instead, the Arab and Persian aristocrats came to the King David.

The Egyptian Queen Mother, Farida, and the Shah's mother and sister were the most difficult. Farida was obsessed with clean linen. She rented the adjoining room for her private launderer and installed a small gas stove. Every day the launderer washed and ironed her sheets and dried them over the stove. The other guests complained of smoke. Mathilde complained that dripping-wet bed sheets ruined the furniture. The Queen Mother ignored her.

The Shah's mother was the reverse, too filthy. She traveled with a pack of aging, blind, incontinent Pekingese. After the dogs left piles of feces and puddles of urine in the corridor, Mathilde ordered them sent to the garden. The Shah's mother refused. "You have plenty of staff," she said. "Order them to clean up after my dogs."

Mathilde had not come to Jerusalem to clean up after blind dogs. Her father had been a hotel manager in Egypt, the Sudan and South Africa and she felt she was carrying on the family tradition. She also wanted "excitement and adventure and escape from Switzerland."

"I wanted to be an interesting person," she said, "not just another provincial Swiss."

The war provided enough excitement. British soldiers drank themselves into stupors. They misplaced guns, uniforms and secret papers. One officer left the plans for British Headquarters in his room. A chambermaid who was half German found them and handed them in a day later. Mathilde was certain she had copied them.

Another officer left behind a pistol. Mathilde saw the same chambermaid hide it. When the military police asked for help in locating it, Mathilde refused. "I'm sorry but I work for the hotel," she said. "Besides, I'm neutral. I'm Swiss."

Other soldiers stole from the rooms. Some Australians took towels, sheets, slipcovers and lamps. Mathilde encountered their chambermaid, who would have to pay for the losses, collapsed on the floor of their room in tears. She ran downstairs and confronted the soldiers in the lobby. "Why did you leave the bed? The chairs?" she shouted. "Why not come back and take it all? The chambermaid will have to pay so why not really rob her?"

They returned everything. When someone threatened the hotel's property, Mathilde was not neutral.

Every morning Mrs. Katherine Grey-Donald put on a wide-brimmed straw hat, picked up a pair of clippers and left her desk at the southernmost corner of the Winter Garden to visit the hotel garden.

She complimented Shlomo the gardener on his roses and cut flowers for the suites. She fed the chickens she kept in one corner of the garden and gathered their eggs to share with the hotel staff.

Everyone loved her. She was an elderly woman who, with her ample bosom and fondness for black dresses with white lace collars, resembled Queen Victoria. Jerusalem's British community thought her "a splendid old girl," and called her "The Queen of the King David Hotel."

She had lived in Jerusalem for forty years and moved into the King David the day it opened. Her husband, a government official, had died in the 1920s. Her only relation was a stepdaughter married to "the little man who runs the Cairo trams."

In exchange for a room and salary she functioned as the hotel's press agent and social director, writing speeches that Hamburger delivered at banquets and notes about guests that appeared in the social columns of Cairo's English-language newspapers. She also settled questions of hotel protocol—which visiting prince was entitled to the best suite? Who should sit to the left of the Coptic bishop?

She knew everyone. She was the godmother of the Arabs working in the accounting department and always was summoned for tea in Queen Farida's suite. High Commissioners invited her to every function at Government House.

The previous High Commissioner, Lord Gort, had written a flattering introduction to her memoirs. The book was never published. Only flimsy gray paper was available because of rationing, so she withdrew the manuscript from the printers until they could obtain thicker, whiter paper. She hated cheaply printed books as much as bad manners and gossip.

A particular enjoyment of hers was taking newcomers on tours. On their first Sunday in Jerusalem, Emile Soutter, the hotel's new assistant manager, and his wife, Anne, visited the Old City alone. Anne returned to the King David in tears. Guides had demanded enormous tips; urchins sat in front of the most sacred Christian shrines cracking nuts and peeling oranges.

The next Sunday Mrs. Grey-Donald insisted on accompanying them. She showed them cellars under the Via Dolorosa where children played bizarre religious games. Rabbis, priests and sheiks greeted them with bows and flattery. The guides shooed away the urchins and produced silver trays of dates, flaky pastries and cups of tea. They plucked keys from chains and opened doors to holy stones and secret relics.

Mrs. Grey-Donald knew their names and their children's names. She knew the history and ritual of every chapel and temple. "In Jerusalem," she explained to the Soutters, "everyone should know the protocol. You have to be a religious diplomat to live here happily."

The Soutters learned the protocol and tried to be diplomatic but they were not entirely happy. Anne Soutter found it eerie and unsettling that some of the Jews she kept seeing in the hotel and on the streets seemed so very familiar, yet she was certain she had never met them. Finally she realized they had all taken refuge in Switzerland during the war. She had recognized them from their pictures on the visa applications they had submitted and resubmitted to the British Consulate in Geneva, where she had worked as a secretary.

She and her husband were also upset by the terrorism. It seemed that every time they visited the bank or post office someone called in a bomb warning. So far all of them had turned out to be hoaxes.

This morning both of them were working in the hotel. He roamed through the building performing miscellaneous tasks such as asking Chef Gaillard to remove *pilaf financière* from the menu. She typed letters and handled Hamburger's correspondence. Her office was a small room behind the reception desk, directly above the kitchen of the Regence.

18

11:55 A.M.–12:10 P.M.

"**J**EWISH TERRORISTS have just blown up the King David Hotel!" This short message was received by the London Bureau of United Press International (UPI) shortly after noon, Palestine time. It was signed by a UPI stringer in Palestine who was also a secret member of the Irgun. The stringer had learned about Operation Chick but did not know it had been postponed for an hour. Hoping to scoop his colleagues, he had filed a report minutes before 11:00. A British censor had routinely stamped his cable without reading it.

The UPI London Bureau chief thought the message too terse. There were not enough details. He decided against putting it on the agency's wire for radio and press until receiving further confirmation that the hotel had been destroyed.

Despite the efforts of Irgun leaders to restrict knowledge of the target and timing of Operation Chick, there were numerous other leaks. Leaders in both the Haganah and Stern Gang knew about the operation. Friends warned friends who warned friends. The King David had an extraordinary number of last-minute room cancellations. In the Secretariat, more than the usual number of Jewish typists and clerks called in sick.

Boris Guriel, the pro-British moderate who was also a high-ranking member of the Haganah Intelligence organization, was spending the morning working in an office in Jerusalem's Histadrut building. He noticed that between eleven and noon a colleague with close ties to the Irgun kept walking upstairs and then returning a few minutes later. Finally, his curiosity aroused, Guriel followed him. He found him standing on the roof, looking at his watch and then staring off in the direction of the King David.

"What are you up to?" Guriel asked.

"Patience," the man answered. "You'll soon see why I'm here."

Ibrahim Mansour trudged up the dirt lane leading from Yemin Moshe to the King David clutching a pack of cigarettes. Every morning he sneaked away to a Jewish grocery to buy a cheap brand. Those sold in the hotel were too expensive for a Secretariat messenger.

As he walked past the French Consulate one of Abu Jilda's porters slipped away from the others and approached him. Mansour's yarmulka and khaki uniform identified him as one of the few Jewish messengers in the Secretariat.

"Tell the Jews to get out of the building," the porter said in Hebrew. "There's going to be an explosion." He whispered so the others would not overhear him giving this unauthorized warning.

Mansour ran. He knew that a Jew masquerading as an Arab had to belong to the Irgun or Stern Gang. The man's warning might have meant that bombs had already been placed in the hotel. If so, they might explode at any moment. He could not risk returning to the Secretariat.

He darted through the gates of the Secretariat Annex, a building leased from the Jesuits and now housing the Office of Food Control. He would call Father Antippa from here and tell him to evacuate the Secretariat.

Gal turned the stolen truck containing the milk churns and the assault unit off the Jaffa Road and onto King George V Avenue. Provided he did not encounter any of the "flying checkpoints" of the Palestine Police, it would take him just under ten minutes to get from Beit Aharon to the King David.

At the top of the hill, he drove past the Jewish Agency. Inside, David Horowitz, Golda Meyerson and others debated what further actions they should take to protest Black Saturday. They considered responses such as a boycott, more demonstrations, or a general strike.

Earlier that morning Horowitz had telephoned Roderick Musgrave and canceled their noon meeting at the Secretariat because, he said later, "I still awaited the outcome of the vigorous debate still proceeding in our field over the issue of administrative and economic noncooperation with the government."

Two hundred yards past the Agency, Gal made a left turn onto Abraham Lincoln, a narrow residential street that curved around the north end of the YMCA soccer field and then intersected Julian's Way just north of the King David. Two lines of barbed wire coils partially blocked the intersection but when Gal drove across it neither opening in the wire was guarded.

Abu Jilda was becoming nervous. Anyone staring out of a window in the hotel might have noticed that for the last fifteen minutes he had been standing in the same shadeless spot in the lane that ran past the French Consulate. He had left the other "porters" a hundred and fifty yards farther down the lane with the taxi. It was their job to carry the churns into the basement. He planned to summon them as soon as he saw Gal drive into the hotel.

A British officer walked by, stared at him, continued walking and then stopped, turned around, and stared again. Afraid the officer had become suspicious, Abu Jilda turned and hurried away from the hotel.

During the seconds that Abu Jilda's back was turned, Gal steered the truck through the barbed wire. He crossed Julian's Way, drove twenty-five yards down the lane leading to the French Consulate and then turned right into the King David's service driveway.

Chiam-Toit had been right. No barriers or coils of wire blocked this driveway. Nobody challenged him or asked for an identity card. The entrance was unguarded.

Abu Jilda stopped and glanced over his shoulder. The British officer was gone. He walked back to his post and waited for Gal to arrive. He had no idea that Gal was already down in the service driveway.

The truck coasted down the concrete driveway. Shaul and Amnon appeared and trotted a few feet in front of it. Gal braked in front of the service entrance and killed the engine. Shaul and Amnon opened the green service door and dashed into the basement.

The phone rang in Father Antippa's office on the first floor of the Secretariat. Father Antippa answered it himself.

"There are bombs in the hotel," Ibrahim Mansour shouted. "There's going to be an explosion!"

"Don't worry," Antippa said. "There's nothing there."

"How do you know? I've just been told!"

"I already received a call about it from a Jewish friend. I sent a military policeman to investigate the basement and he didn't see anything suspicious."

"No, no. Everyone should get out of the building!"

"Calm down and come back to work."

From her post on the corner of Julian's Way and Abraham Lincoln, Yael watched the milk truck turn into the service driveway. She was astonished that her brother Gal was driving.

Once before they had been assigned to the same operation—blowing up sections of track between Jerusalem and Tel Aviv. He had mined one section of track, she another and afterward they had met by accident on a Jerusalem-bound bus. When they arrived he protested the practice of sending more than one member of a family on the same operation. The High Command agreed and adopted a rule prohibiting it.

Now the rule had been broken. Now she had to worry about his safety as well as her own.

Across the street from Yael, Emile Soutter happened to be looking out of the narrow window next to the hotel's revolving door as the "milk" truck arrived. He called over to the concierge, Edward Lang, and pointed it out. "What business could such a battered old wreck have at the King David?" he asked. "And why is it coming here at noon?"

"Must be a special delivery for the kitchen," Lang said. "It happens all the time."

Six floors above Soutter, an army clerk knew without looking that it was noon. Everyone and everything moved more slowly. Arab messengers shuffled between offices in slow motion; typewriters clattered at half speed; dark perspiration stains spread until they covered the backs of khaki shirts; and the overhead fan pushed hot, dry air across the offices, rustling the files stacked on tables but providing no relief from the heat.

The clerk walked to the window and stared out. The sky was blue and cloudless, the sun directly overhead. The city's red tile roofs shimmered and a haze of dust clouded the horizon. It seemed to him the hottest moment of one of the hottest days of the year.

He stared across at the YMCA tower. Just after he arrived in Palestine, terrorists had lobbed grenades from behind the YMCA. They had missed the King David and landed in the olive grove.

Now he watched trucks and taxis crawling along Julian's Way. Like the army offices, Jerusalem slowed down at noon. Most people stayed indoors to escape the heat. The few pedestrians about walked in the narrow shadows of walls and buildings.

Last month terrorists had stolen a taxi and driven along Julian's Way shooting at soldiers with a machine gun. Two soldiers had been killed. Later the clerk had been responsible for drafting letters of condolence to their relatives. He always wrote: "There has been an accident that had to do with the prevailing conditions. . . ."

He leaned out of the window and looked down. An open truck drove into the service yard. Four Arabs were squatting among some milk churns in the rear.

Johannes Constantides, the King David's receiving clerk, became suspicious when he noticed that the Arabs who had just entered the passageway wore their headdresses at a crooked angle. "What are you delivering?" he demanded. "Where are the bills?"

Shaul pulled a revolver from his cloak and Constantides raised his hands. Amnon pulled the clerk's keys from his belt and shoved him into the office. The six men from the milk truck crowded into the passage.

Constantides recognized Gideon, the talkative engineer from the electric company. "What do you want here?" he asked.

Gideon ignored the question. "Is there an alarm system in the basement?"

"No." Constantides lied.

"Crawl under your desk and stay there or we'll shoot you," Gideon ordered.

The receiving office was midway down a short passageway connecting the service door and the main basement corridor. It had a sliding window that looked onto the passageway so a clerk could check deliveries and discourage pilferage without getting up from his desk.

Amnon replaced Constantides in the passageway. He would take prisoner anyone trying to enter the basement. From time to time he glanced into the office to make sure Constantides stayed out of sight.

A button on the wall of the receiving office was connected to an alarm in the Mamillah Road police station, a quarter of a mile away. Constantides wondered how he could manage to push it.

In the ground-floor radio room of the Mamillah Road police station, Assistant Superintendent Ian Proud stared at a wood board studded with light bulbs. Nameplates next to the light bulbs said: BARCLAYS BANK, IMMIGRATION OFFICE, GOVERNMENT HOUSE, MAIN POST OFFICE, KING DAVID HOTEL. . . . When someone pushed an alarm in any of these buildings a bell rang and a bulb flashed in the radio room. The radio operator then alerted the six police vans that cruised the streets in eight-hour shifts. These green vans each carried four officers and were known as the "Jerusalem Operational Patrol."

Proud commanded the Jerusalem Operational Patrol from the Mamillah Road station. Until two weeks ago he had commanded the entire Jerusalem Urban Division. Every illegally parked car, bank robbery, murder and terrorist bombing came under his jurisdiction. Now he was cooped up in the stuffy radio room.

The change was temporary. In a few days he and his family would sail for Britain on their first home leave in seven years. His replacement had already arrived and Proud had shifted to the Mamillah Road command voluntarily. He hoped to clear up his court cases and avoid making any new arrests that could delay his departure.

Meanwhile, he suffered. He disliked the radio room's darkness and noise, its crackling static and the monotonous chatter between dispatchers and cars. Today the noise had given him a headache.

He handed command of the patrols to Inspector Taylor, a pale, hollow-cheeked young man who appeared to have spent his life indoors, and left to get a haircut at the Jaffa Gate police station. It contained the only authorized police barbershop in Jerusalem. Terrorists had attempted to murder policemen as they sat in civilian barbers' chairs.

"If I'd known what was going to happen," he said later, "I'd have delayed my haircut."

*   *   *

The assault unit ran into the main corridor. Gideon had been there before. The other men knew it only from Paglin's diagram: a narrow space with four exits that ran for eighty yards under the hotel and connected the main kitchen in the north with the Regence in the south.

They found themselves in a six-foot-wide, ten-foot-high passage lit by naked light bulbs that seemed as bright as searchlights. The passage smelled of food, sweat and steam and pulsated to machines that rattled, thumped, hissed and flushed behind partitions and closed doors. Pipes, cables and wires sheathed in rubber crisscrossed overhead, disappeared into grates and holes and ended in boxes and dials measuring pressure, kilowatt hours and heat.

Temperatures fluctuated wildly. The green walls and concrete floors were cool near stairways, hot near generators, dry near boilers and humid next to the laundry room.

Doors and short passageways led off to rooms, closets and stairways. There were swinging doors with tiny windows, metal doors that slid on tracks and doors with frosted glass that distorted like fun-house mirrors. Behind one door six female army ATS operators manned a switchboard for the entire military headquarters. They wore earphones and the room was noisy with their chatter. Neither they nor their supervisor, Major Mackintosh, heard anything unusual in the corridor.

Gideon had missed the switchboard when he scouted the basement. Chaim-Toit and Paglin did not know it existed.

A European chef wearing a high white hat pushed through the double doors leading from the kitchen. He saw the "Arabs" and stopped. The morning deliveries had already been made.

"What are you doing here?" he demanded.

Two authentic Arab porters balancing rolled carpets on their heads walked out of the laundry room.

Gideon drew his revolver. "Hands up! Hands up! Into the kitchen," he shouted. His hand shook uncontrollably and the gun waved back and forth between the chef and the Arab porters.

Two other Irgun soldiers took out revolvers. Avidor drew a submachine gun from a sack.

The chef and porters backed through the swinging doors into the kitchen. Gideon and Avidor followed them.

A dozen cooks, busboys and dishwashers looked up from stoves, sinks and worktables. Sauces bubbled and soups simmered. Chopped vegetables and fruits lay on counters. Lunch would be served in an hour.

They dropped knives and spoons and raised their hands. An Arab boy climbed under a table and slapped his hands over his eyes. A cook darted into the walk-in refrigerator and slammed the door. Another cook protested: "Lunch will spoil. None of us has any money. What else do you want?"

"Quiet!" Gideon shouted. "Everyone on the floor. If you move or make a noise we'll kill you."

The workers sat down on the white tiles. Gideon ripped a telephone from the wall, gathered their knives, tossed them into a corner and left. Avidor remained as a guard.

Gal, Yanai and the others ran down the corridor pulling open doors, rounding up waiters, cleaners and housekeepers and herding them into the kitchen. One man turned the handle of the door leading to the army switchboard and pushed. The locked door wouldn't budge. He tried Constantides' keys. When none of them worked he gave up.

Five yards down the hall from the switchboard, a young Swiss headwaiter sat alone in the Regence eating lunch. He was one of the most amusing and popular members of the hotel staff. As a joke, he frequently proposed to Mathilde Papadoupolous. "Marry me," he would implore, "and I'll give you beautiful clothes, take you to beautiful places. Finally you'll be chic." She always refused.

He heard someone rattle the Regence's swinging doors and then fumble with the lock. He thought the sounds signaled a visit from one of his lovers on the hotel staff. He walked over and thrust out his bottom as a joke. Nothing happened. When he turned and saw someone waving a distorted gun at him through the frosted panes of glass he dashed into a storage room and dived under a pile of mattresses.

The assault unit was guarding the exits according to plan: Amnon guarded the receiving clerk and the door to the service driveway; Aharon guarded the service stairs near the kitchen that led to the lobby; Katsina guarded the stairs from the Regence to the lobby; Yanai guarded the door in the middle of the corridor that opened onto the King David's gardens. If troops were summoned from the nearby army camp they would burst through this door.

Gideon and Gal stood by the service door, nervously pacing, checking their wristwatches, and waiting for Abu Jilda and his five porters to appear. Already they were late. The plan called for them to hurry down the French Consulate lane and into the service driveway as soon as the truck arrived with the explosives. Without their help with the churns, the assault unit would have to spend twice as long in the basement. The chance they would be discovered was twice as great.

Gideon had to decide: Should he risk going outside to search for Abu Jilda? Perhaps he had been arrested, and Gideon's men should move the bombs themselves. But if the assault unit unloaded the churns who would guard the basement?

"They're coming!" Yanai screamed. "They're coming. British soldiers are coming through the garden."

Gideon froze and stared at the garden door.

Yanai ran over and pulled him toward the service exit.

"Retreat! Retreat!" he shouted. "Retreat or we'll all be killed."

19

12:10—12:15 P.M.

I N THE King David's military and government offices, Monday was the busiest day of the week. Jerusalem enjoyed a three-day weekend. Moslems took off Friday afternoons, Jews all of Saturday and Christians Sunday. Monday was the first full working day after Thursday.

On Mondays Sir John Shaw always met with the American Consul, Lowell Pinkerton. Today he saw his deputy, Malcolm Hooper. Pinkerton had gone to London a few days before to attend the British-American discussions on Palestine's future.

British civil servants from other parts of Palestine scheduled their Secretariat meetings for Mondays so they could visit friends in Jerusalem over the weekend. Today Bernard Bourdillon was visiting from Nazareth and Ivan Phillips had come up from Ramle.

Noon was the most crowded time of day in the Secretariat. Visitors who had attended early morning meetings were leaving; others were arriving for pre-luncheon meetings.

In George Farley's office a conference on postal security was breaking up. As soon as Postmaster General Gerald Kennedy and the others left, Farley planned to attend a financial meeting in Julius Jacobs' first-floor office. It was scheduled to start at 12:30.

Two rooms down the hall from Farley, Chief Financial Secretary Geoffrey Walsh met with Simon Seidler, a Jewish tea inporter, and Omar Bisharat, a senior member of a noted family of Arab traders. Seidler wanted to negotiate tea prices. Bisharat was asking Walsh to pay more for sheep.

Walsh expected to make additional payments. He knew that Bisharat enjoyed the bargaining and bluffing, and he expected the negotiations would probably continue until lunchtime.

Arabs and Jews, Greeks and Armenians, and representatives of dozens of Christian sects jammed the corridors and rooms outside Walsh's and every other British Secretary's office. They stood in lines, sat on chairs or squatted on the floor as they waited for an audience. They scheduled an appointment with one official in order to get into the Secretariat and then stayed to pursue other business.

They followed the Secretaries down the corridors, thrusting out petitions, waving forms and whispering of wrongs. They bribed government messengers to deliver letters pleading favors for relatives. They protested government projects that bestowed benefits on rival communities.

Many of these noontime visitors to the King David were Jewish.

Joseph Alles, a Tel Aviv lawyer, shuttled between offices pleading for the release of clients arrested during Black Saturday.

On the third floor, Captain Dan Ben-Dor explained the operation of the King David's new fire alarm and sprinkler system to a brigadier general. Ben-Dor, a Jewish architect and inventor from Jerusalem, was a decorated war hero who had designed a bomb-proof, igloo-shaped army barracks constructed entirely of three-and-a-half-foot-thick mud bricks. During the North African campaign his igloos had protected British soldiers from German bullets and bomb splinters.

After the war Ben-Dor was posted to his native Jerusalem where he supervised the construction of fortifications and security systems to protect the British Army from Jewish terrorists. He had designed the turnstile, trip wires, sentry boxes and other devices surrounding the King David.

One floor above, on the top floor of the hotel, Golda Meyerson's special emissary, Harry Beilin, met with Major Ernest Quinn in an office at the southern end of the fourth-floor corridor, just one room away from the partition separating the military headquarters from the Secretariat.

Beilin and Quinn were on excellent terms. Quinn had been among the troops liberating the Belsen concentration camp. What he had seen made him more sympathetic to the Yishuv than most British officers. Even Jewish terrorism had not shaken his sympathy.

Today Beilin was visiting Quinn to reassure him, and through him the British Army, that the Haganah was not planning any military retaliation for Black Saturday. "The 'Old Girl' [Meyerson] had been in touch with the activists," he said, "and has told them not to rock the boat while the 'Old Man' is in London."

Gideon peered out the door leading to the garden. There were no soldiers heading toward the basement. Arab gardeners weeded zinnias and pruned roses. "Calm down," he told Yanai. "No one is coming."

"I saw them . . . troops in the garden running toward us," Yanai said.

"You're scared. You're imagining things. Stay next to me and help carry the churns."

Yanai *was* scared; scared that the operation would succeed and scared he would have to set the fuses. The British would certainly hang whoever touched off the bombs. It was too late to call Max Schindler. His only hope lay in panicking the others into a retreat.

Gideon decided not to wait for Abu Jilda. The assault unit would have to carry the churns. He took Yanai's revolver, gave it to Aharon and orered him to cover the service stairs and the garden door. He, Shaul, Gal and Yanai would carry the churns into the Regence. It meant fewer men to guard the exits, disarm intruders and repulse an attack, and fewer men to move the churns. The operation would take longer than planned.

Gideon and Yanai lifted a churn by the handles and carried it through the service door. It was heavy and they took short, jerky steps.

Yanai continued to protest. "I'm certain I saw British soldiers. We should retreat while we can."

"Stay close to me and nothing will happen to you," Gideon said. He still thought Yanai was only frightened.

They lowered the can onto the floor and dragged it seventy-five yards along the basement corridor, past the locked door of the army telephone exchange where the young female operators manned a switchboard connecting them with every one of the 3,000 British soldiers stationed in Jerusalem, past the storeroom where the headwaiter still hid under a mattress five minutes after being surprised in the Regence, down a short concrete ramp, through the kitchen, and into the Regence.

The room was cool—dark-red curtains had been drawn against the sun—and empty. Its waiters and bartenders were eating lunch in the staff dining room. The floor where Gideon and Yael had danced glistened with wax. The table where they had eaten was covered with a pink cloth and laid with crystal glasses and silver flatware, ready for army officers who favored the Regence's special "businessman's plate."

Slices of lemon, swizzle sticks, a cocktail shaker and an ice crusher were lined up on a clean towel at one end of the bar. The barstools were arranged in an even row and clean ashtrays were centered on copper cocktail tables. The Regence was ready for one of Hamburger's inspections.

Gideon shoved aside tables and kicked the chairs and banquettes away from the two pillars supporting the southwest corner of the building. The pillars were four feet wide and three-foot-high wooden paneling ran around and between them.

He placed the first churn against this paneling and then returned to the truck for another. There were six more: three trips for Gideon and Yanai, three for Gal and Shaul.

The churns' metal bottoms scraped against the corridor's concrete floors and disturbed the ATS operators. Their supervisor, Major Mackintosh, unlocked the door of the exchange and strode into the corridor. He stared at the "Arabs," then at the milk churns. When he saw the Yale locks fastening their lids, he froze.

The hotel's revolving front door turned faster and more frequently. The Regence and the main dining room served lunch at one. Between noon and one, Jerusalem's wealthiest Arabs and Jews, Jewish Agency officials, senior civil servants, journalists and guests from other hotels met in the lobby and bar for drinks. Guests rode the elevators down from their rooms and army officers walked down from headquarters. The lobby's Hittite thrones were filling up.

Leila Canaan pushed through the revolving door ten minutes late for her appointment with Wasfi Tell. As they walked toward the Winter Garden he joked about her lack of punctuality.

"It's a woman's prerogative to be late," she said. She had heard this retort used in a Hollywood movie.

The Winter Garden was ideal for her flirtation. The narrow glass-walled room extended south from the open portion of the terrace to where the Secretariat wing jutted out from the main body of the hotel. It offered a superb view over the hotel garden to Mount Zion, the walls of the Old City and the Jaffa Gate. Yet at the same time it was secluded.

In the main lobby she risked being seen by a family friend or relative. Eighteen-year-old Arab girls were not supposed to meet men for drinks in the King David without a chaperone. Her parents would be scandalized.

Tell steered her to a wicker table at the southern end of the Winter Garden, near the wall of the Secretariat. As soon as they were seated he began flattering her.

"You are just the one I need to help me open the office," he said. "The German-speaking Americans will be impressed because you can speak German and English fluently. They will be amazed that such a pretty Arab girl can speak their languages so well. . . ."

She was certain her parents would never permit her to go to New York and she paid more attention to Tell than to the conversation. He fascinated her. He was urbane and educated, yet he possessed the courage and confidence and the bright, shrewd eyes of a Bedouin.

A waiter appeared and she ordered a gin. A day for firsts, she thought. Her first unescorted date, her first visit to the King David without her parents and now her first gin.

Katy Antonius climbed up Julian's Way from Mamillah Road. Richard Graves, the Chairman of the Jerusalem Council, had invited her and twelve other Arabs, Britons and Jews to lunch at the Regence. It was the first time she could remember him returning her hospitality and she planned to take full advantage.

She had dismissed her driver at the bottom of Julian's Way. She hoped that the walk uphill to the King David and an aperitif in the lobby with Wasfi Tell would give her a huge appetite.

Atallah Mantoura and his police bodyguards drove up Julian's Way to the Secretariat. Except for this morning when his wife had related her unsettling nightmare, the day had been routine. Every Monday he followed a precise schedule: four hours in the District Commissioner's office settling feuds and questions of religious protocol between the various Christian sects, then back to the Secretariat for two hours of work before lunch. At 2:00 he went home.

In the afternoon he escaped from Jerusalem into his garden. He sat in his favorite wicker chair sipping Turkish coffee and staring at a single rose stem, the thorn on a rose stem, a cedar sapling, or a green lizard. He often stared for hours, never talking or moving.

In the evening he escaped again, this time into ancient Greece. He read and reread Greek history and literature. He had even named his sons after Greek heroes—Jack Homer Mantoura, Guy Demosthenes Mantoura.

The only times the boys could remember their father being happy was during a vacation to Cyprus. He sang as they drove between the ancient ruins in an open car.

"I won't leave until you begin fixing my car," Sami Hadawi shouted at the Armenian mechanic. He had left his new Austin 16 at Spinney's Garage at 8:00 that morning. Now he had returned four hours later to find the mechanic had not even lifted the hood.

He was supposed to return to the Secretariat at noon for a meeting with Mantoura and Levi. He had called to apologize and explain he would be late because of the car. It had to be in good working order by 2:00 when he was scheduled to motor to Galilee to assess Jewish property for taxes.

He was the only senior Arab official in the government with important responsibilities in Jewish districts. One of his specialties was the kibbutz fish ponds which were taxed according to the number of fish they held. He counted dead carp floating in the ponds and then reduced taxes accordingly. He had become an expert on the care and feeding of carp and often advised the Jewish settlers how to manage their ponds.

The Armenian mechanic finally lifted the hood and began muttering about the fuel pump. After making him promise to fix it by 2:00, Hadawi started walking up the hill to the Secretariat.

Meyer Levin and his film crew drove up Julian's Way on their way to their Jerusalem headquarters, an office in a dead-end lane directly opposite the

Secretariat. Levin, an American writer and moviemaker, was filming *My Father's House*, a fictional account of a Holocaust survivor's search for his father in Palestine.

Filming in Jerusalem during the terrorist attacks and the British police actions was a strain. Minutes after arriving at his office, Levin left for an appointment with his therapist. His leading actors and film crew remained in their office opposite the Secretariat.

Ivan Phillips, the Assistant District Commissioner for Ramle, walked up Julian's Way toward the King David. Early that morning he had driven his wife and infant son to Jerusalem for physical examinations at the Government Hospital. Afterward he had briefed the Attorney General on land disputes in Ramle and now he had a free hour before meeting his wife for lunch. He planned to spend it in the Secretariat visiting Bob Newton, an assistant secretary for political affairs.

After a visit to Jerusalem two weeks earlier, Phillips had written to his father in England:

> The atmosphere is very electric and we have to prepare for Jewish terrorist retaliation at any moment. Jerusalem is an uneasy city with barbed wire, road restrictions, armed troops everywhere, armoured cars and Bren gun carriers rolling slowly through the streets.
> The country has been ominously quiet during the last ten days. There is no disguising the intense bitterness of Jewish feeling. It seems only a matter of time before the terrorists have another smack on a big scale and when they do it will probably be very unpleasant.

As he walked to the hotel he saw twice as many Bren carriers and army jeeps and twice as much barbed wire as two weeks ago. He thought his letter had been too mild. This Jewish terror was more threatening than the Arab kind. Even when Arab terrorists had shot at him they had proved themselves gentlemen. Once in 1938 they had attempted to kill him as he approached one of "his" villages. He had taken cover in a mud puddle, ruining his new suit. The next day an Arab friend in the same village was sympathetic. "Oh, dear sir," he had said, "that was me doing the shooting but I'd never have fired if I'd known it was you lying there."

Upon reaching the King David's driveway, Phillips decided to get a haircut in the hotel barbershop before seeing Newton. He pushed through the revolving door, walked past the reception desk, turned right and climbed a short flight of stairs. The barbershop was in the south end of the mezzanine, above the Regence.

Aharon saw Mackintosh first. The officer was huge, six feet tall, two hundred pounds and broad-shouldered. Aharon was a thin teenager, not quite five feet eight, under a hundred and fifty pounds and with a narrow build.

He wanted to obey Paglin's order—"Shoot only if your life is threatened." He knew gunfire would alert the army guards. The officer might be taking a break. He might leave. He might not become suspicious.

"What's going on here!" Mackintosh shouted as he unbuttoned his holster.

Aharon drew his Smith & Wesson first. "Hands up!" he ordered.

Mackintosh obeyed. Aharon pulled the service revolver from its holster, tossed it on the floor and ordered Mackintosh into the kitchen. Without the revolver, Aharon reasoned, the huge British officer was just another hostage.

Just before walking through the kitchen's swinging doors, Mackintosh lowered his hands, whirled around and slammed his fists down on Aharon's shoulders.

Aharon staggered but held onto his pistol. Mackintosh dashed for the service stairs.

Aharon lunged, hooked his fingers into the officer's belt and pulled. The officer was so heavy he was dragging Aharon toward the stairway.

He pulled harder. Mackintosh stumbled and fell. Aharon jumped on him, punching, gouging, wrestling, and trying to knock his head against the concrete floor. Anything to subdue him, quiet him, to avoid having to shoot him.

Mackintosh had left the door to the telephone switchboard open. Despite her earphones Sergeant Brown, the senior ATS operator, heard the sounds of the struggle. She peeked out into the corridor. Major Mackintosh and a small Arab boy were wrestling on the floor. Armed Arabs guarded the exits; other Arabs were delivering milk.

She ducked back inside, shoved on her headset and rang the officer at Signals in charge of the switchboard. Signals was located in the old King David annex, fifty yards across the garden from the basement.

Lieutenant Chambers answered the Signals telephone.

"This is Sergeant Brown in the exchange. Armed Arabs are chasing Major Mackintosh around the corridor."

"I'll be right over," he said.

"Don't come through the corridor. The Arabs are still here."

Chambers ordered two test clerks, both corporals, to grab Tommy guns and follow him to the exchange.

Next Sergeant Brown rang the security post in the annex.

Gunner Buckle answered. "Number four security post."

"There are four armed Arabs in the hotel basement. Send someone over immediately," she said.

"I'll come myself."

"Be careful you don't come through the service door."

She rang the orderly sergeant in the Military Police station, East Palestine Subdistrict (EPS). The station was behind Barclays Bank, a five-minute drive from the hotel.

The officer in charge of the EPS, twenty-year-old Lieutenant Ian Tilly, was in the orderly room when Brown rang. The orderly sergeant answered.

"What's it about, Sergeant?" Tilly asked.

"A report from an ATS operator at the K-D. Arab civilians are causing trouble around the exchange."

"Call her back. Tell her to alert the Palestine Police and tell her we're coming over."

Tilly pointed at three corporals. "You, you and you, come with me. We're going to the K-D."

Sergeant Brown followed Tilly's instructions and rang the Palestine Police. A dispatcher sent an armored car from the Mea Shearim police station. The car was manned by a commander, driver and turret machine gunner.

It left for the King David in such a hurry that its gunner, Arthur Miles, had no time to find his Bren gun. He grabbed a rifle instead.

Mackintosh pushed Aharon away, staggered to his feet and stumbled toward the service stairs. Aharon pointed his revolver and fired. Although hit, Mackintosh started up the stairs.

A hotel porter, Mohammed Abu Solob, saw everything. He had been standing on the ground-floor landing. He turned and ran up four flights to report the incident to the military guards at the number-one security post in the army headquarters.

Aharon fired again. This time blood spurted from Mackintosh's side. He clutched his stomach and pitched onto the stairway.

As Mackintosh fell Yanai began screaming, "The soldiers are coming. They're coming. They're coming. . . ." This time they were.

Lieutenant Chambers and his two test clerks climbed through a garden window into the telephone exchange. Seconds later, Gunners Buckle and Barber climbed through the same window. Barber and one of the clerks were armed with Tommy guns. Buckle was unarmed. Lieutenant Chambers had a rifle.

Sergeant Brown told Chambers: "Two shots have been fired and the armed Arabs are still in the corridor."

There was a small window above the door leading from the exchange to the corridor. Barber and one clerk stood on chairs and looked through it into the corridor. A slim, dark-featured man in red-checked Arab Legion headdress cradled a Sten gun in his arms.

He looks like a Jew, Barber thought.

The "Arab" pointed his Sten at the window and shouted something in Hebrew. Barber couldn't understand him. "Get back!" he warned the test clerks. "One of the Arabs has a Sten."

Lieutenant Chambers climbed up and looked through the window. Two "Arabs" pointed their guns at him. He pulled back and ordered Barber to call for assistance.

Sergeant Brown rang the sentry at the number four security post and handed Barber her headset.

The sentry refused to help. "I'm on my own," he said, "and besides, there aren't any weapons, the weapons case is locked."

Barber climbed out the window and ran back to the Signals Annex to fetch reinforcements.

Buckle climbed out and started circling the hotel to the south. He planned to rush the "Arabs" from the service driveway but first he needed a weapon.

Thinking that he had interrupted the first stage of an all-out attack on the hotel by Arabs, Chambers called the Signals adjutant and told him to prepare for a possible breakdown in communications. He and the test clerks remained in the exchange to guard the female operators.

Two Irgun soldiers dragged Mackintosh up the service stairs and laid him on the floor of the gentlemen's cloakroom. Someone would find him and call an ambulance. In wartime real soldiers, honorable soldiers, looked after the enemy wounded.

Downstairs in the basement corridor Gideon grabbed Yanai and hugged him. He was afraid Yanai was having a nervous breakdown; he was also afraid the British would burst into the corridor within minutes, perhaps seconds. Somebody must have reported the shots.

After passing Yanai to another member of the assault unit, Gideon helped Gal drag the last churn into the Regence. When it was in place he knelt down and pulled a glass vial from his pocket. It was four inches long, an inch and a half in diameter and covered with a bulbous wood cap from which protruded an aluminum tip. The vial contained two inches of a brownish liquid—sulfuric acid.

"In Jerusalem someone is always shooting someone," thought Mathilde Papadoupolous as she arranged flowers in one of the first-floor bedrooms. The shots had broken her concentration.

She looked at her watch. Almost 12:15, time to go downstairs for lunch. The senior staff ate in the main dining room before it opened to the public.

She began walking down the service stairs to the dining room. She stopped short when she saw a pool of blood on the ground-floor landing. More blood trailed down the stairs toward the basement. "What has happened here?" she said aloud.

She could not ignore a disturbance that threatened the hotel. There might have been another fight between the Arab and European staff. Rosemarie Polushny might have shoved another Sudanese in the commissary.

The passkey she carried in a locket hanging around her neck unlocked every door in the King David. The key symbolized her responsibility, and reminded her of her duty to investigate disturbances.

She followed the trail of blood down the stairs and into the basement.

*   *   *

Ivan Phillips could not decide where the muffled shots had come from and he did not much care. Shootings and bombings are two-a-penny in Jerusalem, he thought. The barber kept snipping and combing as if nothing had happened.

Upstairs on the third floor, Abu Solob, the porter who had witnessed the Mackintosh shooting, was reporting it to the young blond sergeant in charge of the security checkpoint by the entrance to the military offices.

Solob was so excited he forgot who had shot whom. "An Arab has been shot in the basement," he told the sergeant.

Sergeant Petty walked down the hall and reported the incident to the duty officer, Captain Michael Payne.

"There appears to be some trouble," Petty said. "Someone's been shot and I think you ought to come downstairs."

Gabe Sifrony wondered if the bangs he had just heard were backfires, shots, or a waiter dropping something. He sat at a table in the main bar with two British correspondents. Except for a British officer who stood alone at the bar, they were the only patrons.

Most of the journalists had joined the junkets to the Transjordan and Mount Scopus, leaving the Swiss bartender, Georges Ruchard, without many of his most loyal customers. He and his assistants Ahmed and Taufik busied themselves filling drink orders brought by waiters from the lobby.

Sifrony stopped a waiter. "Ask if anyone knows anything about those bangs," he said. He wanted to remain in the bar. Roderick Musgrave had promised to stop in for a drink. Sifrony planned to ask him if the British were going to release more Jewish detainees today as promised. He liked Musgrave best of all the Colonial officers. He was well informed and candid, loyal to Britain but sympathetic to Zionism.

Sifrony remembered that after the *Struma* sinking Musgrave had said, "To deny those refugees admittance was inexcusable; to allow their ship to sink was a crime."

After the end of the war he had said, "We [Britain] must follow a policy that satisfies the Jews or we will lose Palestine entirely. We lost our Colonial wars against white people and we created the Dominions to avoid fighting whites. Why should the Jews be different?"

After "The Season," when the police had captured many of the Irgun leaders, Musgrave overheard one British official telling journalists, "This is the end of the Irgun. We've got them. Got them all!"

"What does he mean 'got them all'?" Musgrave had asked Sifrony. "Doesn't he understand there'll be others to take their places?"

The waiter returned from the lobby. "What is it?" Sifrony asked.

"One of the Arab kitchen workers went crazy and shot someone in the basement."

Sifrony returned to his gin.

The officer who drank alone at the bar was Colonel Michael Fell, a dapper professional army man in his late fifties with a reputation for being utterly fearless. Fell had proved his bravery at crucial moments in the Empire's history. He had ridden with the Indian Army on the Northwest Frontier and fought in the trenches in Flanders during the First War. During the Second, he had led parties of scouts behind Rommel's lines in the Western Desert. Now he was the head of Palestine's military court. After Andrew Campbell convicted the terrorists, Fell sentenced them, sometimes to death.

In 1946 the Irgun and LEHI both "convicted" Fell of "capital crimes" against the Yishuv and ordered him "executed." He refused bodyguards but his fellow officers watched over him. One noticed that as the terrorists became bolder, he swallowed more and more aspirin with his drinks.

Gideon tipped over the glass vial. The acid began eating into the wooden plug wedged into a hole in the middle of its ebonite screw cap. Paglin, with the assistance of Chaim-Toit, had built this acid fuse. He had filled the vial with acid, sealed it with the screw cap and covered the screw cap with a bulbous wood top.

He had also drilled a hole in the wood top. Into this hole he inserted a three-quarter-inch-long, thin-walled aluminum tube—a number-eight commercial detonator. One end of the detonator—the end inside the wooden cap—was open; the other end—the end sticking outside the cap—was packed with .9 grams of fulminate, a volatile explosive.

Gideon swung the lid off one churn and inserted the vial, taking care to slide the aluminum tip into a four-inch-long, waxed paper cylinder inside the churn. Four grams of gelignite coated the sides of the cylinder. Fifty kilograms of light-brown TNT surrounded it.

He pulled three more vials from his pocket and repeated the process on three more churns. It was 12:13. The churns would explode at approximately 12:43.

Paglin had tested the fuses. It took thirty minutes for the acid to destroy the wood plug, drip into the detonator, and trigger an explosion. He had modeled the fuses on the British Army's acid (or pencil) delay switches.

Each of the army's acid switches was marked by a colored band indicating the amount of time between activation and detonation, twenty minutes for a black band, thirty for a red one, and so on. The Chief Engineer for Palestine, in a pamphlet about explosives, warned that "it is strongly emphasized that these are average times for the Middle East and in hot weather the time may be greatly reduced."

Captain Michael Payne, the duty officer, and Sergeant Petty, the guard alerted by the hotel porter, found Captain Mackintosh lying on the floor of the cloakroom. A crowd of guests and waiters had gathered around him in a circle. Someone had opened his bloody shirt and he was still conscious.

Seeing the hole in the right side of his stomach, Petty kneeled down and asked, "Who shot you?"

"Arabs in the basement," Mackintosh whispered. "I went for one and he shot me."

Someone had already summoned an ambulance. Payne called the officer in charge of the Military Police detectives and went upstairs to report the shooting to his superior, Colonel Mitford-Slade. He assumed Mackintosh had surprised some Arabs as they were stealing from the hotel's storerooms. Every army base in Palestine had problems with Arab pilferage.

"Colonel Campbell, sir, could I please borrow your Browning?"

Andrew Campbell looked up from his desk in the first floor of the Signals Annex. He was preparing for the trial of the terrorists who had attacked the Haifa Railway workshops. He had almost forgotten his conversation with General Barker earlier this morning and the Intelligence tip about a possible attack on the hotel.

His orderly, who stood in the doorway with Gunner Barber, knew he owned a Browning eight millimeter automatic. The army issued Webleys to officers but Campbell considered them wildly inaccurate.

"What do you want my Browning for?" Campbell asked. "What the bloody hell's happened?"

"Barber will tell you, sir."

"Some armed Arabs have got into the basement of the K-D and shot an officer," Barber said.

"Well, if there's trouble, I can assure you I'm not parting with my automatic. What I will do is come with you. Have you notified the security police? They should come along as well."

"Yes, sir, but they can't come."

"Why the bloody hell not?"

"Their arms are locked up. The corporal has gone off for his dinner and he's got the keys to the rifle racks."

"Well, how bloody stupid."

"Yes, sir."

Campbell put on his tartan tam-o'-shanter. "Well, let's go then. Punch You Bugger, c'mon." The dog leaped up and followed him into the garden.

On the other side of the hotel, Gunner Buckle finally found a Tommy gun in the guard's hut near the turnstile. He picked it up and inserted a magazine. Now he was ready to return to the basement.

He circled around the front of the hotel, ran down the service driveway and pulled open the green door. An Arab stood a few yards away. Buckle got a glimpse of a Sten gun before the Arab flattened himself against the wall and signaled to someone behind him.

Buckle retreated. There were more Arabs than he had thought. He needed reinforcements. He ran up the driveway, along Julian's Way and through the hotel's revolving door.

Meanwhile, downstairs in the basement, Aharon had discovered Mathilde. "Go! Go into the kitchen or I kill you!" he shouted in halting English. He tried to point his revolver but his hand, his entire body, trembled. The revolver waved up and down.

Mathilde pulled out one of the kitchen doors and crouched between it and the wall. "I was right," she thought. "Some Arab has gone berserk and is shooting people. He's probably a relative of one of the hotel workers. Perhaps if I hide he'll forget about me."

Aharon yanked open the door. His revolver still shook. "Into the kitchen!" he shouted.

This time she obeyed. The hostages gathered in the kitchen were a good cross section of the staff. She saw Mrs. Aboussouan, the assistant housekeeper, and the Italian sous-chef, Sabatino Girelli. Two Arab porters crouched under a table, their rolled rugs still balanced on their heads. Blood trickled from the head of a Sudanese. He had banged it against one of the iron grilles covering the kitchen windows while attempting to escape.

The kitchen doors swung open again and a French Army chaplain attached to the Consulate stumbled in. A waiter in the lobby had interrupted his aperitif to tell him that a man had been shot in the cellar. He had rushed downstairs to administer the last rites.

"What's happening?" he asked Mathilde.

"What do you mean 'what's happening?'? Can't you see? Terrorists are taking over the hotel."

He spoke to the man guarding the kitchen. "Let me go. I'm a priest."

"No one leaves," Avidor said.

"I give you my word of honor I won't report you. It's the job of a priest to keep secrets. You can trust me."

"I don't care if you're a priest or a watermelon." He pointed to a watermelon on one of the worktables. "No one leaves."

Mathilde began to laugh. She could not control herself. It was too amusing. The porters and their rugs, the scared boy who couldn't hold his revolver straight. Finally he had to grab it with both hands, and now the priest—a priest or a watermelon?

She began to cry. Her daughter, Amerliene, boarded with Italian nuns in a convent next to the courthouse. If this was part of an all-out terrorist attack, the courthouse where terrorists were tried and sentenced would certainly be a target.

She blamed herself. *She* had refused to be another military wife and follow her husband to Cairo. *She* had wanted to continue her career at the King David and keep her daughter in Jerusalem. *She* did not want her child's life to be like her own childhood—educated by tutors and living with aunts. Now Amerliene might not have a life at all. She cried, laughed, and then broke into sobs.

Upstairs, Gunner Buckle met Sergeant Petty in the lobby and told him that the Arab thieves were still in the basement. They walked through the lobby, down the service stairs and peered into the basement corridor. It was empty. Aharon and Avidor were in the kitchen. Gal and Gideon were in the Regence setting fuses. Amnon was in the service passageway. The others happened to be out of sight.

Petty returned to the ground-floor landing and waited. Buckle walked back upstairs, out the revolving door, and stood guard in the hotel's circular driveway. From here he could look down over a stone wall into the service driveway and see the milk truck. If any of the Arabs tried to escape up this driveway he could easily mow them down with his Tommy gun.

In the Regence, Gideon and Gal circled the churns looking for those armed with the antitampering fuses. When they located them, Gideon knelt and slid a two-inch peg from the base of each one.

Paglin had built and designed these fuses. They consisted of brass tubes, containing at one end an exploding cap of fulminate and at the other a striker attached to a spring. The spring was kept tight by a flat pin. If it was removed, the spring would propel the striker into the blasting cap.

Paglin cut a slit into the bottom of each churn and placed the devices inside in such a way that one end of the flat pin filled this slit and lay flush with the bottom of the churn.

Then he drilled a hole in the side of the churn and inserted a two-inch peg through it and into a hole in the flat pin. This prevented the flat pin from falling through the slit when the churn was picked up off the ground. This was the peg that Gideon was removing from four of the churns.

Only the floor of the Regence now held the flat pin in place. If anyone—a waiter, policeman, or army bomb-disposal expert—lifted the churns more than half an inch off the floor, the flat pin, no longer anchored by the peg, would fall out through the slit and release the striker. The striker would shoot through the brass tube and ignite the blasting cap. The TNT would explode.

Gal handed over two cardboard placards and Gideon propped them against the churns. Each carried the same message in Hebrew, English and Arabic: DANGER! BOMBS! WILL EXPLODE IF MOVED. They were meant to stop a hotel employee from touching the churns while the assault unit was leaving the basement, and to guard against the bombs exploding before the hotel had been evacuated.

Gideon relaxed. Operation Chick had succeeded. Now it did not matter if soldiers burst into the basement and killed them. The acid fuses would detonate the churns in thirty minutes; if anyone tried to lift them, they would explode immediately.

In the corridor outside the Regence, Gal gave orders for the retreat. Amnon, Avidor, and Katsina were to form a rear guard and cover the exits while the others casually ambled up the service driveway. Two minutes later they would leave as well. Eight "Arab workers" could not be seen exiting the basement at once.

Near the basement exit, Johannes Constantides, the clerk held hostage in his own office, noticed that his guard had become distracted. He climbed out from under his desk and, keeping his hands in the air, edged along the wall. He stopped when he felt the button that sounded the alarm in the Mamillah Road police station. Facing the window and keeping his hands raised, he pushed it with his bottom.

20

THE ALARM bell rang in the Mamillah Road station. A few seconds later it rang again, and stopped again.

Inspector Taylor stared at the indicator board. The light bulb next to "King David Hotel" flickered in cadence with the stuttering bell. Usually the bell gave one long and steady ring and the light remained lit. This alarm was different, more tentative. Taylor thought it might be a short circuit. The equipment was ancient, a makeshift system patched together during the war by local electricians.

He noted in the log that "the alarm rang sporadically at 12:15." He and the other officers debated how to respond. Ignore it? Dispatch one radio car to the hotel? Or send them all? The six radio cars followed routes taking them past potential terrorist targets at fixed intervals. Diverting them from their itineraries for a false alarm reduced the security afforded other buildings.

Taylor had other options. He could call a "Terrorist Alert" by activating Jerusalem's air raid sirens, or he could call out detachments of the Police Mobile Force (PMF), a paramilitary unit of policemen based on Mount Scopus and equipped with small tanks, armored cars and personnel carriers. The PMF had been trained to erect instant roadblocks and trap terrorists before they escaped from the scene of an "outrage."

The alarm kept ringing fitfully; the light bulb still flickered. Taylor and the other officers continued debating whether it was a real alarm or just a short circuit.

*   *   *

Even if Mamillah Road decided not to respond, there were already more than enough policemen and soldiers at the King David to subdue the Irgun assault unit. However, the soldiers alerted by the calls of the ATS operator thought they were dealing with Arab thieves. There was no need to call for reinforcements or evacuate the hotel simply because Arabs were stealing from the kitchens, and besides, they were having difficulty making contact with these elusive "Arabs."

Gunner Buckle stood in the main driveway, looking down into the service entrance, waiting for the "Arabs" to leave the basement.

Sergeant Petty crouched on the lobby landing of the service stairs, one flight above the basement and in a position to prevent the "Arabs" from bursting into the lobby.

Captain Payne was upstairs on the fourth floor reporting the disturbances.

Lieutenant Chambers and his test clerk guarded the female operators in the basement telephone exchange. They were outnumbered by the "Arabs" in the corridor and their only safe exit was through the window and into the garden.

Colonel Campbell and Gunner Barber were hurrying across the garden from the annex. Also in the garden was Lieutenant Tilly, who had just arrived from the East Palestine Military Police station with four corporals. He had ordered two corporals to circle the north wing of the hotel and search for the "Arabs." He and his driver had run through the turnstile and into the garden. He was friendly with Doris Hather, one of the ATS operators, and wanted to make sure she was safe.

Completely by chance, the soldiers summoned by the ATS operator happened to be blocking all the exits from the basement. Gideon's assault unit was trapped.

Gideon ran into the kitchen and addressed the hostages in English. "Stay here for five minutes, then run away," he said. "We'll shoot anyone who tries to leave sooner. Don't go into the Regence. We've put bombs in there."

He spoke rapidly. Some hostages understood some of what he said. Most did not.

Mathilde did not hear a word. When she saw the only guard had left, she planned her escape—a dash across the corridor, then through the back door and into the garden. She could hide in the basement laundry room of the workers' hostel.

She slipped into the main corridor. The "Arabs" had left. The assault unit's rear guard—Amnon, Avidor and Katsina—had withdrawn into the passageway leading to the service door. A blond soldier—Sergeant Petty—was flattened against the wall of the service stairwell.

"Where are they?" Petty asked.

"Just left," she said.

"Where to?"

She pointed to the service passageway.

In the service passageway Constantides went on pushing the alarm. He kept his arms in the air as the "Arabs" filed by the window on their way out.

At the Mamillah Road station, the bell went on ringing and the light bulb continued to flicker. Finally Inspector Taylor called a radio car on the wireless and ordered it to "investigate an incident at the K-D."

Gideon and Gal walked slowly up the service drive. No one challenged them and the hotel grounds were quiet. There were no policemen or soldiers. Unbelievably, the shots seemed to have gone unnoticed. They walked so calmly and nonchalantly that Gunner Buckle, who could see them from the wall of the main driveway above, had no reason to believe they were not genuine hotel workers, especially since Gideon wore the uniform of a Sudanese waiter.

Gal glanced back at the empty truck. "Let's take it," he said. "It's a shame to leave it behind."

Gideon debated. The plan was to retreat on foot but they could escape more quickly in the truck. The shots might still have repercussions. "All right," he finally said. "Go back and get it but be quick."

He and the others walked up the driveway. The rear guard remained in the basement.

Gal ran back, climbed into the driver's seat and pushed the starter. The engine sputtered and died.

Sergeant Petty turned the corner from the basement corridor into the service passage. An "Arab" stood in front of the service door. Petty pointed his Tommy gun and shouted, "Halt! Halt!"

The "Arab" fired and Petty jumped back into the corridor. Seconds later he peeked into the passage. The service door was open. The same "Arab" now crouched under a truck parked in the driveway. Petty aimed and fired twice.

The "Arab" answered with another burst from his Sten.

Gal heard shooting and then saw the rear guard—Avidor, Katsina, and Amnon—burst through the service door. Bullets slammed into the truck. He pushed the starter again; the engine spluttered and died. He fell to the floor of the cab as the rear guard began running up the service driveway.

As soon as Gunner Buckle heard the shooting he realized he had caught up with the "Arabs" at last. He could see them pulling guns from underneath their cloaks and firing at someone in the basement as they ran up the driveway. They were trapped in his field of fire with nowhere to hide or take cover. High stone walls flanked the seventy-five-yard service driveway. He could pick them off easily.

He unslung his Tommy gun, aimed it over the wall of the main driveway and fired. At the same time an army clerk leaned out of an upstairs window and fired down at the Arabs with a revolver.

Katsina dropped his gun and clutched his leg. A bullet nicked Yanai. Avidor, the prankster who had worn the monocle at Beit Aharon, hugged his stomach and pitched onto the asphalt. Amnon and another soldier picked him up and dragged him up the driveway. Someone in the assault unit exploded a smoke grenade and within seconds clouds of smoke had enveloped the driveway, covering the retreat.

From the window next to the revolving door Soutter and Lang could see the "Arabs" firing machine guns as they ran up the service driveway. "If we only had a gun we could have a shot," Soutter said. "But of course not to kill them," he added. "I'd only want to wound them in the legs."

Lang had worked in the King David much longer than Soutter. "Don't get excited," he said. "In Jerusalem things like this happen all the time."

Downstairs in the main kitchen one of the cooks hiding in the huge refrigerator peered out when he heard the first shots. When the gunfire continued he slammed the door shut.

The Arab rug cleaners remained squatting under the worktable. One of the cooks, Moustapha Attiye, decided to escape. He pushed out a metal grille covering a window and slithered to freedom. A soldier mistook him for one of the other "Arabs" and shot him in the right forearm. Later, the Irgun pointed to this incident as proof that British soldiers had been given orders to shoot anyone trying to leave the hotel.

The wounding of Attiye and the continued shooting outside terrified the kitchen workers. Many remained in the basement, fearful that if they tried to escape, they too would be shot. Because of the distance between workers and managers and the bitterness over recent disputes, the few who did leave the kitchen did not bother to seek out and alert Hamburger, Soutter, or the King David's other senior managers.

A few yards outside the kitchen's swinging doors, Sergeant Petty realized he was outnumbered by the "Arabs." He retreated down the corridor and dived through the open door of the telephone exchange just in time to join the operators as they climbed out the window and into the garden.

Mathilde changed her plan. She dashed back up the rear stairs to the mezzanine floor and pounded on the door of Hamburger's apartment. The maid who opened it had no idea where Hamburger was.

"Lock the door and don't go out under any circumstances," Mathilde warned. "The hotel is being attacked by terrorists!"

Throughout the hotel many came to the same conclusion. The shooting had occurred outside. It was better to stay inside than risk being gunned down in the street. The police guards closed the door of the Secretariat and ordered the frightened Jewish and Arab employees who had wanted to leave to return to their desks.

When Abu Jilda heard the gunfire and saw Gideon's men running out of the driveway, he realized for the first time that he had missed the operation.

Peri threw the taxi into reverse and sped backward down the lane to meet the assault unit. Abu Jilda grabbed the weapons from the men of the assault unit, stuffed them into sacks and tossed them into the back of the taxi. Then he and Amnon lay Avidor on the back seat and jumped onto the running boards as Peri slammed into forward and accelerated toward the Old City.

The other porters and attackers ran and limped in the same direction. The densely settled Jewish Quarter of Yemin Moshe was only a few hundred yards down the hill. Once there, they could hide in the homes and shops of relatives, friends and sympathetic strangers.

From a third-floor window in Military Headquarters, Captain Payne saw the "Arabs" running down the lane. He was reporting on the Mackintosh shooting to a group of senior officers that included General Barker.

Everyone in the room assumed these "Arabs" were the same ones who had shot Mackintosh and had broken into the basement to steal supplies. "It would have been a different story if we'd known that they were really Jews in disguise," Payne said later.

Marion Small and Sir John Shaw's private secretary, Marjorie King, watched the "Arabs" from a window in Shaw's office. It seemed to them that Arabs were always running from someone—the police, vengeful relatives, dissatisfied customers. "It didn't impress us one bit," Mrs. Small said later.

Assistant Financial Secretary William Bradley heard the shooting but could not see its source. His office, Room 115, was a floor below Shaw's but on the south side of the building. He walked next door to Jerry Cornes' office and looked out into Julian's Way. The street was quiet. An army jeep packed with soldiers approached the hotel from the south.

Through a gap in the garden wall, Lieutenant Tilly saw six "Arabs" running down the French Consulate lane. Running men meant crime; running Arabs meant theft. He drew his revolver and ran toward the gap. The barbed wire strung across it prevented him from pursuing them. "Come on!" he shouted to his driver. "Let's go after them!" They dashed back through the garden towrd their jeep.

"Calling Zebra, Charlie, Sugar, Baker."

Officer Evans, the driver and radio operator of the police armored car sent to the hotel from Mea Shearim, answered the call. He had parked in Julian's Way across from the hotel. The crew had heard shooting but decided to follow procedure and wait for orders. Now the orders came.

"Suspects have been reported climbing into a blue taxi near the K-D service entrance," the dispatcher said.

Arthur Miles climbed back into the turret. "God, I won't be much use with only a rifle," he thought.

Tha taxi sped through Yemin Moshe toward the Jaffa Gate. As the armored car closed the distance, Miles shoved his rifle through the slit in the turret and began firing.

Up ahead, two military policemen happened to be reversing a truck into the middle of the road. The taxi swerved around it but the truck kept moving. The driver of the armored car hit the brakes. The truck now blocked the road completely. The taxi had escaped.

No one shot at Gideon. No one stopped or questioned him. He left the driveway seconds before the shooting and turned left toward Julian's Way. His clothes distinguished him from the other "Arab" terrorists. Sudanese waiters often walked in the streets surrounding the hotel.

Upon reaching Julian's Way he waved to Amatzia and Shlomo, the two "Arab porters" who had pushed loaded carts from Beit Aharon earlier that morning. He also waved to Adina and Yael. Adina immediately turned and ran north toward Mamillah Road. Yael missed seeing Gideon's sign. Avinoam had told her to look for Gideon's signal, but he had also ordered her to wait until the last man left the hotel. She knew there was still one more soldier inside, her brother Gal.

She had watched in horror as a British soldier leaned out of a window and fired into the driveway. Her view was blocked so she could not see if anyone had been hit. Now she remained standing at the corner of Julian's Way, waiting for Gal, praying he would walk out of the driveway.

Gal climbed down from the truck's cabin and began walking up the service road.

The two military police corporals sent by Tilly to scout the north wing started down the service road. They met Gal halfway; his blue overalls distinguished him from the other "Arabs."

"Quick," Gal shouted in English. "The terrorists are still in the basement."

The corporals dashed through the service door. Gal continued up the service road. When he reached the top, he was shocked to see his sister standing across Julian's Way. He had not known they were both on the same operation.

Amatzia pulled a waterproof safety fuse from between the milk churns on his pushcart. It was two feet long, would burn for sixty seconds, and led to a detonator attached to a churn. All four churns contained kerosene.

He lit a cigarette, puffed, and touched the burning tip to the end of the fuse. In sixty seconds the gelignite would explode and ignite the kerosene, throwing a sheet of flame across Julian's Way. The diversion would help the assault unit escape. The flames would burn for ten minutes and prevent reinforcements from reaching the hotel from the Allenby Barracks.

Amatzia gripped the handles of the cart and waited for a break in the traffic. He planned to roll the churns into the middle of Julian's Way.

Two hundred yards to the north, Shlomo lit an identical fuse. It led through the melons and vegetables to another four cans of kerosene. This bomb would close Julian's Way to the north and block soldiers or police coming from downtown Jerusalem or the Mamillah Road station.

In sixty seconds the King David would be cut off from the rest of Jerusalem.

The radio van dispatched by Taylor to investigate the alarm sped past the intersection of Mamillah Road and Julian's Way on its way to the King David.

A number-four bus chugged up Julian's Way ahead of the police car. Most of its twenty passengers were Arab women returning to Katamon after shopping in the Old City.

Two RAF nurses, a priest and four airmen were jammed into a jeep approaching the hotel from the opposite direction. The soldiers had driven to Jerusalem from their base near Tel Aviv to order a wedding cake from the YMCA chef. One of the nurses, Kathleen Bailey, was going to marry an RAF engineer in two weeks. Her friends had come along for the excursion. They planned to order the cake and then have a celebratory lunch.

As they passed Salameh's store, Bailey saw an "Arab" push a handcart onto the shoulder of Julian's Way. Suddenly the churns burst into flames. Shards of metal flew toward the jeep. One sliced a gash in Bailey's cheek; blood spurted onto her blue blouse. The driver hit the brakes. The jeep stopped a few yards short of the YMCA.

Someone pressed a handkerchief to Bailey's cheek and stemmed the bleeding. Someone else said, "Come on, Kate, you need a brandy, we'll take you into the K-D."

The blast had also shattered Salameh's windows and rolled the number-four bus onto its side. The passengers clambered out, most with slight injuries. Policemen helped them across the street, through the turnstile and into the canteen opposite the Secretariat.

There were no sheets of flame. Amatzia's bomb had failed to ignite the kerosene; Shlomo's bomb had failed to explode. Julian's Way remained open.

The radio car sped past Shlomo's vegetables and parked next to the remains of Amatzia's milk churns. The police crew thought they had been summoned by Mamillah Road to investigate this disturbance.

21

12:20 P.M.

I NSPECTOR TAYLOR heard the explosion from the radio room of the Mamillah Road police station. He decided immediately to declare a terrorist alert. He called the Police Mobile Force down from Mount Scopus, ordered his radio cars to block streets leading from the King David, and sounded the city's air raid sirens. He noted in the log that it was exactly 12:20.

Seconds after the blast police sirens wailed, ambulance drivers rang bells and leaned on their horns, policemen on foot patrol blew whistles, the buglers of the Mobile Force sounded a charge as they raced downtown in their armored cars, and the air raid sirens screamed their piercing, stomach-churning alternating notes.

Once these sirens announced a terrorist alert, civilian vehicles had to pull over to the side of the road and stop. Automobiles, trucks, even bicycles, swerved into fields and onto sidewalks. Buses halted and passengers disembarked. Men chased sheep and donkeys into empty lots and whipped horses down alleyways. Within a minute Jerusalem's streets had cleared. Violators were arrested or, even worse, mistaken for terrorists.

Jeeps, Bren carriers and radio vans raced to the King David. Tanks and armored trucks swung across the northern and southern ends of Julian's Way and sealed off the King David from the rest of Jerusalem. Soldiers unrolled concertinas of barbed wire across the roads leading to Tel Aviv, Bethlehem, Jericho and Ramallah and sealed off Jerusalem from the rest of Palestine.

The terrorist siren ruptured the truce between British soldiers and Jewish shoppers on the Jaffa Road. The soldiers unslung rifles, formed into impromptu squads, and returned to their barracks.

Jews made last-minute purchases of food and hurried home on foot. Curfews often followed a terrorist alert, curfews that meant daytime imprisonment in sweltering apartments, neighborhoods isolated and families separated.

The sirens also forced Arab drivers off the road. During the Arab revolt, British troops had dynamited entire Arab villages suspected of harboring a single *fedayeen*, and military tribunals had condemned Arab terrorists to death. A hundred and seven were executed. Now the British High Commissioner commuted the death sentences of Jewish terrorists and instead of razed villages there was a siren that forced Jews and Arabs to stop driving.

When they heard the sirens, Britons who had lived in London during the war thought "Blitz," and then remembered it was Palestine six years later and the sirens meant Jewish terrorists, not Nazis, were trying to intimidate and kill them.

Six years ago in London, the sirens had meant an attack was imminent. People worried: "Who will be killed? My husband? My wife? My friends? Me?"

In Jerusalem these sirens meant the attack was over. Now they worried, "Who *has* been killed?"

Joan Gibbs wanted to call her husband but could not; her apartment was without a telephone. Phones were so scarce they were only allotted to political officers. Anyway, he had a strict rule: no calls at the office except in an emergency. But was this an emergency? The explosion sounded close to the King David. Had it gone off inside?

She gathered up her two infant children and hurried out the door. Her neighbors, the Sidney Daweses, had a phone. She could call the Secretariat from there.

In the Secretariat almost everyone rushed into offices overlooking Julian's Way in order to see the remains of the bomb. Two young typists, Eugenie Markarian and Hilda Azzam, edged out onto one of the narrow stone balconies in order to get a better view. In neighboring offices, typists, clerks, messengers, and Colonial officers crowded in front of windows directly overhead the Regence and the milk churns timed to explode at 12:43, in twenty-three minutes.

"They probably wanted to kill a passenger in one of the automobiles," said one of the Arab clerks.

"No. It's an attempt to kill Shaw," said another. Ever since Lord Moyne's assassination the Arabs in the Secretariat had expected terrorists to kill the Chief Secretary or High Commissioner.

The phone rang in Sir John Shaw's office. Marjorie King, who screened all of Shaw's calls, answered. It was Bill Fuller, the District Commissioner for

Samaria. Before he could explain his business, she interrupted and said, "I'm sorry, Bill, but will you please ring off? I think we're under attack." She seemed so calm that Fuller thought he had interrupted a security drill.

The bomb interrupted a meeting in Shaw's office. Peter Smith-Dorrien had been married for only a few months. He hurried off to call his wife. Meanwhile, Shaw walked into his outer office and asked Marjorie King what had happened.

"Some Arabs have let off a cracker in the street," she said. "I saw them running toward the Old City."

Shaw went to the front of the building and joined a crowd gathered by one of the windows. A bus lay on its side and soldiers were helping injured passengers into the canteen. A police car was parked near the remains of the bomb. Its crew was busy examining some blackened milk churns.

Enough police on the scene, Shaw decided. Best to leave matters to them. Too much meddling by a general could lose a battle. He remembered how Montgomery had planned his strategy for the battle of El Alamein and then retired to his caravan to sleep.

He tried to follow the same approach—set a broad policy and then avoid interfering in every minor incident. Almost every day there was another bombing and shooting. It seemed cowardly to worry about them excessively. He returned to his office.

Elsewhere in the building other Colonial officers reacted to the explosion as Shaw had: after taking a brief interest in what appeared to be a minor incident they went back to work.

On the Secretariat's first floor William Bradley told Jerry Cornes, "I'm not going to waste my time leaning out a window. I'm going back to my office."

Bradley had seen enough shooting and bombs in his lifetime. When he lived in Peru in the 1920s, dissidents regularly shot up the streets of Lima. Twenty years later he had fought in North Africa, escaped from a German prison camp and walked to freedom across the Sahara. He saw no reason to look for trouble.

"I think I'll go down and have a look as soon as I finish my files," Cornes said.

On the second floor, John Gutch heard the clerks from the confidential registry run down the corridor to the front windows. He did not join them. He wanted to finish examining and translating the day's quota of Jewish Agency cables before lunch.

He also disapproved of the way people rushed about in a crisis. He made a point of moving around the office as slowly as possible. Some considered his rate of speed to be a reliable barometer of the political climate. "The slower Gutch walks, the worse things are," was a popular office maxim.

Today Gutch stayed at his desk.

Julius Jacobs pulled open the drawer of his desk, grabbed a packet of yellowing letters and stuffed them into a black briefcase. Among them was one from former High Commissioner Harold MacMichael. It said, in part,

It was with the very greatest pleasure that I learned that His Majesty had given directions for your appointment to be an OBE [Order of the British Empire] and I send you my sincere congratulations. The work you have done for the War Supplies Board has been outstanding and of the very greatest value. . . . It is particularly gratifying that recognition should have been accorded to you.

The packet also contained dozens of letters of congratulations from friends. Jacobs was a modest man but this award and these letters had pleased him immensely. At last his decades of service to the Mandate had been appreciated. He wanted to save these precious letters from whatever catastrophe might occur.

Roderick Musgrave's third-floor corner office had been the parlor of a hotel suite. Glass doors opened from it onto a narrow balcony overlooking the street. When Musgrave heard the explosion, he opened these doors and, along with Richard Catling of the Palestine Police, stepped out and surveyed Julian's Way. Before Musgrave left the police force, he and Catling had shared a house in Tel Aviv. Whenever Catling came to the Secretariat he made a point of calling on Musgrave.

Earlier this morning Catling had met with Robert Newton, the Assistant Secretary for Political Affairs, to discuss the papers seized from the Jewish Agency during Operation Agatha. Many of these papers had turned out to be copies of secret and top-secret British diplomatic dispatches stolen by the Haganah from British consulates and embassies in Europe and the Middle East. Agatha had proved that procedures for guarding these dispatches were inadequate.

It had accomplished little else. The original Jewish Agency documents were disappointing and did not prove that the Agency was formally allied with either the Irgun or Stern Gang. They revealed nothing about the Joint Command or the X Committee.

Catling now believed Agatha had been a terrible mistake. It would not help him "whack" any of the underground groups. "Of all the papers we seized from the Jewish Agency," he said, "the few interesting ones filled only two or three briefcases, and these were really of little use."

J. G. Sheringham, a Hebrew-speaking Colonial officer who had been called back from leave in England to translate the captured papers, agreed with Catling's assessment. He said, "I don't think I came across a single piece of paper that was of the slightest interest to anyone—Jew, Arab, or Briton. They were the kind of dull papers you would find if you turned any civil servant's desk upside down."

The Haganah activists had panicked without cause. The papers contained none of the damaging revelations they had feared about the Jewish Agency and contrary to what Sadeh had told Paglin three weeks earlier, and contrary to what Paglin had told the assault unit that morning, most of these papers, unimportant as they were, were not being kept at the Secretariat, but in safes at the CID headquarters in the Russian Compound.

Four days ago Cunningham had taken the more interesting ones to London. The only Jewish Agency papers in the Secretariat at this moment were those being examined by Bob Newton and John Gutch. Newton and Gutch's offices were both in the southeast corner of the King David.

Gideon had placed the milk churns under the hotel's southwest corner, under the Secretariat's economic and personnel sections; under the Attorney General's office on the third floor and the army clerks' office on the fourth; under the offices of Mantoura, Jacobs, Musgrave, Levi, Cornes, Farley, Walsh, and Gibbs; under the "hand-picked darlings" of the confidential typing pool; under the registry where Father Antippa oversaw the dozens of Jewish and Arab messengers and clerks who filed, sorted and delivered forms, letters, reports and memoranda on post office procedures, civil servants' pay scales, land disputes and citrus prices.

The churns were near the military offices and guest bedrooms in the center of the building; near the bar where Sifrony awaited Musgrave, and Fell took aspirin between his drinks; near the Winter Garden where Leila Canaan had her first gin and the Arab Lounge where Mrs. Grey-Donald prepared social notes for the Cairo papers; and near the six-inch earthquake joint intended to prevent the entire building from collapsing.

The churns were also underneath the barbershop where Ivan Phillips was having his haircut; and underneath the windows and balconies to which the diversionary explosion had attracted Eugenie Markarian and workers from throughout the Secretariat. They were under the stone balcony on which Musgrave and Catling were now standing.

Catling saw that the bomb had blackened the street near his automobile. Duncan, his driver, appeared to be missing. "I think I'll just pop downstairs and see what's become of Duncan," he said to Musgrave.

Lubah Wahbeh, the Arab typist who was working today for George Farley for the first time, also decided to go downstairs after hearing the explosion. She wasted no time wondering who had set off the bomb or why. Her first thought was, "There may be another bomb inside the building."

She dashed down two flights of stairs to the ground floor. The side door, the only exit from the Secretariat, was closed and the police guard refused to open it. "We may be under attack," he explained. "We're keeping it closed until we're positive the terrorists have gone."

Sometimes as a child Lubah had become so afraid that her legs shook uncontrollably. Now it happened again, this time so badly that she couldn't walk. She leaned against a dustbin and waited for the terror to pass.

The hotel's revolving door remained open. Guests, soldiers and lunchtime visitors pushed through as if nothing had happened.

Upstairs in the military offices, Major Ernest Quinn leaped up from behind his desk and ran to the window the moment he heard the blast. He saw a WRAF nurse running toward the hotel, her hands covering her face, blood on her blouse.

"Christ, Harry, what's happened?" he asked Golda Meyerson's representative. "Your talks with the dissidents haven't done much bloody good, have they?"

Harry Beilin was just as shocked and surprised as Quinn. "Well . . . well . . . I just can't understand it," he stammered. "I know she did it . . . I know she told them we couldn't do anything to embarrass the Old Man while he was in London."

Down the hall from Quinn, General Barker poked his head into the office of one of his aides and ordered him to "send a man downstairs to find out what all that damned racket is about."

ATS officer Honor Sharman was not as blasé. She had only come to Palestine a few months ago to join her husband. Bombings and shootings still frightened her. She rushed to the balcony of her office and looked down into the garden. An elderly Colonial officer, with revolver drawn, was creeping about peeking under shrubs and peering around palm trees. It struck her as another comic example of the attitude toward security and terrorism, like the recent order that British officers should sleep with a loaded revolver near their beds, preferably under the pillow.

Captain Dan Ben-Dor, the Jewish architect and engineer, adjourned his meeting on fire safety and hurried down to the street to inspect the remains of the bomb. He had a professional interest in the construction of the terrorists' devices.

He elbowed through a crowd and poked at the charred remains with his foot. "An extremely crude, homemade device," he announced.

Gabe Sifrony ran through the revolving door and out into Julian's Way. A wire service photographer was taking pictures of Salameh's store. Dan Ben-Dor kicked at the blackened churns.

"It must have been part of an attack on the hotel," Sifrony said to Ben-Dor. "Apparently it failed."

Ben-Dor opposed terrorism. He suspected that Sifrony did not. As the two men strolled back along Julian's Way, they debated its morality.

Sami Hadawi, the Arab expert on Jewish carp ponds, saw men in Arab dress running down Julian's Way. He assumed they were Arabs afraid of being detained during a police sweep. He was too far from the hotel to see where the bomb had exploded. It could be the David Brothers Building, the YMCA, or the King David. He decided to return to Spinney's garage and wait until Julian's Way calmed before setting out again for the Secretariat.

Katy Antonius continued walking up Julian's Way toward the King David. Bombs were not going to prevent her from attending Richard Graves's luncheon party.

She passed two British officers leaning against the wall of a shop. "Where are you going, Mrs. Antonius?" one asked.

"To the Regence for lunch. At *last* Dick Graves is giving a party."

"Oh you'll never see the K-D again. Don't go any nearer."

Katy saw that he was smiling. A joke. "You mean Graves is going to be let off? This is the first time he's given us a party." She laughed and kept on walking.

A quarter of a mile north of the King David, the bomb rattled the windows of the St. Julian's Hotel. *New York Post* correspondent Richard Mowrer had spent the morning in one of the hotel's small stuffy bedrooms staring at his typewriter. In a few hours he had to cable his weekly column to New York. He was stumped. The last week had been the most uneventful in months.

He was unaccustomed to such calm. He had covered the Spanish Civil War, the German bombing of Warsaw and the important campaigns of the Second World War for the Chicago *Daily News*. He had been injured once, scratched by bomb fragments during the North African battle of Mersa Matrûh.

His paper, the *New York Post*, had a large Jewish readership and followed events in Palestine closely. Of all New York's newspapers, it was the most sympathetic to Zionism and the Jewish underground groups. It frequently carried fund-raising advertisements for the American League for a Free Palestine (ALFP), which was an American front for the Irgun.

The explosion gave Mowrer an excuse to escape from his stifling room. He left the hotel and walked south along Julian's Way toward the King David.

Atallah Mantoura's son Jack heard the sirens from a Jewish optician's shop on the Jaffa Road. He and Oplatka, a Jewish boy his age, had been at the optician's since mid-morning checking the prices of lenses and frames against those permitted by the Price Commission. His father had got him this job after he was expelled from a Jesuit university in Beirut for "misconduct."

He liked working for the Price Commission and spent his salary visiting Jewish cinemas and cafés. In Jerusalem, unlike Beirut, an Arab playboy had to go to Jewish neighborhoods for his nightlife, and he had come to prefer young Jews like Oplatka as companions. They were better educated than Arabs and he liked "talking and drinking with them because they understood things that I understood."

Atallah encouraged these friendships. When Jack was a child his father had often scolded him for playing with Arab street boys. They were "beneath him." He also discouraged his son from befriending the few politically aware Arabs of his generation. They were "wild extremists."

Until recently, Jack Mantoura had found his father cold and unapproachable. Then last summer he had worked in Jerusalem. Every morning, as they walked together to their respective offices, his father explained for the first time why he believed there was no future for Arabs in Palestine, why the British, not the Jews, were their real enemies, and why he nevertheless worked for Britain and accepted its offer of citizenship.

For the first time Jack Mantoura had begun to understand his father, and to love him.

The sound of the explosion carried as far as the Old City. In the Jaffa Gate police station the police barber stopped running his clippers over Ian Proud's neck. Proud ripped off the white smock, rushed to the nearest telephone and called the Mamillah Road Station.

"What's happened?" he shouted into the phone.

"A small bomb has exploded near the K-D," Taylor said.

"I'm on my way."

Twice Proud had nearly been killed by terrorist bombs. In 1944 he had gone to the Eden Cinema to see Tyrone Power in *Blood and Sand*. When the film ended and the house lights went on, he saw that High Commissioner Harold MacMichael's two teenage daughters had been sitting in the row behind him. Two minutes after he left an explosion rocked the theater. The Stern Gang had slipped a bomb under the girls' seats. No one was injured.

A month later the Irgun planted a bomb in a government office. As Proud walked through the door to investigate, another bomb exploded. It was the first and only time he could remember a two-stage terrorist bombing. Usually Jewish terrorists favored short fuses and single bombs. Long fuses and multiple bombs posed a danger to Jewish civilians.

Proud dashed out of the Jaffa Road station. There were no police cars in sight. He suddenly remembered that because terrorists wired explosives to the undercarriages of unguarded police cars the idle ones were parked under guard in a special lot a few blocks away. He decided it would be quicker to run to the hotel.

When Assistant Superintendent Stacey Barham heard the muffled explosion, he looked out his second-floor window in the Jaffa Gate police station in time to see a column of smoke rising over the YMCA tower.

"Salameh! By God, boys, they've done it. They've blown up poor old George Salameh," he said to the three detective sergeants assigned to his criminal investigation squad.

He reached into his pocket. A letter from Arab terrorists threatening Salameh was still there. CID Chief Arthur Giles had handed it to him two days ago.

Last month Arab leaders had announced a commercial boycott. Arabs were forbidden to patronize Jewish stores; Arab merchants were forbidden to serve Jews. George Salameh refused to comply. He had too many Jewish customers. He also had customers among the British police. "Salameh is a friend," Giles had said, "make sure your Jerusalem CID looks out for him."

Until now Barham had almost forgotten the letter. He was chief of

Jerusalem's CID and one of the busiest police officers in Palestine, responsible for investigating common crimes such as robbery and murder as well as terrorism.

His experience in Palestine had prepared him well for the struggle against terrorism. He spoke fluent Hebrew and had spent most of his thirteen years in Palestine working in Jewish districts. He liked the Jews and was especially fond of the farmers—"splendid chaps."

During the Arab revolt, he had ridden on night patrols to isolated Jewish settlements. He still remembered the wine, dancing and song around blazing fires. Jewish terrorism had not changed his fondness for the Jews. He took pains to distinguish among the underground groups.

"The Stern Gang practice random murder. They'd shoot me or any Palestine policeman anytime, anywhere," he was fond of saying. "The Irgun is paramilitary. They'd shoot me if I was in their way. The Haganah are not terrorists. Practically every Jew in Palestine belongs."

He even saw some good in the Stern Gang and Irgun, considering them "half villain and half Boy Scout." He admired the Boy Scout side—the loyalty and honesty among their membership. He learned about the villain side in 1944 when he flew to Cairo to question the Stern Gang teenagers accused of murdering Lord Moyne. He was surprised to find them "literate young chaps from good Jewish families," not like the friendly farmers he had known during the Arab revolt.

"Why did you shoot Moyne so many times?" he had asked one of the young assassins.

"I always shot three bullets in practice," the boy answered. "What's the difference?"

He asked the other boy, "What do you think you could possibly gain from this terrible murder? How do you expect to intimidate the British, a people who have been standing up to all of this incredible bombing?"

"What do you mean?" the boy answered. "The bombing by the Irish?"

Barham realized he had just been given a short lesson in the political philosophy of Abraham Stern and Menahem Begin.

He was certain today's bombing was "an Arab show." The smoke came from the vicinity of Salameh's store and besides, he had the threatening letter in his pocket.

"Come on, boys," he said to his sergeants. "We'd better go and have a look. I want to make sure Salameh is safe."

Colonel Andrew Campbell stood with his dog, Punch You Bugger, in the hotel garden, level with the window of the telephone exchange. An ATS operator leaned out and hailed him.

"What's going on in there?" Campbell shouted. "Did you hear that explosion?"

"Yes, sir. And there's been some shooting in the basement. An officer was shot by Arabs. What should we do?"

"Come out of there."

"Oh, but we can't, sir."

"Well, why not?"

"We've been ordered to stay on duty."

"Nonsense, I'm ordering you to come out at once."

He was worried the "Arabs" might burst in and shoot up the exchange, if they were still in the basement, if in fact they were Arabs. And why would Arabs, he wondered, set off a bomb in the road or shoot a British officer?

Sergeant Petty climbed out the window with the operators. "I saw them, sir," he said. "The armed men dressed as Arabs." He was so excited and spoke so rapidly that Campbell had trouble understanding him.

"But *were* they Arabs?" Campbell asked.

"I don't know. I don't know who they were. One hid under a truck. He's the one that took a shot at me. They shot a Signals officer but they treated him well, carried him upstairs and laid him on the floor of the gents' cloakroom. I saw him there. I don't know what's happening but I know where to find them."

"Where?"

"In the corridor."

"Let's go and have a look. You take me there." He was not sure which part of the hotel Petty meant.

As Petty led Campbell and Punch through the garden and toward the service driveway, officers leaned out of windows above them cheering and shouting encouragement.

"Go on, Andrew, fix the buggers!" one yelled.

"My God," Campbell thought. "They think it's a huge joke."

Just outside the service driveway Campbell flagged down Lieutenant Tilly as he drove by in his jeep.

"Come give us a hand," Campbell said. "Some Arabs have shot an officer and locked themselves in the basement."

"I just saw them jump into a blue taxi and tear off toward the Old City," Tilly answered. "We're hoping to chase them down." He sped off as Campbell and Petty ran down the service driveway. They planned to give the basement a thorough search in case some of the "Arabs" were still hiding there.

Because Campbell and Petty had missed seeing the "Arabs" retreating, they were the only soldiers still searching for them on the grounds of the King David, and the only ones still interested in checking out the basement. Everyone else summoned by ATS operator Smith was chasing the "Arabs" into the Old City or had returned to their normal occupations.

Most of the 400 soldiers quartered in the army camp behind the King David had heard the air raid sirens but not the explosion that preceded them. Bettina Peters, an army film producer from Cairo, was visiting the camp to make a film showing how the troops in Palestine coped with Jewish terrorism. The soldiers thought the alarm was a police exercise staged for her benefit and remained in their camp.

To most, the terrorist siren meant that the worst was over, the damage done. To those in the hotel it appeared that the army had beaten off a raid on the hotel. Now it was up to policemen such as Stacey Barham and Ian Proud to decide what had occurred, write up their reports and perhaps arrest the "Arab" thieves.

Hotel patrons who had walked, drinks in hand, into the circular driveway to see what had happened, returned to the lobby.

Upstairs in the military and government offices, workers tried to finish meetings and files so they could leave promptly for lunch. Workers in the Secretariat went for lunch at 2:00; those in the military offices broke earlier, at 1:00—seventeen minutes after the churns were timed to explode.

22

12:21—12:31 P.M.

ADINA SLIPPED into the Arab pharmacy on Julian's Way. The explosion had drawn the handsome young Arab chemist outside, where he stood in the middle of the street staring at the hotel.

The phone sat on a counter in the rear of the store. She lifted the receiver and dialed 1 . . . 1 . . . 1 . . . 4. After two rings a male voice answered. "King David Hotel."

She spoke rapidly in Hebrew. "This is the Hebrew Resistance Movement. We have placed a bomb in the hotel. The building is going to blow up. You must evacuate immediately. You have been warned." She repeated the message in English, and then hung up and ran out of the store. It was 12:22.

Gideon stopped next to the YMCA soccer field and pulled off his waiter's uniform. Underneath he wore a white shirt and khaki trousers. He rolled the uniform into a ball and stuffed it into a hole near the wire fence surrounding the field. He stood up and looked around. When he was certain no one had seen him he began walking toward King George V Avenue. Just another skinny Jewish boy.

Yael could see Gal clutching his side as he crossed Julian's Way. By the time they met opposite the Shell station he was shaking and almost bent double.

"I'm wounded," he said. "Feel the blood."

Yael slid a hand under his overalls and patted his stomach and chest. She removed her hand. It was wet. "It's perspiration, not blood," she said. "You're not wounded, just excited."

Gal was embarrassed. "I was the last one to leave," he said.

"Give me your pistol and grenades." She knew the penalty for carrying weapons was death. After the explosion it was certain to be enforced. But the British would never hang a girl.

Gal ran behind the YMCA. Yael put the pistol into her handbag and tucked the grenades into her blouse. She stepped back onto her corner in time to see Adina running toward King George V Avenue.

The assault unit escaped. Yanai disappeared into the Old City. Later Gideon learned that the police had arrested and then, mysteriously, released him.

Abu Jilda and Amnon jumped off the taxi's running boards in Yemin Moshe. Peri drove into the Old City with Ariela and the wounded. Amnon hid at a friend's house for a few minutes and then returned to his job at the dental laboratory. Abu Jilda leaped onto a moving bus, got off in a Jewish neighborhood and set off for the prearranged meeting point in Givat Shaul.

Lieutenant Tilly had never come close to catching the fleeing "Arabs." He gave up and returned to the hotel to collect his men.

The corporals he had sent to scout the north wing looked up and down the basement corridor before concluding that the Arab terrorists had escaped. They walked up the service stairs to the lobby without searching the main kitchen or Regence.

Colonel Campbell and Sergeant Petty peered under the abandoned milk truck in the service driveway. Nine-millimeter cartridge cases littered the pavement. One of the "Arabs" had dropped a headdress and a sugar sack. Campbell picked them up and pulled a Sten gun cartridge out of the sack.

"Jews," he thought. "Jews dressed as Arabs." The ammunition convinced him.

"There are bound to be more terrorists inside," he said aloud. He banged on the service door with his fist. It swung open and he and Petty stood back. No one came out.

"Come on," he said. "Let's go in and find them."

Mathilde found Hamburger standing next to the reception desk talking with Fakitas, the accountant. "Be careful," she said. "The hotel is full of terrorists."

Hamburger shrugged. "There's something going on outside, a small bomb exploded in the road. It's nothing to do with us. Things like this happen all the time."

"No! No! I saw them with my own eyes. They took me hostage."

Without a word, Hamburger walked outside to question the army guards stationed in the driveway.

In the main dining room first maitre d'hôtel Naim Nissan made his final inspections. He walked between tables, counting settings, polishing a smudged utensil and rearranging the flowers. He flicked dust from the china and turned each plate so that its emblem, King David's Tower, would face the diner. He examined the linen tablecloths for stains and measured their placement on the table with a ruler.

Meanwhile, the hotel's senior staff was arriving in the dining room for lunch. Fakitas and his wife took seats at a small corner table. Ubelhardt, the reception clerks and others filled the chairs at a round *table de famille*.

The room was strangely quiet. Soon everyone had turned and was staring at the swinging doors leading to the pantry. Usually waiters hurried through these doors bringing up trays of food from the basement kitchens. Today the doors remained closed. There was nothing to eat.

A page appeared from the lobby and said, "There's a call for Mr. Nissan at the switchboard."

The telephone switchboard and two wooden cubicles were jammed into a cubbyhole under the main staircase. Nissan waited for Emile Kary, the young Arab operator, to finish taking a call and direct him to one of the cubicles.

Kary pushed his chair away from the desk. His legs shook and his face was chalk white. "She told me they've put bombs in the hotel," he said, pointing to the switchboard. "She said they're going to blow it up!"

"Who said?" Nissan asked.

"A woman . . . the Resistance!"

Nissan dashed through the lobby, past startled guests, and into Hamburger's office. Hamburger was preparing to leave for lunch. "I've just been at the switchboard," Nissan blurted out. "Someone called and said that bombs have been placed in the hotel."

The army guards had just assured Hamburger that the shootings had occurred outside. The small explosion had also been outside. The hotel seemed to be in no danger. He tried to calm Nissan. "You know there have been so many false alarms in Jerusalem. . . ."

Nissan interrupted. "Why take a chance? Call somebody."

The manager lifted a telephone connected to the military headquarters. Someone answered immediately.

"This is Hamburger. I've received a message that there's a bomb in the hotel." He paused to listen.

"Yes, that's right. The message was phoned into the hotel switchboard." He paused again.

"When? Only a few minutes ago. What shall I do? Shall I warn everyone? Evacuate the hotel?" Another pause.

"Yes . . . yes. . . . Fine. All right. Good-bye."

"What did he say?" Nissan asked.

"He said, 'It's easy to *say* there's a bomb.'"

"Do we evacuate?"

"No. He said it would cause a panic. Don't tell anyone. No one is going to leave."

At the time, Nissan did not ask Hamburger the name of the British officer with whom he had spoken. A few days later Hamburger told Nissan that this Briton had feared the bomb warning was a hoax designed to trick them into evacuating. Once the British were in the street they could easily be ambushed. This possibility had seemed more likely than that the Irgun had succeeded in placing a bomb inside the King David.

By the summer of 1946, so many bomb warnings had turned out to be hoaxes that many British considered them threats meant to terrorize and intimidate rather than genuine warnings given to minimize casualties. They seemed similar to the "warnings" given during the war by Axis propagandists such as "Lord-Haw-Haw" and "Tokyo Rose."

In April, for example, the Irgun had published posters proclaiming:

> WARNING!
> 1. The Government of oppression should WITHOUT ANY DELAY evacuate children, women, civilian persons and officials from all its offices, buildings, dwelling places, etc. throughout the country.
> 2. The civilian population, Hebrews, Arabs and others are asked for their own sake, to abstain from now and until the warning is recalled, from visiting or nearing Government offices, etc.
> YOU HAVE BEEN WARNED!

Clearly, this was more threat than warning. The British, who had not been intimidated by Nazi threats, were likewise determined not to be intimidated by Jewish ones. Hence, by July 1946, many "warnings" were being disregarded, as the Irgun well knew.

Adina bounded up the steep hill separating King George V Avenue from the King David Hotel. The hill was a no-man's land of loose dirt, rocks and wild olive trees. She stumbled, recovered, stumbled again and kept running as if in a race. She had not made a second call from the Arab pharmacy because she feared giving the police time to trace it.

She did not notice Yael following her. Halfway up the hill Yael stopped, bent down, and shoved her brother's hand grenades under a rock. The pistol was too valuable to throw away. She kept it.

Adina reached King George V Avenue and turned left toward the Jaffa Road. The roof of the King David was visible over her left shoulder. The siren had halted traffic and the sidewalks were crowded. She hurried along, darting around pedestrians, a beautiful, dark-haired girl trying to get home before curfew.

She slipped into a telephone booth and slammed the door. All morning she had clutched a token in her fist. She shoved it into the slot and dialed 29.

"Consulat-General de France," a voice answered.

"This is the Hebrew Resistance Movement. We have placed a bomb in the

King David Hotel and warned them to evacuate the building. Open your windows so you will not be harmed by the blast." She gave the warning first in French, then in Hebrew. Without waiting for an answer she hung up and ran north on King George V Avenue toward the Jaffa Road.

It was 12:27.

Benjamin Cohen-Arounoff hurried to the second floor to report the call to Consul-General Neuville. They raced through the Consulate throwing open windows and closing curtains.

Next door to the French Consulate in the Secretariat Annex, Helen Rossi stared out her office window into the King David's garden and worried about Geoffrey Walsh and her other friends in the Secretariat.

She thought that Walsh was "the very best kind of Englishman." For four years they had worked together in the Office of Food Control. At first she had reservations about working for the Mandate. She had emigrated from the United States and, as much as any Palestinian Jew, detested the White Paper. Walsh, however, had won her over.

In her opinion, no Christian-British civil servant in Palestine had done more to promote Jewish welfare. Walsh's greatest achievement had been the encouragement of the Jewish diamond industry. He had founded the Palestine Diamond Board and fought for the admission to Palestine of Jewish refugees who had been cutters and polishers in Antwerp, Amsterdam and other Nazi-occupied European cities.

Ever since hearing gunfire and a muffled explosion she had kept glancing out her window and worrying about Walsh. She had seen the ATS operators climb out their window and mill about the garden and the British soldiers race in and out of the Signals Annex. She worried more than ever when a Christian Arab who worked in the Secretariat joined her at the window and said, "Something is wrong but those bastards guarding the door won't let anyone leave."

Near the lobby reception desk Naim Nissan stopped Emile Kary, who had finished his shift and was leaving for lunch. A young Arab woman, Mathilde Raitan, had replaced him at the switchboard. Nissan asked Kary to repeat the warning.

"She said in two languages, in Hebrew and English, that bombs had been placed in the hotel and it was going to explode. . . . What are we going to do?"

"Nothing," Nissan said.

"Nothing?"

"Don't worry. We've had so many false alarms in Jerusalem. We're certain this is another one. By the way, you remember who called me earlier? You know, the call I never answered."

"It was Mr. Albana. He wants a special table for a party of ten on Saturday night."

Before leaving, Kary reported the warning call to Emile Soutter. He found him standing in the lobby, discussing the shootings with a Jewish guest.

"Mr. Soutter," Kary said. "I've just received a call from a woman who says the hotel is mined with bombs."

Although Soutter had only lived in Jerusalem for four months, he knew all about the bomb warnings. Every day the concierge or his page boys returned late from their errands complaining of being delayed by these warnings. Since the frustrated strike of the Arab and Jewish civil servants in April, the number of these warnings had increased dramatically. The employees or their relatives liked to call them in at about noon. That way, after the police evacuated the building, the workers could go home for an early lunch.

Jews also called in bomb warnings to humiliate the British. It was amusing to see the British civil servants run out of buildings and then stand nervously on street corners waiting for explosions that never came.

Although the King David was one of the few large buildings in Jerusalem that had escaped warnings, Soutter knew all about them from personal experience. Last month he and his wife had been standing in a line at Barclays Bank when a bomb warning forced them to evacuate. A trip to the post office a few minutes later was interrupted by another hoax.

Soutter remembered the panic caused by these sudden evacuations. He did not want to be responsible for a similar fiasco at the King David. Furthermore, there had just been shootings and a bombing in the streets outside. Was it wise to send hundreds of people rushing into Julian's Way?

"Listen," he told Kary. "The post office is mined with bombs every day. Everything in Jerusalem is always mined with bombs and nothing ever happens. The call is another hoax. Forget it."

Adina relaxed. The most important calls had been made. She walked into a Jewish store to make the last one. Yael, who had kept a distance between herself and Adina, waited outside. If Adina was arrested, she had to be free to telephone the warning.

Adina ran from the store and saw Yael for the first time. "Yael!" she said. "The owner stopped me calling when he heard the word 'Irgun.'"

Yael knew what to do. "Come with me," she said. "There's a store nearby where people are sympathetic. One of my brothers works there."

A minute later Adina dialed the *Palestine Post* from the rear of Moshinsky's, a paint and hardware store on the Jaffa Road. She spoke more clearly and recited her message only once and in Hebrew: "This is the Hebrew Resistance Movement. We have placed a bomb in the King David Hotel and have called to warn them. You must warn them as well."

It was 12:31.

As they left, Yael tried to pay for the call with a pile of small coins. The owner, knowing she was on Irgun business, refused to accept her money. The call was free, he said.

Devorah Ledener, the attractive redheaded operator at the *Palestine Post,* dialed the Palestine Police CID.

A busy signal.

She dialed again.

Five rings . . . ten rings. She looked at her watch. Thirty seconds . . . forty-five seconds. . . .

She liked to pass bomb threats on to the police immediately. This was about the twentieth she had received during the last two months. Every one had been a hoax. After the first threat she had run screaming into the editorial offices. Now she reported them to the CID and forgot them. Many of the "targets" were army camps and government offices whose numbers were new or unlisted. Only the CID knew how to contact them.

Sixty seconds. Still no answer. Usually they picked up after a few rings. Thinking she'd dialed a wrong number she hung up and dialed again. For the first time in months she was nervous about a bomb threat.

Stacey Barham stared at the remains of Salameh's window. He was right; they had been after Salameh. The bomb had exploded in front of his store, shattering his windows and damaging his curios.

Salameh knelt on the pavement separating his brass trays, rosaries, olive-wood crosses, Bibles and postcards from shards of glass. He denied being the target.

Barham was incredulous. "How the hell can you say that it's not against you? You had this threatening letter, I've even got it in my pocket, and the bomb's exploded on your doorstep. Look at your bloody shop!"

"It wasn't against me, Mr. Barham," Salameh protested. "There was also shooting down the road, near the hotel."

Barham pointed at the bullet holes in the shutters. "Look at these bloody holes. They're bullet holes and they're in *your* shop."

"No, no, no, Mr. Barham, fragments from the bomb. It's nothing to do with me. There's been shooting elsewhere."

While Barham was talking with Salameh, his three detectives returned from checking the Secretariat and the lobby. One reported that, according to an assistant manager, a British officer had tried to commit suicide in the basement. An ambulance had taken him to the hospital.

Barham saw Dick Catling standing in the hotel's circular driveway. He gave up on Salameh and walked over to discuss the bombing with Catling. He would know if something important had happened.

"What's going on, Stacey?" Catling asked.

"We have a letter threatening Salameh over the Arab boycott but he doesn't think they're after him. Busey and company [the detectives] have been inside the hotel and nothing is going on there, except a shooting incident. Army chap shot himself and he's been taken to hospital."

"What are you going to do?"

"I can't see any purpose in keeping the alarm on. I'm going to blow the all clear."

23

12:32—12:35 P.M.

THE SIRENS blew a long straight blast: all clear. Traffic moved again along Julian's Way and the police guards opened the door to the Secretariat. Workers and visitors telephoned relatives to assure them they were safe. The emergency was over.

A British officer in the Arab Legion even called his wife in Amman. He was afraid she would learn of the incident from someone else and worry.

Eugenie Markarian climbed in off the stone balcony where she had been standing and called her sister, Sophie, who lived a half-mile away on Princess Mary Avenue. Eugenie knew she would have heard the bomb.

"Thank God you called," Sophie said. "Are you sure you're all right?"

"Yes, but what a shock we had. I was cut by some flying glass because our window shattered. But don't worry. They gave me first aid and I'm fine."

"Oh Eugenie, why don't you come home? Why not leave now?"

"Oh, we're safe enough. We've been told we'll be safe if we stay inside. Tell Mother and the aunts I'm all right."

"Look after yourself, dear, and try to come home as soon as you can."

Many people felt as Eugenie did: the worst was over but it was probably safer to stay inside the King David. Work continued and meetings resumed.

Julius Jacobs had scheduled an economic meeting for 12:30 and Smith-Dorrien, Gibbs and Jacobs stood in his office waiting for it to begin. Marion Small, the British woman in charge of the top secret files, arrived in Jacobs' office carrying a stack of economic policy files. Someone apologized for forgetting to request a particular file and she went back upstairs to fetch it.

On the stairway she met the Postmaster-General, Gerald Kennedy, a genial man in his late fifties. She was fond of Kennedy but today she cut short their pleasantries. She had worked all day Sunday and was determined to leave the Secretariat by one o'clock. She had promised her husband, Dennis, an army dentist, to be home for lunch.

A few offices down the hall from Jacobs' office, Geoffrey Walsh and Omar Bisharat ended their negotiations on the price of sheep. Walsh suggested they conclude the deal with a drink at the bar.

The telephone rang as they were leaving the office. Walsh ran back. "This should only take a few minutes," he said, putting his hand over the mouthpiece. "You go ahead and I'll meet you downstairs."

In the street outside the hotel, Sifrony and Ben-Dor finished their argument about terrorism. The roads were open and Ben-Dor wanted to return to the Allenby Barracks for lunch. He walked into the parking lot behind the YMCA. His Great Dane, Assad II, sat patiently in the back seat of the Austin.

Sifrony noticed about a dozen people standing on the steps of the Y. He strolled over and asked Miller, the Y's American director, if he had seen the explosion.

"No," he said. "But what do they want from us? Why would they attack us?"

"What are you talking about?"

"Look, isn't it obvious? The bomb practically exploded on our doorstep."

"Don't be silly. Nobody cares about the Y."

"Oh. . . ." Miller was insulted. "Well, I suppose you're right. Of course we're not involved in anything."

Sifrony decided to return to the main bar. He would report that the army had beaten off a terrorist attack.

As he walked away, Richard Mowrer of the *New York Post* was poking at the remains of the bomb. It had left a black smudge on the pavement and scorched a nearby tree. There was nothing here to fill his column. He started back to his hotel.

Ian Proud picked up a piece of the blackened milk churn, tossed it back on the ground, and then walked over to the turnstile.

The corporal on guard said, "I don't know anything. I just came on duty. Ask the Arab chap."

The Arab Legionnaire said, "I heard shots near the north wing."

Proud gave up. The all clear had sounded. Whatever had happened was over. He started walking back to the Jaffa station. There was still time to finish his haircut before lunch.

Katy Antonius found her daughter sobbing in front of the hotel. She had been near Salameh's when the bomb exploded. Other members of Richard Graves's lunch party were comforting her. Graves had not arrived.

Katy hugged her. "Let's go to an Arab restaurant," she said. "There's too much trouble here."

The others agreed. Katy laughed as they started down Julian's Way. "Well," she said, "I guess Graves has avoided giving us lunch."

The wife of Kenneth Hadingham, Jerusalem's Superintendent of Police, lived on the ground floor of a house near the olive grove that separated the German Colony from the King David. After the explosion, an Arab woman from the second floor ran downstairs to her apartment and said, "Come join my family. If we stand on the roof we can see what's happening."

Mrs. Hadingham accepted. She knew the blast would bring her husband to the King David.

Superintendent Hadingham stood in the driveway of the hotel surrounded by the handful of soldiers, waiters, and guests who had not yet bothered to return to the lobby. No one could explain the ambulance Hadingham had seen leaving the hotel a few minutes before. No one had been in the basement and no one had seen the explosion of the incendiary bomb in front of Salameh's.

Hadingham had often faced this type of exasperating situation since joining the Palestine Police thirteen years before. He had been "fed up with working in a London office" and now, at the age of thirty-three, he was superintendent of the Jerusalem District, in military terms a rank equivalent to Lieutenant Colonel. His command encompassed Proud's Urban Division, Barham's CID and numerous other departments and adjoining rural areas.

He loved Palestine so much he was planning to buy a house there for his retirement. In his opinion, the Palestine Police were performing a mission "that had challenged men for thousands of years, that of bringing peace to the Holy Land." He saw himself facing the same problems that had confronted Roman Legionaries two thousand years before, "the same troublesome atmosphere, the same troublesome people."

Hadingham looked over the heads of the waiters and guests in the driveway to see Hamburger striding toward him. He thought the manager appeared "concerned but not terribly worried. Despite the heat, his trousers had kept their crease and his hair was slicked down, perfectly parted."

"An army officer has been shot in the basement," Hamburger said. "He's already been taken off to hospital."

Before Hadingham could react, a European cook pushed through the crowd and shouted, "Ten Jews dressed as Arabs held me and the other kitchen workers hostage in the basement."

Without a word Hadingham turned on his heel and, with Hamburger following, hurried toward the service entrance. To get there he had to walk seventy-five yards down Julian's Way, twenty-five yards down the lane, and then another seventy-five yards down the service driveway. It would take at least ninety seconds.

It was 12:33.

In the basement corridor a crowd of kitchen workers gathered around Campbell, Petty and Punch. They shouted, waved their arms, jumped in the air and pushed each other aside to get their attention. They spoke in Arabic, Greek, Italian, Hebrew and French. Some yelled almost unintelligible phrases of English.

". . . said we'd be killed. . . ."

"Who said?" Campbell asked.

"Men in Arab clothes."

"Where are they now?"

"Milk cans."

"Where are they *now*?" he repeated.

It was no use. No one spoke enough English. Campbell and Petty did not speak any foreign languages. They glanced up and down the corridor. The terrorists had escaped but one had dropped a Sten gun. Campbell picked it up. A round was jammed in its breech.

He tried questioning the workers again. The same answers. He gave up and went outside to find an interpreter.

"CID."

Devorah Ledener relaxed. Finally she had reached the police. "This is the *Palestine Post* operator. I've just had a call informing me that a bomb has been placed in the King David."

The officer thanked her and hung up.

About a minute later she dialed the King David. Mathilde Raitan, the hotel's switchboard operator, was a friend and she wanted to be sure she learned about the warning.

The phone kept ringing. It was impossible. She had never known the King David not to answer.

Six years before, Mathilde Raitan had received one of Hamburger's famous disciplinary notes. It criticized her for writing telephone messages on the wrong kind of paper. "You have specially printed forms at your disposal," it said, "and I am at a loss to understand how you presume to use any kind of already used paper for the transmission of such messages to one of our guests."

It also criticized her for taking too long to transmit these telephone messages. "Although this message was taken by you in the morning, it was not delivered to Captain Rosselli until late afternoon."

Hamburger fined her half a Palestine pound and threatened that if it happened again, he would "not hesitate to dismiss [her] from the services of the King David Hotel."

Emile Kary had told Mathilde about the bomb warning when he turned over the switchboard. She wanted to be certain that this important message was properly transmitted. She left the switchboard to deliver it to one of the managers in person.

She found Soutter in the lobby. "We've received a call about a bomb in the hotel saying that we must evacuate," she said.

"Thank you very much, but I've heard that one before," he said. "Go back to your switchboard."

Soutter immediately reported the call to the concierge, Edward Lang. "They play that game all over Jerusalem just to create panic," Lang said.

A minute later Mathilde Raitan returned to the lobby. Soutter saw she was trembling. "W . . . we j . . . just received another call about a b . . . bomb," she stuttered. The police had forwarded Devorah Ledener's call from the *Palestine Post*.

Suddenly Mathilde Papadoupolous ran into the lobby and told of being taken hostage in the basement.

For the first time Soutter entertained the possibility that there *were* bombs in the hotel. The warning was probably a hoax, he thought. But did he dare take a chance? He had seen some Arab thieves running away, shooting at the British. Could they have left the bombs?

"Gather up everyone in the lobby," he ordered Mathilde Papadoupolous. "Take them upstairs and make them lie on their beds, away from the windows."

Surely no bomb could be powerful enough to reach the King David's bedrooms.

Mathilde ran through the lobby interrupting conversations, shaking opened newspapers and begging people to follow her upstairs. Some people took her advice but most preferred to remain in the lobby.

Soutter looked for people staying in the hotel. "We've received a bomb threat. Please return to your rooms. Pull your beds away from your windows and lie on them," he urged.

"Send someone to the barbershop and tell them to close at once," he told the reception clerk. The barbershop was the public area nearest to the Secretariat.

He saw his wife, Anne, standing in the lobby. "Go back to your office," he said. "I'm sending the guests upstairs. We've had a bomb threat but I don't know if it's genuine."

He rushed down the back stairs. The kitchen workers would know if terrorists had mined the basement.

One of Father Antippa's daughters who worked for the hotel ran into the barbershop and shouted, "Mr. Soutter wants the barbershop closed because of the disturbances." The two barbers folded their straight razors and removed towels from customers' necks.

"Is this really necessary?" one man protested. "Can't he finish me first?"

Ivan Phillips thought he would look "damned funny walking about with half a haircut." When he reached the lobby he looked at his watch. It was 12:32. He was due at the Pollocks for lunch in less than half an hour. The hot towels had relaxed him. Instead of climbing up to Bob Newton's office he decided to have a drink.

He was surprised to see fewer than ten people in the bar and only one, Colonel Fell, that he recognized. Usually it was packed at this time of day. He took a table by himself. A waiter appeared and he ordered a pink gin. Through the open window he could see his driver, Bader, sitting on the stone wall bordering the YMCA.

Soutter found the busboys sitting on the floor of the kitchen. None of them moved. They seemed in a trance, paralyzed by fear. "They're gone," he said. "There's no one in the basement. I saw them run away."

He heard someone moving inside the icebox. He opened it. A cook stood shivering under a carcass. "Hey," he shouted. "I don't want you to be the King David's fresh meat. Get out of there."

One man said, "They told us they'd shoot us if we moved."

One of the Arabs sitting on the floor blurted out a garbled story about milk cans and a warning that the hotel would explode.

Soutter ran upstairs. There *were* bombs in the hotel. He had to find Hamburger.

Hamburger and Hadingham joined Campbell, Petty and the kitchen workers who had followed Campbell from the basement. They stood in the service driveway, between the milk truck and the service door. Campbell asked Hamburger to translate what the workers were saying.

Constantides spoke first.

"He says he was held up by armed men and then locked in the receiving room," Hamburger translated.

Another man shouted.

"He says a number of men dressed like Arabs unloaded milk churns from this lorry."

"Ask him where they put the churns."

"Where did they put the churns?" Hamburger asked in French.

The man answered.

"In the basement, he says."

"Where in the basement?" Campbell asked.

The man spoke again.

"He doesn't know where they left the churns. He and the others were in the kitchen but he says he saw them being dragged along the corridor."

Hadingham turned to Hamburger. "It seems terrorists have carried bombs into your hotel."

"Yes."

"Well, for Christ's sake," Campbell said. "We'd better go find them."

"Yes, we'd better," Hadingham agreed.

"Punch You Bugger," Campbell shouted. "Come on!"

Campbell and Hadingham hurried to the service door. Petty and Punch followed. Hamburger ordered one of the workers to pull the fire alarm.

It was 12:36, twenty-three minutes after Gideon had tipped over the bottles of acid.

The hot weather had increased the speed of the reaction. The wood plug separating the acid from the explosives was almost gone.

24

12:36 P.M.

GIDEON RAN into his mother and sister near the Shaere Sedek hospital.
"Why are you so pale?" his sister asked. "What's the matter?"
"In a few minutes you'll understand," he said.

Adina met two schoolmates outside Moshinsky's hardware store. They invited her to join them and the three girls strolled along the Jaffa Road window-shopping, gossiping and holding hands.

Yael arrived at her father's store in Mahane Yehuda as he was pulling down his metal shutters and closing for the afternoon.
"Be quick," she said. "We have to catch the bus. There may be a curfew." She wanted to get home before the army blocked roads, stopped buses and searched passengers. She still carried Gal's pistol.

Amnon slipped on a white smock and climbed onto his stool in the dental laboratory. His employer said nothing.

Peri's taxi crawled through the narrow streets of the Armenian Quarter behind a slow-moving truck. Blood gushed from Avidor's wound, drenching Ariela's clothes and spreading over the floor. Ariela was afraid he would die before they could reach the synagogue and summon an Irgun doctor.
"Can't you pass that truck?" she screamed at Peri.

"Shut up," he whispered, "no one in this neighborhood should hear you speaking Hebrew."

He was too late. A pedestrian ran to find a policeman.

No one had warned Doris Katz about Operation Chick. She was married to Samuel Katz, the South African Jew who was the Irgun's chief of propaganda. A few minutes after the all clear she drove along Julian's Way and noticed groups of people standing alongside the road near the King David. She assumed someone famous was about to arrive at the hotel.

Dan Ben-Dor turned right onto Julian's Way and drove past the main driveway. His Austin was a convertible. In five seconds he would be directly opposite the Secretariat.

Ian Proud passed a young army sergeant near the entrance to the hotel driveway. The sergeant was tall, bronzed and good-looking. His sleeves were rolled up and the blond hairs on his arms glistened in the sun. "What a fine looking man," Proud thought. "At least these army chaps stay fit and healthy in Palestine."

Lieutenant Tilly had parked his jeep near the turnstile and stayed to direct traffic during the terrorist alert. After the all clear sounded he decided to wait in Julian's Way until "someone turned up to tell me what to do." He could not ask for advice or report on what he had seen because his jeep was not equipped with a radio.

Roderick Musgrave waved down to Stacey Barham from his third-floor balcony. "What's up, Stacey?" he shouted.

"I don't know for sure," Barham said. "We think they're after George Salameh. The bomb exploded in front of his store."

"The Regence will be open in a few minutes. I'll see you there for a drink."

"All right."

Two ATS girls peered over the roof of the Secretariat. They had sneaked up to get a good view of the commotion on Julian's Way. It was a lovely day and they decided to stay on for a few minutes and sunbathe.

As soon as Eugenie Markarian finished talking to her sister on the telephone, she walked onto a balcony for a last look at Julian's Way. Her friend Hilda Azzam joined her.

Lubah Wahbeh managed to stop her legs from shaking. When she returned to her office, George Farley handed her a sheaf of longhand notes and said,

"These are the minutes of this morning's meeting on postal thefts. Do you think you can manage to type them before lunch?"

She fed a sheet of paper into her typewriter and began: "Minutes of the Attorney General's meeting. . . ."

Marion Small returned to Julius Jacobs' office with the missing file. She placed it on Jacobs' desk and turned to leave.

Mohammed, one of the Secretariat's messengers, did not know that Sergeant Woodward had opened the Secretariat's door after the all clear. Worried there might be more explosions, he had devised a plan for escaping the building. He grabbed a stack of files from a table in the ground-floor registry, slapped an "Immediate" slip on them and ran six steps up to the doorway.

"Urgent telegrams from the Colonial Secretary," he shouted.

The guard waved him by. He ran out into the yard between the Secretariat and the canteen.

Jerry Cornes finished writing a letter refusing every request made by the Armenian Patriarch ("or someone like that"). Under the circumstances it amused him to sign himself, "Your Beatitude's most obedient servant." Now he could go see what had caused the excitement in Julian's Way. He left his office and walked downstairs.

Sergeant Bill Jennings and Sir John Shaw's Armenian chauffeur were drinking cups of tea in the canteen. The Arab bus passengers injured by the diversionary explosion took up most of the other chairs. When Jennings finished his tea he decided to check with Shaw to see if the small explosion would delay his departure from the Secretariat.

Gunner Barber and the ATS operators from the basement switchboard walked across the garden toward the hotel. The operators had been ordered to return to the basement and resume working.

Joan Gibbs dialed the Secretariat as soon as she reached the Dawes's. As she waited for the operator to answer, she worried about how to explain the call to her husband.

The switchboard usually picked up on the third or fourth ring. After waiting over a minute for an answer, she hung up. "Everyone is trying to reach her husband," she thought. "The switchboard must be jammed with calls."

Devorah Ledener yanked the plug connecting her to the King David's switchboard and walked into the corridor. "There's been a warning about a bomb at the King David," she said to a friend, "and now their switchboard doesn't answer. Do you think this time there really is a bomb?"

In Major Quinn's office on the top floor of the hotel, Harry Beilin was saying, "And I can assure you, Ernie, that everything is going to be quiet. There won't be any trouble from anyone. . . ."

Also in the army offices, a major ordered Staff Sergeant Caswill and the other clerks working in the top-secret registries to leave their offices near the Secretariat and gather in the middle of the corridor by the marble staircase. There another officer told them to use this staircase if an evacuation was ordered. The Palestine Police had just forwarded the warning from Devorah Ledener. They also called the Secretariat switchboard where one of Father Antippa's daughters took the call. It was too late.

Caswill suddenly remembered he had left top-secret files sitting in a pile on top of his desk. He ran back to lock them in a safe. ATS Sergeant Ella Smith ran after him. Although Caswill had arrived in Palestine only a week ago, she was already fond of him.

Two floors below, in room 105, *Daily Express* correspondent Peter Duffield was writing a feature entitled "Dateline King David." He typed, "A country [Palestine] in which it is always a closed season on sweet reason. . . ."

Outside Duffield's room Mathilde Papadoupolous sat on the floor of the corridor with the guests she had persuaded to evacuate the lobby. A woman left her room and almost tripped over her.

"What's the matter? You look ill," the woman said. "Come to the bar and have a brandy."

Mathilde refused. The woman shrugged and started down the stairs to the lobby.

Ivan Phillips drained his pink gin and decided to leave the bar. He looked out the window. Bader was still sitting on the wall waiting to drive him to the District Commissioner's for lunch.

At another table Kathleen Bailey held a handkerchief to her cheek and drank the brandy brought by her friends on the wedding-cake expedition.

Just outside the bar, in the lobby, Sifrony, Catling, Nissan and other police, employees and guests stood near the reception desk discussing the bombing and shootings.

Across the lobby in the Winter Garden, Leila Canaan found herself paying less attention to Wasfi Tell's compliments.

Tell had ignored the explosion and the sirens. She had not. She was afraid the curfews and searches would trap her in the King David. Her father would discover she had come to the lobby unescorted to meet a man. Her family would be disgraced, they would have to leave Jerusalem forever and it would be her fault. She wished she had never come to the King David; she wished she was home with her father. Suddenly she burst into tears. "I want to go home, I want to go home, I want to go home . . ." she sobbed.

The disturbances persuaded Mrs. Grey-Donald to postpone her visit to the garden. She remained at her desk in the Winter Garden; her straw hat stayed on the corner of her desk. For security the army had instlled heavy iron grates over the window between the Winter Garden and the Secretariat. One of them was directly over her head.

The lobby filled up despite the efforts of Mathilde and Emile Soutter. British civil servants, army officers, Arab traders and politicians, Jewish dignitaries and Christians and Zionists on pilgrimages to Jerusalem had gathered for their aperitifs. Sudanese waiters circulated among them taking orders, delivering drinks on silver trays, and passing bowls of olives and platters of the King David's famous hot cheese puffs.

The lobby looked as it had on every day for the past fifteen years; as it had on that day ten years ago when Weizmann and the Mufti had met there by chance; and as it had when Mountbatten, Churchill and Montgomery had relaxed on its thrones.

An Arab bellboy ran over to Soutter and said, "I've seen Mr. Hamburger standing in front of the hotel."

Soutter dashed through the revolving door. No Hamburger in the main driveway. He leaned over the wall and looked into the service driveway. Hamburger was crouched on the ground, peering under the milk truck.

"Watch out," Soutter yelled. "There may be bombs down there. . . ."

25

12:37—12:40 P.M.

FIRE ALARMS clanged in the basement. Campbell and Hadingham rounded the corner of the service passageway and ran into the main corridor. The Regence was fifty yards straight ahead.

The acid ate through the wood plug and dripped onto the detonator at 12:37, six minutes before schedule. The explosion of the fulminate in the blasting cap lasted one twenty-five-thousandth of a second. A full second later the TNT exploded.

Three hundred and fifty kilograms of TNT became 250,000 liters of hot gas. At the center of the explosion, the gas expanded at a velocity of 160,000 MPH, heating the air to over 3,000°C. and exerting a pressure of 500,000 pounds per square inch, thirty-four thousand times normal atmospheric pressure. The pressure burst the hearts, livers and lungs of the clerks working on the floor above.

A bright orange light flashed at the end of the basement corridor, burst into flames and swept toward Campbell and Hadingham. A bang stabbed their eardrums. A wave of scorching air slammed Campbell against the wall and flung him onto the floor. Hot blackness smothered him.

Hadingham somersaulted into the air. Jagged pieces of iron pelted him, ripping his uniform and slicing wounds in his hands and arms. "I've seen this happen to my men and I've scraped up bits of bone and flesh afterward," he thought. "Now it's happening to me. In a second I'll be nothing but bloody pieces." As his wife's face flashed in front of him, he smacked into a wall farther down the corridor.

The blast was equivalent in force to a direct hit from a 500 kilogram aerial bomb. The churns disappeared and the pillars in the Regence supporting the Secretariat disintegrated.

The Secretariat became alive. Its outer stone walls bulged, swayed, convulsed inward and, with a thunderous roar, vanished into sheets of flame and clouds of smoke. The roof shot into the air and plummeted to earth like an elevator out of control, pitching the sunbathing ATS women into the garden and crushing those on whom it landed.

An elliptical shock wave swept into Julian's Way from the center of the explosion. Those standing close to the hotel felt the blast before they heard it. First they were slammed by a thrust coming from the blast and then, a split-second later, a reverse pressure, a suction pulling them toward the hotel.

The suction ripped off clothes, tore rings from fingers and watches from wrists. It sucked the window panes out of nearby buildings, spewing shards of glass into the street. Automobiles rolled over, small trees were uprooted, and cypresses and palms bent backward as if battered by hurricane winds. Ivan Phillips' driver was blown onto the metal spears of the YMCA's ornamental gate.

In the courtyard between the Secretariat and the canteen the shock wave pitched Mohammed the messenger backward and Jerry Cornes forward onto the ground. Cornes looked up and saw "bodies falling down off the roof and winging through the air."

The shock wave shook the "milk truck" standing in the service driveway and tossed Hamburger against a wall, concussing him. Across the street from the Secretariat it blew in the door and shattered the windows of Meyer Levin's office. One of his cameramen raced into the street and began filming.

Lieutenant Tilly was standing nearly opposite Salameh's store when he heard a rumbling like that of a subway train approaching a station. The train seemed to get closer, the rumbling became louder and louder.

The King David was turned into a gigantic cannon and Julian's Way was its field of fire. Small pieces of concrete shot out of the smoke at the speed of sound, spraying the street like buckshot. Large concrete blocks flew into the air at speeds of up to a hundred miles an hour. They punched holes in the roof of the Signals Annex, smashing cars, blasting craters in the street and burying half the canteen. Many of the Arab bus passengers who had been wounded by the first Irgun explosion were killed by the second one.

Debris showered Julian's Way. Sheets of paper from top-secret files fluttered in and out of the smoke like white birds; slivers of glass shot from shattering windows; chunks of cement crashed into pedestrians; bodies were blown into the street.

If the Irgun's warning had been heeded, hundreds of evacuees would have been standing in Julian's Way, in the path of these deadly missiles. The death toll would have been even higher. As it was, dozens of those who happened to be driving or walking near the hotel were killed or injured.

A block of rose-colored stone hit *New York Post* reporter Richard Mowrer in the leg. A pane of glass decapitated an Arab bus passenger standing outside the canteen. An office safe hurtled out of the smoke, spinning in the air and emptying its secret papers before flattening an Arab woman walking along Julian's Way.

Chunks of red stone smashed into the hood of Dan Ben-Dor's Austin convertible as he drove past the YMCA. He jammed on the brakes and threw his arms over his head. A stone splinter gouged his elbow and a rock crashed into the back seat. His dog, Assad II, howled in agony and a bystander thought a human passenger had been hit. The dog's sobs were indistinguishable from those of the people who lay dying in the road.

Postmaster-General Gerald Kennedy had been walking down the Secretariat path to the turnstile. The blast tossed him into the air, blew him a hundred and fifty yards across the street and smacked him against the wall of the YMCA. His body slid to the pavement, leaving behind a bloody silhouette. His head stuck to the wall, too high off the ground and too far from a window to be easily removed.

In the building itself, six floors of reinforced concrete slapped against one another and pancaked to the ground with a crash. More than fifty rooms and a hundred and fifty lives were trapped between the slabs. Trapped were Leah Bachrach's beautiful ankles, the top-secret files Marion Small had just brought downstairs from the registry, Roderick Musgrave's address book with the names of his Irgun friends, Atallah Mantoura's favorite brown wing-tip shoes, Julius Jacobs' letters of commendation from the High Commissioner.

In that split second after 12:37, thirteen of those who had been alive at 12:36 disappeared without a trace. The clothes, bracelets, cufflinks and wallets which might have identified them exploded into dust and smoke. Others were burned to charcoal, melted into chairs and desks or exploded into countless fragments. The face of a Jewish typist was ripped from her skull, blown out of a window, and smeared onto the pavement below. Miraculously it was recognizable, a two-foot-long distorted death mask topped with tufts of hair.

Those in the Secretariat who survived this first, frozen split second endured a moment during which they understood what had happened—a bomb—and what might happen next—death. Then they were slammed by a hurricane of hot air, dust, and flames; knocked down, thrown up, somersaulting, sprawling, rolling, spinning, and helpless; blinded and choked by clouds of smoke and plaster, blistered by heat and deafened by clanging girders and exploding walls.

Blocks of stone, tables and desks crushed heads and snapped necks. Coat racks became deadly arrows that flew across rooms, piercing chests. Filing cabinets pinned people to walls, suffocating them. Chandeliers and ceiling fans crashed to the floor, impaling and decapitating those underneath.

In his office on the third floor, Sir John Shaw heard a dull thud. Papers and files flew off his desk and he looked up to see his chandelier swinging wildly. Clouds of dust billowed into his office, turning it pitch black and blinding him. Gasping for breath, he stumbled toward the door.

Down the hall, William Bradley thought, "Another bomb in the street." He wrote two more words on a file before his windows exploded and the wall separating his office from Father Antippa's disappeared.

The sound reminded Marion Small of a matchbox cracking. She hurtled backward from Jacobs' office into the corridor. "Why isn't anyone from Jacobs' meeting coming out to help me?" she wondered.

In George Farley's office, Lubah Wahbeh shot out of her chair. A door swung off its hinges knocking her down and a cabinet toppled onto the door. She could hear masonry crashing into the cabinet.

Eugenie Markarian and her friend Hilda Azzam grabbed each other's hands and screamed. The stone terrace on which they stood exploded and, still holding hands and screaming, they tumbled into a cloud of smoke.

In the military headquarters, Honor Sharman told her husband, "I think I'd better ring off now, it sounds like there's a fire or something." As she hung up clouds of smoke enveloped her office.

Down the corridor, Major Ernest Quinn and Harry Beilin saw sheets of flame shoot past their window. Quinn's filing cabinet fell one way and, luckily, Beilin fell the other.

"Stay here!" Quinn shouted. He ran into the corridor and peered into the smoke. He stood a few feet from where the earthquake joint was straining to absorb the stress of the explosion.

In the army office nearest the Secretariat, Sergeant Caswill and his ATS girl friend jumped under a table. The blast swept away Caswill's top-secret papers.

On the other side of the partition separating Caswill's office from the Secretariat, John Gutch jumped under his desk as his walls exploded, shooting plaster into his eyes. Suddenly he was blind. The roaring stopped. There was a brief, eerie stillness and then he heard a sound louder and more piercing than the initial blast—the shrieks and sobs of his friends suffocating and dying under tons of rubble.

Downstairs in the main lobby lights flickered and died. The fire alarm stopped clanging. Pillars supporting the ceiling swayed and plaster and cement showered guests. Cracks appeared in the walls and floor nearest the Secretariat. They grew longer, became wider, and split open as the bulding shook with the blast.

The pressure bent the iron grilles surrounding the cashier's windows. Women's stockings burst open at their seams, drinking glasses rattled and then shattered in hands. The arms smugglers, Arab merchants, army officers, priests and spies rose out of their chairs and pitched forward onto the rugs symbolizing the twelve tribes of Israel. Some of the marble slabs covering the floor rose, allowing sand from underneath to shoot like geysers into the air. The view of the Holy City through the picture window dissolved into shards of glass that flew across the lobby, cutting deep wounds that gushed blood onto the green leather of the Hittite thrones.

Richard Catling threw himself down near the reception desk. As Gabe Sifrony was blown onto the floor, he could see glass flying over his head and slicing into guests. In the Winter Garden, Wasfi Tell felt the first tremor from below. He slapped Leila Canaan to stop her sobbing, grabbed her by the arms and shoved her under their wicker table just as the Winter Garden's glass walls exploded.

In the lobby office next to Hamburger's, Anne Soutter jumped up from her desk and grabbed her dog, RAF. The next moment, slabs of marble fell off the wall, digging craters in the floor around her. A glass showcase tumbled onto her desk and shattered. She stood in the middle of her office, paralyzed with fear, hugging her dog to her chest. She had chosen the only safe patch of ground in the entire room.

Next door in the bar Ivan Phillips felt the floor "tremble as if a train were passing underneath." Bottles tumbled off shelves and smashed into the wood paneling. As the wall behind the bar vanished, Phillips thought, "I can't see. I'm blinded. I'll be crushed by the masonry. Will I die? Can I escape? Is the entire building collapsing?"

Outside the bar, a dense plume of brown smoke, plaster and pulverized cement spiraled into the blue sky, blocking the sun, enveloping the building and concealing the destruction. The smoke chased terrified pedestrians down side streets and muffled the sound of crashing steel girders, police whistles, and death wails. Onlookers choked on its bitter fumes and coughed up dark-gray phlegm. The cloud of smoke expanded, billowing out and becoming larger and larger until it shadowed an area a quarter mile square and brought a gray twilight to Julian's Way.

Everyone within a few miles of the King David saw the smoke or heard the blast. Paglin, Spector and Chaim-Toit were driving through Abu Gosh, an Arab village several miles west of Jerusalem, when they heard it. Spector had taken a circuitous route out of the city so he and the others could be within earshot of the King David. As they smiled and congratulated one another, Spector accelerated. The army would soon throw up roadblocks and Paglin was in a hurry to reach Tel Aviv and brief Begin on their success.

Almost everyone in Jerusalem knew or was related to someone who worked in the King David or had reason to visit it. Many remember experiencing the same emotions: first a sudden, uncontrollable elation—they had survived; and then a convulsion of nausea—someone they loved might be dead.

The shock wave blew Joan Gibbs across the Dawes's parlor. The Arab maid

Left, Roderick Musgrave *(Bodleian Library, Oxford)*; *right*, Joan and Brian Gibbs with their son, Robert, several years before the explosion *(Author's collection)*

Colonel Andrew Campbell *(left)* and "Punch You Bugger" receiving his award for valor at The Victoria Dog Show in London *(Imperial War Museum, London)*; *right*, Atallah Mantoura. *(Jack Mantoura)*

Some of the "hand-picked darlings" of the Secretariat typing pool at a wedding a month before the explosion. Eugenie Markarian is second to the left. Hilda Azzam is between the bride and groom. "Father" Antippa is next to the bride. *(Author's collection)*

Above left, seconds after the explosion, smoke billows from the King David. A policeman (left) raises his whistle to this mouth *(Imperial War Museum, London)*; *right*, Police on Julian's Way examine a body minutes after the blast. *(Imperial War Museum London)*; *below*, the King David Hotel after the explosion *(Illustrated London News)*

Above left, D. C. Thompson is pulled from the rubble twenty-four hours after the explosion. Sir John Shaw is at left in civilian clothes *(Israel State Archives, Jerusalem)*; *above right*, wounded Arab messenger is carried away from the hotel by rescue workers *(Israel State Archives, Jerusalem)*; *below left*, rescue workers search for survivors *(Israel State Archives, Jerusalem)*; *below right*, body of Secretariat typist *(Author's collection)*

Left, blood stain on YMCA wall left by one of the bodies blown from the King David *(Central Zionist Archives, Jerusalem)*

Begin (*right*), Yael and Gideon at a 1972 press conference in Tel Aviv *(Author's collection)*

ran around the room, crying hysterically. Her nephew was a file clerk in the Secretariat. Joan Gibbs prayed, "Oh God, I hope Brian had the sense to leave the King David after the first explosion."

Jerry Cornes' wife saw clouds of smoke billowing up, obscuring the top of the hotel and the olive trees. "The Secretariat!" she screamed, as she ran for the telephone to call her husband.

From the roof of her building in the Greek Colony, Mrs. Hadingham saw what she thought looked like "miniature colored parachutes" fluttering in the breeze outside the King David. They were the dresses of the female office workers who had been blown through windows.

Meyer Levin grabbed his camera, ran to the third-floor window in his therapist's office and began snapping pictures of the rising smoke over the King David. "You have excellent rapid-functioning reactions," said the therapist.

In the Allenby Barracks, Marion Small's husband, Dennis, was busy on a patient's teeth. He asked his assistant, Sergeant Hughes, to "climb up on the roof and see where that enormous bang came from."

Eugenie Markarian's brother, Nubar, rushed to the front door of the Secretariat Annex where he worked.

"It's the K-D," the policeman guarding the door told him. "It's gone."

Even though Andrew Sharman had been talking to his wife, Honor, on the phone when the bomb exploded, he still wanted to be certain she was safe. He was one of the few officers who had managed to circumvent army regulations and get his wife into Palestine. They frequently upset the senior officers by holding hands in the corridors of the King David. As he ran out of his office, a Cockney sentry warned him against going to the hotel. "Cor blimey, sir," he said. "The whole building's gone for shit."

"My God, this time they've really done it," Devorah Ledener said to someone as the shock wave hit the Palestine Post building. Seconds later her switchboard exploded with lights and bells.

The blast rocked the optician's shop where Jack Mantoura and his Jewish friend Oplatka were checking prices. "It must be the David Brothers Building," Oplatka said. "They're probably after the Palestine Information Office."

Mantoura disagreed. "That doesn't make any sense. Too many foreign journalists use that building. They wouldn't want to risk killing them." He hoped he was right. His sister, Iris, worked as a typist in the Information Office.

The blast was so loud that Sami Hadawi thought a bomb had exploded inside the garage where he waited for his car to be repaired. He crouched down behind the nearest pillar, afraid that the ceiling would collapse. He remembered hearing that this was the safest place to be during an explosion, next to a pillar.

Three hundred yards north on Julian's Way, in the army offices in the Triangle Building, a young Arab clerk named Zehdi Terzi felt his desk shake. The other Arab file clerks who worked for the army stopped working and stared at each other. Finally one broke the silence and shouted, "My God! It must be another terrorist explosion!" Terzi ran downstairs to see which building the terrorists had hit.

Closer to the hotel there was no doubt about the target, only about the damage and death toll. Across the garden in the Secretariat Annex, Helen Rossi and the other employees gathered at the windows. They had screamed and sobbed as the walls bulged and collapsed on their British, Arab, and Jewish friends. Now as the smoke cleared they could begin to see the extent of the damage. They assumed they would know within minutes which of their friends had perished. They would not. It would take days to establish conclusively who had lived and who had died. The question of who was responsible would be debated for decades.

PART FOUR

July 22, 1946–June 1980

26

July 22, 1946
12:40–9 P.M.

"THERE'S A bloody great hole in the King David!" Sergeant Hughes shouted as he ran downstairs from the roof of the Allenby Barracks. Dennis Small left his patient in the dentist's chair, hurried to a telephone and dialed his wife's number at the Secretariat. No answer.

The "hole" Sergeant Hughes had seen was in the Secretariat. The earthquake joint had contained the blast. The center of the hotel and the southeast corner of the Secretariat remained standing. The six stories and twenty-eight offices in the southwest corner of the hotel had become a three-story pile of twisted iron, cracked cement, red stone blocks and corpses.

The Irgun had destroyed half their objective, half of the government's headquarters—the equivalent of half the White House or half of Parliament. Their faces caked with dust and streaked with blood, the wounded crawled and staggered out of the rubble and into Julian's Way. One man moved his hands back and forth over his ears and screamed. He was trying to block out the cries for help from his friends trapped underneath.

A naked woman scrambled over the wreckage kicking the dust, tossing rocks and muttering oaths as she searched for her engagement ring.

An Arab clerk knelt weeping in Julian's Way. He clasped his hands and repeated a prayer: "My sister is under there. Lord, send her out alive. Lord, send her out alive. Send her out alive. Send her out alive."

The dead and wounded lay on sidewalks and in the street. A chunk of bloody flesh blocked the turnstile. A belt and revolver identified it as the remains of a Palestine policeman.

Ian Proud ran back toward the hotel. He found the handsome blond soldier lying on the pavement, his head crushed by a slab of stone. The blond hairs on his arms still glistened through the gray dust.

Lieutenant Tilly pointed to an elderly white-haired man lying in the road. "This is the first person I've ever seen killed in action," he said to no one in particular. In fact, he realized, it was the first dead person he had ever seen.

He dragged a Jewish newspaper photographer to the body and shouted, "There! Take a picture of that and put it in your bloody newspaper."

Richard Mowrer struggled to stand up. A flying piece of concrete had fractured his thigh. One leg was twisted out of shape "like a Javanese dancer's."

"Someone make that man lie still," a policeman yelled. As Mowrer was being carried to an ambulance, he looked up at the King David and recognized the neat surgical slice of a direct hit: part of the building reduced to rubble, the rest standing. It reminded him of hundreds of buildings in Spain, Poland and Germany. "What a terrible anticlimax for me," he thought. "To survive so many wars and revolutions and then to be wounded so randomly. I could have been anybody."

The rooms and corridors nearest the Secretariat suffered the greatest damage. The basement resembled the hold of a torpedoed ship. Hadingham, Campbell and Petty clawed their way out through a maze of twisted pipes and crackling electric wires.

Hadingham was the most seriously wounded. His hands and arms dripped with blood and he was in shock. Nevertheless, when he reached the street he began pulling people from the rubble.

As someone led him to an ambulance he shouted, "Curfew! Curfew! Put the city under an immediate curfew."

Inside the hotel, Ivan Phillips groped over upturned tables and smashed chairs to the door of the bar. He staggered through the lobby and into Julian's Way. Bricks had dented his car. His driver, Bader, hung on the YMCA's gate, impaled through the chest.

Kathleen Bailey, now injured for a second time, was led into the garden. Blood still seeped from the first wound, drenching her shirt. Some Jews who had been in the hotel lobby recognized her uniform and spat on her.

Colonel Fell lurched into Naim Nissan in the lobby. "Bloody people," he muttered. "They've blown up the bar."

Other guests struggled out from under upturned tables and chairs and hurried into the garden or Julian's Way. Everyone feared another blast.

Tell led Leila Canaan out of the Winter Garden. Both were bleeding from numerous cuts.

Mrs. Soutter ran into the Winter Garden. The window grate had fallen on Mrs. Grey-Donald's desk, slicing it in half. Mrs. Grey-Donald crawled out from underneath. "I'm perfectly all right, my dear," she said, as she knocked dust from her straw hat. She jammed it on her head and strode outside to inspect the damage to the garden and her chickens.

Gabe Sifrony stumbled through the revolving door. "What happened to Musgrave?" he asked a British police officer. "Is he all right? Does anyone know what's become of him?"

The officer pointed at the rubble. "He's under there," he said. "His 'friends' finally killed him."

On the first floor of what remained of the Secretariat, Marion Small watched in amazement as the door of the staff lavatory flew open. Jabri, an Arab messenger who had a perpetual squint, walked out. The squint had vanished and his curly black hair stood straight up in the air.

"How fascinating," she thought. "It's true what they say, fear *does* cause hair to stand on end." She could not see that her own was doing the same. It stayed on end for the next three days.

Jabri lifted chunks of cement and plaster from her legs and helped her up. She could not stop staring at his hair. "Oh, Mrs. Small," he said, "do you think we can go home now?"

"Yes, Jabri," she said, "I think we can."

Because of the smoke and dust Sir John Shaw could feel, but not see, his arms and hands. When he realized he was uninjured he began groping his way along the walls of his office. A few feet away he heard his secretary coughing and gagging on the dust.

"Are you all right, Marjorie?" he shouted.

"Yes. All right. What's happened?"

"Hang on. I'm going to see."

He edged slowly into the hallway, scuffing his shoes on chunks of masonry and stirring up more dust. A light appeared and he shuffled toward it. A few feet outside his office, a woman—he thought it was Marion Small—blocked his way.

The dust settled and the "light" became blue sky. The blast had cut the hallway in half and he and Mrs. Small stood on the edge of a precipice. He yanked her back to safety. He had to get the survivors out of the building. Others might fall into this chasm. He knew too that fires often followed explosions.

The blast had punched a small hole in the concrete security wall separating the Secretariat from the rest of the King David. A few weeks before he had insisted that sledgehammers and axes be placed in boxes on both sides of this wall to allow for evacuation during a fire. Now he broke into the box and grabbed a sledgehammer. Five minutes later he had succeeded in battering down the rest of the wall and crawling into the hotel corridor.

The door to room 123 had been blown off its hinges. Inside, Jack Keegan, the TWA representative, sat at his desk, stunned by the explosion.

"Good afternoon, Keegan," Shaw said. "Care to give me a hand?" For the next thirty minutes Keegan and Shaw smashed through partitions on the other floors and rescued others who had been trapped.

On the first floor William Bradley tumbled into what remained of a typing pool. The ceiling had fallen in and he counted six girls lying in the rubble. He grabbed one, shook her and shouted, "We have to leave, the rest of the building may collapse." He made the survivors hold hands and walk away from the blast zone. When they reached the end of the hallway he lowered them through a window and onto a desk in the Winter Garden.

A brigadier handed Honor Sharman a revolver and ordered her into the corridor. She wondered what good the revolver would be if, as she feared, the terrorists had planted a second bomb under the army's headquarters.

Soon more soldiers joined her in the corridor. They stood silently, revolvers drawn. Some would later admit they were secretly hoping for an evacuation order.

Some officers still joked. Major Payne ran into a young Guards lieutenant in the third-floor corridor. The lieutenant pulled down the visor of his cap so it covered his eyes, pointed downstairs to the lobby and, thinking of the display cases full of jewelry, grinned and said, "Looting."

Covered with plaster, Captain Alan Day and Joan Chapman from Intelligence ran into Major Quinn's office. They had been working next door in one of the offices cut open by the blast.

"My God, what happened to you?" Quinn asked.

"We were teetering on the edge of the building," Day said. "Luckily the door was at my rear so I could pull Joan back from the edge and we could escape."

Quinn suddenly noticed that Harry Beilin was still in his office. "Well, Alan, I guess you'd better see Mr. Beilin off the premises," he said.

"Thank you," Day said. "I'd be bloody pleased to."

An impenetrable wall of dust at the end of the corridor blocked General Barker's view of the Secretariat. As soon as he learned the extent of the damage, he returned to his office and hastily wrote an order for circulation to every British officer in Palestine. The order concluded:

> I am determined that they [the Jews] shall suffer punishment and be made aware of the contempt and loathing with which we regard their conduct. . . .
> Consequently, I have decided that, with effect from the receipt of this letter, you will put out of bounds to all ranks all Jewish places of entertainment, cafés, restaurants, shops and private dwellings. No British soldier is to have any social intercourse with any Jews and any intercourse in the way of duty should be as brief as possible, and kept strictly to the business at hand.

I appreciate that these orders will inflict a measure of hardship upon the troops, but I am confident that, if my reasons are fully explained to them, they will understand their propriety and that they will be punishing the Jews in a way the race dislikes as much as any, namely by striking at their pockets, and showing our contempt for them.

Outside Barker's office the air raid sirens sounded again. Police vans mounted with loudspeakers cruised the streets blaring "Curfew! Curfew! Curfew in thirty minutes!"

People jammed into taxis and buses. Automobiles accelerated and then slammed on their brakes at roadblocks. Policemen and soldiers demanded drivers' licenses, registrations and identity cards. They ripped open parcels and dumped the contents of purses and briefcases into the gutter. They were furious with every Jew and every Jew was panicked, afraid of being detained or of missing the curfew.

At police headquarters, CID officers contacted the suspects on the "terrorist supervision list." They called Amnon minutes after he returned to work at the dental laboratory. His employer reported he had been at work all morning.

Ian Proud stood in the middle of the Jaffa Road trying to untangle traffic so ambulances could get through. An American woman, a Jew, pulled alongside Proud and complained, "I hope you're going to get us out of this jam quickly, officer. I haven't had my lunch yet."

"I'm terribly sorry, madam," he said, "but neither have I, and the blood on my uniform comes from people who will never have lunch again."

A traffic policeman flagged down Peri as he was driving to collect the Irgun doctor. He jumped out and escaped into the crowd hurrying home for the curfew.

The officer searched the taxi and found eight revolvers, a Thompson submachine gun, rounds of ammunition, medical supplies, four Arab costumes and a puddle of blood. Two of the revolvers had been fired and one, it was later determined, had killed Major Mackintosh.

Yael's bus stopped at a roadblock near Givat Shaul. A major climbed on and ordered everyone to disembark. Yael looked out the window. The passengers of an earlier bus were being separated and searched. Men and women filed through different gaps in the coils of barbed wire. On the other side soldiers and police matrons frisked them and opened parcels and handbags.

She grabbed her father's arm. "I have a revolver in my bag. Pretend you're ill and lean against me." She slid her handbag between them, put her arm around his shoulder and helped him out of the bus.

"Men and women separate," the major ordered.

Yael refused. "My father is old and sick and he's just been injured in a collision between one of your armored cars and another bus. He'll collapse unless I hold him up."

The major relented and they hobbled through the same checkpoint. No one searched them.

Later, when she showed her father the revolver, he was proud. "Look," he said to his wife. "Our daughter knows how to handle a gun."

The army and police also searched automobiles at frequent points along the Jerusalem–Tel Aviv highway. Outside Abu Gosh, cars backed up the road from an army roadblock. Spector stopped the Irgun getaway car a few hundred yards away.

"Let's abandon it and walk into the hills," Paglin suggested.

Spector disagreed. Arab villagers might report them. He swerved into the oncoming lane, blew his horn, and raced toward the barrier. At the last minute he slammed on the brakes and skidded to a stop.

"CID officers," he shouted at the bewildered soldiers in a British accent. "Open the barriers. We have to get to Tel Aviv at once."

They raised the barrier and Spector sped through.

Thirty minutes after the explosion: glass, dust, blood and rubble; ambulance sirens and parades of stretcher-bearers; the injured writhing in agony under blankets and blood dripping from stretchers; the khaki shirts of rescue workers soaked with perspiration; handkerchiefs covering the faces of the dead and the mouths of policemen; rattling jackhammers cutting into mountains of wreckage.

The first rescue workers were a collection of survivors, soldiers, army engineers, police constables, doctors from Government Hospital, laborers from the Department of Public Works, Arab post office linemen and the anxious relatives of Secretariat workers.

The Arab linemen and army engineers burrowed into the rubble with picks and jackhammers, cut away steel rods and metal furniture with acetylene torches and attempted to lift concrete slabs with their hands.

An army doctor jumped into a crevice and shot morphine into someone trapped below.

An ambulance attendant lowered tin cups of water tied on strings into holes in the rubble.

The Arab linemen ripped out a wire security fence and dumped wreckage into the olive grove. One looked up and saw a body hanging in the branches of a cypress tree. Another body was draped over a coil of barbed wire. Near the turnstile were two corpses, their legs crossed as if they were still alive and sitting in chairs.

Sir John Shaw stood on top of a hill of rubble shouting encouragement to someone trapped below. A cipher officer ran up and said, "Don't worry, sir. I've rescued the ciphers and locked the safe."

Dennis Small stopped an army chaplain who was circulating among the workers handing out glasses of lemonade. "Where's Marion?" Small asked.

"I don't know," the chaplain said. "But the death toll is something terrific. Have some lemonade."

Over the chaplain's shoulder Small could see Kennedy's head sticking to the wall of the YMCA. "I don't want any of your bloody lemonade; I want my wife."

He ran over to Shaw. "Sir John, do you know where Marion is?"

"No. But I do know that she's had a miraculous escape." Relieved, Small went home to wait.

Police Sergeant "Blackie" Smith heard shouts from a pile of concrete slabs near the remains of the canteen. Smith was in his forties but he had boxed professionally and his arms were strong. He jumped into an opening and began burrowing. Within a few minutes he had dug a tunnel that almost reached the victims.

Suddenly, the tunnel collapsed. He crawled out unharmed, a rescue worker rubbed his back with liniment and he reentered the tunnel. An Arab welder cut away the canteen's metal file cabinets with his torch. Half an hour later Smith emerged again. Two wounded men crawled after him. He was later awarded the George Medal.

Campbell escaped from the cellar with minor cuts and a ripped tam-o'-shanter. Punch You Bugger had also survived. Campbell moved along Julian's Way, stopping to look at bodies. Most were unrecognizable, their clothes shredded or missing, their faces burned or crushed by stone blocks. If a body moved, he shouted for a stretcher-bearer.

Across the street, Stacey Barham identified the remains of Gerald Kennedy. Arab janitors at the YMCA pulled his head off the wall and tried to hose away the red splotch. Bits of flesh and blood were embedded in the stone.

Thirty minutes after the explosion relatives of Secretariat and hotel workers were already scrambling over the rubble, shouting for wives and husbands, mothers, fathers, brothers and daughters, asking the rescue workers and each other: "Has anybody seen . . ."

A delegation of doorkeepers from the Old City came to ask after their beloved Mrs. Grey-Donald. The father of a young Arab messenger ran all the way from Bethlehem. He stood opposite the rubble panting, sobbing and begging to be shown his son. A Jewish woman wailed uncontrollably in front of the YMCA first-aid station. Marion Small asked why she was crying.

"I'm crying for all the dead people, for the tragedy," she answered.

Mrs. Small became enraged. "Do something. You should do something. Not waste your time wailing."

Doreen Farley ran from one group of people to another asking strangers, "Has anyone seen George Farley?" She asked friends, "Have you seen my husband?"

"It's my father I'm worried about," Rosemarie Walsh said.

Richard Catling pointed toward an ambulance. "I thought I saw George over there helping load people into the ambulances."

A young Arab typist confirmed the good news, "Yes, yes. I've seen him helping around the ambulances."

She ran to the ambulances. No sign of him. "What can I do now to save him?" she wondered. "What can anyone do? If they're right and he's survived, then where is he?" Reluctantly she went home to wait.

Many wives stayed at home and called the Secretariat. When the switchboard didn't answer they called the police. Finally, they called one another.

Joan Gibbs did not want to leave her children alone. She stayed at her neighbors and rang John Gutch's wife, Diana, every thirty minutes and asked, "Any news? Have you heard anything from your John?"

"No, nothing" was the answer to each call.

Diana Gutch had already called everyone she knew whose husbands worked at the hotel. They were all as scared as she. One acquaintance reported that she had been standing on the roof of the German Hospice when the Secretariat disappeared. "Don't worry, my dear," she added. "I'm sure your John is all right."

Diana Gutch slammed down the phone, furious at such a "stupid, fatuous remark." An hour later a policeman appeared at the front door. "This is finally it," she thought. "He's dead." She held her breath.

The officer said, "Your husband sent me to tell you he's survived but will be late for lunch."

Gerald Kennedy's wife flagged down Sami Hadawi. She was walking her dog. Hadawi's car had finally been repaired and he was driving home to reassure his family.

"Where was that explosion?" she asked.

"The King David."

"How terrible! Was anyone killed?" She did not know her husband had been attending a meeting at the hotel.

Hadawi had just seen Gerald Kennedy's head on the wall of the YMCA. He could not bear to be the one to tell her the truth. "I expect there must have been casualties," he said.

Zehdi Terzi stood in the doorway of the Triangle Building, looking up Julian's Way and worrying about his friends who worked in the Secretariat. There was Charles Moghanam, Adi Bittar, his classmate in law school, and Hilda Azzam, such a beauty, such high spirits. Terzi tried to imagine their terror when the bomb went off. Seven years ago, when he was fifteen, the Irgun had exploded a bomb in the Jerusalem radio station while he and other boys in a school choir were singing hymns for a popular children's hour.

An hour after the blast, police cordoned off the Secretariat and turned back relatives or suggested they gather in the YMCA courtyard. Nubar Markarian left the police barricade and ran to his sister Sophie's house on Princess Mary Road.

He and Sophie called their aunts, mother, cousins, friends and the family doctor. They told everyone the same thing. "There's been some trouble at the King David. We haven't heard from Eugenie yet. All we can do is wait."

The family gathered in Sophie's apartment. The invalid aunts whom she supported cried. Everyone kneeled and prayed, stared at the front door and asked one another the same questions again and again. "Is she going to come home? Is she trapped up there? Is she safe?"

Every few minutes Nubar ran into Princess Mary Road. Survivors were stumbling home. "Have you seen Eugenie?" he asked each one.

"No, but I've seen . . ." one said.

"Yes. I saw her standing in the rubble," another said.

"Yes. I saw her. There was a group of girls on the balcony. We heard them screaming as the balconies fell on top of one another."

Jack Mantoura returned home to find his mother standing on the doorstep, sobbing. "For God's sake, go to the King David," she wailed. "It's been blown up and your father was there."

Jack threw his briefcase on the ground and ran. When he produced his identity card the police let him through the Julian's Way checkpoint.

He took up position sitting on the low stone wall bordering the YMCA. He could see the workers digging into the heaps of rubble across the street. His father had to be pulled out alive. What happened to other families could not happen to them. They were different. Nevertheless, he had to struggle to keep from staring at the red stain on the YMCA wall and wondering, "Could that have been him? Could that have happened to my father?"

Leila Canaan and her parents rushed to the YMCA to inquire about their friend, Atallah Mantoura. Leila's father had given her first aid at home. He had been too stunned by the tragedy to scold her for meeting Tell at the King David.

When they arrived, he pointed across the street at the King David and said, "The Irgun did it to kill Arabs. Mr. Mantoura is under there, so is Grace Baramki, so is Hilda Azzam, so is . . ." The list went on and on. It included the families of her school friends, close friends of her father, prominent men, the chauffeurs and servants of prominent men. She began to cry.

Throughout the afternoon and evening the families of Secretariat workers gathered in the courtyard of the YMCA and stared across the street at the King David.

At 4 P.M. they saw the Arab linemen and public works employees replaced by a squadron of Indian sappers from the 6th Airborne Division. An hour later a Royal Air Force bulldozer arrived and began pushing the rubble on Julian's Way into mounds.

After sunset powerful arc lights illuminated the wreckage. Like spectators at a gigantic outdoor theater, the relatives stared, transfixed, as rescue workers pulled one body after another from underneath the twisted iron and shattered masonry.

"Have they found him?" "Have they found her?" They asked one another. "How many have died?" "How many have they found?" "Where are they taking the bodies?"

They answered: "He's survived, thanks be to God." "Yes, but she's a terrible mess." "We're still waiting."

They traded stories about the explosion:

—A female clerk standing on a fifth-floor balcony landed on top of the rubble without a scratch.

—As the smoke cleared, someone saw a British secretary sitting in a chair balanced on the edge of the building.

—An Arab boy ran out of the rubble and did not stop until he reached his home in Ramallah, eleven miles away.

—Lubah Wahbeh survived but her sister died. It was God's will that one sister be spared.

—They took Rashid Sbeitan to the mortuary and told his relatives he was dead. Then one of the attendants saw him move. He was revived and sent home!

"Jules Gress was in the Secretariat," someone said.

"Gress had to be there," another answered. "The explosion couldn't have taken place without him." He was famous for his bad luck.

One Arab said: "Why did they only call the French Consulate? The YMCA is much closer to the Secretariat."

"Because only Arabs go to the YMCA," someone answered. "They wanted to murder Arabs. That's why they exploded bombs in the street, to lure everyone onto the balconies so they'd be killed."

Everyone standing in the YMCA could see Sir John Shaw towering over the other rescue workers as he carried the wounded to ambulances and identified the bodies of his friends. During the afternoon a messenger brought him a coded telegram from the Colonial Secretary in London. Shaw and the cipher officer went into the lobby, swept dust and glass from the grand piano and decoded it.

The Colonial Secretary wanted a full report on the explosion. The cable ordered Shaw to send an immediate estimate of casualties, damage and security measures taken. This was the kind of "bureaucratic bunk" Shaw detested. To ask for this kind of information now, and to send the message in code, seemed incredible. "As usual," he thought, "the Colonial Office doesn't understand the situation."

Since the explosion he had been sending messages on the only available stationery, a roll of toilet paper. He ripped off more sheets for his reply to the Secretary. "I have no staff, no office, no stationery, nothing," he wrote. "But if you must have a report, here is the best I can do. . . ."

"For God's sake," he told the cipher officer when he finished, "forget the damned code and send it in clear."

London was two time zones behind Jerusalem. The second, and this time correct, UPI report of the explosion had arrived shortly after 11 A.M.

That afternoon Baffy Dugdale had tea at the Dorchester with Chaim Weizmann and his wife, Vera. Weizmann was so upset and sick he was scarcely able to speak. After the meeting Dugdale wrote in her diary that the explosion "confirms Chaim's worst fears about what might happen after he left Palestine, and may change the whole course of affairs."

That same afternoon Chaim Weizmann summoned his nephew, Ezer Weizman, to his room at the Dorchester and asked him, "Nu, what do you think of it?"

Although Ezer had been sent to study in London he was known to be sympathetic to the Irgun. He could sense the tension in the room and imagined his Aunt Vera thinking, "Now we'll see what Yechiel's son thinks of his friends murdering Englishmen."

Finally he answered his uncle, "Not at all a bad idea."

His aunt's face contorted in fury. "If you think it's such a good idea," she said, "why don't you go back to Palestine and shoot a few Englishmen?"

"Aunt Vera," he replied, "that, too, is not at all a bad idea!"

The atmosphere in the room had been poisoned. According to Ezer, the meal that followed was shortened to a tenth of its normal length. "When I got up to go," he said, "no one bothered to try and ask me to stay."

In a more modest London hotel, the Pembridge Carlton, Julius Jacobs' daughter returned to her room to find her mother and Mrs. Levi sobbing in each other's arms.

"Your father and Mr. Levi have been killed," her mother said.

In fact, the women had been told only that their husbands were missing. Mrs. Jacobs assumed the worst. A Jewish friend later called to report a rumor that the Irgun valued Jacobs so highly that they had kidnapped him just before the explosion. Mrs. Jacobs refused to believe it. She was convinced he was dead.

The next day, she received his last letter. In it he again refused to heed her pleas to leave Palestine and accept a Colonial Office job in London. "My decision to stay in Palestine is final," he wrote. "You are not to worry about me. My heart lies in Palestine."

In Amman, Jon Kimche was interviewing King Abdullah when someone called to report the explosion. The King turned to Kimche and his British aide, Colonel Broadhurst, and said, "If the King David is not safe, then no place in

Palestine is safe from the Jews." He asked if he should surround Amman with barbed wire to protect it from Jewish terrorists.

Late that afternoon in Tel Aviv, Paglin reported to Begin: "As far as the Operation is concerned, everything happened according to plan. The explosion took place on the minute. This means that the British had thirty minutes to evacuate. I cannot believe they did not obey our warnings and leave the building." Paglin did not know that Abu Jilda's porters had failed to join the attack, nor that the bombs had exploded in less than thirty minutes.

Begin reassured him. "I understand the casualties were out of your control. You should not blame yourself, we all share the responsibility."

27

July 22—July 31

THE RESPONSIBILITY weighed heavily on Begin. In the hours following the explosion he became depressed and overwrought as the names of the dead and wounded were heard over the radio. Finally the Irgun's Chief of Staff, Haim Landau, became so concerned that he turned off the radio in Begin's apartment. "This must stop," he insisted. "You must not listen to these reports."

Throughout the afternoon and evening almost every Briton, Arab and Jew in Jerusalem who was not standing vigil in the YMCA courtyard listened to the government radio station, the Palestine Broadcasting Corporation. At 9:30 P.M. an announcer read the first official casualty lists. In many households people fell silent, turned up the volume and prayed.

There were 45 dead, 46 injured, and 55 missing. People were incredulous. The announcer said, "The following officials in the Secretariat at the time of the morning's outrage are known to be *safe*, repeat *safe*: Sir John Shaw, Mr. Gibson, Mr. J. Gutch, Rhi Bey Abdul Hadi, Mr. J. Cornes, Mr. A. M. Dryburgh, Mr. J. Smith, Mr. M. Browne, Mr. Bradley, Mr. Ford, Mr. N. W. McClellan, Mrs. Small, Miss M. King, Mrs. Cassell, Miss R. Walsh, Mr. Antippa, Mr. Forrest, Mr. Bayliss and Mr. R. Newton."

The announcer read a list of those known to be dead. It included Postmaster-General Kennedy; Ezra Sperling, an American Jew who wrote numerous articles on Palestinian life for Hebrew newspapers; Yehuda Yanovsky, who had joined the Secretariat only a month before; Shmuel Yeshayahu, a noted Hebrew scholar; Zvi Shimshi, one of the highest ranking younger Jews in the civil service; Claire Russo, the young Jewess who answered the Secretariat's switchboard; Jamil Bader, the seventeen-year-old son of the main doorkeeper, who had accompanied his father to work for the first time; Jamil Ayyub, who served tea in the canteen; Jules Gress, an Arab treasury worker who had rushed back from an errand at Barclays Bank in order to attend the meeting in Jacobs' office; Lubah Wahbeh's sister Nadia, who typed in the fourth-floor army offices; eight soldiers who worked in the fourth-floor offices, all clerks and none higher in rank than sergeant; and twenty-five clerks, messengers, cleaners and drivers.

The list of those missing included Musgrave, Gibbs, Mantoura, Farley, Levi, Jacobs, Walsh, Eugenie Markarian, Hilda Azzam, Leah Bachrach, ten members of the public and dozens of clerks and laborers. Until their bodies were recovered and identified, no one, least of all their families, wanted to add their names to the list of the dead. Army doctors had admitted it was conceivable they were still alive, trapped underneath the rubble. There was still hope.

After reading these three lists the announcer said, "Three unidentified bodies have been recovered and relatives of persons whose names are on the list of missing from the King David bomb outrage are requested to telephone 4437, extension 5, and give full descriptions and full names of the missing persons, together with details of the clothes they were wearing and of any jewelry or other identifiable articles in their possession when last seen."

Relatives calling extension 5 reached a ground-floor room in the YMCA where Lady Shaw had created a bureau of policemen, doctors and volunteers to identify bodies and compile casualty lists. The police had turned another YMCA room into a temporary morgue.

While the relatives in Jerusalem listened to the radio, Menahem Begin received a note from Israel Galili, asking him to announce that the Irgun alone had carried out the attack and promising that the Haganah would refrain from comment.

Begin complied with Galili's request. On the morning of July 23, Irgun soldiers plastered Tel Aviv with posters explaining the operation and omitting any mention of the Haganah's involvement. The posters said:

> Yesterday at 12:05 P.M. soldiers of the Irgun Zvai Leumi attacked the central building of the British power of occupation in Palestine. Before the attack the bombs were placed so as to explode half an hour later. Immediately after that the telephone operator of the KD, several newspapers, agencies, and the French Consulate were warned by telephone. Also a little alarm bomb which could do no harm was placed before the KD and exploded so that the hotel could be evacuated in time. The tragedy which happened in the offices of the

Government is not the guilt of the Jewish soldiers who have received orders to spare human lives and they fulfilled that order. But this tragedy came through the fault of the British Tyrants who played with human life on the advice of the military experts who said that they would be able to disarm the bombs and therefore there was no need for evacuation. On every bomb a placard was placed written in three official languages warning that any touch on the bombs would set them off. Despite this they tried to disarm the bombs and the explosion happened. The warnings by telephone were given between 12:10 and 12:15 so that the British had 22 minutes to evacuate the building and therefore the whole responsibility falls on the British and should it be necessary we will give further particulars. . . .

The Government Information Office immediately denied that any warnings had been received by anyone in a position of authority. Shaw told one of the Jewish widows, "I would never risk ignoring a warning. I have a wife and young children. I wasn't told. Maybe the hotel was warned."

Even as the Irgun's posters were going up in Tel Aviv, the Haganah's radio station, Kol Israel, was announcing that, "the Hebrew Resistance Movement denounces the heavy toll of lives caused in the dissidents' Operation at the King David Hotel." The Haganah made no mention of its own complicity.

Begin was outraged. He had been betrayed. Several hours after the Haganah broadcast, a messenger appeared at Bin Nun Street with a letter from Galili:

23 July 1946 9:00
To M., Shalom!
The serious consequences of your operation in Jerusalem have led to developments which were unforeseen. The reactions as published disregarded our guidance and were unavoidable under the present circumstances.
The situation creates tragic and serious complications for the continuation of our struggle. In order to avoid this it is important for us to meet at 9:00 P.M. tonight. . . .

By midmorning of the twenty-third the rescue work had settled into a routine. The army sappers worked on a schedule of sixteen hours on, eight hours off. Many refused to fall out when it was their turn and worked until they collapsed. One airman fainted after driving the bulldozer for twenty consecutive hours. Inspector Hadingham returned to the King David after being discharged from the hospital and lifted slabs of cement with his bandaged hands.

The rescue workers labored frantically and without rest because, just when it seemed impossible that anyone could still be alive, they would find another survivor.

At 8:00 the night before they had found Jamais, an Arab messenger. They reached four more survivors during the night and at 11 A.M. extracted an Arab constable. Several minutes later they heard another moan and then a tapping.

An officer blew a whistle. The sappers shut off drills and acetylene torches; rescue workers froze with their pickaxes in midair; YMCA helpers balancing trays of lemonade stopped where they stood; the relatives in the YMCA courtyard turned and stared intently at the rubble. Everyone was silent. An officer lowered an oversize stethoscope into a crevice and listened.

"Maybe it's Eugenie who's moaning; maybe it's her they're digging out alive," thought Nubar Markarian.

Jack Mantoura prayed it was his father.

The news that someone was alive spread quickly. More relatives gathered at the Y. Even if the moans did not belong to their own, they proved it possible to survive for twenty-four hours entombed in the wreckage. Others might still be found.

Throughout the afternoon rescue workers followed this procedure: they worked for fifteen minutes, an officer blew a whistle, they froze, the stethoscope was lowered into the hole, the trapped survivor tapped his stick and, having again pinpointed his location, they resumed work.

By midafternoon the sweet stench of decomposing bodies had mixed with the acrid odor of dynamite to create an unbearable smell. Medical officers squirted disinfectant through crevices and soldiers dipped handkerchiefs into it and tied them over their mouths and noses.

By 7 P.M. they had cleared a ten-foot hole in the rubble. The moans and tappings grew louder and part of a body became visible. An officer bent over, cupped his hands over his mouth and shouted into the hole, "Are you a wog?"

"Yes, a wog named Thompson," came the answer. It was Donald Thompson, a popular fifty-five-year-old assistant secretary who was due to retire in several weeks.

"My head's wedged between two slabs," he said. "There's another man here and I believe he's alive. I can't see him but I can see his stomach moving." He was wrong. It was his own stomach.

Gently, carefully, the soldiers cleared away more rubble. When the hole was large enough, John Gutch jumped in. "I'm sorry, John," Thompson said, "but it appears I won't be able to report for work tomorrow."

At 8:00 the soldiers began to free him. One fed him a brandy and water solution through a rubber hose while another tied ropes around his waist. The rescue workers rested on shovels and axes as he was raised from the hole. "Thanks, chaps," he said.

Shaw was waiting for him. "Hello, Topper old chap, are you all right?" he said.

"Yes, sir, but I'm sorry to have troubled you all so much."

"Nobody's troubled, old boy. We'll take care of you."

Thompson was loaded into an ambulance and driven to Government Hospital. Despite being buried for thirty-one hours without food or water, he was conscious and appeared uninjured. The next day he died of shock.

Thompson's miraculous recovery from the rubble encouraged other relatives. Jack Mantoura was pleased it was Thompson the soldiers had found. If the fifty-five-year-old Thompson could survive for so long, so could his father.

Some relatives were more realistic. "What do you really think?" Joan Gibbs asked William Bradley. "Do you think there's any hope for Brian?"

"No," he said. "None at all."

Begin and Galili met at 9 P.M. on July 23 in Tel Aviv.

"What does this Kol Israel broadcast mean?" Begin demanded. "Don't you know what and who caused the 'heavy toll'? Why do you denounce us? The plan was agreed between us, our men carried out their instructions precisely, the warning was given. Why don't you tell the truth?"

"The members of the Executive weren't informed," Galili replied. "You must understand that most of our people are still in detention camps and we don't have regular contact with the few on the outside. The people who condemned you weren't aware that it was done with our knowledge and concurrence."

Galili did not tell Begin the truth, that the X Committee had canceled the operation. Instead, he repeated the rumor that Sir John Shaw had received one of the Irgun's warnings. According to Galili, when a policeman told Shaw about the warning he had replied, "I'm not here to take orders from Jews; I'm here to give them."

Begin demanded that Kol Israel immediately broadcast this account and Galili agreed. In fact, the story was a baseless rumor promoted by the Haganah in order to mollify the Irgun and fix responsibliity for the carnage on Shaw.

Before leaving, Galili pulled a note from his pocket and handed it to Begin. It was from Yitzhak Sadeh, the Haganah's Chief of Operations.

Begin read it and then, according to him, "everything seemed to go black." In it, Sadeh accused Paglin of going back on his promise to carry out the attack between two and three in the afternoon when most Secretariat workers would be at lunch.

Begin protested to Galili that never once, when he and other members of his High Command reviewed the plan, had Paglin ever mentioned that the Haganah insisted the operation occur during these hours. In fact, given the nature of the plan, it would have been impossible to attack between two and three. The Regence would have been full of lunchtime customers. He was positive Sadeh was wrong. Before parting he and Galili agreed that Paglin and Sadeh would have to submit to an official inquiry of the Joint Command.

On Wednesday evening, sixty hours after the explosion, army doctors announced there was no possibility anyone trapped in the rubble was still alive.

The officer commanding the engineers predicted it would take four more days to reach bottom and recover all the bodies.

The government radio broadcast the latest casualty figures: 61 dead, 45 injured, and 59 missing. Only sixteen bodies had been recovered since Monday evening, among them that of Roderick Musgrave. Eight of the sixteen corpses remained unidentified.

Coroners determined that the victims had died of snapped spinal cords, crushed or fractured skulls, internal or external bleeding, and nervous shock. Practically all had multiple contusions and lacerations; many were so mutilated and decomposed as to be unrecognizable.

Lady Shaw relied on clothes and personal effects to make identifications. Every night she carried the wallets, rings, watches and bracelets home and, kneeling on the floor of the German Hospice bathroom, wept as she washed them in a tin basin to remove the blood and flesh before showing them to the relatives.

Mrs. George Baramki identified her sister's clothes and false teeth.

Mrs. Bahai Tewfik was shown a man's suit and a cross. Her husband's body was so badly mutilated that Lady Shaw was determined to prevent her seeing it.

Khalil el Ahari was given a sealed coffin containing his brother's remains and ordered not to open it.

Geoffrey Walsh, the popular Financial Secretary who had encouraged the Jewish diamond industry, was identified by his gold cufflinks.

An elderly Arab sheik worried that the body of his son, a Secretariat messenger, might never be recovered. "Please find me something," he begged Lady Shaw, "one little finger, a toe, anything."

"Why do you want just a finger?" she asked.

"Because unless some part of his body is buried he'll never see heaven. I must have something."

Sir John Shaw noticed a fancy crocodile wallet with gold corners lying in the rubble. When he bent over to pick it up he saw to his horror that it was smeared with blood. Inside were letters identifying it as belonging to Bernard Bourdillon, the young Colonial officer who had wanted to return to Nigeria. Until now, no one had suspected that Bourdillon had been in the Secretariat. His wife, who was home in England, thought he was in Nazareth.

With so many bodies to be identified, mistakes were inevitable. A soldier named V. A. Hadford lay his shirt over the face of a dead girl. He had left his paycheck in the shirt pocket and the name of Miss V. A. Hadford appeared on the list of the dead.

A Mr. Cohen from Tel Aviv called the YMCA almost hourly to inquire about his wife and daughter. He was convinced they had been at the Secretariat on Monday. Finally on Wednesday he found them. They had been visiting his wife's mother in Nahariyya.

"Congratulations, Mr. Cohen," Lady Shaw shouted into the telephone when he called with the good news. Afterward everyone in the YMCA laughed uncontrollably. It was the only amusing event of the week.

One Jewish victim remained unclaimed despite frequent broadcasts of his description: "Height, 184 centimeters; face may have been slightly deformed naturally; eyes, pale blue; hair, black; age, approximately thirty-five years; teeth, artificial both upper and lower; Charlie Chaplin mustache with gray hairs." Some Jews assumed there was no one to claim him because his family had perished in the Holocaust. If this was true, he was not the only victim without blood relatives. Leo Baum, a Jewish administrative assistant, had been the last surviving member of his immediate family. His mother, brother, and sisters had all been gassed by the Nazis.

Throughout the week Jewish newspapers, organizations and individuals condemned the explosion and mourned the loss of life.

In Paris, David Ben-Gurion told a reporter for *France-Soir*, "The Irgun is the enemy of the Jewish people. . . ."

In London, Baffy Dugdale described Chaim Weizmann as being in an "irrational frenzy of anger. He refused to go to the Zionist office or discuss anything calmly on the telephone," she said.

The main targets of his rage were Ben-Gurion and Moshe Sneh. "He considers that he has been deceived and defied about the Haganah," wrote Dugdale.

Several days later Weizmann met Richard Crossman, a British Labour Party politician whose experience on the Anglo-American Committee had made him sympathetic to Zionism. Weizmann was touched that Crossman had come to his suite in the Dorchester Hotel. His other British friends were boycotting him because of the explosion.

Their conversation showed Weizmann's ambivalence about Jewish violence. He condemned it, but sympathized with its causes. As soon as Crossman mentioned the King David tears began streaming down Weizmann's face. "I can't help feeling proud of our boys," he said. "If only it had been a German headquarters, they would have gotten the Victoria Cross."

In Palestine, the Jewish newspaper *Mishmar* appeared to call for another Haganah war against the Irgun: "What next? Are we to leave the fate of our people in the hands of an evil gang of fascists? Is it not our duty to purge our own camp before it is too late?"

The newspaper *Hatsofeh* said, "We must see and point out the yawning abyss into which desperate men among us have plunged and are pulling us after them. This tragedy is sabotage committed against us and the integrity of our struggle."

According to *Haaretz*, "In the piles of debris many dear lives were buried

yesterday. Who knows whether many other things were not buried there too."
In a second editorial the paper said:

> We came to this country not only to save ourselves from anti-
> Semitism and persecution, but to build a new and better life, based on
> the principles of justice which have been Israel's great contribution to
> world civilization.
> Has it been decreed that we should be guilty of all the sins and
> crimes of our enemies before attaining a haven of peace, the striving
> toward which has been the main motive force of Zionism? And if these
> are birth pangs of the Messiah, was that ancient Sage not right who
> said, "Let the Messiah come but I do not wish to see him"? The
> purpose for which those who committed yesterday's crime and their
> associates are striving, so they tell us, is a Jewish State. Even if murder
> could get us a State—which is more than doubtful—would that State
> be really Jewish? What would such a State be worth if we had had to
> blind ourselves to all the moral values of our Jewish tradition and break
> all the commandments in order to attain it? The best of the Yishuv
> stands with weakened forces, facing a rising tide of criminal, insane
> bloodshed. In very truth, the price is too great.

The Executive of the Jewish Agency and the Executive of the Vaad Leumi
expressed "their horror at the dastardly crime perpetrated by the gang of
desperadoes who today attacked the Government offices in Jerusalem and shed
the innocent blood of Government Officers and other citizens, British, Jewish
and Arab." They also extended "their deepest sympathy to the relatives of those
who have been murdered and those who have been injured. The Yishuv in
Palestine is called upon to rise up against these abominable outrages."

The Histadrut (the Jewish Labor Organization) adopted a resolution expressing shock at "the revolting massacre." "Jewish labor . . . condemns this
appalling crime and from its very depths abhors it and its perpetrators."

Chief Rabbi Ben Zion Uziel declared, "From the depths of my heart, I call
on all who have had a hand in this sin: cease from this dangerous path which is
forbidden by the law of Israel, and from which there can be no returning for
those who take it."

Doctor Canaan's Jewish friends told him, "This is not how we wanted to
build the Jewish State."

Pauline Mantoura's Jewish dressmaker telephoned to express her sorrow. She
did not dare come in person, not because she was afraid of the Irgun, but
because she was so ashamed of the Jews she could not bear to face Mrs.
Mantoura.

One member of the Irgun slipped a message through the window of Nissim
Levi's sister's house apologizing for the operation and saying, "I join your
sorrow."

On the afternoon of the twenty-third, Begin met with members of the High

Command. Among them was Samuel Katz, who later wrote that Begin appeared saddened and angered at the British for bringing about the unnecessary loss of life. At one point Begin said that "among those killed in the explosion were sympathizers with the Irgun including Julius Jacobs."

Adina appeared in Richard Mowrer's hospital room and laid a bunch of roses and an envelope on his bed.

"Who are you?" he asked.

She shook her head and vanished. Inside the envelope was a letter from Begin. It said:

> We are at a loss to find words that will adequately reflect our deep sorrow over the fact that you suffered an injury as an outcome of our action against British headquarters.
>
> We hope that you have ascertained the facts connected with this action and are now fully convinced that every opportunity existed to prevent the wounds which you personally received and all the other tragic casualties among the civilians which nobody regrets more than we do. For our part we did everything possible to avoid just such a human sacrifice as did occur.
>
> Yours Sincerely, Begin.
Irgun Zvai Leumi.

This American reporter, the representative of a strongly pro-Zionist American newspaper, was the only person to receive a letter of condolence from Begin.

Two days after the explosion, the Irgun's "Voice of Fighting Zion" broadcast a communiqué:

> The British Department of Information published the content of our announcement of July 23rd and said that the Irgun Zvai Leumi had announced that it "mourned the high number of victims," etc.
>
> This is a distortion. We wrote that "we mourn for Jewish victims" and we meant—as always—what we said. It is true that the objective of our attack was in this case not any person but the destruction of the objective itself, and all the victims who fell, fell because of the guilty negligence of the British. However, the British did not mourn at all for the six million Jews who lost their lives, because of them, during the war; they did not mourn for the fourteen thousand rescued Jews who perished in their concentration camps in the period following the "Liberation"; they did not mourn for the *Struma* and the *Patria*. They did not mourn for the hundreds of Jews who were murdered in Poland because the British did not allow them to enter the despoiled Jewish homeland. They did not mourn for the scores of pioneers and the Jewish fighters whom they, the British, murdered with their own hands, without warning and in cold blood. They did not mourn. On the contrary, they were glad, and they blessed the hands of the murderers.
>
> Therefore we leave the mourning for the British victims to the

British themselves. We shall mourn for our victims, the Jewish victims, and we, together with their families, shall mourn for them all our lives.

And with this mourning and with this anger over the deep Jewish tragedy we shall continue going our way, the way of suffering, the way of struggle.

And the God of truth will be at our side.

The broadcast failed to mention that the majority of the victims were neither British nor Jewish, but Arab. For the Irgun, the Arabs were invisible.

Funerals for the Arab victims occurred at a rate of five a day throughout the week. On the afternoon of the twenty-third, Arab shops and cafés in Jerusalem closed and as many as ten thousand mourners marched in funeral processions. In Beit Jala the entire population turned out for the funerals. At Lydda three thousand attended the funeral of Ivan Phillips' driver, Bader.

Some funerals resembled political demonstrations. The dead were hailed as martyrs to the cause of Arab Palestine and young men carried banners and chanted slogans attacking the Jews, Britain and, in a new development, the United States and President Truman, Zionism's newest champion. Young men clapped their hands and shouted in unison a curse learned from the British soldiers, "Bugger Truman! Bugger Truman! Bugger Truman!"

Speakers at the victims' graves made appeals for vengeance and stressed that Arabs, not Britons, had been the intended targets of the bomb. A graveside oration by Emile Ghoury struck a theme repeated at many Arab funerals: "Your death in this treacherous manner has done our cause much good and has strengthened our morale, but be sure that we will avenge you, and our revenge will be terrible."

Many of the victims had belonged to prominent and respected Arab families, families that until now had been only marginally involved in Arab politics. Later, when the Irgun revealed the role of the Haganah, these moderate Arabs learned, according to the relative of one victim, "an important lesson about the treachery of so-called 'moderate Zionism.'"

The Arabs later came to regard the King David explosion as the beginning of a new phase of Jewish terrorism, a phase in which its goal would be to intimidate and eventually drive them from Palestine. This terror proved to them the truth of Antonius's prediction that the Jews could not win Palestine "except by dislodging or exterminating the nation in possession."

The British were no more impressed than the Arabs with Jewish proclamations of sympathy and outrage. Sir John Shaw refused to accept a message of regret from the head of the Revisionist Party (the New Zionist Organization), Dr. Arieh Altman, and wrote in reply that:

I have received your letter of July 24th addressed to me by name which purports to express grief and sympathy in respect to the dreadful event of Monday July 22 which massacred more than one hundred of my faithful colleagues and friends.

According to their own published boast this revolting crime was perpetrated by a national military organization (Irgun Zvai Leumi) which is associated with your New Zionist Organization. In these circumstances I find myself unable to accept the expressions of regret and sympathy which emanate from the central office of the New Zionist Organization.

Most British believed that the test of the sincerity of Jewish outrage would be the extent to which Jews cooperated in tracking down those responsible.

They were soon disappointed. The authorized Jewish leadership did nothing beyond publishing verbal attacks on the Irgun. Even moderates within the Agency, knowing that anyone convicted of the bombing faced certain execution, could not bring themselves to cooperate with the police. A year after the Holocaust, few Jews could bear to condemn others to death, no matter how heinous their crimes or grave their political differences. More important, there was only one Jewish organization which could deliver the Irgun soldiers responsible—the Haganah, which was itself deeply implicated.

Most of those responsible for Operation Chick were never apprehended. Police and army searches of the Old City netted only the two wounded Irgun soldiers hiding in the Tachemoni School. Aharon was taken into custody and Avidor's body taken to the morgue. The rest of the assault unit escaped by catching Arab buses to Jaffa and then slipping into Tel Aviv. Only Gideon and Abu Jilda remained behind and they avoided capture by posing as inmates of an insane asylum.

Eight days after the explosion, the army cordoned off Tel Aviv and conducted a four-day, house-to-house search. By chance one group of soldiers camped in Begin's garden and frequently visited the kitchen to ask for water. Begin escaped capture by hiding in a secret compartment. He stayed there for almost four days, never moving or eating.

When the operation ended, eight hundred Jews had been arrested and sent to detention camps. None were responsible for the attack on the King David.

The remorse of the Yishuv and the revulsion of the world at the Irgun's deed was soon blunted by the publication of the letter General Barker had written minutes after the blast. By mistake, one of Barker's aides had circulated it with only a restricted classification. A British officer removed it from the notice board of his mess and slipped it to Jon Kimche. Kimche's newspaper refused to print it but he persuaded an American reporter to send it to his paper.

The anti-Semitism in Barker's last sentence—"punishing the Jews in a way the race dislikes as much as any, namely by striking at their pockets"—did Britain's position in Palestine grave harm throughout the world, particularly in the United States. By giving credence to Zionist allegations of British anti-

Semitism it distracted attention from the King David outrage, provided some with justification for Jewish terrorism and did more to undermine British rule in Palestine than the explosion itself.

On Thursday the twenty-fifth, the day General Barker circulated his letter, rescue workers recovered fourteen more bodies from the wreckage. They found Leah Bachrach wearing her new shoes. They found Shaw's bodyguard, Sergeant Jennings, and his doorkeeper, Ibrahim Bader, buried in the same hole. They found Hilda Azzam and Eugenie Markarian clutching each other's hands. The explosion proved to Nubar Markarian the Jews' determination to rule Palestine and he and his family, seeing no future for Armenian Christians in a Jewish State, began making preparations to leave Jerusalem.

They had not yet found Atallah Mantoura. His son, Jack, continued his vigil on the wall of the YMCA, still optimistic. He had learned to tell when the soldiers discovered a corpse. They shut off their drills, gathered around a hole and, sweating and naked from the waist up, became quiet. An ambulance backed up onto the sidewalk and Shaw crossed the street to inform the victim's family. There were wails and sobs, people collapsing from grief.

Mantoura had witnessed the same scene again and again. This time Shaw walked over to him and said, "I think we've found your father, Jack, but I'm not completely positive." His voice left no doubt; Atallah Mantoura was dead.

Mantoura remembered: "I followed Shaw and an American from the YMCA across the street and into the rubble. They pointed to a small hole. I said I couldn't see anything and they pointed again.

"Most of him was under the rubble; the only thing showing was one side of his shoulder and his face. His bifocals were still on his nose and I was amazed they hadn't been broken, only a bit twisted. What shocked me the most was his suit, it was torn at the shoulder and I could see its padding. Later someone told me his arm had been severed and never recovered."

Shaw's voice brought Mantoura out of his trance. "Do you recognize him?"

"Yes. It's him."

He walked back across the street and burst into tears. When he recovered he saw his father being loaded into the ambulance. He begged to be allowed to ride with him but they refused. His last glimpse was of his father's shoes, the brown wing-tips with rubber soles.

The remaining bodies were recovered and identified over the weekend. Lady Shaw, accompanied by Greek, Arab, Hebrew and Armenian interpreters, visited the home of every bereaved family and expressed her condolences. The visits took so much of her time that her young son began asking, "Don't you ever visit anyone but widows?" "Are you a widow?" he asked every woman he met in the following weeks. "Mother only visits widows."

Joan Gibbs never visited the hotel. She was pregnant and wanted to stay with her children. "I told them he had gone to Aden but they learned the truth from their friends."

On Sunday, six days after the explosion, they found her husband's body. A beam had fallen across his head, fracturing his skull.

"I'm going to the Colonial Office right away," she told John Gutch after learning the news. "If I get there while I'm still pregnant they'll probably give me more help in raising and educating the children."

Other wives clung to the impossible hope that, five or six days after the blast, their husbands might be rescued. One widow became so hysterical when she learned the truth that Lady Shaw offered her a sleeping pill. "Who the hell do you think you are to go around offering pills to people," the widow screamed.

One Jewish widow stared at Lady Shaw without speaking. Lady Shaw left as soon as possible, shocked by the intensity of the woman's hatred and afraid that "the explosion had destroyed our fragile and carefully built friendship."

Doreen Farley refused to believe Lady Shaw's news. Two people had claimed to have seen her husband after the explosion. She herself had been to the morgue the day before and could not identify him from among the unclaimed dead. She continued to hope he had been stunned and then wandered away from the hotel with amnesia.

Lady Shaw tried to convince her that his badly mutilated body had finally been recovered. She handed her the contents of his pockets: a wallet, a checkbook, and a toy airplane. The night before Lady Shaw had cried uncontrollably as she washed them.

Doreen Farley handed back the airplane and said, "No, no, it's impossible. This couldn't be his. We never had anything like it."

Lady Shaw held it in front of her face. "But the children, perhaps he bought it for the children?"

"No. Impossible. He's still alive."

"How about the wallet?"

"It's not his."

"The checkbook?"

She examined it. It *was* his. "He must have dropped it. He's still alive. I know it."

Lady Shaw became frantic. "Dear woman, I must make you believe that he's dead. You must accept it."

She held out a bunch of keys in the palm of her hand. "These are the keys found on his body. Lock me out of your house. If I can open the front door with these, then will you finally believe your husband is dead?"

Doreen Farley agreed. She locked the door and waited. Lady Shaw had once lived in the Farley's house. She knew which key opened the front door. She slipped it into the lock and turned. The door swung open and Doreen Farley burst into tears.

This was Lady Shaw's last visit. On July 31, the government announced the final toll: 91 dead and 46 injured. Of these 91 dead there were 21 first-rank government officials, 13 soldiers, 3 policemen, and 5 members of the public. The remaining 49 were second-rank clerks, typists, and messengers, junior members of the Secretariat, employees of the hotel, and canteen workers.

By nationality there were two Armenians killed, one Russian, a Greek, an Egyptian, twenty-eight Britons, forty-one Arabs and seventeen Jews.

EPILOGUE

August 1, 1946–1980

THE KILLED and wounded were not the only casualties of the King David explosion. Weizmann's dream of a nationalism untainted by violence, a nationalism unlike any other, was also mortally wounded.

Weizmann's attempt to prevent Operation Chick proved the penultimate time he would try to exercise authority as President of the World Zionist Organization. The last time he spoke out was six months later at the twenty-second World Zionist Conference in Basel, Switzerland. Even though the majority of the delegates were no longer in sympathy with the type of moderate Zionism he had come to symbolize, he delivered a speech condemning violence and urging them to retain a belief in "the victory of peaceful ideals."

An American delegate interrupted this phrase with a shout of "Demagogue!"

Weizmann looked up from his notes and removed his spectacles. The hall quieted. He had been reading his words slowly and haltingly. Now, in a loud, booming voice, he said:

> Somebody has called me a demagogue. I do not know who. I hope that I will never learn the man's name. *I* a demagogue! I who have borne all the ills and travail of this movement! The person who flung that word in my face ought to know that in every house and stable in

Nahalal, in every little workshop in Tel Aviv or Haifa, there is a drop of my blood. You know I am telling you the truth. Some people do not like to hear it—but you *will* hear me. I warn you against bogus palliatives, against short cuts, against false prophets, against facile generalizations, against distortion of historic facts. . . .

If you think of bringing the redemption nearer by un-Jewish methods, if you lose faith in hard work and better days, then you commit idolatry and endanger what we have built. Would that I had a tongue of flame, the strength of prophets, to warn you against the paths of Babylon and Egypt. "Zion shall be redeemed in judgment—and not by any other means."

Overcome with emotion, most of the delegates rose to their feet and applauded. Weizmann left the podium and walked slowly down the aisle, half-blind, old, and exhausted. He embraced his wife and was gone.

Several days later, knowing he could not be reelected, he withdrew his name from consideration as President of the Zionist movement. After independence he was appointed to the ceremonial office of President of the State of Israel. He asked Moshe Shertok, the Foreign Minister, to describe his duties as President.

"Just to be a symbol," Shertok replied.

The King David explosion also mortally wounded the alliance between the Irgun and Haganah. Because of the dispute between Sadeh and Paglin over the timing of the attack and because of the operation's appalling casualties, the Joint Command collapsed in bitterness and recriminations. It was never re-formed.

At the meeting of the Jewish Agency Executive in Paris held a month after the explosion, Ben-Gurion ordered the Haganah to refrain from further attacks on British installations and confine itself to smuggling illegal immigrants and procuring weapons. These operations would prepare the Yishuv for what he believed was the "probable eventuality" of a war with the Arabs. He was certain that this war, not the revolt against the British, would determine the survival of a Jewish State. He considered the Irgun's obsession with expelling the British immediately and unconditionally short-sighted and dangerous. If the British left too soon the Arab attack might occur before the Haganah had marshaled sufficient arms to repel it.

The Irgun defied Ben-Gurion and continued its revolt against the Mandate. Freed from the Haganah's restraint, its attacks became increasingly ruthless and brutal. It took hostages and executed them, placed bombs in the British Embassy in Rome, attempted to assassinate British officials, and blew up buildings without warning.

In March 1947, an Irgun assault unit detonated bombs in a Jerusalem officers' club. No warning was given and the building collapsed. Seventeen soldiers and three civilian telephone operators died.

In July the Irgun kidnapped two British sergeants, held them hostage for seventeen days, and then hanged them in an orange grove in retaliation for the execution of three Irgun members the day before. Paglin placed the nooses around the sergeants' necks.

Also during the summer of 1947 Begin ordered General Barker assassinated. Barker had now returned to England. His last official act in Palestine had been to confirm the death sentences of three Irgun members.

Before the two Irgun members assigned to the Barker assassination could perfect a plan, suspicious Scotland Yard detectives ordered them to leave Britain. One of the two frustrated assassins was Chaim Weizmann's nephew, Ezer. In 1977 Ezer Weizman became Minister of Defense in the new Begin government.

The Irgun also tried to kill Andrew Campbell, the military lawyer who had prosecuted its soldiers. Campbell's life was saved by Punch You Bugger, who heard the assassins sneaking around outside and barked, waking the household. As they fled, one of the terrorists shot Punch. He survived his wounds and was awarded seven medals at the Olympia Dog Show.

Two months after the King David explosion, Sir John Shaw was appointed High Commissioner to Trinidad and Tobago. The Irgun immediately sent a letter bomb to his new post. It was intercepted in the mails and dismantled.

The Irgun's revolt—in particular, the King David bombing and the hanging of the two sergeants—accelerated but did not cause Britain's departure from Palestine. The Second World War, not the Irgun, had robbed Britain of the resources and will to maintain an empire.

In 1947 Britain asked the United Nations to make recommendations for Palestine's future. At the end of November, the General Assembly voted to partition Palestine into Jewish and Arab states, reserving Jerusalem as an international city. Britain announced it would terminate the Mandate and withdraw its armed forces by the middle of May 1948.

The Palestinian Arabs were outraged by the UN plan. Arab mobs and organized terrorist bands began attacking Jewish civilians. By the end of 1947 they were murdering an average of fifty a week.

The Irgun retaliated. On December 29 an Irgun bomb exploded near Jerusalem's Damascus Gate killing fifteen Arabs. The following day Irgunists hurled a bomb at Arab workers standing outside a Haifa oil refinery. A week later they rolled an oil drum packed with TNT and scrap metal into a group of Arabs waiting at a Jerusalem bus stop. Seventeen died.

The most notorious Irgun operation directed against Arabs took place in April 1948, when Irgun and Sternist units attacked the Arab village of Dir Yassin killing 254 men, women, and children. The Haganah and Jewish Agency condemned the attack, calling it a massacre. Begin claimed that the village had been a legitimate military objective and that the Irgun had brought up a loudspeaker mounted on a truck in order to warn civilians to flee. The truck, however, fell into a ditch and the warning was not heard by the villagers. Another Irgun warning had failed.

Five weeks after Dir Yassin, Britain withdrew from Palestine and Ben-Gurion proclaimed the State of Israel. Immediately the new state was invaded by the armies of neighboring Arab countries. During the war that followed, it was the Haganah's superb training and the men and weapons it had smuggled into Palestine during the closing years of the Mandate that proved decisive and ensured Israel's survival.

In June 1948, only a month after Britain's departure, the cold war between the Irgun and Haganah suddenly exploded into a hot one. Sixteen Jews were killed and seventy-five wounded during a brief battle between the two organizations for control of a shipment of Irgun weapons on board the S.S. *Altalena* anchored off Tel Aviv. During the fighting, Paglin made an unsuccessful attempt to seize the offices of Israel's legal government.

The bitterness between the Irgun and Haganah persisted long after they were disbanded in 1948. For the next twenty-nine years, Israel was governed by the founders and heirs of the left-wing labor movement, leaders such as David Ben-Gurion, Moshe Sharett (Shertok), Levi Eshkol, Yitzhak Rabin and Golda Meir. They had approved "The Season," condemned the King David operation, and opposed the Irgun during the *Altalena* incident. Most never lost their dislike and distrust of Begin. In their speeches and writings they often referred to him as a terrorist and a threat to Israel's democracy.

Golda Meir, for example, said in her memoirs: "But I feel that it would be dishonest for me not to make crystal clear my own attitude to the methods (and philosophy) of the Irgun Zvai Leumi and the Sternists. I was and always have been unalterably opposed—both on moral grounds and tactically—to terror of any kinds, whether waged against Arabs because they are Arabs or against the British because they were British. It was, and has remained, my firm conviction that . . . they were wrong (and thus dangerous to the Yishuv) from start to finish."

Meir, like Ben-Gurion, Shertok and most others who led Israel in its infancy, had belonged to the activist wing of the Jewish Agency. Although they had differed with Weizmann over the application of Havlagah, they continued, throughout their political careers, to be influenced by his vision of a nation based on a uniquely Jewish agrarian socialism, a nation unlike any other.

Begin did not share this vision. He wanted a state *like* every other, a state that would make another Holocaust impossible, a state that included the entire east and west banks of the Jordan River. Begin was also opposed to socialism and found his greatest support among the populations of Israel's cities. His attack on the King David Hotel had shattered Weizmann's hope that, despite the Holocaust, the Yishuv could return to its earlier belief in a nonviolent nationalism. His election as Prime Minister, in 1977, was evidence of the waning influence of those who still hoped that Israel might someday fulfill Weizmann's utopian vision.

Begin never abandoned his vision of a greater Israel. After the 1948 war, he muted his claims to the east bank of the Jordan River but continued to claim that the lands west of the river rightfully belonged to Israel. After Israel occupied these lands in the 1967 war, he began referring to them as "The Estate of our Forefathers." His election as Prime Minister ten years later finally put him in a position to encourage extensive settlement on this "estate," and to implement his lifelong vision of "the entire land of Israel." For the moment, his Zionist vision, not Weizmann's, was in ascendancy.

For many former members of the Irgun, Begin's election seemed a vindication of the struggle they had waged three decades earlier. It also alleviated the discrimination they had been subjected to by the Israeli Army, civil service, and labor organizations. Yael, for example, had been dismissed from her position in the Histadrut after she appeared with Begin and Gideon at a public meeting in 1972.

This meeting was one of many occasions at which Begin has attempted to convince Israeli and foreign opinion that, British denials notwithstanding, the Irgun transmitted a warning to the King David Hotel. He believes that this warning completely absolves the Irgun from any responsibility for the casualties caused by its bombs. In fact, he often points to the King David warnings as proof that the Irgun was not a terrorist organization.

Begin is sensitive to being called a terrorist since it appears to place the Irgun in the same category as the Palestine Liberation Organization (PLO). His sensitivity is somewhat justified. As a rule, acts of terrorism committed by the PLO have tended to be more ruthless than those of the Irgun. The PLO has never adhered to even the most flexible moral code. It does not attempt to minimalize casualties. Rather than seeking to warn civilians, it seeks them out.

The similarities between the Irgun and contemporary terrorist organizations such as the PLO are, however, more numerous than their differences.

All have employed the same terrorist techniques: taking hostages, attacking embassies, and bombing civilian targets.

All have employed these techniques systematically. The Irgun's participation in the King David operation was part of a systematic strategy to force Britain to leave Palestine; the Haganah's participation was an aberration.

Most of the victims of these techniques have been innocents. In the case of the King David explosion, they were messengers and clerks; thirty years later the PLO attacked Jewish shoppers, schoolchildren, or tourists boarding an airplane.

The members of these organizations are usually not psychopathic murderers; not Charles Mansons but Adinas, Gideons and Chaim-Toits—people of considerable courage and patriotism to whom terrorism seems a compelling necessity.

Terrorists tend to exaggerate the importance of their acts. A successful terrorist campaign may, as in the case of the Irgun's revolt, accelerate an historical process; only rarely does it cause it to happen. Thus the King David explosion was to have its greatest impact not on the fact of Israel's independence, but on its timetable, and on the internal dynamics of Zionism and on the lives of the widowed and wounded, and the survivors.

Sir John and Lady Shaw live in retirement in a small village in Sussex. In 1977 Lady Shaw said of her husband, "He's never completely recovered from the shock of the explosion; from losing so many of his friends and then being unjustly blamed for not heeding a warning."

Shaw has continued to deny the falsehood that he rejected an Irgun warning and ever used the words, "I'm here to give orders to the Jews, not to take them." As late as 1977 Israel Galili, recently Israel's Minister of Information, was unable to provide any proof that the warning was passed on to Shaw and that he made these remarks. Nevertheless, this story, the one Galili related to Begin the day after the explosion, has been repeated in numerous articles and books.

One American author, William Ziff, wrote a book in 1948 entitled *The Rape of Palestine,* in which he embellished Galili's story with the lie that Shaw had scrambled out of the building minutes before the blast, leaving his friends behind to die. Shaw sued for libel. Lawyers in Israel were unable to find evidence supporting Ziff's allegations. The publisher withdrew the book from circulation and apologized to Shaw.

The truth—that the Irgun *did* send warnings which were received and then disregarded, not by Sir John Shaw but by Emile Soutter and others—has been made known for the first time in this book.

On the twentieth anniversary of the explosion Victor Levi's son, Michael, told a reporter for an Israeli newspaper, "I will revenge the blood of my father and of Julius Jacobs." He has not.

In the same article Levi's daughter, Sheila, said, "For years I couldn't understand that my father, who was so loyal to the Yishuv, could be killed by other Jews."

After 1948 Julius Jacobs' house in Rehavia became the official residence of Israel's first Prime Minister, David Ben-Gurion. Long after the explosion, Mrs. Jacobs held Ben-Gurion and the Haganah responsible for her husband's death. When a friend innocently mentioned that the Prime Minister was now occupying her former home, she replied bitterly by telling the biblical story of Naboth, who was killed so King Ahab could seize his vineyard.

Thirty-two years after the explosion Roderick Musgrave's widow, Celia, wrote, "The King David explosion broke my heart, orphaned my daughter and left me widowed at twenty-two after a year of blissfully happy marriage. I have been trying ever since to rebuild my life."

Bernard Bourdillon's widow, Joy, said, "I still love the Middle East even though it wrecked my life."

Doreen Farley said, "In many ways my life stopped with the King David explosion." She raised her two sons alone and still cannot bear to hear the sound of pneumatic drills. They remind her of the drills used by the workmen as they extracted bodies from the wreckage of the King David.

Joan Gibbs also raised her children alone. After the 1967 war she visited Israel and the occupied West Bank for the first time since her husband's death. She saw that the King David's south wing had been rebuilt and two upper floors added. Everywhere she encountered the relatives of Arabs killed in the explosion. "They treated me like a long-lost friend," she said.

Immediately after the explosion Jack Mantoura resigned from his government job and stopped seeing his Jewish friends. He said, "I suddenly became politically conscious. I wanted to know why my father had died so I learned about the Balfour Declaration and Zionism."

In January 1948 he married his next-door neighbor, Leila Canaan, and went to work for Jack Keegan in the TWA office. Two months later he was detained by Haganah soldiers as he walked through a Jewish neighborhood. They searched him and found a small pistol he carried to protect the airline's cash.

The Haganah held him captive in a building next to the Palestine Post building. That evening Arab terrorists, assisted by two British deserters, exploded a bomb in front of the *Post's* offices. Mantoura escaped in the confusion. The following day he and his wife fled to London where they have lived ever since. Atallah Mantoura had been right: the day *had* come when his son needed a British passport.

Wasfi Tell became Jordan's Foreign Minister. In 1971, Palestinian terrorists belonging to the "Black September" group assassinated him as he walked through the lobby of the Sheraton Hotel in Cairo.

Zehdi Terzi, the Arab army clerk who lost so many friends in the explosion, became the first Permanent Observer for the Palestine Liberation Organization to the United Nations.

Some Palestinians insist that the son of one of the Arab messengers killed in the King David was among the Palestinian terrorists responsible for the attack on an El Al plane at the Zurich airport in 1969. Others place the son of a King David victim at other terrorist outrages committed by Palestinians in Israel and Europe.

These stories have proven difficult to verify. Even if they are untrue, they are fitting parables for the way in which terrorism has ricocheted between Jews and Arabs, Arabs and Jews, all the time gaining velocity and becoming more ruthless.

The Irgun bears some responsibility for this continued violence. In order to impress and intimidate the Arabs, it described its successful operations in detail on posters and in leaflets printed in Arabic. As Begin has said, "Their [the Arabs] curiosity to find out what the Irgun was saying was very marked." And also, as Begin has said, "We actually provided the example of what the urban guerrilla is, we created the method of the urban guerrilla."

Those in the Irgun who planned and executed the attack on the King David have not escaped terrorism's deadly ricochet.

Yitzhak Avinoam named his only son Gal, in honor of Yael's brother, who died heroically during the 1948 Arab-Israeli war. Avinoam's Gal was killed by Palestinians while serving with Israeli occupation forces in Gaza. According to his friends, Avinoam has never recovered from the shock. The walls of his study are covered with pictures of the handsome boy.

After the 1948 war Adina met and married the King David's headwaiter, Naim Nissan. For many years they operated a hotel in Cyprus, itself the scene of a bitter civil war and numerous terrorist atrocities. Finally they closed their hotel and it was expropriated by the United Nations peacekeeping force. They returned to Israel and now live in Nahariyya, a town near the Lebanese border that has often been the target of attacks by Palestinian terrorists.

Once Israel became independent Paglin returned to his family's bakery oven business. In 1972 he and Rabbi Meir Kahane, the leader of the American-based Jewish Defense League (JDL), were arrested by Israeli police and charged with attempting to smuggle arms to the United States concealed in Paglin's ovens. It was alleged that the weapons were to be used to murder Soviet diplomats in New York.

Five years later Prime Minister Begin chose Paglin to be his special assistant in charge of antiterrorist activities. In 1978, shortly after being interviewed for this book, Paglin was killed in an automobile accident.

Meir Kahane went on to found a right-wing political organization in Israel known as "Kach!" ("Thus!"). The organization's emblem was a clenched fist held over a map of Israel, the West Bank, and Jordan. (The Irgun's motto had been "Ra Kach!" ["Only Thus!"]. Its emblem had been a fist holding a rifle over an identical map.)

In May 1980, Prime Minister Begin ordered Kahane arrested and detained under the authority of emergency laws first promulgated by the British to combat the Irgun and Stern Gang. Instead of repealing these laws, successive Israeli governments had used them to imprison Arab terrorists and activists without placing charges or holding trials. Kahane was the first Jew detained under these laws since the end of the Mandate.

The Begin government was afraid that Kahane was on the verge of launching a terrorist campaign against Arab targets in retaliation for Arab attacks on Jewish settlers in the West Bank. After Kahane's arrest Jewish terrorists exploded car bombs, crippling two Arab mayors sympathetic to the PLO.

Several weeks after the King David explosion Yanai surrendered to Palestine Police officers Richard Conquest and Max Schindler. In exchange for immunity, a new identity, a British passport, and passage out of Palestine at a later date, he agreed to become a police informer.

He soon reported that the Irgun planned to attack the Jerusalem railway station. The police trapped the attackers and afterward arrested other members of the Irgun identified by Yanai. Among them was Yitzhak Avinoam.

Avinoam was sent to a detention camp in East Africa. Yanai fled to Belgium. A year later an attempt by the Irgun to kill him was thwarted by the Belgian police. Since then his whereabouts have become a mystery. According to one rumor, he is in Hong Kong. Another rumor puts him in China, another in New York, another in Jerusalem, dressed as a Christian priest and with deep scars running across his neck.

"If you find Yanai, let me know where he is," Avinoam said, upon learning efforts were being made to locate him. "I'd like to give him something—a bullet in the head."

Amnon still works in Jerusalem as a dental technician. He is the only Irgunist involved in the King David explosion and interviewed for this book who admits to feelings of remorse and responsibility.

"To this day I am not happy about the operation," he said. "I know that it ruined many lives and destroyed families and I often think and dream of this. . . . I was ashamed when I first heard how many had been killed. If I had fought against soldiers and killed them in combat it would not bother me, but these were office workers. I am still sad, I have never been able to escape my guilt and I never mention this episode to my friends. I think that the life of one person is very important. A person is the symbol of God."

New York
August 1980

Chapter Notes

PROLOGUE

The account of Allenby's entrance into Jerusalem is based on Gardner's *Allenby of Arabia*, Wavell's *Allenby–Soldier and Statesman*, *The New York Times*, *The Times*, and the official army report on Allenby's campaign. The reaction of Jerusalem's Christians is described in Vester's "What Is the American Colony?" Tuchman's *Bible and Sword* explains the British fascination with Palestine.

Support for the position that the Balfour Declaration was motivated by idealism can be found in Laquer, *A History of Zionism*, and Stein, *The Balfour Declaration*. Many Arab and Jewish historians prefer the explanation that the Declaration was made to enlist the support of Russian and American Jewry in the First World War. Zionists like this theory since it turns the Declaration into a simple *quid pro quo*; Arabs because it shows the Declaration to be motivated by British self-interest.

Documents recently released from Britain's Foreign and Colonial offices indicate that some British officials tried to prevent Jewish refugees from reaching Palestine because they sincerely believed that the White Paper was crucial to the war effort. Others enforced it because of sympathy with the Palestinian Arabs or anti-Semitism. Bernard Wasserstein's *Britain and the Jews of Europe* is an excellent account of Jewish immigration during the war.

Other sources for the Prologue: Bethell, *The Palestine Triangle*; Hurewitz, *The Struggle for Palestine*; Sykes, *Crossroads to Israel*.

CHAPTER 1

The opening passage about the Irgun is based on interviews with Avinoam and Chaim-Toit.

Throughout the book most material about the Irgun is based on the author's interviews with former Irgunists Avinoam, Adina, Yael, Gideon, Paglin, Amrami, Spector, Chaim-Toit, Amnon and Begin; interviews with Irgunists that have appeared over the years in Israeli newspapers; Niv's *History of the Irgun*; Shay's book about the explosion, *The Milk Cans Roared*; and transcripts of interviews on file at the Jabotinsky Institute in Tel Aviv and at the Hebrew University's Oral History Archives in Jerusalem. In future chapter notes these sources will be referred to as "Irgun sources."

The details of Sir John Shaw's walk to the King David are drawn from two lengthy interviews conducted with Shaw and his wife, from Shaw's papers in the library of Rhodes House, Oxford, and from a profile of Shaw published in the *Daily Telegraph* three days after the explosion. The author also retraced Shaw's route and found that the German Hospice continues to accommodate guests and the olive grove still enjoys the same panoramic view.

The description of the security devices and procedures protecting the King David is compiled from interviews with Sir John Shaw, Emile Soutter and Dan Ben-Dor, the engineer who designed many of the devices. In *Behind the Silken Curtain*, Crum describes the security surrounding the Secretariat. Shaw's letter comes from the Israel State Archives (D/70/45). These archives also contain the files of the Mandate's Department of Public Works which was responsible for erecting the searchlights and barbed wire concertinas. The passes used to enter the Secretariat are among the papers of Sir Donald MacGillivray at St. Antony's College Middle East Centre, Oxford.

CHAPTER 2

Irgun sources (see Chapter 1 notes) are the basis for the material about the early morning briefing of the assault unit in Beit Aharon. There is some disagreement among those interviewed about the order in which the Irgun commanders addressed the unit. The sequence described is that remembered by the majority of sources.

There are numerous versions of the Irgun oath. The oath taken by Amnon is a composite of these versions and of the oath described in Frank's *The Deed*.

An interview with Emile Soutter is the source for the story of the menu ritual he and Hamburger followed every morning. Soutter believes, but is not certain, that *pilaf financière* was discussed between them on the morning of July 22.

The biographical material about Max Hamburger is based on interviews with Anne and Emile Soutter, Naim Nissan, Mathilde Papadoupolous, Victor Shaer, Mrs. Max Hesse (the widow of a Jerusalem restaurateur friendly with Hamburger) and Mrs. Emmanuel Propper (the widow of the King David Hotel's doctor). These interviews were also important sources of information for the passages on the history of the King David.

Other sources for the hotel's history include: the private archives of Ami Federman (son of the current owner); the King David's leather-bound "Golden Book" which lists the famous guests who have stayed at the hotel; articles from the *Palestine Post* and its successor, the *Jerusalem Post*, and particularly an article in its weekend magazine of August 8, 1975; and the "Note on Interior Decoration of the King David Hotel," which still hangs on a pillar in the King David's lobby.

Dan Ben-Dor, Alan Park, and Stacey Barham—the police officer in charge of investigating the explosion—all provided information about the hotel's construction and its expansion joint. The *Palestine Bulletin* quotation about the hotel's opening is from the issue of December 19, 1930. Victor Shaer, who worked for the Secretariat in 1946 and for the hotel in 1978, was kind enough to give the author a tour and point out how the hotel's interior had changed over the years.

The details of the expropriation of hotel space by the government and army come from the Mandate's Department of Public Works files now available at the Israel State Archives. The contract between the government and the King David Hotel can also be found at these archives (W/104/46 Vol I).

CHAPTER 3

Most of this chapter is based on a long interview with Amihai Paglin. Transcripts of Paglin interviews with other researchers available at the Jabotinsky Institute and the Hebrew University Oral History Archives were also helpful.

Gerold Frank relates the story of the *Struma* demonstration and Paglin's free-lance terrorist group in *The Deed*, his account of the Moyne assassination. This author read excerpts from Frank's book to Paglin. Except for a few minor points, Paglin confirmed the accuracy of Frank's material and the author has therefore borrowed from it several details and phrases.

Other written sources for the histories of the Irgun and Stern Gang are: Bethell's *The Palestine Triangle*, Bell's *Terror Out of Zion*, Sykes's *Crossroads to Israel* and Katz's *Days of Fire*. Interviews with Katz and with the official Irgun historian, David Niv, were also of great assistance.

The poem by Abraham Stern comes from an undated article by Arthur Koestler, "Middle East Underground," in *Britain Between East and West* (London: Contact Publications).

Teddy's Kollek's role in warning the British about the Irgun's attempted rocket attack on the King David was mentioned by Richard Crossman during a speech to the House of Commons on July 1, 1946. A few weeks later Kollek acknowledged the truth of Crossman's account in a letter to *The New Statesman*.

The author could not find any evidence that the British had installed the automatic machine guns that Paglin referred to in his briefing. However, Paglin was so convinced of their existence at the time that he eliminated this plan.

CHAPTER 4

The most important single source for the passage about the King David as a center of intrigue is an interview with Gabriel Sifrony. Interviews with Naim Nissan, Mathilde Papadoupolous, Martin Charteris, John Briance, Jon Kimche, and numerous other policemen, army officers and journalists are used to portray the postwar atmosphere at the King David.

Crossman's description of the King David terrace at twilight comes from a letter to his wife located among his private papers at St. Antony's College Middle East Centre, Oxford.

Most of the material describing Gideon's briefing is from two lengthy interviews the author conducted with Gideon and interviews with Paglin and Avinoam.

CHAPTER 5

During a long interview Paglin described Begin's Tel Aviv hideout and the bicyclist who brought messages to him from the Haganah. Descriptions of the house on Bin Nun Street are also found in *The Revolt*, Begin's account of his war against the British, and in Haber's biography of Begin.

Samuel Katz supplied information about Begin's house, his domestic life, and how he spent his time during this period of voluntary incarceration. Katz's book, *Days of Fire*, was also useful.

Arthur Koestler's evaluation of Begin was made during an interview with the author.

The metaphor with which Jabotinsky dismissed the Arab problem comes from an interview with Azkin, a Revisionist politician, conducted by Bernard Wasserstein and available at the Hebrew University Oral History Archives.

Begin's own comments about the Arabs are on page 89 of *The Revolt* (New York: Dell, 1977). The Irgun leaflet "To Our Arab Neighbours" is included in a collection of Irgun propaganda material on file at the Jabotinsky Institute.

Principal sources for the section on Begin's "reality": author's interview with Begin; Haber's *Menahem Begin;* and *The Revolt.* The reference to Jabotinsky is from *The Revolt,* page 32; the passage about hating one's enemy is on pages 26 and 27.

A copy of the note Begin received on the morning of July 22 is on file at the Jabotinsky Institute.

CHAPTER 6

General Barker's orders for Operation Agatha can be found among Cunningham's papers at St. Antony's College, Oxford.

Principal sources for the account of Black Saturday: *Under the White Paper,* Trevor; *Cordon and Search,* Wilson; *State in the Making,* Horowitz; the article "Black Saturday" in the *Jerusalem Post Magazine,* June 25, 1971; the *Palestine Post* account of June 30, 1946; the Jewish Agency Press Digest for the first two weeks of July 1946; the 31st Infantry Brigade Operational Order (Britain's Public Record Office—PRO: WO 169 23005); the wireless logs of the army units participating in Agatha (PRO: WO 169 23221).

Additional material about the search of the Jewish Agency is from interviews with Sir Martin Charteris, Kenneth Hadingham and Sir Richard Catling. Catling also related the story of his face to face meeting with the Irgun leaders several years earlier.

Interviews with Dov Joseph and David Hacohen are the basis for the details of their arrests on the morning of June 29.

Sources for the passage about the search at Yagour and other agricultural communities: interviews conducted by the author with six members of Yagour present on the morning of June 29, among them the mayor; an article, "Yagour Revisited," by Meyer Levin in *Commentary,* February 1947; the testimony of settlers detained during Agatha as compiled by the Jewish Agency and now on file in the Central Zionist Archives in Jerusalem; the Operational Reports of the army units involved in the Yagour search (WO 261 315).

The material about the British assessment of Agatha comes from interviews with Joan Gibbs, Sir John Shaw and Ivan Phillips. Shaw's press conference on the morning of Black Saturday is described in the *Palestine Post* and the Jewish Agency Press Diary. Shaw's own feelings about the Agency can be found in his testimony to the Anglo-American Committee on March 23, 1946, and in a letter he wrote to John Martin at the Colonial Office in November 1945 (CO 733 456).

The story of the meeting of the Haganah and dissidents on June 10 is contained in a Strategic Services Unit (the successor to the OSS and precursor of the CIA) cable of June 11, 1946 (A-70034), at the National Archives in Washington.

Cunningham's reluctance to move against the Jewish Agency is shown in his cables to the Colonial Office and in his handwritten letter to Sir John Shaw of December 20, 1945. They are among his papers at St. Antony's College. Cunningham's change of mind and Montgomery's role in promoting Agatha is described in Bethell's *The Palestine Triangle*.

CHAPTER 7

The description of the meeting between Weizmann and Cunningham is based on Vera Weizmann's autobiography, *The Impossible Takes Longer*, and on a summary that Cunningham cabled to London, now among his papers at St. Antony's College. American Intelligence agents of the Strategic Services Unit also filed an account of the meeting. It is available in the National Archives (A-70035).

The comment about Weizmann's ability to handle British statesmen was made by Richard Crossman.

The biographical material on Cunningham comes from a collection of press clippings and press releases amassed by the Palestine Information Office and now on file at the Israel State Archives in Jerusalem.

Sources for Weizmann's views on violence: his autobiography, *Trial and Error*; Vera Weizmann's *The Impossible Takes Longer*; *Chaim Weizmann: A Biography by Several Hands*, Weisgal and Carmichael (eds.); and particularly the piece, "Bridge to a Statehood" by Jon Kimche; *So Far*, Weisgal; *A Nation Reborn*, Crossman; *Weizmann*, Litvinoff; *The Diaries of Blanche Dugdale*, Rose (ed.).

The story of the bomb that killed Weizmann's brother-in-law is taken from the *Palestine Post* report at the time of the explosion. Bethell's *The Palestine Triangle* contains a good account of how the Moyne assassination damaged Weizmann's friendship with Churchill and the possibility of a Jewish State immediately after the war.

Sources for the material about Havlagah, the differences between the Haganah and Irgun, and the Haganah's activists and moderates: *The Revolt*, Begin; *Terror Out of Zion*, Bell; *Days of Fire*, Katz; articles on Havlagah and the Haganah in the *Encyclopedia Judaica*; the report of the Peel Commission as described in Bethell; *Seven Fallen Pillars*, Kimche; *Promise and Fulfilment*, Koestler; *Palestine Mission*, Crossman; and the author's interview with the official Haganah historian, Colonel Gershon Rivlin.

Weizmann's letter to Churchill about terrorism was sent on April 14, 1946. This letter and drafts of his letters of resignation to Shertok are unpublished but available in the archives of the Weizmann Institute in Rehovot.

CHAPTER 8

Because the Irgun did not keep dated, written records of its activities, the author has relied on interviews to determine the dates on which certain preparations were made for the attack on the King David. Hence the dates indicated for Irgun meetings and actions in Part Two are based on the best recollections of the participants.

The Irgun and Haganah propaganda after Black Saturday is taken from material found in files in the Museum of the Haganah and the Jabotinsky Institute. Much of the Irgun material is from a booklet, "The Hebrew Struggle for National Liberation: Selected documents on the Irgun submitted to the United Nations in 1947."

The principal source for the July 1 meetings of the Haganah High Command and the X Committee is an unpublished autobiographical tape-recording made for his biographer, Yair Tsaban, by Moshe Sneh shortly before his death. Mr. Tsaban read and translated a transcript of this recording for the author. Other important sources are interviews with Israel Galili and Gershon Rivlin and Slutsky's *Official History of the Haganah*.

Galili and Rivlin were both extremely helpful in explaining the workings of the X Committee. Other material on the X is found in Israeli's *Underground Emissary*. In *My Life* (p. 190) Golda Meir describes the closeness of the vote in the X Committee and Levi Eshkol's importance as the deciding swing vote.

The passages about the Irgun are based on long interviews with Paglin, Adina and Gideon. The letter from Sneh to Begin authorizing Operation Chick is on file at the Jabotinsky Institute. Samuel Katz's wife makes the complimentary remark about Adina in her book, *The Lady Was a Terrorist*. The information about the Betar comes from an interview with Gideon, the *Encyclopedia Judaica* and Schechtman's *The Vladimir Jabotinsky Story*.

CHAPTER 9

Interviews with Adina, Chaim-Toit, Avinoam, and Yael are the sources for the opening passage about the Irgun preparations.

An interview with Jon Kimche is the principal source for the meetings between Kimche and Weizmann and Kimche and Shaw. Kimche's role as an intermediary is also mentioned by Horowitz in *State in the Making*.

The material about the visit to the Regence is based on interviews with Gideon, Yael, Chaim-Toit and Avinoam. Other details about the Regence are taken from advertisements and articles found in Ami Federman's private archives.

CHAPTER 10

Sources for the opening passage describing the Rehovot meeting: *My Life*, Meir (p. 190); *History of the Haganah*, Slutsky.

The meeting between Shaw and Weizmann is summarized in telegram 1117 from Cunningham on July 8, 1946, which is among Cunningham's papers at St. Antony's College and available at the Public Records Office (FO 371 52538).

The account of the meeting between Paglin, Sadeh and Sneh is based on Slutsky's *History of the Haganah*; author's interviews with Amihai Paglin, Israel Galili and Gershon Rivlin; and on the tape Sneh recorded for Yair Tsaban. Begin's statement about hating is from *The Revolt* (p. 26). Bell gives a good account of "The Season" in *Terror Out of Zion*. An Irgun pamphlet published in 1947, "Background of the Struggle for the Liberation of Eretz Israel," gives reasons for the bitterness between the Irgun and the Haganah.

Israel Galili and other former Haganah members deny that the destruction of the papers seized from the Jewish Agency was one of the purposes of Operation Chick. Paglin and other former Irgun members insist that the opposite was true. The most likely explanation for this disagreement and the one I have incorporated into the text is that Sadeh and Sneh mentioned these papers in passing to Paglin and that he and the Irgun blew their importance out of proportion.

Interviews with Begin and Paglin are the most important sources for reconstructing the meeting between them. Arthur Koestler in *Promise and Fulfilment* discusses the Irgun's moral code. Bowyer Bell's *Terror Out of Zion* contains examples of operations in which the Irgun violated its own moral precepts. Other examples are found in the Epilogue to this book.

CHAPTER 11

The description of the Kielce pogrom is based on newspaper accounts that appeared in the *Palestine Post*, *The Times*, *The New York Times* and on an article, "Between the Mill Stones in Poland," *Commentary*, August 1946. The dangers faced by Jewish refugees who tried to remain in Europe, particularly eastern Europe, are also documented in the April 1946 *Report of the Anglo-American Committee of Inquiry*.

Sources for Weizmann's press conference in the Eden Hotel are Vera Weizmann's *The Impossible Takes Longer* and Trevor's *Under the White Paper.* A complete transcript of the conference is among Weizmann's private papers at the Weizmann Institute.

The passages about the Irgun's preparations are based on interviews with Paglin, Chaim-Toit and Avinoam. The material about the Irgun's obsession with its weapons comes from the transcript of a Paglin interview found at the Hebrew University Oral History Archives.

The account of the disputes among the King David's staff is based on employment files still kept in storage at the hotel and on interviews with Emile Soutter and Mathilde Papadoupolous.

Sources for the meeting between Weisgal and Sneh are: Sneh's testimony to Tsaban; Litvinoff's *Weizmann;* Weisgal's autobiography, *So Far;* and an interview with Weisgal's daughter, Helen Amir.

CHAPTER 12

The section about Julius Jacobs and Victor Levi is compiled from interviews with Sir John Shaw, Lady Shaw, Mrs. Julius Jacobs and Jacobs' daughter, Ruth Kedar, and from an article about the two men in the *Jerusalem Post* of July 22, 1966.

Interviews with Boris Guriel and a former Haganah commander who wishes to remain anonymous and who now lives in self-imposed exile in the United States are the basis for the passage about the dilemmas faced by the moderates following the war.

The most important source for the material about Yanai is a file of Yanai's letters and papers located at the Jabotinsky Institute. These documents were seized from Yanai's apartment by Irgun Intelligence agents shortly after he defected to the British. Other sources are interviews with Avinoam, Chaim-Toit, Gideon and Arieh Eshel, Yanai's biographer.

An interview with Katy Antonius is the most important source for the section describing her party; also used are interviews with some of her frequent guests: General Evelyn Barker, John Briance, Sir Richard Catling, Sir Martin Charteris, Jon Kimche and Gabriel Sifrony. There is also a description of one of her parties in *O Jerusalem!* by Collins and Lapierre.

The sources for the stories illustrating Jerusalem's divided loyalties are (in the order used): interviews with Boris Guriel, the mayor of Yagour, Sir Martin Charteris, and Thomas Buchanan; interview with Ernest Quinn; Bernard Fergusson's book, *The Trumpet in the Hall;* an interview with Stacey Barham.

CHAPTER 13

In *My Life*, Golda Meir says that Levi Eshkol cast the vote that reversed the earlier decision of the X.

Sneh's testimony to Tsaban and interviews with Menahem Begin and Israel Galili are the principal sources for the material about Sneh's failure to inform Begin of the decision of the X Committee. Dov Joseph's comment about stopping the operation was made during an interview with the author.

The sources for the section about the journey of the explosives are interviews with Avinoam and Chaim-Toit.

An interview with Ernest Quinn and Golda Meir's autobiography are sources for the passages about the efforts of the Jewish Agency leaders to comply with Weizmann's orders.

David Horowitz recounts his meeting with Roderick Musgrave in his book *State in the Making*. Moshe Rosenberg described his friendship with Musgrave during an interview. Other material about Musgrave's career comes from interviews with Sir Richard Catling, John J. O'Sullivan and numerous other former Palestine policemen, and from Musgrave's obituary in the *Palestine Post*. Musgrave's widow, Celia Douglas, also supplied some personal details about her husband.

CHAPTER 14

Joan Gibbs related the story of her July 20 party during an interview. Material about the young Colonial officers and the problems of Anglo-Jewish relations is from interviews with Ivan Phillips, Joy Bourdillon, Doreen Farley, Sir John and Lady Shaw, Sir John Gutch, Leah Ben-Dor, John Briance and Jerry Cornes. Bernard Wasserstein also interviewed Phillips about the same subject and a transcript is available at the Hebrew University Oral History Archives.

Richard Crossman recounted the sentiments of the police inspector in charge of training during an address to the Royal Institute of International Affairs in 1946. The speech is available in his papers at St. Antony's College. The Begin quotation about the "British Master Plan" is from *The Revolt* (p. 67). The story of Sir John Shaw's premature departure from Palestine is reported in the *Daily Telegraph* of July 25, 1946.

Baffy Dugdale's account of Weizmann's visit to the London Zionist office is from her diaries. The letter Weizmann wrote to the Chief Rabbi is among his papers at the Weizmann Institute. The handwritten notes Cunningham penned before his meetings in London are in his papers at St. Antony's College.

The material about Gal and his aborted briefing is based on interviews with

Zvi Bar-Zel and Gal's sister, Yael, who also supplied copies of her brother's poems.

The notes Begin received from Sneh are on file in the Jabotinsky Institute. His reaction to the first is recounted in *The Revolt* (p. 293). During an interview with the author, he explained his reasons for not wishing to postpone the operation further.

CHAPTER 15

The entire chapter is based on interviews with Joan Gibbs and with Jack and Leila (Canaan) Mantoura.

CHAPTER 16

The author's interview with Begin is the source for explanations of why he could no longer postpone the operation.

Irgun sources (see notes to Chapter 1) are the basis for the account of the last minute preparations at Beit Aharon and the account in later chapters of the attack on the hotel. In instances where these sources are contradictory, the author has chosen the account that is most likely in the light of the other available material, such as police reports, journalists' accounts and the eyewitness testimony of those in or near the hotel on July 22.

The assumption that Yanai had not decided to betray the Irgun until July 22 is supported by the testimony of John J. O'Sullivan, one of the policemen who handled Yanai's defection. Yellin-Mor's book describes the problems of coordinating the LEHI and Irgun attacks.

The description of the meeting between Campbell and Barker is based on an interview with Campbell. Barker now has no recollection of this meeting nor of the Intelligence tip about Operation Chick and believes Campbell is mistaken. Nevertheless, the author has chosen Campbell's version. Campbell has a clear, detailed recollection of this meeting and is absolutely certain it occurred. In every other matter Campbell's testimony has proven to be completely accurate.

Barker's quotations about Palestine are taken from an interview with the author. The Teddy Kollek quotation is from Bethell, *The Palestine Triangle* (p. 323). Military documents in the Public Records Office (WO 261 382) give details of the elaborate roadblock and pass system used in Jerusalem. Kimche's *Seven Fallen Pillars*, Wilson's *Cordon and Search* and the weekly and quarterly reports of the army regiments based in Palestine (available in the Public Records Office) are sources for the security and morale problems faced by the army in Palestine.

CHAPTER 17

Passages about the departure of the assault unit for the King David are compiled from Irgun sources (see notes to Chapter 1). The author also retraced the route taken by Nissim and Amatzia. The inventory of Ariela's medical kit and the types of weapons taken by the assault unit come from the official police report located at the Public Records Office in London (CO 537 2290).

An interview with Leila Canaan (Mrs. Leila Mantoura) is the source for the section describing her activities on the morning of July 22. Adina and Yael's experiences are also reconstructed from interviews with them. The sources for the material about the typing pool are interviews with Marion Small, Nubar Markarian, and an Arab typist who wishes to remain anonymous.

The interviews and written sources for the material about Max Hamburger, Naim Nissan, Mathilde Papadoupolous, and Katherine Grey-Donald are the same as those used for the passages about Max Hamburger and the King David Hotel in Chapter 2. An interview with Andrew and Honor Sharman provided some information about Mrs. Grey-Donald.

CHAPTER 18

An article in *The Guardian*, January 11, 1972, is the source for the story about the premature wire service report of the explosion. Interviews with Ibraham Mansour and Boris Guriel are the basis for the subsequent stories of premature warnings.

David Horowitz recounts the debates within the Jewish Agency on the morning of the 22nd in his book, *State in the Making*.

Irgun sources (see notes to Chapter 1) are the basis for the details of the arrival of the milk truck and the entrance of the assault unit into the basement. Johannes Constantides testified about his experiences at an inquest that was reported in the *Palestine Post* throughout September. A copy of the final findings of the inquest is available at the Israel State Archives. The author paced off the basement corridor and Victor Shaer provided information as to how it had changed since the explosion.

The material about the Mamillah Road police station is taken from an interview with Ian Proud and the testimony of Inspector Taylor at the inquest.

The story of the Swiss headwaiter is from an interview with Mathilde Papadoupolous. She also described the different hostages—the Arabs balancing rugs, etc.—whom the assault unit herded into the kitchen.

There is no single authoritative source for the timing of the events leading up to the explosion. The author has reconstructed the most probable sequence and timing based on interviews with eyewitnesses, testimony at the inquest and official police and army reports. The author has also retraced and timed many of the routes taken by the various characters.

CHAPTER 19

Sources for the opening passage about noon at the Secretariat: interviews with Sir John Shaw, Helen Rossi, Victor Shaer, Dan Ben-Dor and Ernest Quinn.

Irgun sources (see notes to Chapter 1) are the basis for the account of the Irgun carrying the churns into the basement. Gideon's testimony is the most important of these sources.

The description of noon in the hotel comes from interviews with Leila Canaan, Katy Antonius, Jack Mantoura, Sami Hadawi, Meyer Levin and Ivan Phillips.

Irgun sources and reports of the inquest are the basis for the details of the Mackintosh shooting.

Interviews with Andrew Campbell, Arthur Miles and Ian Tilly and the official reports of the police and army (CO 537 2290), particularly the affidavits of Sgt. Petty, Lt. Tilly, Gunner Buckle and Lt. Chambers attached to the army report, are important sources for re-creating the calls for help sent out by ATS Sgt. Brown after the Mackintosh shooting.

These affidavits are considerably more reliable than the texts of the army and police reports which contain statements and conclusions at variance with the weight of eyewitness testimony, news reports and the inquest. Another factor calling into question the reliability of the army report is that the two most important affidavits, those of Colonel Campbell and Gunner Barber, were not attached to the final report submitted to the High Commissioner and sent to the Cabinet in London. These missing affidavits contain crucial testimony that does not reflect well on security at the King David. Campbell kept both affidavits and gave them to the author in 1979. It is clear that they were typed on the same typewriter as the other affidavits.

Sources for the reaction to the sound of gunfire in the basement: interviews with Mathilde Papadoupolous, Michael Payne, Ivan Phillips, and Gabriel Sifrony.

Material about the fuses is based on interviews with Eliahu Spector and Amihai Paglin. A written source is a British pamphlet published in Palestine in 1946, "Terrorist Methods with Mines and Booby Traps."

Sources for the reaction to the Mackintosh shooting: interviews with Michael Payne, Andrew Campbell, Mathilde Papadoupolous; the affidavits of Barber, Buckle, Campbell, Chambers and Petty.

Irgun sources (see Chapter 1 notes) and the report of the inquest are the basis for the description of the fusing of the anti-tampering devices and Constantides' successful attempt to ring the alarm.

CHAPTER 20

The scene in the Mamillah Road police station is based on the report of the inquest and an interview with Ian Proud.

Sources for the scenes in the basement and the service driveway: Irgun sources (see Chapter 1 notes); interview with Mathilde Papadoupolous; affidavits of Sgt. Petty and Gunner Buckle; interview with Emile Soutter; official army and police reports.

Sources for the Irgun's retreat: Irgun sources; interviews with Michael Payne, Marion Small, Sir John Shaw, William Bradley, Ian Tilly, and Arthur Miles; official army and police reports (CO 537 2290).

Sources for diversionary explosion account: Irgun sources; official army and police reports; interview with Kathleen Bailey; *Palestine Post* of July 23, 1946. In *The Revolt*, Begin claims that the purpose of the preliminary bombs was to keep innocent pedestrians away from the hotel. This version is contradicted by both Paglin and Gideon.

CHAPTER 21

Sources for the passage about the terrorist alert: interviews with Ian Proud, Kenneth Hadingham and Stacey Barham; *Palestine Post*, July 23, 1946; official army and police reports (CO 537 2290).

Sources for the material about the reaction to the explosion: interviews with Joan Gibbs, Nubar Markarian, William Fuller, Mrs. Every, Sir John Shaw, William Bradley, Sir John Gutch, Ruth Kedar, Sir Richard Catling, J. G. Sheringham, Ernest Quinn, Honor Sharman, Andrew Sharman, Dan Ben-Dor, Gabriel Sifrony, Sami Hadawi, Katy Antonius, Richard Mowrer, Jack Mantoura, Ian Proud, Stacey Barham and Andrew Campbell; affidavits of Andrew Campbell and Sgt. Petty.

CHAPTER 22

Sources for the account of the transmittal of the warning: Irgun sources (see Chapter 1 notes) and interviews with Adina and Yael. Adina did not realize that Yael was following her while she gave the first two warnings.

Sources for the description of the Irgun's retreat: Irgun sources (see Chapter 1 notes), principally interviews with Yael and Gideon.

Sources for the descriptions of activity in and around the hotel: affidavits of Campbell and Petty; interviews with Ian Tilly, Andrew Campbell, Mathilde Papadoupolous, Naim Nissan and Helen Rossi.

In addition to the testimony of Naim Nissan, the author has found the following evidence that confirms that warnings were received by the staff of the King David Hotel and by members of the military:

1) In an interview with the author, the Swiss assistant manager, Emile Soutter, admitted that he had been notified of warnings by the King David's switchboard operators on three occasions. Soutter is not Jewish, in fact, his wife is British. He has nothing to gain by making the truth known after so many years.

2) In a letter to the author, Max Hamburger's widow (Hamburger died in 1975) has confirmed that her husband was told of a warning before the explosion.

3) Sgt. Caswill, who worked on the top floor of the military headquarters, told the author in an interview that he and other members of the military staff were told to gather by the main stairway in case it was decided to order an evacuation.

4) In a letter written to a friend in 1946, Dudley Skelton, the head of a hospital in Palestine, claims that he was in the King David's bar on July 22 and heard a warning passed on to some army officers who dismissed it as "Jewish terrorist bluff." Skelton seems a reliable source since he had been a major-general in the British Army until retiring in 1937. However, because this letter has been lost by its original recipient, the author has not included this story in the text.

The account of Devorah Ledener's reaction to the warnings is based on her interview with the author.

The account of the warnings in the official police report (CO 537 2290) claims that the warning was received at the hotel two minutes before the explosion. This is contradicted by Soutter, who is positive that the first warning arrived at least ten minutes before the explosion. Soutter's testimony is corroborated by that of Mathilde Papadoupolous and Naim Nissan.

The police report also claims that the warning was received by the French Consulate five minutes *after* the explosion. This is extremely unlikely in view of the fact that five minutes before the explosion members of the Consulate staff were seen to throw open the windows of the Consulate. This was reported by eyewitnesses in newspaper accounts and to the author in the course of several interviews.

The police report further claims that the call was not received by the *Palestine Post* until after the explosion. This is contradicted by the testimony of Devorah

Ledener (who was not an Irgun supporter) and by Leah Ben-Dor, who was a *Palestine Post* editor. Ledener says that after the explosion the Palestine Police put pressure on her to change her testimony. "They kept trying to get me to say that I had gotten the call after the explosion," she said.

CHAPTER 23

Sources for the scenes following the all clear: Interviews with Mrs. Every, Nubar Markarian, Marion Small, Helen Rossi, Victor Shaer, Gabriel Sifrony, Dan Ben-Dor, Richard Mowrer, Ian Proud, Katy Antonius, Kenneth Hadingham and Andrew Campbell; affidavit of Andrew Campbell. Since Campbell wrote his affidavit only days after the blast, I have relied on it in cases where it conflicts slightly with interviews conducted thirty-five years later.

Sources for the passages about the warnings: interviews with Devorah Ledener, Emile and Anne Soutter, Mathilde Papadoupolous, Ivan Phillips, Kenneth Hadingham and Andrew Campbell.

The letter criticizing Mathilde Raitan is among the hotel's papers in the possession of Ami Federman.

CHAPTER 24

Sources for the scenes at 12:36: Interviews with Gideon, Adina, Yael, and Amnon; Irgun sources (see Chapter 1 notes); Doris Katz, *The Lady Was a Terrorist*; interviews with Dan Ben-Dor, Ian Proud, Ian Tilly, Stacey Barham, Nubar Markarian, Marion Small, I. Brin, Jerry Cornes, Sir John Shaw; affidavit of Gunner Barber; interviews with Joan Gibbs, Devorah Ledener, Ernest Quinn and Sgt. Caswill; *Daily Express*, July 23, 1946; interviews with Mathilde Papadoupolous, Ivan Phillips, Kathleen Bailey, Gabriel Sifrony, Sir Richard Catling, Naim Nissan, Leila Canaan, and Emile and Anne Soutter.

CHAPTER 25

Sources for the account of the explosion: reports in the *Jerusalem Post, The Times, Daily Telegraph, New York Times* of July 23, 1946; *Terror Out of Zion*, Bell; interview with explosives consultant George Tresher; interviews with Andrew Campbell, Kenneth Hadingham, Meyer Levin, Ian Tilly, I. Brin, Jerry Cornes, Richard Mowrer, Dan Ben-Dor, Marion Small, Sir John Shaw, William Bradley, Nubar Markarian, Honor and Andrew Sharman, Ernest Quinn, Sgt. Caswill, Sir John Gutch, Sir Richard Catling, Gabriel Sifrony,

Leila Canaan, Anne Soutter, Ivan Phillips, Eliahu Spector, Chaim-Toit, Amihai Paglin, Joan Gibbs, Dennis Small, Devorah Ledener, Jack Mantoura, Sami Hadawi, Zehdi Terzi, and Helen Rossi.

CHAPTER 26

Sources for the scenes describing the reactions to the explosion: interview with Dennis Small; report of the inquest, official army and police reports (CO 537 2290); Irgun sources (see Chapter 1 notes); newspaper accounts of July 23, 1946 (see Chapter 25 notes); interviews with Ian Proud, Ian Tilly, Richard Mowrer, Kenneth Hadingham, Andrew Campbell, Kathleen Bailey, Ivan Phillips, Gabriel Sifrony, Leila Canaan, Anne Soutter, Marion Small, Sir John Shaw, William Bradley, Honor Sharman, Michael Payne, Ernest Quinn, Sir Evelyn Barker, Amnon, Yael, Amihai Paglin, and Eliahu Spector.

A copy of Barker's letter is among Cunningham's papers at St. Antony's College.

Sources for the account of the activity at the King David in the hours following the explosion: newspaper accounts (see Chapter 25 notes); interviews with Dennis Small, Sir John Shaw, Stacey Barham, Andrew Campbell, Marion Small, Doreen Farley, Joan Gibbs, Diana Gutch, Sami Hadawi, Zehdi Terzi, Nubar Markarian, Jack Mantoura, Leila Canaan, and Lady Shaw.

Sources for the scenes in Weizmann's room at the Dorchester: Baffy Dugdale's diary and Ezer Weizman's autobiography, *On Eagles' Wings*. Julius Jacobs' widow and his daughter, Ruth Kedar, provided the material for the scene at the Pembridge Carlton Hotel.

Interviews with Amihai Paglin and Jon Kimche are the basis for the two passages at the end of the chapter.

CHAPTER 27

Transcripts of the radio announcements are available in the files of the Palestine Information Office at the Israel State Archives.

In *The Revolt*, Begin repeats the note from Galili; a copy is also on file at the Jabotinsky Institute as is a copy of the poster giving the Irgun's version of the explosion.

Sources for the passages about the rescue work at the hotel: newspaper accounts of July 24, 1946 (see Chapter 25 notes); interviews with Kenneth Hadingham, Sir John Shaw, Ian Proud, Jack Mantoura, Sir John Gutch, and William Bradley.

Sources for the account of the Begin–Galili meeting: *The Revolt*, Begin;

282 • By Blood and Fire

interviews with Menahem Begin and Israel Galili. Paglin's version of the earlier meetings between him and the Haganah leaders is the most credible, particularly because it would have been impossible for the Irgun to have placed the bombs in the Regence after two o'clock since the restaurant was then always full of customers.

During an interview with the author in 1977, Israel Galili was unable to provide any evidence whatsoever that Shaw had received a warning. During an interview with author Nicholas Bethell, Galili claimed that his informant for the Shaw story had been Boris Guriel and that Guriel had received the information from Carter Davidson, an American journalist who represented the Associated Press. Davidson died in 1958. Boris Guriel told this author that he was not the source for this rumor.

The material about identifying victims is based on interviews with Sir John and Lady Shaw, the files of the Palestine Information Office, and the *Palestine Post*, July 23–30, 1946.

Sources for the various condemnations of the explosion: *Palestine Post*, July 23–30; *A Nation Reborn*, Crossman; *Diaries of Baffy Dugdale*, Rose (ed.); the Jewish press digests kept by the Jewish Agency and available at the Central Zionist Archives; *Days of Fire*, Katz; interviews with Samuel Katz, Jack Mantoura, Leila Canaan, Richard Mowrer, and Menahem Begin.

Sources for the Arab and British reactions: Kirk, *The Middle East 1945–50*; *Palestine Post*, July 23–30, 1946; interviews with Sir John and Lady Shaw and Leila Canaan.

The accounts of the British search operations following the explosion are based on the official army and police reports (CO 537 2290); *History of the Irgun*, Niv; *The Milk Cans Roared*, Shay; *The Revolt*, Begin.

Sources for the final scenes at the rubble and with the families of victims: *Palestine Post*, July 23–30, 1946; inquest report and files of the Palestine Information Office at the Israel State Archives; interviews with Jack Mantoura, Joan Gibbs and Lady Shaw.

EPILOGUE

Sources for the acts of Irgun terror that followed the King David explosion: *Palestine Triangle*, Bethell; *Terror Out of Zion*, Bell; *Crossroads to Israel*, Sykes; *Palestine Post 1947–48*; *The Revolt*, Begin.

There is an excellent account of Dir Yassin in *O Jerusalem!* by Collins and Lapierre that is based on eyewitness accounts and a Red Cross report.

The quotation about Begin is from Golda Meir's biography, *My Life*, page 188.

Walter Laquer's *Terrorism* has a good discussion of how the Irgun fits into contemporary terrorist history.

Bibliography

NOTE

Nicholas Bethell's *The Palestine Triangle* and Christopher Sykes' *Crossroads to Israel* are recommended to readers seeking a more detailed history of Britain's Palestine Mandate. Those wanting to learn more about Zionism should consult Walter Laquer's *A History of Zionism*. *Terror Out of Zion* by J. Bowyer Bell and *Days of Fire* by Samuel Katz both contain extensive material about the Irgun. Gerold Frank's *The Deed* is a good account of the assassination of Lord Moyne. Bernard Wasserstein's *Britain and the Jews of Europe 1939–1945* and Arthur Morse's *While Six Million Died* describe the failure of Britain and the United States to rescue the European Jews. George Antonius' *The Arab Awakening*, although written prior to the Second World War, remains the best statement of the Arab viewpoint on Palestine.

Antonius, George, *The Arab Awakening*. London: Hamish Hamilton, 1938. New York: G. P. Putnam's Sons, 1946.

Begin, Menahem, *The Revolt*. London: W. H. Allen, 1951. Los Angeles: Nash, 1972. New York: Dell (paper), 1977.

——, *White Nights: The Story of a Prisoner in Russia*. Tel Aviv: Steimatsky's Agency, 1977.

Bell, J. Bowyer, *Terror Out of Zion: Irgun Zvai Leumi, LEHI and the Palestine Underground, 1929–1949*. New York: St. Martin's Press, 1977.

Berlin, Isaiah, *Chaim Weizmann*. New York: Farrar, Straus, 1958.

Bethell, Nicholas, *The Palestine Triangle*. London: Andre Deutsch, 1979. New York: G. P. Putnam's Sons, 1979.

Cohen, Geula, *Woman of Violence: Memoirs of a Young Terrorist 1943–1948*. London: Rupert Hart-Davis, 1966. New York: Holt, 1966.

Collins, Larry and Dominique Lapierre, *O Jerusalem!* New York: Simon and Schuster, 1972.

Crossman, Richard, A *Nation Reborn*. London: Hamish Hamilton, 1960.

———, *Palestine Mission*. New York and London: Harper & Brothers, 1947.

Crum, Bartley C., *Behind the Silken Curtain*. New York: Simon and Schuster, 1947. London: Victor Gollancz, 1947.

Dekel, Efraim, *Shai*. London and New York: Thomas Yoseloff, 1959.

Esco Foundation for Palestine, *Palestine: A Study of Jewish, Arab and British Policies* (2 vols). New Haven: Yale University Press, 1947.

Fergusson, Bernard, *The Trumpet in the Hall*. London: Collins, 1970.

Frank, Gerold, *The Deed*. New York: Simon and Schuster, 1963.

Gardner, Brian, *Allenby of Arabia*. New York, Coward-McCann, 1966.

Graves, R. M., *Experiment in Anarchy*. London: Victor Gollancz, 1946.

Great Britain, Army, *Egyptian Expeditionary Force: A brief record of the advance of the Egyptian Expeditionary Force under the command of General Sir Edmund H. H. Allenby*. London: H. M. Stationery Office, 1919.

Haber, Eitan, *Menahem Begin: the Legend and the Man*. New York: Delacorte, 1978.

Hadawi, Sami, *Bitter Harvest: Palestine Between 1914 and 1967*. New York: New World Press, 1967.

Hirst, David, *The Gun and the Olive Branch: The Roots of Violence in the Middle East*. London: Faber and Faber, 1977.

Horowitz, David, *State in the Making*. New York: Knopf, 1953.

Hurewitz, J. C., *The Struggle for Palestine*. New York: Norton, 1950.

Hyamson, H. M., *Palestine under the Mandate*. London: Methuen, 1950.

Israeli, Joseph, *Underground Emissary* (in Hebrew). Tel Aviv, 1972.

Katz, Doris, *The Lady Was a Terrorist*. New York: Shiloni, 1953.

Katz, Samuel, *Days of Fire*. London: W. H. Allen, 1968. New York: Doubleday, 1968.

Kimche, Jon, *Seven Fallen Pillars*. London: Secker and Warburg, 1950.

Kirk, George, *A Short History of the Middle East*. London: Methuen, 1948.

———, *Survey of International Affairs 1939–46: The Middle East in the War*. London and New York: Oxford University Press, 1952.

———, *Survey of International Affairs: The Middle East 1945–50*. London and New York: Oxford University Press, 1954.

Koestler, Arthur, *Promise and Fulfilment*. London and New York: Macmillan, 1949.

———, *Thieves in the Night*. London and New York: Macmillan, 1946.

Laquer, Walter, *A History of Zionism*. New York: Holt, Rinehart and Winston, 1972.

———, *Terrorism*. Boston: Little, Brown, 1977.

Levin, Meyer, *In Search*. New York: Horizon Press, 1950.

Litvinoff, Barnet, *Weizmann: Last of the Patriarchs*. New York: G. P. Putnam's Sons, 1976.

Marlowe, John, *Rebellion in Palestine*. London: Cresset Press, 1946.

———, *The Seat of Pilate*. London: Cresset Press, 1959.

Massie, W. T., *Allenby's Final Triumph*. London: Constable, 1920.

Meir, Golda, *My Life*. London: Weidenfeld and Nicolson, 1975. New York: G. P. Putnam's Sons, 1975.

Monroe, Elizabeth, *Britain's Moment in the Middle East 1914–1956*. London: Chatto and Windus, 1963.

Montgomery of Alamein, Field Marshal Viscount, *Memoirs*. London: Collins, 1958.

Morse, Arthur, *While Six Million Died*. New York: Random House, 1968.

Niv, David, *The Irgun Zvai Leumi (vol. 4): The Battle for Freedom 1944–1946* (in Hebrew). Tel Aviv: Klausner Institute, 1973.

Patai, Raphael, *The Jewish Mind*. New York: Scribners, 1977.

Rose, N. A. (ed.), *Baffy: The Diaries of Blanche Dugdale 1936–1947*. London: Vallentine Mitchell, 1973.

Samuel, Edwin, *A Lifetime in Jerusalem*. London: Vallentine Mitchell, 1970.

Schechtman, Joseph, *The Vladimir Jabotinsky Story (vol. 1): Rebel and Statesman*. New York: Thomas Yoseloff, 1956.

Shay, Abraham, *The Milk Churns Roared* (in Hebrew). Tel Aviv: Hadar, 1977.

Slutsky, Yehuda, *History of the Haganah Vol. III: From Resistance to War* (in Hebrew). Tel Aviv: Am Oved, 1973.

Stark, Freya, *Dust in the Lion's Paw*. London: John Murray, 1961.

Stein, Leonard, *The Balfour Declaration*. London: Vallentine Mitchell, 1961.

Sykes, Christopher, *Crossroads to Israel*. London: Collins, 1975.

Trevor, Daphne, *Under the White Paper*. Jerusalem: Jerusalem Press, 1948.

Tuchman, Barbara, *Bible and Sword: England and Palestine from the Bronze Age to Balfour*. New York: Knopf, 1956.

Wasserstein, Bernard, *Britain and the Jews of Europe 1939–1945*. New York and London: Oxford University Press, 1979.

Wavell, Archibald Percival, *Allenby–Soldier and Statesman*. London: G. G. Harrap, 1946.

Weisgal, Meyer W., *So Far: An Autobiography*. New York: Random House, 1972.

——— and Joel Carmichael (eds.), *Chaim Weizmann: A Biography by Several Hands*. London: Weidenfeld and Nicolson, 1962.

Weizmann, Chaim, *Trial and Error*. London: Hamish Hamilton, 1946. New York: Harper & Brothers, 1949.

Weizman, Ezer, *On Eagles' Wings*. London: Weidenfeld and Nicolson, 1976.

Weizmann, Vera, *The Impossible Takes Longer*. New York: Harper & Row, 1967.

Wilson, Major R. D., *Cordon and Search: With the 6th Airborne Division in Palestine*. Aldershot: Gale and Polden Ltd., 1949.

Yellin-Mor, Nathan, *Israel, Israel . . . History of the Stern Group 1940–1948*. Paris: Presse de la Résistance, 1978.

PAMPHLETS, ARTICLES, OFFICIAL DOCUMENTS

Anglo-American Committee of Inquiry, "Report to the United States Government and His Majesty's Government in the United Kingdom." Lausanne, Switzerland, April 20, 1946.

Irgun Zvai Leumi, "The Hebrew Struggle for National Liberation, selected documents on background and history." Submitted to the United Nations. Palestine, July 1947.

Irgun Zvai Leumi, Selected pamphlets, posters (unpublished). Available in the archives of the Jabotinsky Institute, Tel Aviv.

Palestine and Transjordan, Government of, Chief Engineer, "Terrorist Methods with Mines and Booby Traps." Jerusalem: Government Printing Press, December 1946.

Palestine and Transjordan, Government of, Chief Secretary, "A Survey of Palestine" (2 vols.). Jerusalem: Government Printing Press, 1946. (Submitted to the Anglo-American Committee of Inquiry)

Vester, Bertha Spafford, "What is the American Colony?" Jerusalem: Greek Convent Press (undated).

ARCHIVES

Israel

Central Zionist Archives, Jerusalem
Haganah Archives, Tel Aviv
Hebrew University Oral History Archives, Jerusalem
Jabotinsky Institute, Tel Aviv
Jerusalem Post Archives, Jerusalem
Israel Army Archives, Tel Aviv
State of Israel Archives, Jerusalem
Weizmann Institute, Rehovot

Britain

Imperial War Museum, London
Public Records Office, London
Rhodes House, Oxford
St. Antony's College Middle East Centre, Oxford
Weiner Library, London

U.S.A.

National Archives, Washington

Acknowledgments

The research for *By Blood and Fire* took almost two years. I conducted interviews and consulted archives and libraries in Israel, Jordan, the United Kingdom, Europe, Canada and the United States. During this time I was shown innumerable kindnesses by the hundred or so individuals with whom I discussed the King David explosion. They met me at trains, planes and buses, fed me, gave generously of their time and relived events which, for many, were extremely painful. To thank them individually would require several chapters. Nine of those I interviewed have asked not to be named in this book and I have respected their wishes. The others are:

Sarah Agassi (Yael)
Arieh Altman
Helen Amir
Yaacov Amrami
Brigadier R. C. B. Anderson
Katy Antonius
Yitzhak Avinoam
Stacey Barham
General Sir Evelyn Barker
Haim Bar-Lev
Zvi Bar-Zel
Menahem Begin
Dan Ben-Dor

Leah Ben-Dor
William Bradley
John Briance
I. M. Brin
Joy Bourdillon
Thomas Buchanan
Andrew Campbell
Sir Richard Catling
Henry Cattan
Sir Martin Charteris
Jerry Cornes
Ari Disenchick
Shraga Eliss (Chaim-Toit)

Arieh Eshel
Canon Everly
Mrs. Everly
Doreen Farley
Israel Galili
Joan Gibbs
Shlomo Guber
Boris Guriel
Sir John Gutch
Lady Gutch
David Hacohen
Sami Hadawi
Kenneth Hadingham
Assiya Halaby
Mrs. Max Hesse
E. P. Horne
David Horowitz
Mrs. Julius Jacobs
Dov Joseph
Samuel Katz
Ruth Kedar (Jacobs)
Rhoui Khatib
Jon Kimche
Arthur Koestler
Devorah Ledener (Sudensky)
Israel Levi (Gideon)
Ibrahim Mansour
Jack Mantoura
Leila Mantoura (Canaan)
Nubar Markarian
Adina Nissan
David Niv
Anwar Nusseibeh
John J. O'Sullivan

Amihai Paglin
Mathilde Dupont (Papadoupolous)
Alan Park
Michael Payne
Ivan Phillips
Edward Pollock
Mrs. Emmanuel Propper
Ian Proud
Ernest Quinn
Gershon Rivlin
Moshe Rosenberg
Helen Rossi
P. A. E. Russell
Shoukri Saleh
Victor Shaer
Andrew Sharman
Honor Sharman
Sir John Shaw
Lady Shaw
Max Seligman
J. G. T. Sheringham
Gabriel Sifrony
Douglas Small
Marion Small
Anne Soutter
Emile Soutter
Eliahu Spector
Zehdi Terzi
Ian Tilly
Yitzhak Tobiana (Amnon)
Yair Tsaban
Archdeacon C. Witton-Davis
Y. R. Yaron

The following discussed the King David explosion over the telephone and by letter:

Nicholas Andronovich
Kathleen Bailey
H. Caswill
Celia Douglas (Musgrave)
William Fuller
Betty Hamburger

Meyer Levin
Arthur Miles
Richard Mowrer
Major A. C. S. Savory
D. C. H. Sweeting
K. W. Woodward

Particular thanks are due to Menahem Begin for taking forty-five minutes out of his demanding schedule to discuss the King David explosion; Helene Bachrach and Joe Ben-Meir for their superb work in translating letters, articles and transcripts from Hebrew; J. Bowyer Bell for pointing me in the right direction; Margaret Bullard, a natural sleuth, for tracking down people in England whom I had despaired of finding; Victoria Bullard for her persistence in picture research; Ruth Dayan for her invaluable help in Israel; Ami Federman for making his personal archives on the King David Hotel available; Jamie and Damaris Fletcher for their generous hospitality in London; Nancy Bruff Gardner for her editorial and typing skills; Hugh Howard for his support in the early stages of the research; Phillip Jones for allowing me to consult the useful files and indices he has assembled at the Anglo-Palestine Research Centre; Gabriel and Delia Khano for their help and hospitality in Jerusalem; Louise Mendelsohn for arranging an interesting interview in San Francisco; Walter Rappeport for being the first to say "what a good idea"; Gershon Rivlin, the official Haganah historian, for the time he took to educate me in the history of the Haganah; Victor Shaer for giving me a tour of the hotel and pointing out how it had changed during the last thirty-five years; Vivienne Schuster, my London agent, for finding a British publisher so quickly and expertly; Michael Sieff and Alexander Zvielli for their help at the *Jerusalem* (formerly *Palestine*) *Post*; George Tresher, an explosives consultant, for taking an afternoon to explain the effects of 350 kilograms of explosives on a building the size of the King David; Yair Tsaban for sharing with me a transcript of his interview with Moshe Sneh; Benjamin Tsuk of Kibbutz Yagour for arranging interviews with members of the kibbutz who were present on Black Saturday; and Judith Yehieli for letting me roam about the King David Hotel and consult its employment records.

Above all I am grateful to my agent, Julian Bach, for his enthusiasm and encouragement over the last several years; to Judy Wederholt for her skillful and sensitive editing; and to my wife, Antonia, for everything.

Index

302 • By Blood and Fire

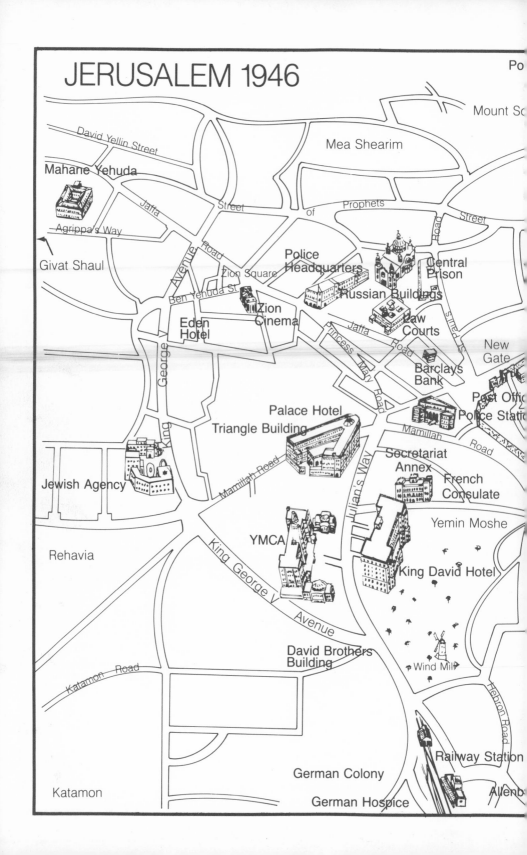